THE FACE
OF A ROGUE

ABSORBING LIVES
SERIES
BOOK 2

LT ANDERSON

Published in the United States by Rogue Street Entertainment.

The Face of a Rogue / Les and Taylor Anderson (LT Anderson)
Summary: Banishment from the Punks forced Krystal to seek friends within the Changers Underground. Defection from the Changers had cast Krystal as one of many Rogues. Courtesy of Dr. Felix Yaz, she was a special Rogue. Felix's experimental procedure reversed the Change, giving her enhanced eyesight, hearing and physical prowess. Forcing her way back into the Punks would give her access to Curtis Dyer.

Edited by Lisa Gilliam – lisagilliam.com
Cover Design by Dane and Team – ebooklaunch.com
Interior Design and Format by Lisa Gilliam – lisagilliam.com
Beta Read by John Kozina

ISBN: 978-1-7321795-3-0 (hardcover)
ISBN: 978-1-7321795-4-7 (paperback)
ISBN: 978-1-7321795-5-4 (ebook)

Visit us on the Web – ltanderson.com

Also by LT Anderson

ABSORBING LIVES
A world where the cost of immortality is your neighbor's life.

THE FACE OF A ROGUE is dedicated to the Protectors of the small, the weak and the bullied, the victims of abuse, ridicule and scorn.
To the Comforters of the lonely.
To the Voice of Strength for the fearful.
To the Warrior who fights for these.

CHAPTER 1

The Return

THE PEOPLE WHO HATED KRYSTAL Peterson more than anyone in the world were about to welcome her with open arms. Forsaken, deserted and abandoned by family and friends, and targeted for death by her enemies, this outcast was poised and confident. She stood atop the hill outside the Punks' headquarters at Checkpoint One.

The Punks. Only a few months ago, Krystal had been one of them, held in high esteem. But she was also a Changer. The two don't mix. So she was branded and banished from the Punks' organization.

After the Information Age, the Changers controlled all information and technology. They had harnessed immortality and the ability to change their appearance at will. But to retain their immortality they must absorb innocent human lives. So they had erased state boundaries and walled off sections of the country to control the human population as a life source.

The Punks objected to the absorption of the innocent to feed the elite, and they rebelled. After years of fighting and countless deaths, the Changers and the Punks established a treaty. Until recently, the Punks had protected the Bystanders from the

Changers. Their method was simple: control the food source to control the Changers.

Growing weary of the Punks' power over their lives, the Changers devised high-tech AI weapons, hybrid Changers, to eliminate the Punks. And the Chybrids attacked.

The underdog Punks had refused to be intimidated. With a rag-tag group of misfits and society's rejects, the Punks fought back. But their casualties numbered in the thousands. They were losing the battle. Until Krystal Peterson returned.

From day one, Krystal had been defiant, a misfit, a blemish. She didn't fit in with anyone, with any group. She had been rejected her entire miserable life.

But today was a new day, and Krystal had chosen sides. Despite the cold breeze, the warmth of the rising sun heated her back. Her leather duster whipped randomly, furling and unfurling like a black flag.

She gazed intently down the muddy incline before her. Remnants of AI humanoid mechanical creatures ascended methodically, deliberately. The battlefield behind them was strewn with chunks of metal—vehicles that were once the backbone of the Punks' armored fleet. Bodies and limbs of the dead and dying filled in gaps between the vehicles, rocks and sagebrush. Beyond that, the imposing Perimeter Wall and Checkpoint One.

A remote-controlled drone hovered directly in front of Krystal's face. Two AR-15 rifles hung on custom straps—one on each shoulder. She lifted the rifle on her right and cracked off a shot, disabling the drone. The damaged aircraft spun wildly in the air as she glanced at a cell on her wrist. "Time to accept the unacceptable, Punks."

Expressionless, she watched the drone crash to the ground as the wind swept her light brown hair from her scarred face.

Punk headquarters at Checkpoint One remained in shambles. Word of the Punks' defeat had spread quickly through the Bystander grapevine. As the Bystanders accept free homes and technology from the Changers, they question the necessity of a Punk presence.

The world was in a new stage of disarray. The eternal Changers were preparing to launch the next phase of their quest for global dominance. The wounded Punks were picking up the pieces of their once-formidable war machine.

Banishment from the Punks had forced Krystal to seek friends within the Changers' Underground. Defection from the Changers had cast her as one of many Rogues. But courtesy of Dr. Felix Yaz, she was a special Rogue. Felix's experimental procedure reversed the Change and gave her enhanced eyesight, hearing and physical prowess. Forcing her way back into the Punks would give her access to Curtis Dyer.

Curtis. Krystal's reason for living. Her thoughts turned to the night she had broken away from him. Her last words to him echoed in her mind. "*And I love you, too,*" she had said. "*But I don't need you now, Curtis.*"

I'm so sorry! she thought. *I do love you. And I do need you.* She wiped the tear before it fell and stepped toward Punk headquarters.

CHAPTER 2

Insider Out

IN THE SOUTHERN CALIFORNIA DESERT, two and a half miles from the Colorado River, Curtis Dyer slowed his armored Chevy van and turned off Interstate 10 at the Highway 95 junction. He headed north toward the Changers' Underground City. Thankful he was no longer facing the rising sun, he flipped the driver's visor up as he glanced in the rearview mirror.

Johnny Logan sat in a jump seat behind the security screen that divided the front buckets from the rear of the van. "So you're actually hauling me to the Underground?" He yawned. "What makes you think I'm not gonna just turn you over when we get there?"

Curtis smiled. "Because I got you figured out, Logan. You're not as dumb as you look."

Johnny pressed his face to the screen. "You're right about me not being dumb. And I'm devilishly handsome, if I do say so. Why would I change my looks to be anything other than handsome?"

Curtis couldn't help shaking his head when he rolled his eyes. "Yeah, anyway. I'm about to make you look good to your boss if you play things my way."

"How's that?"

"Easy. You're going to get me into the Underground because you're going to tell your boss I'm defecting. I want to receive the Change."

"Ha!" Johnny fell back in his seat. "The Change is expensive, man. And I didn't hear your name drawn at the Lottery." His eyes widened, and he leaned forward again. "Hey, you didn't suddenly come into a bunch of cash or something, did you?"

"You may not be dumb, Logan, but you're a little slow on the uptake." Curtis rolled the driver's window up. "I hold rank with the Punks. You guys need me. I know the Punks' organization inside and out. If you're the guy to bring me to your boss, you'll be looking good with the Changers. That's better than just turning a Punk over to be killed. Anyone could do that."

Johnny smiled his characteristic full-toothed smile. "Sure, okay. If that's the way it is, me and you are gonna hit it off just fine."

Curtis turned the heater on and pointed the vents downward. "Think whatever you want. Just know I'm your ticket to the big time."

"You're sure putting this little operation of yours on a heck-uva pedestal, buddy. From what I heard, you're a demoted Punk. Fourth level, right? You're not much of a prize anymore. Me, I'm different. I mean, after you guys blasted Scotty back in Tremayne, I got word I'm in Levi's inner circle now." Johnny sat up straight and puffed out his chest. "That's about as high as a guy gets in the Changers, you know."

"I'll give you that. But consider this. Since I used to be higher-ranked in the Punks' organization, I know a lot. If someone else in your boss's inner circle brought even a *former* high-level Punk to the Underground and sponsored him to be a Changer, wouldn't that individual rise in the eyes of your leadership?"

"Yeah, gotta say he would. Gotta say he would."

The highway expanded to eight lanes about a mile and a half from the main entrance to the Changers' Underground City. Curtis took the far-left lane and accelerated the van to ninety miles per hour. "Never been this close to your city."

"Of course not." Johnny smiled again. "You'd be dead meat if you ever had."

Developed after the Punks' rebellion, this underground city was the Changers' headquarters and home to all Changers in the western sector of North America. The thirty-foot-high main entrance was a quarter of a mile wide. Several layers of reinforced high-strength steel framed the entrance. Triple-thick bullet-proof glass served to defend the opening against incursion by the Changers' enemies.

"Impressive," Curtis said as he glanced up to read a series of electronic signs stretched across the highway.

CHANGERS NORTH AMERICA
UNAUTHORIZED NON-CITIZENS PROHIBITED
PREPARE TO SURRENDER WEAPONS AND VEHICLES

Johnny leaned forward to see out the windshield. "Best let me drive before we reach that wall up there. No offense, but the way this looks, they'll shoot you and then ask me what's going on. It won't be the other way around."

A fourth aerial structure appeared as a faint blue light spanning all eight lanes. As the van passed under the structure, the blue changed to bright orange, then back to blue.

"We just got scanned," Johnny said.

The ten-foot-high, three-foot-thick wall blocked all lanes into and out of the Underground City. It extended beyond the highway on both sides. Each end connected seamlessly to perpendicular walls that tapered upward to thirty feet high, where they blended with the city's massive entryway.

Curtis glanced in the rearview mirror. It was filled with Johnny Logan's smiling face. Nervous butterflies roiled Curtis's stomach. He slowed the van and pulled over. He sat and stared at his 9mm Beretta handgun on the dash.

"I wouldn't try anything with the nine," Johnny warned. "They've already got cameras on us. They can see right on into this buggy."

"Right," Curtis said. He gripped the steering wheel to prevent his hands from trembling.

"There's no turning back, buddy. From here, they already know your eye color. Once you get up to the gate where those guards are, they'll have a retina scan done on you before you say hi to the greeter guard."

Curtis flipped the heater off and opened the driver's window. The faint scent of gasoline in the van's interior sickened him. He welcomed the early winter wind that swirled into the cab. The sweat trickling down his temples turned to ice water.

Johnny sat back in his jump seat. "The longer we sit, the more nervous they'll get."

"Okay, already." Curtis unlatched his seat belt. He hoped the vibration from the van's idling motor was enough to hide his trembling. *What the hell, muscles.* "Just remember, I want to be a Changer. I'm on your side now."

Johnny sat up and waited for Curtis to open the side door of the van. "Oh, I remember. Just let me do all the talking."

Curtis exited the van and walked around the back to the passenger side. He unlocked the door and swung it open. For the first time in years, he wished he could ditch his Mohawk.

Johnny stepped out and held the side door for Curtis.

"What?" Curtis said. "I'm riding shotgun, right?"

"Aw, no way, buddy. I'm bringing you in to the top brass, remember? I can't have it be like we're friends or something."

Curtis locked eyes with Johnny. "I could have taken you back to Punk headquarters like…" He choked. *Dammit!* "…like Ryker ordered me to." He swallowed hard. "You know that, right?"

Johnny stepped forward. His huge hand gripped the back of Curtis's neck. "Get your fuckin' ass in the back of that van. Why you being so dense, dude?"

"*Attention, citizens. Attention, citizens. Remain where you are. A security team has been dispatched.*" A male voice from the high-powered PA system seemed to come from directly above the van.

"What'd I tell you? Now get in there!" Johnny shoved Curtis into the back of the vehicle and slammed the side door shut. He locked it from the outside and turned toward the city entrance. Curtis pressed his face against the security screen and gazed through the windshield as Johnny stood still with his arms extended to the sides.

Moments later the PA sounded again. *"Attention, Changer. Body scan is complete. Proceed to the security checkpoint immediately."*

Curtis pulled himself off the floor and climbed into the jump seat. He glanced around the interior for something, anything. *I don't even know what I'm looking for.* He'd cleared the area before taking custody of Logan back in Tremayne. *Stay cool. Keep your eye on the prize. I'm coming, Krys.*

EIGHT GUARDS—FOUR ON EACH SIDE of the security house— stood at attention as Johnny rolled the vehicle to a stop at the City's entrance. A ninth guard saluted as the Changer leaned out the driver's window.

"You're good, man. Relax." Johnny smirked and bobbed his head in mock seriousness. "As you were."

"Good day, sir." The guard completed his salute and crossed his hands behind his back. "Will you need a valet today?"

"Nah. I'm gonna park in the structure." Johnny caught Curtis's eye in the rearview mirror and winked. "The *executive* section."

"Very well, sir. And your passenger?"

"Yeah. He's with me. I'll be his escort."

The guard stepped back as three steel-reinforced concrete pylons descended into the ground in front of the van. Johnny guided the vehicle to the left toward a four-lane ramp into an underground parking garage. An orange beam scanned the van when it passed under the entrance. The parking garage was nearly full. Exotic vehicles—mostly electric—lined the outer walls of the first level.

Curtis eyed the array of Mercedes, Fiskers, Aston Martins, Bugattis, Porsches, Teslas, Audis, Koenigseggs and McLarens. *Wow*, he mouthed.

An electronic banner overhead directed drivers to additional parking and to various locations in the Underground. Beyond the banner was a rectangular tunnel covering a four-lane concrete roadway. Johnny steered the van into the tunnel and accelerated to sixty miles per hour.

"Dang, Johnny," Curtis said. "You people actually have *roads* underground?"

Johnny shrugged. "Cities have roads, right?" He followed the smooth thoroughfare for about a half mile before slowing down. "Well, by golly, my friend, here's our turnoff."

"I thought you said you were going to park. Executive section, remember?"

Johnny pressed the brake and glanced at Curtis in the mirror. "I did say that. One thing you're gonna have to do is trust me. I'm good for my word." He grinned. "Everybody knows that."

Curtis felt nauseous, and his stomach burned. He fought to keep his voice from shaking. "So is this where I get to meet your leader?"

Johnny frowned. "Dude, I said we're parking." He turned in to an opening in the tunnel wall. Sensors activated overhead lights in an expansive room. Johnny drove the van toward the far wall in front of him. He guided the truck into one of twenty glass-walled cubicles and threw the shift lever into Park. He turned off the ignition and shifted in his seat to face Curtis. "See? Parked."

The lights in the room slowly dimmed as the glass cubicle glowed steadily brighter around the ceiling and floor. The indirect glow changed from red to purple to blue.

The van moved downward as the cubicle descended. Curtis felt lighter as the high-speed elevator accelerated. Fifteen seconds later, the movement slowed. "Where are we?" He gazed out the windshield through the security screen in front of him. The cubicle lighting dimmed. The highly polished room was blue— floor and walls. The ceiling was bright white. One wall housed a row of lockers and an unmarked door with no handle. Curtis noticed a control panel to the right of the door. *Some kind of keyless access. Palm scanner or something.* The wall to the right was all glass, covered with blue vertical blinds, and a door to the left of them. Tiny slits between the blinds revealed a lighted hallway beyond the glass.

Two security guards approached the van. "Good day, sir," the lead guard said.

Johnny opened the driver's door and climbed out of the vehicle. "Hey."

"We've been advised you have a passenger—an outsider—on board."

"Yeah." Johnny tossed the keys to the second guard. "Get him into lockup. Don't hurt him. We got plans for this one."

Curtis's jaw dropped. He heard a metallic jingle against the side of the van as the guard pushed the key into the lock. His stomach knotted. "Johnny?"

A well-dressed man approached Johnny from the far side of the room. "Mr. Logan. Will you be having refreshments at this time?"

Johnny glanced across to the far side of the room, opposite the van. Five people sat on barstools, engaged in casual conversation. Two male bartenders busied themselves behind the expansive countertop. "Yeah, get me a shot of the usual. I'll down it on my way out. I'm not stayin' today." He puffed out his chest. "I gotta get cleaned up for a big meeting with Levi."

Curtis provided no resistance when the two guards pulled him from the back of the van. One of the guards grabbed a wad of collar on Curtis's leather jacket and pushed him against the side of the vehicle.

"Oh, he's clean, guys," Johnny said. "No need for that."

An attendant in blue coveralls greeted Johnny. "We'll have the vehicle cleaned and detailed for you, sir."

Johnny smiled, full-toothed. "Of course." He glanced at Curtis. "Go ahead and gut the inside. Nothing in there is worth keeping."

The attendant nodded. "As you wish." He stepped into the cubicle and waved his hand over a palm reader on the wall.

Curtis stood in handcuffs and watched the last evidence of his existence as a Punk descend into the floor.

CHAPTER 3

Disturbance

THE HOPEFUL AND VIBRANT CITY of Tremayne sat silent in the early morning hours the day after the Chybrid attack at Checkpoint One. As the sun peeked above the horizon, optical sensors turned off LED lights in empty parking lots. A cold breeze hissed through downtown between buildings, past vehicles and around dumpsters.

Nico perched in his Lenco BearCat and stared at a hand-drawn MISSING DOG sign stapled over a thousand other staples on a nearby utility pole. The corners of the paper fluttered in sync with each gust of wind.

He started when his two-way radio crackled. *"Nico, it's Will. Do you copy?"*

Nico swiveled his mouthpiece downward. "I copy, Will. Go ahead."

"Hey, Dion told me to let you know things are under control here at headquarters."

Nico paused. "Say again, Will?"

"Yeah. Almost all the Chybrids are down, killed."

"But how?"

"You'll never believe it, partner. Krystal Peterson, *that's how,"* Will said. *"Things are moving fast, man. Me and the other two*

amigos got our own BearCats now. Dion wants us to meet you in Tremayne and help set up security. We're packing now."

Nico pushed himself up in his seat. "I can't wait to hear about it. I'm at the city center, at the intersection of Habiliment and Main."

"We're on our way."

Nico adjusted the rearview mirror to check his look. *You don't seem so badass. How can you lead the Three Amigos, let alone all these other Punks? Dion was crazy to promote me.* He scowled at his reflection, shoved the mirror back into place and stared out the windshield.

A rude gust of wind whipped into the cab and pushed his straight bleached-blond hair into his eyes. He reached across his waist and grabbed his left wrist, pulling the paralyzed arm into his lap before unlatching the door. *Might as well wait outside.*

Nico hopped down the single step on the armored truck and stood in the street next to the vehicle. Using a custom-made Velcro strap at his waist, he secured his left arm to his side. He faced the wind to sweep the hair back off his face and grabbed a red-and-black beanie from his back pocket. With his chin tilted slightly upward, he slapped the beanie onto his head before closing the driver's door.

He stepped to the sidewalk and ambled toward the intersection of the city's two main streets. He was thankful his beanie covered his ears as his cheeks and nose flushed pink from the cold wind. The sunlight flickered off and on as clouds moved in to gray the day. He stopped at the corner and peered left.

A group of children loitering at the alley between Main and First Street caught Nico's attention. *One, two, three, four, five...six,* he counted. *Two girls.*

One of the boys bent down and picked up a small rock. The kid threw the rock into the alley, igniting the group into a clatter of oohs and ahhs as the rock clanged off something metallic.

Nico guessed from the sound the rock hit a trash dumpster—probably empty.

"Hey," he yelled.

The activity stopped, and the six kids looked in Nico's direction. After a quick impromptu conference, the group of youths turned and walked swiftly toward Nico.

"Hey, yourself," the tallest kid said as they approached. "Are you a Punk?" The kid wore jeans, athletic shoes and a loose-fitting polo shirt.

A skinny girl with dirty-blond hair pulled back in a ponytail stood next to him. "He's a Punk all right." Her olive drab sweater appeared at least one size too small. Her blue knee-length skirt looked awkward with red tennis shoes and no socks.

Her girlfriend, a short-cropped brunette with glasses, whispered in her friend's ear.

The blond girl giggled and looked at Nico. "Yeah. My dad said the Changers were gonna whip you guys. He always said you Punks aren't as tough as you think you are."

"What are you guys doing out here, anyway?" Nico asked.

A pudgy kid with his baseball cap on backward spoke up. "Don't have to tell you, man."

"Yeah," another kid said. "And we're not all *guys*, in case you didn't notice."

"Okay, kids, that's enough." Nico swallowed. "It's probably best if you head on home."

The tall guy meandered around behind Nico and pretended to look in a storefront window.

Nico glanced toward his empty BearCat as the other five youths formed a loose semicircle on the sidewalk in front of him. He spoke into his shoulder mic. "Unit Two, it's Nico. Do you copy?"

The response was immediate. "*Go ahead, Nico.*"

"Yeah, get a couple of units headed in my direction."

"*10-4. What's going on?*"

"Nothing yet, Two. Just roll a couple."

"*You got it, bro.*"

Miss ponytail put her hands on her hips and giggled. "You calling for backup? You scared of us kids?"

Nico stepped back toward the building behind him.

"Ow!" The big kid hopped around in feigned pain as if the pressure from Nico's boot had somehow broken his ankle. "That's assault, man."

"Sorry, guy. Didn't see you."

"Hey, you know what, Mister Punk?" The pudgy kid took a step toward Nico. "My dad says we don't really need you guys. You didn't protect us from the Changers during the Lottery. They didn't just attack you Punks, they attacked us regular citizens."

"Yeah, the Punks are sissies," the brunette girl said. "We really don't need Punks in our town. Why don't you just leave?"

"What's up with your arm, anyway, dude?" The pudgy kid slapped Nico's paralyzed arm.

When Nico flinched, the tall kid saw an opening and took a swing. Nico ducked and swiped his foot at the youth's ankles, knocking the boy to the ground. Before the big guy had a chance to inhale the breath that was knocked out of him, Nico's knee was in his chest. He grabbed the boy's throat and pinned him to the sidewalk.

Two Lenco BearCats rolled slowly into the intersection. *"Attention. Everyone move away. All parties move away."* The PA speaker from the lead truck reverberated off the buildings.

A big punk leaned out the driver's window of the first vehicle. "Saw it all, bro. Hold him there."

THE THREE AMIGOS GUIDED THEIR newly assigned BearCats down the highway toward Tremayne. Will led the miniconvoy, followed by Adam and Joey. A new billboard—courtesy of the Changers—caught Will's eye just outside the city limit sign.

ADOPT A CHILD TODAY.
GOOD FOR TREMAYNE.
GOOD FOR THE SOUL.

Hmm, that's new. Good for the soul? He shook his head. *Those people are weird.* He tapped the brake to release the cruise control when he saw the REDUCED SPEED AHEAD sign.

At Habiliment Avenue, he turned right and cruised the vehicle at thirty miles per hour. He glanced at the time on the dashboard clock: 9:35 a.m.

"*Will, Adam. Do you copy?*"

"Go ahead, Adam."

"*That's four straight green lights, and I've seen a few groups of kids playing around on the side streets. Dion hasn't sent the all clear to the city manager yet. What gives? Why are these kids out of their homes?*"

"*Break, guys. Joey here. Do you copy?*"

"Go, Joe," Will replied.

"*Yeah, seems like those kids you're seeing are checking us out. Every time we pass a group, they run out in the street and stand there staring at the back of my truck.*"

"Something's up, guys," Will said. "Don't know what it is yet, but we got activity at Nico's location."

With zero traffic, Will felt comfortable pulling to a stop in the middle of the intersection at Habiliment and Main Street. Adam parked two truck-lengths behind and to the right of Will's truck. Joey stopped the same distance to the left.

The trio exited their vehicles and met Nico dead center in the intersection. The four young Punks bumped fists.

Will looked past Nico at the big Punk in Unit Two and his crew, now involved in an animated discussion with two youths. "What's happening here, partner?"

"Well," Nico said. "It didn't start out as much. The kids were throwing rocks in that alley—no big deal, right? When I confronted them, they were a little belligerent, so I suggested they go on home." He shrugged. "They didn't like that, so they challenged me." He turned around and motioned to the tall kid in handcuffs. "After I called for backup, the big guy made a move on me, so I took him down."

"Hey, I know that guy," Joey said. "His name's Tim. Everyone calls him *Little Man.*"

Adam wandered back to the alley to have a look. Tall buildings on both sides still blocked the day's new sun. A piece of paper—crumpled by some anonymous fist and powered by the wind—crawled up to his boot like a tumbleweed. He bent down and picked up the crinkled wad. He held it momentarily before untangling the indiscriminate folds.

Faint giggling in the narrow passage between the buildings pricked his ears. Adam glanced toward the intersection. Will, Joey and Nico remained engaged with the situation on the street. He stuffed the paper into his pocket before stepping into the darkened passageway. Grit under his boots and the now-continuous breeze muffled the distant laughter as he strained to pinpoint the source.

He stopped and squinted. The green dumpster ahead on his left was out of place. *What the heck?* Adam's instinct pulled him to the opposite side of the alley into a small alcove—the rear entrance to an electronics repair shop. He moved quietly past the dumpster and crouched in the shallow recess before turning back to face the garbage bin.

Without the wind swirling in his ears, the voices became clear.

Giggling children in quiet conversation. "Try to make it in her mouth."

Clink splat.

Clink clink splat.

"You keep hitting that eye, stupid. Gimme one."

Bang splat.

"Shh, you idiot. That's too big."

"Made it, didn't I?"

From his vantage point, Adam saw four children he guessed to be around twelve years old. They'd obviously made themselves comfortable on top of an abandoned mattress and a pile of flattened cardboard boxes. Two girls leaned against the brick wall of the building opposite Adam. The other kids, both boys, squatted on the mattress, facing the crevice between the dumpster and the wall.

He watched one of the boys reach into a box and pull out a potato-sized rock.

"Aw, that's no fair, man," the other boy said. "That's way too big."

The girls laughed. "Do it, stupid," one urged.

The boy tossed the rock.

Splat.

"Whoa, I think you broke her tooth!" one of the girls cheered.

More laughter.

"Gimme one!"

Her? Adam frowned. He stood and walked swiftly toward the children. As he approached the small group, the reality of the scene punched him in the gut. The blood rushed from his face as his skin turned cold. "What—?" He suppressed a gag as every hair on his body prickled. Lack of oxygen squelched his attempt to scream. His muscles went weak. He knew the feeling—like the last time he tried to scream in a dream. "Hey…hey!" he whispered hard, trying to catch his breath.

A forty-something-year-old woman was propped up in the corner between the garbage bin and the brick building. Her expensive skirt was hiked above her knees, her silk blouse torn down the front. The red pump on her left foot contrasted sharply with her pale skin.

Blood trickled from one of her open eyes and the corners of her mouth.

Adam found his voice. "Hey!"

The four children scrambled to their feet.

Adam rushed to the woman and knelt beside her. He grabbed her wrist. *Pulse!*

When he turned around, the kids were gone.

"Nico, it's Adam! Do you copy?"

"*Hey, Adam. Go ahead.*"

"I need medical assistance in the alley! Now!"

CHAPTER 4

Security Shuffle

BLINKING RED LIGHTS AT EACH ceiling corner of every major corridor throughout the Changers' Underground reminded residents the city was still on high alert since the Chybrid offensive on the Punks' headquarters. Guards stationed at specific checkpoints kept activity to a minimum as citizens were redirected back to their homes or escorted to their places of employment. Not one restaurant, lounge, bar, shopping establishment, theater or game center was open for business during the lockdown.

Tension remained high inside the conference room adjacent to the Changers' War Room. Levi Aldrich paced back and forth between the executive wet bar and an array of flat-screen monitors on the opposite wall. As leader of the Changers in North America, Levi had recently made decisions that would take the organization in a new direction. His new program and personnel changes would not be popular with his present inner circle.

"Leader, please sit down," Silver Long insisted.

Levi stopped pacing long enough to stare down his second-in-command. "Yours is the last voice I want to hear at this moment, Long."

Ivan Duncan pushed his chair back and stood. "Leader, if I may."

Levi smoothed his hands over the lapels on his royal-blue suit coat and then through his jet-black hair. "You may." He resumed his pacing.

"I think a recap of the events leading up to the defeat of our Chybrids is in order. If we analyze the timeline of events, it will assist us in rooting out the weak points of our plan."

"And who was responsible," Marvellus Macey added.

Levi stopped and inhaled deeply. He closed his eyes and exhaled.

"Leader, please," Ivan said, motioning to Levi's chair at the head of the conference table.

A muscular six foot three, Levi's presence intimidated even his closest confidants. He moved slowly to his chair and sat down, his eyes locked on Silver. "I know where our weakness is, and who's to blame."

"That does it!" Silver slammed her stylus onto the tabletop. "There's no way in hell I'm responsible for the defeat of your little *robots*!" Her hand shook as she pointed at Levi. "*You* were the supreme overseer of that project from its inception. The whole thing was *your* idea. I wasn't even involved."

"She has a point, sir," Ivan said. "The Chybrid project was developed by Garrison and Dennis, headed up by yourself."

"It's not the Chybrids that failed us, Duncan," Levi said. "Their purpose has been realized, the objective complete."

"But the Punks have not been eliminated—"

"The Punks!" Levi's fist landed hard on the table. "They have been severely crippled. It will take them years to recover from the damage inflicted by my Chybrids."

Silver pushed her chair back and folded her arms. "Hmph."

Levi stood and leaned across the table toward Silver. "Don't be so smug, Long. My disappointment is not in the execution or outcome of the Chybrid project. My issue is with your total failure regarding the security of the Changers' organization."

Silver pressed herself back into her chair. "What security?"

Levi sat back down. "You are..." He looked around the conference table. "...or *were*, head of security, correct?"

Silver's eyes narrowed. "Up until now, I thought I still held that position. Why, Levi? Why would you take that away from me?"

Levi stood again and surveyed his top leaders and commanders. "Ladies and gentlemen. I have made an executive decision with regard to security. We recently experienced the worst breach in the history of our organization. I'm sure you all remember the defector, Krystal Peterson—"

"Ha!" Silver mock-laughed. "That wasn't my doing. I suspect Dr. Yaz had a hand in that."

Levi turned to Silver, expressionless. He blinked slowly once before turning back to his commanders. "As I was saying, Peterson escaped the Underground right under our noses. This would not have happened under a competent security chief."

"Dr. Yaz is your inner circle, Levi," Silver said. "Your accusations are misplaced."

"I am addressing the Dr. Yaz angle with our new head of security."

Silver raised an eyebrow. "Who's your new security chief? And where's Yaz now?"

"This is not question-and-answer time, Long. But for the sake of those present, I will say that we have a lock on Dr. Felix Yaz's position as we speak. Of course, he is still in the Underground, and security personnel are en route to apprehend him for questioning."

Silver persisted. "Who's the new security chief?"

"I can assure you, you will not approve of her—"

"Her? Oh that's rich. Has to be a woman, right, Levi? You couldn't handle things without a strong woman to hold you up."

Levi's ire rose. "Enough!"

Silver surveyed the Changers at the table. "You know I wear the pants around here, Levi. You've never made a move without consulting me first. It's time everyone knows how weak you really are."

"Weak?"

"Sure. This has nothing to do with any security breach. This has everything to do with your pride. Your ego has been damaged by Krystal Peterson. You can't get over the fact you were outdone by a woman."

"Let's be honest, Long," Levi said. "It was a woman—you—that allowed Peterson to escape the Underground. So you yourself were outdone by that same woman."

"She couldn't have done it without Felix. I feel it in my bones. I may have been outsmarted, but it wasn't by Peterson. I'll give the nod to Yaz."

Levi smiled. "However you choose to look at it, my dear. Peterson got over on you."

"But she never completed the simplest of assignments," Silver said. "She never absorbed a high-ranking Punk."

"As if we need that now," Levi said. "My Chybrid project damaged the Punks adequately. Need I say more?"

"Sir." Marvellus raised his hand. "Long has a point. Peterson failed her assignment. However, would it not be beneficial had she completed the task? As crippled as the Punks are, surely the loss of a high-ranking official within their organization would reap great benefits to us now."

Silver leaned forward. "I could have completed that assignment with one hand tied behind my back—"

"But you couldn't complete your own assignments or fulfill the obligations of your position as head of security," Levi said.

"At least I remained loyal. You had a defector in your inner circle. Dr. Yaz is your man."

Levi shook his head slowly. "Look around the table, Long. Who else is missing from here?"

Ivan raised a hand.

"Never mind," Levi snapped. "I'll tell you. Garrison and Dennis. Those two Rogues were under your authority in lockup." He pointed at Silver. "They were your responsibility."

Silver swallowed. "I blame Dr. Yaz for that as well."

"Always deflecting, Long. A good leader accepts responsibility and takes action."

"Then you accept responsibility for Peterson, as well as Garrison and Dennis?" Silver asked.

"I do. And I am taking the necessary actions to correct the problem. That's why you're out as security chief. And nobody cares." He pressed a button on the table's surface. "Lift the high-security alert."

"*Yes, sir.*"

Silver stared at Levi. "I don't need to prove anything to you or to myself. I know how good I am. And I am loyal to the Changers' organization and to our cause. You'll regret all of this."

CHAPTER 5

Outsider In

Behind the Perimeter Wall, inside the Depot at Checkpoint One, Ryker studied a flat-screen monitor. "Hey, Dion. She's at the walk-through."

Dion stepped across the room and stood next to his best friend. "That's her, all right. Do we have audio?"

Ryker pressed a touch pad to power up the voice-activated communication system at the main gate.

"Krystal?" Dion said.

"*Long time, no see, Dion.*" Krystal's voice was crisp, clear and strong.

Dion looked at Ryker and shrugged. He mouthed, *Now what?* The two Punks stared at Krystal's image on the monitor.

Krystal surveyed the exterior of the imposing thirty-foot-high structure. Dried mud mixed with blood accentuated the heavy gouges left by Chybrids in the wall's surface. The marks and scratches extended to the top of the wall. *Damn*, she thought. *Almost made it over.* She glanced at the intercom by the walk-through. "Well?"

"*Krys, it's Ryk. Stand by a sec.*"

Krystal swung the two rifles off her shoulders and leaned them butt-down against the wall. She turned around and faced the combat zone. A cold gust of wind rushed between her back and the wall. *What a loss*, she thought as she fastened the two middle buttons on her duster. She scanned the terrain, the hunks of metal and debris, the bodies. Wind against numerous communications antennae atop the destroyed vehicles whispered a disconcerting tune. *Even sounds like death*, she thought. Her ears prickled at a faint sound—distinct from the wind noise. She turned her head ever so slightly, her left ear to the battlefield.

Slluurrpp. The sound was weak, vague and distant. *Slluurrpp.* But there it was again.

Krystal held a hand to her ear to determine the direction of the sound. "Hey," she shouted.

"Help," a voice whispered.

Krystal turned toward the voice. Or was it only the wind? She squinted and panned the area. Her eyes locked on a swollen mound of mud about fifty yards from the wall. The blob seemed foreign against the flattened ground around it. But the blob moved.

"Hey," Krystal shouted again, her eyes on the blob.

The intercom speaker by the gate popped. *"Hang on, Krys."* It was Ryker again.

Krystal ignored Ryker and ran toward the voice on the battle-field. Her steps were deliberate and firm as she pivoted between the seemingly endless debris over the muddy ground. She used a free hand to assist the occasional vault across oversized wreckage as she made her way to the location of the voice. A few feet from the mud mound, she slowed her approach. "Holy shit," she said. "You're alive."

THE ATMOSPHERE INSIDE THE DEPOT had devolved from exhilaration to pandemonium. With the highest-ranked Punks, two Rogue Changers and a number of agitated, low-grade loyalists present, the debate raged about how to handle the arrival of Krystal Peterson. Punks from the compound outside forced the door open and crowded in.

Dion stood with his back to the communications console facing the door. He grabbed a wad of sleeve on Margot's leather jacket. "Go out there and get a handle on the troops. This has gone beyond crazy."

"You got it, boss," the level three commander said as she pushed her way between bodies.

"And lock that door behind you," he shouted.

Unconsciously, the crowd had loosely segregated itself into four groups. The smallest faction was in favor of Krystal's current sentence—allow her to live, but only outside the Perimeter. Two groups were equally divided between those in favor of allowing her back into the Punks' organization and those advocating an immediate death sentence. The largest group consisted of the undecideds.

Dion looked at Ryker. "Shut down the monitors."

The array of flat-screens across the wall above the communications console displayed real-time video from outside the Wall. Ryker took one last glance at Krystal kneeling in the distance and tapped the power button on the video control panel. As the monitors flashed black, the crowd in the Depot erupted.

"No!" came a voice from the back of the room. "She's scavenging parts!"

"We can't let her go," another said.

"She could be setting traps for us."

"We need to keep an eye on her. We can't trust her!"

"Let's bring her back so we can put an end to this!"

Pops made his way to the side door leading to the Hangar. "If she's coming in now, we can let her in through the Tunnel. It'd take a while to move all those trucks away from the main gate."

Raymond stepped between Pops and the door. "Hold on a sec," he challenged. He placed a hand on Pops's shoulder and looked at Dion. "We're not teaming up with Peterson, are we?"

Pops took a long look at Raymond's hand on his shoulder, then stared him in the eye. His posture stiffened.

Raymond held firm. "Dion?"

Dion had a hand in the air for thirty seconds before the din began to decline. The Punk leader glared at Raymond. "Everybody listen up. I hear you. You all know this isn't the way we do things."

"But—" Raymond protested.

"Back down, Ray," Dion said.

KRYSTAL HELD THE INJURED PUNK behind his head and wiped the mud from his face. "I don't know you," she whispered.

His eyes were slits, his face swollen and red. "I…I…"

"Don't try to talk right now." The mud was cold on Krystal's knees. She felt the man's forehead. *You're freezing*, she thought as she glanced to her left at the remains of a nearby BearCat. "I'll be right back," she said, laying his head gently onto the cold mud.

She jumped up and hurried to the vehicle. Its doors had been completely detached from the body. The tires were gone. The truck was tilted to the right, half its body buried in the muck. She hurried around to the back and hopped inside. *Yes*, she thought, grabbing a titanium canteen from the floor of the vehicle. She snatched a large first aid kit off a side shelf before backing out.

Krystal rushed back to the prone Punk and lifted his head again. She trickled the water from the canteen over his eyes before holding it to his mouth. "Try to drink." Most of the refreshing liquid drained out of the Punk's mouth, washing away the mud and gunk from his cheeks. But he drank.

"Where are you injured?" Krystal asked.

"My…legs. I was pinned…under my truck…" His voice trailed off, and he closed his eyes.

Krystal opened the first aid kit and unwrapped a temporary thermal blanket. She spread the blanket over the Punk and tucked the sides down into the mud. "Now hang in there. I'll be back."

RYKER REFUSED TO ALLOW THE tension in the room to seep into his psyche. "Look," he said to the crowd. "You've all trusted us in the past to lead you. We make decisions based on all the information we have. Sometimes we miss, but we always put the safety and survival of all of you first. This can't be a free-for-all. So trust us now."

Dion stood next to Ryker, arms folded across his chest. "He's right. Now, I want everyone who's undecided on what to do about Krystal to raise your hands."

The undecideds raised their hands.

"Winter, Jimbo." Dion nodded to his two top commanders. "Escort these people outside to the compound. All of you, report to Margot when you get outside. She'll have your assignments."

Shadows on the battlefield disappeared as the morning wind shoved the clouds back over Checkpoint One. Misty silver and blue highlights from the rising sun changed to a soggy gray, and the carnage blended back into the muck. Krystal re-shouldered her rifles and pounded a fist on the intercom button at the walk-through gate.

"Ryker!" She turned to eye the fallen Punk in the distance as she pounded the button again. "Ryk! You got people out here!"

"Stand by, Krys. Pops is gonna open the tunnel hatch. Head east about fifty yards and stay near the wall. You won't miss him."

Krystal looked east and spotted the hatch, already open. She trotted toward the opening, her gait smooth and firm across the slippery terrain.

Pops stood on the thick concrete shelf inside the tunnel opening, his arm in the air. "Come on in, girl."

Krystal descended the small ladder to the shelf and hopped onto the tunnel floor.

When Pops closed the hatch behind her, he couldn't help smiling. He hustled down the ladder and turned to face Krystal. "I gotta say I'm happy to see you, Krys."

"Last time I was allowed here, there was only one person glad to see me."

Pops glanced toward Checkpoint One. "There's more than that now. C'mon, I'll show you."

Krystal followed the old Punk through the four-person-wide

corridor. "You guys have at least one person out there on the hill, still alive. There could be more."

Pops stopped to wait for Krystal. "Damn, Krys." He studied her face for the first time since he'd participated in her expulsion from the Punks' organization.

Krystal gazed at the senior Punk. He looked older than she remembered. He needed a shave, and his clothes looked like he'd slept in them for a week. *Eyes are weak, Pops,* she thought. *You look tired.*

"You know," he began. "I've always regretted not going to bat for you that night."

"The past is passed, Pops. I'm not the same person I was that night. I suspect none of us are."

"Me and Geezer always loved you. You have to know that. We—"

Krystal waved her hand. "That's enough. I know who's on my side, and I know why. Right now, you have a man down out there. He's going to die of exposure if we don't get him out of that field."

Pops turned. "C'mon, walk beside me, Krys."

The two locked eyes.

"It'll make me feel better," he said.

Krystal's heart softened ever so slightly. "Let's go."

The pair walked swiftly toward Checkpoint One.

"I gotta tell you, girl. There's still some of 'em want you dead."

"Yeah, well, they'll just have to get over it."

Pops smiled to himself. "You know we got a couple of your old friends at Checkpoint One?"

"I didn't know. What old friends would that be?"

"Some Changers. Names are Fred Garrison and Thomas Dennis."

Krystal raised an eyebrow, suppressing her genuine surprise. "Been a long time. They'd be about the only friends I think I'd be able to count on today. So how'd they end up with you guys?"

"Well, it's kind of a long story. But I can tell you they came willingly. Had a lot of help from our people gettin' 'em outta the Underground."

Krystal stopped walking. "They won't last long on the surface, Pops. Not without having to absorb someone. You all know that, right?"

Pops squinted under one of the tunnel lights. "You know, Krys. We gotta rely on the fact they know what they're doing. We don't know all the ins and outs of the Changers. We just know these two guys don't want to be Changers anymore and they offered their help to us."

"So you helped them get out of the Underground? Now what?"

The two resumed walking. "Well, a lot of that's up to them. I can say they weren't much help when the battle was goin' on outside the Perimeter. But they're willing. Maybe we'll see what they have to offer now that it seems to be settling down some."

"Fred and Thomas are good men," Krystal said. "With good hearts."

GEEZER WAITED IN THE INSPECTION pit inside the Hangar. He gazed through the tunnel opening while he held the hatch up. "They gotta be comin' pretty soon, Dion. Don't take that long to walk fifty yards."

Dion stood next to Ryker, arms folded across his chest. Ryker leaned against Pops's pride and joy—a classic boattail Buick Riviera—thumbs hooked in the front pockets of his jeans. Jimbo and Winter stood adjacent to the inspection pit. Jimbo mirrored Dion's stance. Winter paced, her hand resting on the 9mm pistol at her waist. Lace and Jasper sat atop the main workbench next to Dion.

Fred Garrison and Thomas Dennis stood on the other side of Lace and Jasper.

Raymond leaned against the door that led to the compound outside. "So are we gonna make a decision before she gets here?"

"Hang loose, Ray," Dion said. "We'll make the decision when I say."

"Sounds like you're wussing out on us, man," Raymond said.

Jimbo spun a quick one-eighty to face Raymond. "Care to back that up, dude?" He unfolded his arms and dropped them to his sides.

Raymond took a step forward. "You know this is all bullshit, Jim." He pointed at the tunnel opening. "That bitch is a Changer, man, just like those two assholes." He pointed at Fred and Thomas. "She's got no place here."

Geezer propped the hatch open. He took his spectacles off and snatched a rag from the back pocket of his coveralls. "My money's on Jim, Ray." He motioned at Jimbo with his glasses before rubbing them with the rag. "He'll kick yer ass."

"Nobody's kicking anyone's ass," Dion said. "Both of you settle down."

Geezer glanced down into the pit. "Hep." He put his glasses back on. "Here they come."

Pops trotted up the ladder from the tunnel opening inside the inspection pit. Krystal followed. The two stood side by side and looked at Dion.

Dion nodded once. "Krystal."

"Dion."

The bullet from Raymond's 9mm slammed into Krystal's form-fitting helmet, ricocheted up into the I-beam rafters and clinked off the steel ceiling before falling to the floor at Pops's feet.

Krystal spun toward Raymond, simultaneously rotating both rifles vertically around her back. She stopped the movement on the upswing, both barrels pointed at Raymond's chest, her fingers resting on the triggers.

Pops glared at Raymond. "I oughta shove that pistol up your ass."

Winter glanced at Ryker. He held both hands out, palms down. *Be cool*, he mouthed.

Jasper and Lace slid slowly off the workbench.

Dion stepped between Jimbo and Raymond. "Put it away, Ray," he said. "Now."

"Dion, we got a man down in the field out there," Pops said. "Krystal says he's alive."

"Where abouts?" Dion said.

"About two hundred yards northeast from the walk-through," Krystal said. "Right next to Zane's vehicle."

Ryker's eyes widened. "It's not Zane, is it?"

"No. I talked to the guy. I don't know him."

Dion looked at Jasper.

"I'm on it," Jasper said. He grabbed his leather jacket from the vise on the workbench. "I'll need some help, Lace."

"Good idea," Dion said. "Take whoever you need from the compound and get that guy back here. On your way out, tell Margot to form a search team. We need to scour the battlefield for survivors." He looked at Krystal. "Now that it's safe to go out there."

Raymond stepped aside as Jasper and Lace headed for the door. Jasper held the door for Lace and turned back to Dion. "For the record, don't hold the meeting for me and Lace." He glanced at Krystal, then Raymond. "We both vote to let her back in with us."

CHAPTER 6

The Appointment

Two hours after Levi lifted the high-security alert, citizens of the Underground had resumed most of their normal activities. Maintenance technicians busied themselves placing new electronic signs and billboards throughout the City, announcing the leadership's newest initiative. Strategy from the Changers' governmental marketing arm dictated the advertising go up before the official announcement. Building curiosity and excitement was key to Levi's plan to obtain universal buy-in from the Changers' population.

The technicians worked in groups of four to eight, as determined by the size of the sign. In the main thoroughfare on Level One, a small group of Changers stood watching the construction of a large electronic billboard. A safety buffer of bright orange stanchions and warning tape gave the eight technicians room to work unmolested by lookie-loos. The billboard depicted a well-dressed young couple in their early twenties standing next to a late-model electric sports car. The background of the picture changed continuously from city to country to poolside.

A young woman hung on the arm of her boyfriend. "Wow," she said, pointing at the sign. "If those are Chybrids, they sure look different."

"Yeah," the boyfriend replied. "They look absolutely human."

Three teenage girls crowded in to the front of the group. "That guy's hot. Look at those ripples."

"Not like your boyfriend couldn't change to make himself look that way," her friend said. Then she giggled. "If you had a boyfriend!"

"This is a far cry from the beasts that destroyed the Punks," a woman at the back of the crowd said.

"From what I heard, the Punks weren't destroyed," a man replied.

The woman looked down her nose at the man. "Our leadership knows what they're doing. *Destroyed* doesn't have to mean *disappeared*. The Punks are out of commission. That's all that matters."

"Hey lady," the boyfriend said. "If you're so smart, what's SOUL stand for?"

"Yeah," his girlfriend agreed. "What's a SOUL Chybrid?"

The woman turned to leave. "You'll find out soon enough, kids. Have fun drooling on the sign. For me, I can't wait to see the real thing."

Two stainless-steel doors swished quietly closed behind Levi when he reentered the main executive conference room in the Underground. "Greetings again, everyone. My apologies for being fashionably late." He sat down and poured water from a pitcher into his monogrammed wineglass. "But it's better you wait on me than vice versa. I trust you all enjoyed the brunch served by our master chefs."

The Changers' department heads occupied twelve seats around the shiny black table. Silver Long was noticeably absent. Levi smiled broadly and addressed the attendees. "As all of you should know by now, our lopsided treaty with the Punks has come to an end. The Chybrid project was successful in destroying the Punks' mighty military machine, thus humiliating the Punks emotionally and spiritually. Their days are numbered, and they have nothing in their arsenal with which to retaliate. They are down, and now is the time to kick them."

A mild applause from the group accompanied smiles and nods. Levi held up a hand, both to accept the credit and squelch the clatter.

"Before we discuss our next phase of dominance and independence, I'm sure some of you have noticed we have some new faces here. Allow me to make some introductions." Levi motioned to his right. "Here is a face to which you will all become accustomed. She is the new head of security and will assume the role of my right-hand person. I want to be clear, she and her two assistants have my utmost trust and confidence. Ladies and gentlemen, let me introduce to you, Angelica DeMone."

Angelica pushed her chair back and stood to address the Changers. Her presence was commanding. Shoulder-length dark brown hair complemented her black formfitting pantsuit, while her ebony eyes displayed a friendly sparkle.

She smiled. "Leader, ladies and gentlemen, thank you for the warm welcome. As the new security chief, I am here to guarantee you will not witness the same disgraceful performance from this department to which our people were subjected under the previous management. As you might imagine, necessity dictates changes, not only within this department, but in all departments. I will address these changes with some of you individually. Others I will discuss in this meeting." She glanced at Levi. "Thank you, sir."

"Thank you, Ms. DeMone," Levi said as Angelica took her seat. "Seated next to Ms. DeMone are two of her most trusted aides, whom I will introduce shortly. Additionally, as you no doubt have observed, we have another new member of our team. Outside of Ms. DeMone and myself, this person is not familiar to anyone here. Because Dr. Felix Yaz has become unreliable—" Levi held up a finger. "Let me rephrase. Because Dr. Felix Yaz has become a liability, we have found it necessary to replace him."

A thick fog of silence engulfed the room. Department heads and military leaders exchanged glances but avoided locking eyes with anyone in the room. The silence settled over the table and pressed down on the attendees like a migraine. Felix had been highly regarded as a modern day Einstein. Each person in the room felt the weight of the statement. If Felix was out, anyone was expendable.

Levi raised an eyebrow. "I can see I have struck a nerve. At this time, I am beyond explaining my decisions. This is a new chapter, a new beginning for the Changers. It is a new world, my friends. You will either join us, or be left behind."

He stood and turned to his left. "With that, please indulge me to introduce the new Minister of Research and Development, Dr. Xander Rasmus."

Angelica joined Levi in starting the applause for Dr. Rasmus. The others around the table nodded and clapped dutifully.

Levi motioned to the doctor's left. "Dr. Rasmus has added two members to his elite scientific research and development staff."

Dr. Rasmus stood and placed his hands behind his back. His custom-fit dark blue three-piece suit was the antithesis of the bedraggled khakis and lab coat worn by Dr. Felix Yaz. His black slicked-back hair reflected the ceiling lights and clung to his skull like a formfitting cap. He scanned the attendees, nodded twice, and sat back down.

Levi smiled broadly and glanced at Angelica. "Let's get down to business, shall we?"

"Yes, let's." Angelica glanced at an electronic tablet in front of her. "Before we address the top security plans, I'd like to announce a few minor personnel changes." She looked up. "Ivan Duncan and Marvellus Macey?"

Ivan and Marvellus raised their hands.

"You two are out."

The two distinguished scientists exchanged glances. "But—" Ivan began.

Marvellus appealed to Levi. "Leader, you approved this?"

Levi leaned forward. "I believe everyone in the room heard the same three words I did from Ms. DeMone. You. Are. Out."

Angelica stared emotionless at the two. The sparkle in her eyes was gone. "Security, please remove these men from the room."

Levi sat back and clasped his hands behind his head.

The two security guards at the conference room door swiftly moved behind Ivan and Marvellus.

"All right!" Ivan said, standing.

The two moved toward the exit, and the doors swished open. Marvellus stepped into the war room outside.

Ivan stopped at the door and pivoted to face Levi, Angelica and Dr. Rasmus. Involved in quiet conversation, none of the three watched Ivan and Marvellus. Ivan turned and stepped across the threshold, and the doors closed quietly behind him.

LEVI RUBBED HIS HANDS TOGETHER and smiled as he looked around the conference table. "I must say I am pleased and enthusiastic about our new team. We have assembled the new best of the best. Welcome, all of you, to the circle of the most elite team in the history of our organization. We are on the cusp of something most special." He sipped his water, just enough to wet his lips. "Now, are there any questions before we get started?"

"There's an empty chair," Xander said, motioning across the table.

Levi's smile faded ever so slightly. "Yes, that is for Mr. John Logan. I'm so very anxious for our new team to come together. Mr. Logan is our top field commander. My understanding is he is on his way back from Tremayne as we speak."

"And his role is?" Xander asked.

"Commander Logan has just completed a successful six-month mission as a spy for our organization. He infiltrated the Punks, evaded their identification system and led a successful demoralization campaign. He faced extreme odds and performed in an exemplary manner for the Changers. He has been inside the city of Tremayne for the last forty-eight hours and should be with us shortly."

Dr. Rasmus remained emotionless. "And his role for *this campaign* is?"

Levi held up his hand. "It would not be appropriate to discuss in detail an absent team member's assignment at this time. I will brief you all on his role momentarily, Doctor." He looked around the table. "Are there any other questions before we begin?"

Without a word, everyone looked at Levi.

"All right, then," he said, clapping his hands together once. "I must commend the artist who devised the images for the new billboards around the city. I noticed on my way to this meeting that our corporate marketing team has worked overtime to complete the new campaign."

The head of marketing smiled and nodded. "Thank you, sir. And yes, we have worked overtime. At no additional expense to the organization, of course," he added.

"Well, the images are splendid," Levi said. He turned to Dr. Rasmus. "Are the images an accurate depiction of the new SOUL Chybrids?"

"They are not an artist's rendition. They are actual photos of the new SOUL Chybrids," Xander said.

"Even better," Levi said. "And they are currently disposed to our target location, correct, Doctor?"

Xander made a weak attempt to hide his elation. "At this time they have been deployed to the City of Tremayne, sir."

"Excellent." Levi folded his hands and placed them on the table. "Team, unbeknown to Dr. Felix Yaz, the defector, I enlisted the services of Dr. Rasmus to improve upon our Chybrids. The new SOUL Chybrid is an exact replica of human perfection. There is not a flaw, a blemish, a hair or pore out of place on this magnificent AI specimen."

"What's the purpose of this, Leader?" a uniformed officer asked. "And what does the SOUL part mean?"

"I'm glad you asked. First, let me give credit where credit is due." Levi gestured toward Xander. "The development of the new SOUL Chybrid has been expertly guided by our own Dr. Rasmus from the project's inception."

Xander nodded once to the group.

"First of all, Mr. Logan will be intimately involved with the SOUL Chybrid program and its deployment. We will discuss timing and strategy when he arrives. Secondly, the prefix has been attached for two very specific reasons. SOUL Chybrid serves to distinguish the new breed from the previous. The label 'SOUL' is an acronym, which stands for Specter of Ultimate Life. There is much to be gained from a proper name, team. When the effect of the SOUL Chybrid is realized in the city of Tremayne, I expect the very sound will strike fear into the hearts of the Punks. The SOUL Chybrid marks the beginning of the end for the Punks, and the birth of the Changers' global breeding farms."

CHAPTER 7

About Felix

Dr. Felix Yaz tapped a small control panel on top of the sleek black desk in his private library. A six-inch-tall holographic image of Silver Long appeared on the desktop. He tapped another key on the panel to answer the call. "Greetings, Ms. Long."

"*Yaz, where are you? My locator can't get a lock.*"

"I'm comfy and cozy in a safe place," Felix said. "Who wants to know?"

"*I do. Did you know Levi demoted me?*"

Felix reclined in his plush office chair and placed his hands in his lap. He raised an eyebrow. "And you imagine I would know such a thing? I myself am now in our leader's outer circle, so to speak."

The hologram of Silver paced back and forth within the confines of the display. "*So what are we going to do?*" she asked, stopping momentarily.

"I wasn't aware there was a *we* between you and me," Felix said.

Silver turned to face the doctor. "*There has to be. Levi's bringing in others to take our places. There's strength in numbers. We need to team up, starting with you and me.*"

"That's an interesting proposition, Ms. Long. I have done well all these years as a team of one." He interlocked his fingers behind his head and closed his eyes. "What might you bring to this new team?"

"*Do I really have to answer that?*" Silver asked. "*You know I have intimate knowledge of this entire organization.*"

"As do I," Felix said, his eyes still closed.

"*Dammit, Yaz! No one, not even you, knows Levi like I do. We'd make a great team.*"

Felix took a deep breath and exhaled. "Hmm. You haven't convinced me."

"*Look, Doctor. That, that…wench he brought in to replace me must be stopped. Did you know the first thing she did was fire Duncan and Macey?*"

Felix's eyes shot open. He stared at the ceiling.

Silver pointed at Felix. "*Ha! You didn't know that, did you?*"

A soft female voice sounded on a ceiling speaker in Felix's library. "*Security Team One, the subject has been located on the seventh level, sector one. Coordinates have been dispatched to your mobiles. Please respond immediately.*"

"*I heard that,*" Silver said. "You *are the subject, Doctor. You'd best move.*"

"I'm not there, Long. As always, you underestimate me."

"*Where the hell are you, Yaz?*"

"That isn't information I'm inclined to provide you." Felix sat forward. "Tell me more about the disposition of Duncan and Macey."

Silver chuckled. "*Oh, no. This is a two-way street. You want anything from me, you meet me someplace where we can talk in person.*"

"I am somewhat concerned regarding the fate of Ivan and Marvellus. Is your tracking circuit still active?" Felix asked.

"*Of course it is.*"

"We can't meet unless you disable it."

"*How the hell am I supposed to do that? Dig it out of my neck with a steak knife?*"

Felix swiveled in his chair and opened a large drawer in a cabinet behind him. "I have a device that will facilitate the disabling of the GPS circuit in your chip."

"*So how do I get it if you don't tell me where you are?*"

"I'm going to leave it someplace in the city where it will be accessible to you. Then I'll message your cell with the location."

Silver threw her arms up. "*Fine, Yaz. And how do I use it?*"

"I'll set the parameters. You will need to take the device and press it against your neck where your chip was implanted. When the device is firmly in place, press the power button."

Silver smiled. "*Seriously? That's it?*"

Felix held up a finger. "Sounds simple, but it will be mildly uncomfortable when the device powers on."

"*Fine. Just do it, then message me. And do it fast.*"

"Goodbye, Ms. Long."

"*But—*"

Felix pressed the disconnect on the holophone.

IVAN AND MARVELLUS SAT AT a table in the center of the Executive Dining Room on Level Seven. A black-tuxedoed waiter wiped the small round electric-blue tabletop.

"Have you decided?" the waiter asked as he tucked the cleaning cloth into a back pocket.

"I'll have the usual," Ivan said, looking at Marvellus.

"Me, too."

The waiter bowed, hands behind his back. "I'm sorry, gentlemen. "The 'usuals' are reserved in the database for senior personnel. We have been informed you are no longer ranked as seniors. Your information has been wiped from our database."

The two exchanged glances. "Okay, then," Ivan said. "I'll have a chicken Caesar salad—heavy on the dressing—one slice of garlic bread and ice water."

Marvellus shook his head slowly and refused to look at the waiter. "Give me the personal-size veggie pizza, a side salad with ranch and a diet soda."

The waiter bowed again, turned and left without another word.

"What are we gonna do?" Marvellus asked. "Wait for Dr. Rasmus to give us new assignments?"

"I don't see another option." Ivan ran a hand over his head. He looked around the dining room. "These people just go on about their business, like nothing happened."

"Nothing did for them," Marvellus said. "They all have jobs. Some of them are on their lunch breaks, some are taking a break from shopping…" His voice trailed off.

"I feel like shit, you know?"

Marvellus nodded. "I guess when you're out, you're out."

"Yeah," Ivan said. "Makes you wonder who else is out."

"And what they're doing right now."

SILVER SAT AT A LARGE desk in her office on Level Three of the Underground. She tapped a virtual keyboard and signed in to her administrative profile. She quickly scanned the holographic display.

SILVER LONG
ADMIN LEVEL: TBD
SECURITY LEVEL: 4

Her ears burned. "Security level *four*? One up from the bottom? That's the thanks I get for all my hard work and loyalty?" She pulled up a second display. *Let's see who else is at my level.* Her eyes narrowed. *Of course, Duncan, blah, blah, blah, and Macey…* She scrolled the remainder of the level four personnel list. *…and a bunch of losers I've never heard of.*

She moved her finger smoothly over the virtual mouse pad and selected the heading YOUR LEADERS. *Uh-huh*, she thought as she scrolled again. *Levi Asshole, Dr. Rasmus, Angelica Asshole, John Logan— Wait, Logan?* That *idiot?* She pounded the power button to shut down the display and pushed her rolling chair away from the desk.

"You're going to pay for this, *Leader*. Ohh, how you're going to pay!" She stood and snatched her cell from the desk. *In the meantime, I guess I should try to get some real info for Yaz if I expect anything from him.* She flipped through her contacts. *Duncan. Now where are you? Level Seven.*

THE RESTAURANT MANAGER MET TEN security guards at the entrance to the Executive Dining Room. "We've tracked a high priority security risk to this location, sir," the lead guard said.

"Of course," the manager said. "Feel free—" The lead guard pushed him aside as he motioned to the others. The guards separated into five pairs and pressed into the crowded establishment.

Ivan looked up from his salad. He motioned toward the entrance. "Hey, check that out. Someone's in serious trouble."

Marvellus turned to see the activity. "Yes, someone is." He shrugged and turned back to his pizza. "We know it's not us. We're peons now."

Ivan couldn't resist a smile. "Ha! Speaking of peons, Silver just walked in."

Silver stood just inside the restaurant next to the maître d' station and panned her cell around the dining room. *Where are you, Duncan?*

Marvellus glanced over his shoulder. "She's tracking something, or someone."

"And she's walking this way," Ivan said, raising his napkin to wipe the corners of his mouth.

Silver dropped her cell into a front pocket as she approached the pair. She nodded to the scientists as she sat down in one of two empty chairs. "Duncan, Macey. What are you losers up to?"

Ivan sat back and folded his arms across his chest. "Sure, have a seat, Silver."

Marvellus sucked a gulp of his soda through the straw. "Guess that makes three losers at the table."

"Fine, whatever," Silver said. "What's the status with you guys? Where do you go from here?"

"What?" Ivan raised his brow in mock surprise. "Is there actually something the all-knowing, all-powerful Silver Long doesn't know?"

"Sure, toy with me now, Duncan. I may be down, but I'm not out. Not by a long shot."

"Can we not play cat and mouse, or whatever it is that's going on here?" Marvellus swiped at the leftover ranch dressing with a piece of pizza crust. "What do you want from us?"

As the restaurant manager strolled by, Silver turned and snapped her fingers. "Something to drink, please."

The manager stopped. "Pardon, ma'am, I'll send a waiter."

Silver's eyes narrowed. "I don't need a waiter. Just send my usual drink."

Ivan smiled at Marvellus.

The manager motioned to a nearby waiter and pointed at Silver as he walked away.

"What are you two smiling about?" she said.

"You're about to find out what being on our level truly means," Ivan said, looking up at the waiter.

The waiter bowed. "Ma'am?"

"Yes, my usual drink, please." She turned back to Ivan and Marvellus. "Let's get something straight. I'm not on your level. You two are barely level four security."

"We've seen the database," Ivan said. "You're level four just like us."

"Excuse me, ma'am. There are no 'usuals' flagged to your account. What would you like to drink?"

Silver paused and closed her eyes. "Well, haven't they just thought of everything." She turned and looked up at the waiter. "I'll have a large ice water with two lemon wedges."

"As you wish."

"Told you," Marvellus said. "You're just like the rest of us peons now."

"I still have a special assignment from Levi," Silver said. "Have either of *you* been given assignments?"

"Still trying to get information from us?" Ivan dropped his napkin on his plate.

"All right," Silver said. "Have you spoken to Dr. Yaz? I have."

Marvellus froze mid-bite with the last morsel of pizza crust. His mouth remained open as his eyes locked on Ivan's.

THE LEAD SECURITY GUARD EXITED the kitchen and hurried past the trio's table as he spoke into his shoulder mic. "…tracker led us to a salt shaker in the kitchen…" His voice faded as his pace put distance between himself and the three demoted Changers.

Silver looked at Ivan. "They were looking for Yaz, you know. I tried tracking him myself. My locator just kept spinning."

"How do you know they were looking for Felix?" Ivan asked.

Silver leaned forward and looked around. "Because I've spoken with him. I don't know how he's doing it, but he can't be located. I think he's still in the Underground, but I can't prove it."

Marvellus tossed the last pizza bite into his salad bowl. "Why should we believe what you're telling us?"

Silver sighed and threw her hands up. "Believe what you want. Why would I lie about this? You want proof? I'll get back in touch with you after I meet with him."

Now Ivan and Marvellus leaned forward. "Wait," Marvellus said. "Aren't you being tracked, just like us?"

"Sure," Ivan agreed. "You'll just lead them to Felix. He would never allow that to happen."

Silver smiled through half-closed eyes. "Best get on the right side, boys. Dr. Yaz has made arrangements to disable the tracker in my chip. I'll meet with him when it's disabled."

"Only Felix could do that," Ivan said. "And you're not smart enough to have thought of it on your own." He looked at Marvellus. "Sounds convincing."

"Okay," Marvellus conceded. "If you actually meet with Felix, let him know we're waiting to receive new assignments from Dr. Rasmus. For the time being, we've been granted minimal access as volunteers in the junior high school lab. We get to help the teenyboppers."

Silver snorted. "Good." She slapped the tabletop. "I'm leaving. When that stupid waiter gets here with my water, tell him never mind." She stood to leave. "Service around here has really gone downhill. I'll be in touch."

CHAPTER 8

Majority Rules

RYKER SMOOTHED HIS LONG BROWN hair behind his ears and tied a black bandanna around his head. He surveyed the Punks in attendance at the impromptu meeting in the Hangar. "Okay, partner." He looked at Dion. "Only one not here that matters is Margot. She's still out in the compound."

Dion took a mental roll call. "Jasper and Lace already voted. Jimbo, have you heard back from Griff and Nevada?"

"Yep. Decisive, both of 'em, but they don't agree."

"What's their votes?" Dion asked.

"Griffin says let her back in. Nevada says let her live but kick her out."

Dion glanced at Raymond. "Get Margot in here."

Geezer stood by the inspection pit, his hands jammed into the pockets of his black parka. His bony legs shivered inside the legs of his tan overalls when the wind swept in as Raymond exited. "Shut the damn door, Ray," he cackled.

Pops smiled. "Get some meat on them bones, old-timer, and you won't be so sensitive."

"Hey, Pops," Dion said. "Anyone you can think of that we need to have in on this vote?"

Pops stuffed a wad of chew into his mouth. "Depends on exactly what the vote means." He looked around the room. "Is this an *up or down*, *keep her or not*? Or are we talking about life or death like last time?"

Geezer raised a hand. "I'm votin' keep her, Dion."

"We're not voting right now," Dion said. He looked at Pops. "I'm keeping the discussion short. I want to hear *in* or *out*, *live* or *die*. And I just want to get a quick opinion from everyone. I don't want to rehash all the BS from the last few months. Whichever way you vote, I want to hear your reason." He eyed Winter. "Not that anyone's reason would nullify their vote. If you just have a good or bad feeling about it, I want to know."

"You've been damn quiet, Win," Ryker said. "What're you thinking?"

Winter stood next to Pops, hands on her hips. "You know me best, Ryk. I wanna hear everyone else's reasons and votes first."

Raymond walked in from the compound with Margot. "Why's that, Winter?" he asked. "You gonna vote based on someone else's vote?"

Geezer's face soured. "Shut the damn door, Ray!"

Winter turned to face Raymond. She dropped her arms to her sides. "You know what, Ray? You've been my right hand for the last two years. Don't be stepping up on me now."

As intimidating as Winter appeared, Raymond backed down out of respect for her authority over him. "Just asking, Win. I think we should all be free to voice our opinions without any reprisals." He crossed his arms and turned to Dion. "Right, boss?"

Dion ignored the question. "Okay, looks like we got everyone here. Everybody agree?"

Ryker strolled over to his dirt bike and half sat, half leaned on the seat. "I think Pops has something on his mind."

Dion looked at Krystal, still standing next to Pops. He raised an eyebrow. "Well?"

Pops glanced back and forth between Krystal and Dion. "Well…"

"Go ahead, Pops," Ryker said. "It's just us."

"Well, I think the Three Amigos should be in on this."

"No fuckin' way," Raymond protested.

Margot smiled. "Whadda you got against the Three Amigos, buddy? I kinda like the idea."

"They don't hold any rank," Dion said.

"They're loose cannons," Jimbo agreed.

"Wait," Krystal said. "Who are the Three Amigos?"

Geezer took off his glasses and pulled the rag out of his back pocket. He pointed his spectacles at Krystal. "They's the ones told us about you, for starters. You know 'em. They talked to you when you were holed up at that Changers outpost."

Krystal's eyes narrowed. "Those guys? Wow. Seems to me they must be in pretty good standing for you people to even be debating whether they get a vote in this."

"Hep," Geezer said. "Lemme tell you who wouldn't be standing here if'n not for the Three Amigos." One at a time, he pointed his rag at Ryker, Winter, Raymond and Dion. "Him, her, him and him. Those guys pulled all yer asses out of the fire."

"He's right," Pops agreed.

Ryker caught Dion's eye. "Can't argue with that, partner."

Dion motioned to Jimbo. "Get Will on the radio. Get a vote from them."

Jimbo walked swiftly to the door leading to the Depot. "In or out?"

Dion grabbed Jimbo's arm. "In, out, live or die."

"You got it."

"That's bullshit," Raymond said. "We should all get to decide if they can even vote."

Dion snapped his head in Raymond's direction. "When you rise up as the leader of this organization, you can vote on whatever you want. I say they get a vote."

Raymond scowled. "This is no fucking organization. It's not even organized anymore."

Margot stepped over and stood next to Winter. "'Sup with your partner, sister?"

Winter stared straight ahead. "He's being an ass."

"Being an ass and digging a hole for himself all at the same time. Two and two says that makes him an asshole."

"You got that right."

Dion held up his hand. "All right, everyone." He looked at Krystal. "It all comes down to this vote, here and now. Everyone gets a vote. The vote is final." He looked around the room at each Punk before turning to Raymond. "And everyone accepts the final vote. This will include the two Changers, Garrison and Dennis, sitting in my quarters right now. They'll go the way of Krystal. If she's voted in, they're in, and vice versa." He shifted his gaze to Winter. "And for the record, I'm voting last."

Winter nodded.

Ryker raised his hand and stood up from the dirt bike. "I'll go first." He deliberately faced Dion, not turning to see the faces of his comrades or Krystal. "I vote she lives. I vote we bring her back in as one of us." Now he turned to Krystal. "I also suggest we promote her to second level commander."

Dion raised an eyebrow. "Reasons?"

"She saved our asses. The Chybrids were as good as over the Perimeter Wall until she showed up. She didn't have to do what she did."

Jimbo stepped into the Hangar from the Depot. He nodded at Dion.

"I'll vote," Pops said. "Me and Geezer vote the same as Ryk, for all the same reasons."

Geezer whipped his specs off and snapped his head toward Pops. "Hep, I'll vote for myself, you old fart."

Pops spit his wad into a mason jar and smiled.

Geezer looked across the room at Dion. He motioned to Pops with his glasses. "What he said. And that's *my* vote!"

Dion looked at Raymond. "Ray?"

"Kill. Out." He folded his arms across his chest.

"Margot?" Dion asked.

"I'm gonna have to halfway agree with Ray. I say out, but let her live."

"I'm with Margot," Jimbo said. "Out. Live."

Dion looked at Winter. "You're up, Win."

Winter glanced at Jimbo, then Ryker. She adjusted the 9mm pistol on her hip. "Out. Live."

"So it's up to me, then," Dion said. He walked to the center of the Hangar and faced Krystal. "I'm going to stick with my original decision. Thank you, Krys, from the bottom of my heart, and on behalf of all of the Punks, for everything you did for us. I vote to keep you out of the Punks, but let you live."

Raymond clenched his fist and flexed his body. "Yes!"

"That's six to six, people," Dion said. "Anyone disagrees, correct me, but here's my count. The Punks voting to let Peterson live and to bring her back in are Ryk, Pops, Geezer, Griffin, Jasper and Lace. That's six. The votes to keep her out of the organization are me, Jimbo, Winter, Margot, Nevada and Raymond. That's six." He looked at Pops. "But there's a tiebreaker. The Three Amigos have voted. With three votes, there will be no tie."

He turned to Jimbo. "Jim?"

"Well, you're right about there being no tie. The Three Amigos' vote was unanimous."

Krystal adjusted the rifles on her shoulders. She didn't know these guys, and she had no reason to hope one way or another.

Pops looked at the side of Krystal's face.

Winter folded her arms across her chest to mirror Raymond's stance.

Margot leaned against the workbench, thumbs hooked in the front pockets of her vest.

Geezer removed his glasses again.

Jimbo gazed around the Hangar. "They all voted *live* and *in*."

"Bullshit!" Raymond shouted. He turned, stormed out of the Hangar and left the door open.

Geezer scowled at the open door. Then he looked at Pops and cackled. "Hep."

DION WALKED OVER TO KRYSTAL. "Well, Krys." He smiled and held out his fist. "Welcome back."

Krystal pounded a fist on top of his. "Thanks, Dion." She

looked around at the roomful of Punk commanders. "I'd like to say a few things, then I have some questions."

Ryker stood and strode over to Krystal. She held out a fist. He bumped it and immediately embraced her in a full two-armed hug. "Welcome back, Krys."

She returned the hug with one arm.

Ryker turned to Dion. "Rank?"

"Second level commander," Dion said, eyeing Krystal. "Now, you have something to say?"

"First, I want to let everyone here know you won't regret this vote. I made a mistake becoming a Changer. I also want all of you to know I never compromised the Punks in any way, despite the fact that was my assignment from the Changers."

"I believe her," Pops said.

"So do I," Ryker agreed.

Krystal un-shouldered her rifles and leaned them against Ryker's dirt bike. "There's one more thing. I'm not a Changer anymore."

Winter's eyes widened. "Wait." She looked at Lace, then back to Krystal. "We all thought that was irreversible."

"It's a long story, and it's not something that's ever happened before. I was the first."

"You must have some contacts pretty high up in the Changers, then," Lace said.

"I do," Krystal agreed. "Which brings me to some questions I have." She looked at Dion.

Dion nodded. "Ask away."

"First of all, where's Curtis?"

The room fell silent. Everyone deferred to Dion to respond. "Basically, Krys, he's AWOL. The last we heard from him, he was in Tremayne the night of the Chybrid attack on Checkpoint One. He was on a roll, Krys. He exposed Stringer as a Changer and took him out."

Krystal raised an eyebrow. "Sounds like he was doing what he does best."

Dion looked down at his feet. "There's a lot more to it."

"Okay?" Krystal said, looking around at the somber faces in the Hangar.

"His team also took down two pretty big-name Changers. They were both spies. One was masquerading as a Bystander—the mayor's liaison. I'm ashamed to say the other one was yet another spy in our organization."

"Van Buren and Logan," Krystal said.

Dion looked up. "You knew?"

"Yeah, I knew. But I'm not answering to anything I knew or did before today. So where are they now?"

Ryker sat back down on his dirt bike. "Scotty Van Buren is dead. Curtis's crew took him out."

For the first time, Krystal showed a hint of emotion. She suppressed a smile. "Good. And Johnny Logan?"

"That's the bitch about it," Ryker said. "Far as we know, he's alive. So is Curtis. We just don't know where they are."

"Whadda you mean, you don't know? I can't imagine Curtis would have it in him to go AWOL."

Lace pulled herself up onto the workbench, her feet dangling. "No one thought that. Till I talked to his crew after everyone came back from Tremayne."

Krystal glanced quickly back and forth between Lace, Ryker and Dion. "All right, already. Spit it out, somebody!"

Ryker got up and walked to Krystal. He put a hand on her shoulder. "We all heard about how you broke up with Curtis. Pretty much nuked his world. I gave him orders to take Logan into custody and bring him back here. Last thing he said was 'Will do.'"

The only sound in the Hangar came from the increasing wind outside.

Krystal remained stone-faced as a tear rolled down her cheek. "Where's Garrison and Dennis?"

Dion lit a cigarette and clinked his Zippo shut. "My quarters."

"I need to see them." Krystal locked eyes with Dion. "Now."

CHAPTER 9

Location Unknown

SILVER WALKED SWIFTLY THROUGH THE crowded pedestrian expressway on level seven. Citizens of the Underground immersed themselves in the many shops, eateries and other businesses lining the thoroughfare. Several people, obviously unaware of her demotion, greeted Silver with the same respect she was accustomed to receiving as security chief. Government employees were a different story. Guards walking in pairs looked past her with no apparent recognition, if they looked at all.

Two electronic alert tones sounded throughout the City's global intercom system. Silver recognized the pattern and pitch as a security alert. "*Security Team One, the subject has been located on level nine, sector three. Coordinates have been dispatched to your mobiles. Please respond immediately.*"

Silver smiled to herself. *Another Yaz decoy*, she thought as she stopped to browse the display in a jewelry store window. She had decided to go inside the store when her cell vibrated. She glanced at the screen. *Hmm. Text from a private number.* She tapped the screen to check the message.

Level three.
Executive parking.

Receiving room.
Your locker.

Yaz. What the hell? I don't even know if I'm allowed there any-
more. And how'd you get into my locker? Silver deleted the message
and slipped her phone back into her pants pocket. She stood at
the entrance to the jewelry store, panned the expressway and
made a quick decision to head east to the nearest elevator.

A group of four people hustled out as the elevator door opened.
One man nodded to Silver and smiled. "Greetings, ma'am."

"Hello."

The man was obviously oblivious to Silver's new status. She
looked at the uniformed elevator attendant. "Level three."

The short man nodded and pressed a button on the keypad.

When Silver stepped out of the elevator on level three, no one
was in the hallway. She turned right and headed away from the
main city area toward the executive parking reception room. The
guard at the door spread both legs to shoulder-width and blocked
the doorway as Silver approached.

Ignoring the guard's attitude, Silver attempted to enter the
room. "Excuse me, please." She swiped her hand over the palm
reader on the wall. The panel emitted a low buzzing sound indi-
cating her identification was not recognized.

"Ma'am," the guard said. "This room is for authorized personnel only."

Silver glanced up and down the corridor before looking at
the guard's face. "Okay, I'm no longer authorized for entrance
here, but I have some personal effects I left in my locker. I need
to get them now. Surely I'm authorized to remove my personal
belongings."

The guard stared straight ahead. "One moment, ma'am." He
spoke into a communications device on his wrist. "Base, this is
Station Three-A."

"Go ahead, Three-A."

"A citizen is requesting entrance. States she has personal
effects to retrieve."

Silence.

"*Stand by, Three-A. We're processing the citizen's data via GPS.*"

The guard remained still, hands behind his back, eyes staring straight ahead above Silver.

"*Three-A. We're obtaining third level approval. Stand by.*"

Third level approval, Silver thought. *A week ago I'd have had your job with a wave of my hand, Mister Third Level. Whatever. Just get me in.*

"*Base to Three-A.*"

"Three-A."

"*Entry is approved, with escort. Be advised, approval has a five-minute time limit.*"

"10-4, Base."

For the first time, the guard made eye contact with Silver. "Right this way, ma'am." He turned around and waved his hand over the palm reader, and the door clicked open.

Silver pushed past the guard and hurried across the room to the wall of lockers. She quickly found hers and used the fingerprint panel to unlock the door. She swung the blue titanium door open and peered inside. An electronic device about the length of a touchscreen stylus—and three times the diameter—sat on the top shelf.

Silver glanced up at the guard. Thankful he was standing with his back to the locker, she snatched the device and dropped it into her pocket. She slapped the door shut and turned to leave. "Thanks, I'm done," she said as she walked briskly to the door.

Two sharply dressed security guards approached Silver as she exited the Executive Receiving Room. One guard held her hand in the air.

Great, she thought. *Now what?*

"Ma'am," the guard greeted.

Ah. Silver recognized the guard as a member of her personal staff when she was head of security. "Hello, Steph."

Steph and the other guard stopped in front of Silver. "So, what brings you out this way? Still have executive parking privileges?"

Silver smiled. "No, not anymore. I just had to collect some personal items from my locker."

"Oh. Well, I know things aren't the same as they used to be. But if you ever need anything, don't hesitate to give me a ring."

"Hey, I might just do that," Silver said. "Well, I gotta go. It's been good to see you, really."

"Same here, ma'am. See you around."

Silver continued down the corridor toward the City. *Nice to know I may still have some friends in higher places*, she thought. *After all, what good are friends if you can't use them for your own purposes? As long as no one gets hurt.* She smiled to herself.

She rounded a curve in the hallway and spotted a door with a tiny vertical wire-mesh window to her left. There was a sign on the door.

FACILITY 301 – AUTHORIZED PERSONNEL ONLY.

Hmm. This is as good a place as any if I can get in. She swiped her hand across the reader. The door clicked. *Yes. Level four security accessible!*

She stepped through the doorway and allowed the door to close behind her. She found herself in a small ten-foot by ten-foot room. The walls were painted a hideous pale green. There was a small desk on one side of the dimly lit room. On the other side was a wall with only a bulletin board containing various safety fliers and a clipboard with a sign-in page attached. The far wall, if you could call it a wall, was mostly a portal into a larger area with no lights. The only actual surface on the wall was just wide enough to hang a small fire extinguisher on one side, with a light switch on the other.

Silver stepped across the room to the portal and flipped the light switch. Ceiling lights in the darkened area illuminated the spacious room, revealing row after row of pipes and valves of varying sizes. She gazed around the room. *Perfect place to disable a GPS chip.*

Glancing to her right, she noticed a huge pipe about twenty-four inches in diameter running parallel to the wall. A quick look behind her into the tiny green room proved using the pipe for a seat would put her out of view to any passersby in the corridor. She removed the device she had retrieved from her locker and walked over to the big pipe.

Silver sat down and examined the gadget, remembering Felix's instructions. *Press it against your neck where your chip was implanted. When the device is firmly in place, press the power button.* She shrugged. *Simple enough.* She ran her fingers under her hair at the base of her skull and probed around for what seemed like sixty seconds or more. *Got it,* she thought. She pressed the business end of the apparatus hard against the chip and pushed the button.

"Aaagh!" Silver screamed. The lightning-like pain was excruciating, but she held firm to the device, forcing her head against her hand. When the power stopped, she opened her hand. The apparatus bounced off the pipe and onto the floor as Silver's head jerked backward. She heard her head smack against the concrete wall behind her before losing consciousness and slumping to the floor.

CHAPTER 10

Changing Curtis

CURTIS SAT QUIETLY ON A polished titanium bench in a ten-foot by ten-foot cell in the Changers' Underground. He gazed at the white floor and walls, and the tiny window in the handleless door. Two security guards stood sentry in the hallway outside the cell.

Curtis was alone with his thoughts. *I love you, Krys. Soon, we'll be the same.* He'd always wondered how long it took to effect the Change on a person. So many had gone before him—loners, geeks, rich people, lottery winners. *Krystal.*

He ran a hand over his wilted Mohawk. *Guess I'll have to find a new style.* He felt out of place in his jeans. He stretched his arms out, palms down. *Wonder if my tats will survive?* His vision blurred as his eyes locked on Krystal's name on his left bicep. *Dammit!* He swiped the tears from his cheeks.

The lock on the door clicked. Curtis hopped to his feet as the door slid sideways into the wall.

"Say, what's up, dude?" Johnny smiled broadly at his new protégé. "You been cryin'?"

Fucking Logan. "Nah." Curtis mashed his palms into his eyes. "Just tired. I was kinda drifting off."

"Well, wake up, buddy. We gotta make you presentable. There's some people I want you to meet."

"Okay, well, I'm ready." Curtis snatched his leather jacket from the end of the bench and walked toward Johnny.

Johnny stood in the doorway and held up a hand. "Oh, sorry, but you gotta be cuffed. Security." He shrugged. "You know."

Curtis held his wrists out to the lead guard. The other guard stepped past Johnny and quickly slapped a metallic strap around Curtis's neck. Attached to the strap was a shiny lightweight alloy pole about four feet long.

The guard handed the pole to Johnny. "Thank you, sir." Johnny looked at Curtis and grinned. "It's only temporary, dude."

Curtis heard the whining of a small motor as the collar tightened around his neck. He reached up in time to jam his thumbs between the collar and his throat. "Gah!" He looked at Johnny.

"Man, your face is turning red," Johnny said.

"I…can't…breathe…" Curtis managed to choke out three words before he felt the blood pounding in his head.

"Hang on a sec," Johnny said. He checked the far end of the pole and spun a small roller switch with one thumb.

Curtis heard the little motor again and yanked his thumbs out from under the collar. He bent over, hands on his knees, and sucked in a lungful of air. The metallic pole followed his awkward movement, flipping into the air before clinking against the floor.

"Hold up, hold up," Johnny said, reaching for the pole. "Dude, I had it just right. You gotta calm down."

Curtis stood upright, feeling the slight head rush of relief he expected. "Seriously, Logan? I don't feel like much more than an animal right now."

"It's just protocol, man." Johnny motioned to the lead guard. "We're gonna need an escort. The, uh, *citizenry* isn't going to react kindly to the prisoner." He eyed Curtis. "He's got Punk written all over him."

The guard nodded and spoke into his wrist mic.

Prisoner? Curtis thought. *What the hell?*

"Let's go, man." Johnny tugged on the pole and guided Curtis to walk in front of him.

Curtis's steps faltered as he attempted to match Johnny's gait. He moved swiftly down the narrow corridor, feeling the nudge at the back of his neck with each awkward step.

"That elevator up ahead," Johnny said.

Two guards met the pair at the elevator. Curtis was thankful for the break. At least standing in the elevator he wouldn't have to endure the constant tugging at his neck and throat.

The guards followed Johnny and Curtis onto the elevator.

"Ten," the lead guard said to the attendant.

Johnny wrangled Curtis around toward the front of the elevator. He reached over the attendant and pressed the number seven button on the control panel. He looked down at the back of Curtis's head. "Thought you might want to take a little tour of the business sector before meetin' my boss."

"Actually, I'd just like to get the formalities out of the way—"

"Ah, you'll like this." Johnny smiled. His eyes widened. "Hey, you'll get to see what living the good life really is."

The two guards glanced at each other, expressionless.

Curtis's muscles tightened as he stared at his distorted reflection in the stainless-steel elevator door. *What the hell, Logan. What the fucking hell.*

When the elevator door opened, Curtis felt the less-than-gentle prodding he had come to expect at the back of his neck. He stepped into a wide hallway and glanced both ways.

"Head on left, buddy," Johnny urged. "Hear that? That's the sound of the good life!"

Johnny's enthusiasm was lost on Curtis. The sound of people—laughter, shouting, casual conversation—was low on Curtis's list right now. He wanted to meet the leader of the Changers, be changed, and find Krystal.

When the pair reached the end of the short corridor, the walkway widened onto what appeared to be a city street. *Holy fuck.*

The three-way intersection was filled with people, cars and bicycles. The two streets visible to Curtis consisted of two lanes, each with a center turn lane. Shops and businesses lined the streets as far as he could see. Numerous offices, restaurants, and jewelry, electronics and clothing stores were open for business. Everything seemed to be constructed of ultrasmooth concrete, polished steel and glass. Anything not white glowed some shade of blue.

People crossed the streets at will. There were no crosswalks and no pedestrian signals. But lighting was plentiful and bright. Curtis looked up at what appeared to be clear blue sky above the buildings.

Johnny grinned. "You like?"

Curtis reached up and grabbed his metal collar to ease the pressure on his throat. "This is as clean and bright as any city I've ever seen."

"Let's go across the street," Johnny prodded. "I wanna show you something." He pushed the titanium pole against the collar around Curtis's neck.

Curtis stumbled off the curb into the street in front of an oncoming car. His mind flashed between pulling hard on the pole to yank Johnny across with him, and shoving backward to avoid being roadkill.

Johnny held firm, forcing Curtis to remain dead center in the path of the car.

Curtis's mind raced as he thought of every place he'd rather be. His nerves were shot as the car approached. He squeezed his eyes shut, braced for impact and lost control of his bladder. The pressure of the collar pulled him down as laughter filled his ears—Johnny Logan's laughter.

Johnny was doubled over, hands on his knees. When he caught his breath, he stood and pointed at Curtis. "Dude, you peed your pants!"

When Curtis looked up, there was a ten-foot cushion of air between the stopped car and his legs. He looked at Johnny. "Fuck you, Logan."

"Dude, all the vehicles on this level are self-driving. We got sensors in the road that caused that car to stop in time." He chuckled. "Oh, and they're all electric, too. You don't smell any fumes around here. Betcha didn't notice that, huh?"

Several small groups of people stopped to watch the commotion caused by the two. The pedestrian sensors held traffic at a standstill as additional people crowded into the street to check the scene and offer opinions.

"Sure enough wet his pants."

"Poor kid."

"What's he doing shackled up by his neck like that?"

"That's Mr. Logan. He knows what he's doing. Bet the guy's a criminal."

"Look at him. He looks like a Punk."

"Probably gettin' a grand tour on his way to the Arena!"

Subconsciously, Curtis blocked the banter and the din. He looked at Johnny, his eyes silently pleading.

Johnny held up his free hand to the crowd. "All right, everybody. There's nothing happening here. Everybody just go back to your business." He tugged on the pole. "Let's go, buddy. You've seen enough."

Johnny guided Curtis back to the sidewalk and into the hallway leading to the elevator.

Although Curtis's leg was cold from the wet and his neck raw from the ill-fitting collar, he was thankful to be back into the safety and dignity—if you could call it that—of the empty corridor.

A soothing female voice emanated from the overhead speaker in Levi's conference room. "*Pardon, Leader. Mr. Logan is in the city and en route to your location. ETA is approximately two minutes.*"

Levi scanned the table. "Our SOUL Chybrid initiative is designed to take advantage of the lowly Bystanders, who continue to do what they do best—nothing. This does not mean they will not see what is coming at them. They will not only see it, they will embrace it. John Logan will head up a vital part of this project. Specifically, he will work closely with the youth of Tremayne."

A sharp-dressed member in uniform raised his hand.

"Yes, General."

"Why the youth? We recently destroyed the Punks' organization. It was Changer against Punk. Adult against adult. Need I say we prevailed? There were no youth involved in any battle or altercation."

Levi smiled and looked around the table. "Suffice it to say we believe that when we capture the minds of the youth, they will be ours forever."

"So, what good is our mighty Changers military machine?"

A low murmur of agreement spread among the military members present.

Levi stopped smiling. "I have debated that myself, General."

Angelica raised her eyes to assess the general's reaction.

Dr. Rasmus jotted notes into an electronic tablet.

The military fell silent.

Levi clapped his hands once, then rubbed them together. "With that, before Mr. Logan arrives, I am going to ask all but my inner circle to adjourn to your regular duties. I thank you for your attendance."

Changers military personnel and attendees from the corporate marketing team rose and pushed their chairs in under the table. They dutifully shuffled out the double sliding doors and into the War Room.

Angelica smiled at Levi. "I do detect a bit of unrest among the military, Leader."

"I trust you have protocol in place to manage any issues that might arise."

"My department is embedded in the military, sir."

Levi smiled. "Of course it is. Good work."

CURTIS PAUSED MOMENTARILY OUTSIDE ANOTHER set of slick stainless-steel doors. The metal sleeve around his neck dug into his collarbones as he pulled down on the top of it to relieve pressure on his throat. Blood seeped from the cuts on his neck and soaked into his T-shirt. His signature Mohawk had long since flattened.

Johnny guided his prisoner-on-a-stick through the round multi-tiered War Room. Technicians at computer terminals paused to view the spectacle. Johnny gazed around the room, looking up and smiling as he waved to the technicians.

A computer operator in the top tier nudged the man next to her. "What a jerk, you know?"

The man shook his head. "Last time I witnessed anything so degrading was when they paraded Krystal Peterson through here." He lowered his voice and leaned in to his coworker. "In a way, I'm glad she escaped."

"Better watch what you say," the woman said. "We could both get in trouble for that comment."

Two guards entered the conference room in front of Curtis and Johnny. Conversation at the table came to an abrupt end as all parties present looked up.

Levi stood. "Logan. What's this?"

Curtis surveyed the Changers around the table. His stomach churned.

"Hello, Levi," Johnny said. "I've brought a prisoner. A high-ranking Punk." He glanced at Curtis and smiled. "At least he used to be high-ranking."

Angelica didn't hide her irritation. "Why?"

Johnny locked eyes with Angelica. "First of all, I don't answer to you."

"But you answer to me," Levi said. "Why is this dreg in my conference room? And I suggest you weigh your answer carefully." He shot a look at Angelica. "This is a security breach."

"Leader," Angelica said. "This man has the highest security clearances. He could have brought the entire Punk leadership in here and no one would have questioned it."

"Logan?" Levi said.

Johnny tuned his demeanor specifically for the moment. "Leader, this is Curtis Dyer. He is formerly a second level commander in the Punks' organization. He is a defector from the Punks and wants to undergo the Change. There is no doubt in my mind that as a former Punk, he would be valuable to us."

Levi sat down. "Ms. DeMone, what are your thoughts?"

"On the surface it sounds like a positive development. However, he would have to undergo comprehensive debriefing to gain approval from my department."

Levi appeared irritated. "I don't know, Logan." His voice took on a whiny tone. "This isn't the same scenario as Peterson. She basically grew up in our organization. She wasn't embedded so deeply in the enemy camp when she came to us." He flitted his hand in the air. "There's so much for this one to learn."

Xander cleared his throat. "If I may. We are well beyond primitive Neural Lace technology. We can teach this man everything he needs to know in a matter of minutes."

"Is that wise?" Angelica asked. "If we allow this man to become one of us, why not feed his brain what he needs to know incrementally? As he proves his worth and loyalty, provide him with additional information. I see no sense in bringing an unknown up to our level of knowledge."

"I agree," Levi said. "Doctor?"

"That sounds reasonable. I wasn't suggesting we accelerate his knowledge to our level. Only that we have the capability. It wouldn't be such a waste to bring him into our organization."

Johnny smiled. "Exactly what I was thinking."

Levi eyed Curtis up and down. "Remove the man's shackles, Logan. He looks barbaric."

Johnny spun the electronic thumb wheel at the base of the pole and unlatched the collar. He handed the pole to one of the guards.

"He smells," Xander said.

"The smell of a Punk," Levi said. "We'll have the office disinfected when we're done here." He looked at Curtis. "Have a seat, Mr. Dyer."

Thank God, Curtis thought as he seated himself at the chair nearest him. He felt the grit inside his shirt on his back despite the plushness of the chair. He knew the smell was from dried blood, sweat and urine. He looked at Levi. "Thank you, sir."

Levi smiled. "Well, we're off to a proper start. So you want to be a Changer. Have you made any financial arrangements to pay for the procedure?"

Curtis kept his hands in his lap. His mind raced. He thought of Dion and Ryker. He thought of his parents. Mostly, he thought of Krystal. He measured his words. "Well, sir. I don't have any money to speak of. But I believe what I can bring to this organization in terms of intelligence about the inner workings of the Punks will more than pay for itself."

"How so?"

"Well, as far as I know, the Punks don't know my whereabouts. The last they knew, I was working for them. I know their modes of operation and their emotional tendencies, down to the individual."

"And what do you have against the Punks? Why the change?"

Curtis looked at Angelica and Xander and their assistants, then back at Levi. "I was recently demoted by the Punks, sir. And I believe the demotion was unfair and unwarranted."

"Why did they demote you?" Angelica asked.

This will seal my deal, Curtis thought. "Because I prevented them from murdering a Changer."

Angelica glanced at Dr. Rasmus.

Levi raised an eyebrow. "Well, Ms. DeMone? Doctor?"

Xander nodded once.

Angelica shrugged. "It may be worth a shot. But if we ultimately allow this Punk to become a Changer, my team will be watching him closely. He won't be able to wipe his ass without us knowing about it until I get a warm and fuzzy."

"Very well," Levi said. "Guards, get this man cleaned up. We have much to discuss with him before a final decision is made. The Change is not something to be taken lightly."

He looked at Johnny. "Have a seat now, Logan. Time will tell if your little gamble pays off. In the meantime, I have some people I want you to meet."

CHAPTER 11

Connecting Dots

A GUST OF WIND ACCOMPANIED KRYSTAL as she entered Dion's quarters at Checkpoint One. Fred Garrison and Thomas Dennis, engaged in quiet conversation, sat comfortably on an eight-foot-wide leather sofa facing the door. They looked up as the door swung shut.

"Peterson!" the two scientists said in unison.

Krystal suppressed a smile. "Not meaning to sound trite, but you two look like you've just seen a ghost."

Fred stood and walked around the large glass coffee table to Krystal. "Krys. I don't know whether to hug you or look for an escape route."

Krystal finally smiled. "Hugs are fine."

The hesitation Fred had displayed moments before was gone. He embraced Krystal and smiled.

Krystal returned the hug, one-armed.

Fred stepped back and held her shoulders. "I have to say, you are absolutely the last person I expected to see."

Thomas strode across the room and hugged Krystal. "It's so good to see you, Krystal."

"I can't believe you two," Krystal said. "What are you doing here, anyway?"

Thomas shook his head. "No place else to go."

"I can think of plenty of places I'd rather be," Krystal said. "How'd you get out of the Underground?"

The pair looked at each other. "Felix," Fred said.

"Me, too," Krystal said.

The trio stood in silence for several moments.

"You really did a number on the Chybrids," Thomas said. "I take it that was Dr. Yaz's doing as well?"

"It was. I think you guys know he developed the skull-buster bullets for the AR-15. I used a shit-ton of those bullets to take down the Chybrids. And there's plenty left over to provide to the Punks for any future attacks."

Fred gazed deeply into Krystal's eyes. He stepped back. "Either you're not a Changer anymore, or I'm not." He glanced at Thomas. "Check her eyes."

Thomas looked at Krystal's eyes, then Fred's. "We're Changers. She's not."

"Felix reversed the Change," Krystal admitted.

"Wow," Fred said. "I knew it was possible." He looked at Thomas. "We brought the procedure out of the Underground with us, along with a lot of other information, when we left. But the Change has never been reversed on anyone. At least not until now."

"Felix has the procedure memorized," Krystal said. "Too bad he can't reverse the Change on himself. He wants out pretty bad." She hoisted herself onto a nearby barstool. "So, like I said before, what are you two doing here?"

Fred hopped onto an adjacent barstool. Thomas strolled across the room and leaned against the back of a leather love seat.

"It's a long story, Krys," Fred said. "Probably as long as yours. Suffice it to say, we got busted for talking to you after you escaped the Underground. We knew we were as good as dead—"

"Or worse," Thomas said.

"Yeah, or worse. We knew we had to choose sides." Fred shrugged. "While we were in lockup, Felix came with these three little Punk kids and broke us out."

"Yeah," Thomas said. "Those little kids drove us back here. But not before making a detour and rescuing a company of Punks who were under attack by the Chybrids."

Krystal smiled. "The Three Amigos. They're badasses for as young as they are."

"Call 'em what you want," Thomas said. "They saved our butts and a lot of Punks, too."

Fred fidgeted with a cork coaster on the bar top. "So, anyway. We knew we had to choose a side. No one hates the Changers more than we do, Krys. We came to help the Punks in any way we can to defeat the Changers."

Krystal stood and removed her duster. She walked to the far side of the room and laid it neatly onto the pool table. She turned around, folded her arms across her chest and leaned against the table. "I'm here to help the Punks as well. But I have something else on my mind that's more important to me than the Punks' organization."

"Let's hear it," Thomas said.

"As long as you two have been here, have you heard anyone mention a guy named Curtis Dyer?"

Fred and Thomas exchanged glances.

"Just that no one knows where he is," Fred said. "From what we've heard, he's thought of pretty highly. I guess he took out a couple of our people—I mean Changers—who were embedded as Punks. Scotty Van Buren was one of them."

Krystal raised an eyebrow. "Right. I heard."

"Yep," Thomas said. "Courtesy of your Curtis Dyer. Because of that, we heard Mr. Dyer was restored to his previous rank, second level."

"Yeah," Krystal said. "And he's just gone. Just like that."

Fred stood up and walked behind the bar. "Beer anyone?"

"Me," Krystal and Thomas said in unison.

Fred popped the tops on three beer bottles and handed one each to the two. "So what's your interest in Curtis?"

"I'm in love with him."

Fred's eyes widened. "Seriously? From what you're saying, you had to have been in love with him when you were a Changer. That's strictly forbidden."

"Screw the Changers and their rules," Krystal said. "It happened. So what? The Changers can't touch me now."

"So what do you want, Krystal?" Thomas asked.

Krystal chugged three heavy swallows of her beer. "To make things right between Curtis and me—the way they should have been before I fucked up."

"How'd you mess up, Krys?" Fred asked.

Krystal stared at her bottle. "Last time I talked to him, I was way too hard on him. Look, guys, I was hard for a reason. I didn't know what I was getting myself into. I knew I was heading back to literally save the Punks from the Chybrids. But the new me— my body, my weapons, my resolve—was all unproven. I didn't know if I was going to live or die. I figured if I died, I wanted Curtis to think I wasn't worth having. You know, so he could move on without me, just in case."

Fred slid his beer around the moisture that had condensed under his bottle on the bar top. "Wow, Krys. That's tough."

Krystal guzzled the last of her beer. "No shit, Garrison. So, now that I'm no longer a Changer, I have to talk to him. We can be together now that we're both free and totally human."

Krystal looked up when Dion and Ryker entered the room. "Hey, guys. You're just in time." She underhanded her empty bottle toward the pair. When Dion sidestepped the projectile, Ryker snatched it mid-flight.

"Damn, girl," Ryker said. "You want another one?"

"I'm good with one," Krystal said. "So what's our next move?"

Dion glanced at Fred and Thomas. "Did Krys tell you two we voted to keep you?"

"What's that supposed to mean?" Thomas asked.

Ryker reached behind the bar and grabbed two bottles of beer. "We took a vote. If Krystal stays, you stay. You're all staying."

Dion looked at Krystal. "To answer your question, no one believes the Changers are done with their shenanigans. No doubt they know we slaughtered the Chybrids." He nodded at Krystal.

"Thanks to you. Best we can guess is they'll come back at us with so many Chybrids we don't have enough of your special bullets to stop them all."

Krystal shook her head. "You're way off base. My bet is they're hoping you think that so they can attack with something else."

"That makes more sense than what you said, Dion," Fred said. "The Changers are in a constant state of development. Even if they thought they would defeat you with the Chybrid attack, their research and development is ongoing."

"So translate that for us," Ryker said, handing a beer to Dion. "Are you saying there will be a wave of new and improved Chybrids?"

Fred shrugged. "I don't know. But by now, they know the Punks are still standing. And even if they weren't, the Chybrid project never stopped. The next wave, if there is one, will be with an upgraded version of what they just sent."

"I'll take another one," Thomas said. "Get with the program, people. You need to change your way of thinking. You need to be more forward thinking."

"Meaning?" Dion asked.

"Meaning just because you got lucky and Krystal saved your asses this time doesn't mean you can let your guard down."

Two-way radio banter caught Ryker's attention as he stood behind the bar. He turned up the volume on the overhead speakers.

"*The whole day started weird. Once I found out the Chybrids were down at Checkpoint One, the absence of people in Tremayne didn't sit right.*" The voice was Nico's.

"*Copy that, partner,*" the Unit Two Punk replied. "*We're taking Little Man into custody now. We'll bring him to headquarters and see if he knows anything.*"

"*10-4. In the meantime, get that Jane Doe to the hospital ASAP. I'll follow up with Adam for additional details.*"

"*She's en route now, Nico. You might want to have someone meet her at the hospital for whenever she regains consciousness.*"

"*That'd be me,*" Nico replied. "*I'll head there shortly.*"

"*Sounds good. I'm out.*"

Jimbo broke in from the Depot at Checkpoint One. *"Nico, it's Jimbo. Do you copy?"*

"Go, Jim."

"Sounds a little hectic there. Contact Dion ASAP. Let him know what's happening."

"Will do, Jim. Dion, it's Nico. Do you copy?"

Dion stepped behind the bar.

Thomas caught Fred's attention and nodded. "Changers bullshit. Just like I was talking about."

Dion frowned and looked at Thomas. "You can't possibly know that."

"It's exactly what I just said. You people need to correct your vision, the way you look at things. If something's out of place, assume it's the Changers first. If it's not, you're out nothing. If it is, you're prepared. Mark my words."

"Nico, it's Dion. I copy. Go ahead."

"Hey, Dion. Quick synopsis. Kids are acting strange. No adults present except a woman we found in an alley. She's been beat up pretty bad. Some kids were at the scene with her, but they ran off."

"Thanks for that, Nico." Dion looked up at Thomas. "First off, we haven't put out the word in Tremayne that the Chybrid threat is contained. The adults have their families holed up in their homes. They won't resume business until we make that announcement."

"Copy that, Dion."

"Secondly, kids will be kids, right?"

"Negative, Dion. I'm not on board with you there. The kids aren't just being kids. They're downright weirded out. Something's messed up about the way they're acting."

"Copy that, Nico. I'm gonna send Winter and Lace to the hospital to speak to that woman if they're allowed. Leave Unit Two in charge and head back here. We'll talk then."

"10–4, Dion. I'm out."

Dion lit a cigarette and looked at Fred and Thomas. "Okay, so let's assume what's happening in Tremayne has something to do with the Changers. What are your thoughts on it?"

"I don't have any specific thoughts," Fred said. "But I can say I agree with Thomas. This sounds very Changer-esque. Mostly because it's not something you would expect."

"Then how can we confirm anything?" Ryker asked. "I mean, Punks run on adrenaline and instinct. But we can't throw pure guessing into the mix."

"I still have a reliable contact inside the Changers' organization," Krystal volunteered.

Thomas walked over and flopped down on the leather sofa. "If you're thinking about Dr. Yaz, he's off the grid. We haven't been able to make contact since we left the Underground."

"I have direct contact, any time, twenty-four seven," Krystal said. "If this activity is due to the Changers, he'll know. And he'll tell me."

Ryker smiled at Dion. "Shoulda voted to keep her, bro."

"I'm changing my vote," Dion said. "I vote to keep her now." He tipped his chin at Fred and Thomas. "Even if it means keeping these two slugs as well." He looked back to Krystal. "Reach out to the doctor. We've been in the dark for so long, we can't afford to take any chances."

CHAPTER 12

Unlikely Allies

Four Changers security guards made their last round of the evening on Level Three of the Underground City.

"I'm about beat, boss," one of the male guards said.

"Yeah," a female coworker agreed. "Hey, Steph. How long are we going to be doing twelve-hour shifts, anyway?"

Steph shrugged. "Got me. Until we receive the order to resume business as usual, I guess."

The four stopped in the hallway at a nondescript door marked FACILITY 301 – AUTHORIZED PERSONNEL ONLY. Steph checked the door handle and peered inside its small window. "Hold up. Light's on inside."

Steph passed her hand over the keyless identification panel as a woman in a lab coat approached the quartet.

The woman waved her hand at the guards. "Excuse me. I'm presently working in there. No need for intervention."

Steph smiled at the woman. "Sure, no worries. We noticed the light is on inside. In keeping with the organization's conservation policy, please remember to turn out the lights when they're not needed."

The woman nodded. "Yes, ma'am. My apologies."

"Well, good night, and have a nice evening," Steph said.

"And to you." The woman opened the door and stepped inside the small green room.

When the door closed and latched, the woman peeked out the small window. She pressed her cheek against the door and watched the guards disappear around a corner in the corridor. Satisfied that the hallway was now empty, she turned and leaned back against the door. Her body vibrated momentarily before she ventured into the spacious room beyond.

JUST INSIDE THE ENTRANCE TO the right, Silver lay slumped forward on top of a large pipe. A hand gently shook her shoulder. Her eyes fluttered open, and she felt the blood pounding in her head. Gingerly, she touched the egg-sized bump at the back of her skull. *Ow.* She rubbed her neck. The hand on her shoulder was persistent.

"All right already," she said, looking up. She squinted at the figure standing in front of her. "Felix." She rubbed her neck again. "How did you find me here? Did your little device not work?"

"Be sensible, woman," Felix said. "I tracked you until your chip was disabled. I knew exactly where you were, but I was unable to leave immediately."

"How long have I been here?"

"At least eight hours. It's evening. We must leave at once."

Silver stood, her wobbly legs steadied by an eighteen-inch-diameter pipe on one side and Dr. Yaz on the other.

"Before we enter the corridor, we must change," Felix said.

Silver rolled her eyes. "Fine."

The two separated, changed their appearances and exited the pipe-filled room looking like two middle-age males. Silver glanced at Felix and smirked. "Great minds still think alike, Doctor."

Felix removed his lab coat and handed it to Silver. "Utility workers don't wear pantsuits. Put this on." He snatched the clipboard off the bulletin board as Silver picked up a nearly empty toolbox from the small desk.

Felix checked the hallway before the two stepped out. "This way."

He led the way down the corridor and stopped at a small passageway on his right. A wire-mesh gate blocked the opening. Felix unlatched the gate, and Silver followed him into the passageway.

"Where the hell are you taking me, Yaz? I thought we'd be going to your quarters."

Felix ignored Silver's blather and continued walking. When they reached the end of the passage, he stopped and opened an unmarked door. He stepped into a small room and motioned Silver to follow. Looking up, Felix grabbed a thin chain and yanked. A single LED bulb illuminated the tiny space.

Silver looked around. The little room was filled with cleaning supplies and tools, with a floor-length locker on one wall. The room reeked of various chemicals, mold and air freshener.

Felix opened the locker and waved his hand over a warranty sticker on the back wall. The wall at the back of the locker opened, and Felix motioned to Silver to step inside. He turned around, switched off the overhead light, closed the locker door and followed Silver through the opening.

When the portal closed behind Felix, a narrow hallway was illuminated by blue strips of light along the corners of the walls and ceiling.

Felix turned to Silver. "*Now*, we're going to my quarters."

Silver looked around as she touched the wall. "What is this, some kind of smooth metal?"

"Of course," Felix said. "This acts as a type of Faraday cage. Detection by electronic means is virtually impossible."

"Honestly, Yaz. Must you be so secretive about all this? With your intellect, surely you could have come up with something more high tech."

"Exactly why I don't use methods you would think of. It's what *great* minds would expect me to do. *Greater* minds think differently. Remember I said that. It may help you one day."

"Whatever. So I get that your quarters is under tight security. Isn't the interior of your quarters monitored as well?"

Felix stopped walking and held up a finger. "I'm going to tell you something. Please keep in mind the only reason I tell you anything from here on out is not because I trust you. It is because time is of the essence. You, Ms. Long, are in more danger than I."

"Why? Aren't you a more valuable prize if you're captured?"

"Yes. But I am smarter. And I have more resources at my disposal than you could ever imagine."

"Hmph," Silver snorted.

"You are riding on my coattails, my dear."

"Fine," Silver said. "I agree. So, why are we so pressed for time?"

Felix slowed the pace as the two continued down the long passageway. "I have had numerous communications from allies outside the Underground. Allies you must resolve to work with. Former enemies of yours."

Silver smiled nervously. "How bad can they be, Felix? I can get along with anyone, you know that."

Felix stopped at a blank wall at the end of the passage. A wave of his hand opened the wall, revealing a small elevator. He gestured to Silver. "After you, my dear."

When the elevator door closed, Silver turned to Felix. "Enemies? Who are these people I'm supposed to work with? Worst case."

Felix pressed a button on the elevator's keypad and clasped his hands behind his back. "Worst case?" He smiled. "Krystal Peterson."

Silver leaned back against the wall as the elevator descended. She folded her arms across her chest. "Oh, no. Not her. No way."

WHEN THE ELEVATOR STOPPED, THE two changed back to their previous appearance.

Felix turned to Silver. "What are your loyalties, Ms. Long?"

Silver remained with her arms crossed leaning against the back of the elevator. She raised her eyebrows, deliberately avoiding Felix's gaze. "What do you mean?"

"I think you know," he said. "I know what the Changers are capable of. More than that, I know what their plans are. I need to know right this moment whose side you're on."

Silver reached down and tapped several times on the keypad. "What's with this door anyway? Doesn't it open when this thing stops?"

"Only I can open it. Now, you must answer my question." Felix folded his arms.

Silver sighed and dropped her hands to her sides. She looked at Felix. "Fine. I'm on your side, okay?" She glanced up at a small red light blinking above the door. "Now open up. I'm getting claustrophobic."

Felix closed his eyes. "You have not convinced me. If you are still loyal to the Changers, I will take you back out and release you into the Underground. You will be on your own."

Silver mock-laughed. "Oh, no. I'm not on my own. Not by a long shot."

Felix opened his eyes and held up an index finger. "You are, my dear. You obviously don't know this. But you are."

Silver folded her arms again—tighter this time. "Well, you sure as hell can't turn me loose down there. I'm a dead woman walking if you do that."

Felix smiled. "There is always the surface. You might make your way to Blythe before the Changers catch up to you."

"I'll go to Tremayne. At least I can change, and I could blend in."

"What I'm hearing makes me believe you are still loyal to the Changers," Felix said.

A rare case of nervousness overcame Silver. "I…I'm still trying to decide."

Felix turned to her and placed his hands on her cheeks. "Now. *Now* is the time to decide."

Silver brushed Felix's hands from her face. "Get your hands off me! How dare you?"

Felix shoved his hands into his pockets. "You no longer hold rank here, Ms. Long. You see, you have no friends here in the Underground."

Silver thought of Steph. Her mind raced, but she could think of no one else. "You'd be surprised."

"No one with any authority or power," Felix said. "I have many loyal followers, despite having been rejected by Levi and the appointment of Xander Rasmus."

"Xander Rasmus?"

Felix nodded and stared at the floor. "A great mind. Dr. Rasmus is a force with which to be reckoned."

Silver smiled. "So he's your replacement? Never heard of him." Her eyes widened. "Who's mine?"

"Her name is Angelica DeMone. I must say, I believe she is more ruthless and conniving than you."

"Not a chance," Silver said. She tapped the elevator pad again. "Hello? Are we ever getting out of here?"

"Your answer, Long?"

She looked into Felix's eyes. "I don't have any choice. You're right, I don't have any real decent contacts here anymore. I'm with you." She breathed deeply once. "I'm with the Punks."

"Very well." Felix tapped the keypad once again.

Silver swayed involuntarily sideways as the tiny cubicle moved. She braced herself against one wall. "What, this thing moves laterally?"

Felix clasped his hands in front of him. "It is my transportation cube, not merely an elevator." He closed his eyes again. "I am able to travel anywhere in the Underground undetected."

Silver slid down the back wall of the cubicle and sat on the floor, knees up. "Maybe I *have* underestimated you."

CHAPTER 13

Irony

THE ROOM WAS COLD. THE floor and walls were white. A single computer station extended down from the ceiling, supported waist-high by a sturdy rod.

Curtis stood silently and stared at the seven-foot-tall cylindrical pod in front of him. The pod was made of smooth brushed metal. He noticed a panel on one side—obviously a touch-pad-type control console—with numerous lights and buttons. The huge glass door on the front of the pod matched the curvature of the cylinder.

Three Changer attendants stood with Curtis, one on each side and one behind him. The Changers dressed in hospital blues, sterile masks, caps and safety glasses.

"You'll have to remove your underwear now." It was the female attendant at his back.

Curtis slowly hooked his thumbs under the elastic waistband of his shorts. He hesitated momentarily, then slid his underwear to the floor and quickly brushed them to the side. He clasped his hands in front of him and gazed at his reflection in the glass door. *What have you done?* A momentary wave of jealousy swept over him as he wondered if Krystal had gone through the same procedure when she had become a Changer.

A loud *whoosh* snapped him out of his trance. The curved door on the pod popped outward and slid to the right, revealing the inside of the cylinder. A soft blue glow illuminated the interior. The inside was made of the same smooth metal as the exterior. The floor contained thousands of tiny, evenly-spaced holes. In the center of the floor were two large, solid metal, shoe-shaped pads.

"Step inside, sir," the attendant said. "Stand on the foot pads."

Curtis stepped forward and placed one foot on the edge of the pod while he braced himself, one hand on each side of the door. His legs were shaking ever so slightly.

"Are you scared, sir?" The attendant's voice seemed sharp against the dead silence of the white room.

Curtis's voice quavered. "Just kinda cold."

"You are not undergoing the Change, sir. This is sterilization."

"Please move into the pod, sir," a male attendant to his side urged.

Curtis stepped into the cylinder and turned around to face the door.

"Drop your hands to your sides and stand on the foot pads, please."

Curtis complied, and the door slid closed. He watched the Changers through the glass portal. The female attendant stood in front of him holding an electronic tablet. The other two moved out of his view—he assumed to manage the controls and the computer.

The pod's interior turned noticeably warmer as the air swirled around Curtis's body. Static electricity filled the cylinder, and the hair on his arms stood up. His body felt lighter. *What is—? What?* He looked down at his feet. *Hair?*

Thousands of strands of hair whirled around the cylinder and down to the floor. The fibers seemed to disintegrate into—or through—the tiny holes in the platform. Curtis looked at the raised hairs on his arms. As he ran his hand over his forearm, the hairs detached from their pores and swirled downward. He fought the panic welling up in his gut. He reached up to his head. *Bald. My Hawk!* Tears pooled in his eyes, only to be evaporated by the chamber's atmosphere. He looked down in horror and watched the last vestige of his outward personality turn to fuzz and disappear through the holes at the bottom of the pod.

A HEAVY MIST DESCENDED WITH the night inside the Perimeter at Punk headquarters. Outside the communications Depot, the ground at the compound quickly dampened.

Krystal allowed herself a moment of repose as she gazed at the embers floating skyward from inside a burn barrel. She had lived a lifetime in the month since the Punks had booted her from their organization. That was the night she lost the only real family she'd ever had. That was the beginning of discovering herself—and losing Curtis. *Curtis.* She'd be dead if not for him. He had discovered the real Krystal before she did. *Miss you, Curtis. I'm sorry. I really fucked us up.* The stiff evening wind plastered her duster against the back of her legs. She buttoned the front and turned up the collar.

Ryker tossed another log into the barrel. "You look a million miles away, kid."

She blinked and looked up. "I'm sorry, Ryk. What?"

"Aw, nothing." His eyes sparkled in the firelight. "You're starting to look like your old self. I like that."

"A lot's happened, Ryk." She looked up from the embers. "You wanted me dead that night."

Ryker slipped his bandanna off his head and ran his fingers through his hair. He untied the knot in the bandanna and shook out the creases. "I was stupid, Krys. We all were."

She wrapped her arms across her chest and hugged herself. "Curtis wasn't."

Ryker looked around the compound. Sodium vapor lights cast a soft glow on the concrete walkways and benches. Punk security guards walked in pairs, dutifully patrolling the area. "Dion sent word to Tremayne that we're lifting the red alert."

Krystal zoned on the burn barrel. "How could you guys lose tabs on Curtis?"

"So you wanna talk about Curtis?"

She looked up again. "He had more sense than any of you. Hell, he had more sense than me. I could've not showed up for the acid test. I knew I'd fail, but I still showed up. I never thought the Punks would want to kill me."

Ryker turned to face the wind and retied his bandanna. "We had a rule, Krys. We'd been killing Changers with a bullet to the head for so long it was instinct. Winter just reacted."

Krystal frowned. "Yeah? So did Curtis. Thank God for that."

"He loved you."

Krystal knew it would happen—she didn't try to stop the tears trickling down her cheeks. "And I loved him, Ryk." She looked away. "I still do."

Ryker shoved his hands into the pockets of his leather jacket. "We'll find him." His eyes moistened. "I promise."

"MY SKIN IS SO SMOOTH. I've never felt anything like it." Curtis ran his hands over his head, his cheeks and down his chest.

"Slippers on the feet. And put this on," the female attendant ordered.

Curtis stepped into a pair of heel-less satin slippers and turned around as the Changer helped him slip his arms into a heavy satin robe. He welcomed the warmth the garment provided against the cool room temperature. His skin tingled as he tied the sash at his waist. He smiled at the attendant. "This is nice."

"Right this way, sir." Her monotone voice matched her deadpan demeanor. She led Curtis to a door at the side of the room and pressed a button on the wall. When the door clicked open, two security guards strode in and stood next to Curtis.

"The subject has been sterilized." The female looked at her tablet. "Orders state he is to be delivered to the War Room."

The lead guard nodded. "Ma'am."

The security guards each grabbed a bicep and guided Curtis out the door into a narrow hallway. The pace was slightly faster than his usual gait. He struggled to keep the slippers on as the guards shuffled him to a wide, brightly lit corridor. He was thankful the swift walk to the elevator was short. The guards retained their grip on his arms as they entered the large cubicle.

When they turned to face the doors, Curtis looked up at the lead guard. "So, what level are we on now?"

The emotionless Changers remained silent.

Curtis felt a downward rush as the elevator descended. *All business, I guess.* After the sterilization process, a good portion of his modesty had left him. He felt more at ease.

The doors opened a fraction of a second before the elevator glided to a stop. Four additional security guards met the trio in a short passageway. At the opposite end of the hall was another door. Two of the guards from the hallway led Curtis and his escorts toward the stainless-steel portal. The other two fell in behind. A quick palm swipe by one of the guards opened the shiny silver door.

The group walked into the familiar computer-filled War Room and stopped in the center of the main aisle. The lead guard walked to the alcove and stepped up the short platform leading to Levi's conference room. When the conference room door opened, he turned around and motioned to Curtis and the other guards.

The guards hurried Curtis up the steps and released their grip on him.

Curtis stood in his satin robe and slippers and stared at the Changers around the conference table.

Johnny Logan stood and walked to the door. He smiled. "Welcome back, my friend! Come on in and sit with us."

Curtis chose one of the plush executive chairs at the end of the table opposite Levi. He folded his hands on the table in front of him.

Angelica DeMone and Dr. Rasmus gazed at him from either side of their leader while Johnny seated himself next to the doctor.

Levi stood and looked at Curtis. "So, you want to become a Changer."

"Is this a private party?" Dion strode up to the burn barrel and stopped opposite Krystal and Ryker. He held three open bottles of beer.

Ryker glanced sideways at Krystal.

"Nah, we're done." Her eyes softened. "Is one of those for me?"

"You bet." Dion handed her and Ryker each a bottle.

"Damn cold," Ryker said. "You can smell winter in the air."

"Speaking of." Krystal nodded toward the Depot. "Here she comes now."

Ryker glanced behind Dion. He squinted into the darkness. Dim lights from inside the Depot outlined four silhouetted figures approaching the trio. "Who's that with Winter and Jim?" He shielded his eyes from the fire. "Is that the two Changers?"

Krystal looked at the four. "They're Rogues. They ditched the Changers, so they're called Rogue Changers."

"Is that what they call you?" Dion asked.

"Yep."

Ryker looked at Krystal. "Even though you're not a Changer anymore?"

Krystal shrugged. "I don't make their rules. Might as well call us all dead as far as the Changers are concerned."

Winter and Jimbo stepped up to the burn barrel next to Dion. Fred and Thomas walked around and stood on either side of Krystal.

Jimbo held his hands over the fire. "We need another barrel, guys. Temp's dropping big-time."

Winter motioned to Fred. "Gimme a hand?"

"Sure," Fred said.

He followed Winter across the compound where another barrel sat next to a concrete bench. The barrel was about half full of partially burned wood.

"This'll work," she said.

The two grabbed opposite edges of the barrel and shuffled it over the concrete walkway to the others. Winter shoved her boot against the bottom of the cold container and wedged it against the other barrel.

Jimbo dropped an armload of logs into the container and held a small branch out to Dion. "Light 'er up."

Dion flipped his Zippo lighter open and lit the small end of the branch.

Jimbo strategically placed the sapling into a crevice between two larger pieces of wood in the cold barrel. He shoved his hands into his jeans pockets and looked at Dion. "Well, boss. Here we are."

Fred shivered. He breathed warm air into his hands and held them over the fire. "You guys always have your big meetings out here? It's damn cold."

"Not always," Ryker said. "We just need to regroup and give our minds a break."

Winter eyed Krystal and the other two. "We like it. We've had too many formal, around-the-table meetings inside lately. We're tired."

"Yeah," Jimbo agreed. "This is our element. Punks do their best putting on a strong front for the public. But we hurt, too."

Fred glanced at Thomas. "We're not doubting that. And we're not questioning your feelings. I know the Changers really did a number on you guys."

Ryker took another swig of beer. "We do what we have to do, Fred. On the outside, Punks are fighting their asses off protecting themselves and others. But times like this…" He looked around his circle of friends. "Whatever toughness you think you see, every one of us is crying inside."

"Well, we're here to do whatever we can to help," Fred said.

Dion looked over the fire at Krystal and the other two Rogue Changers. "Krys. You said you were going to contact the doctor in the Underground. Was he able to give you any information about what the Changers are up to?"

"His name is Dr. Felix Yaz. And, yes, he gave me some solid intel."

Winter frowned. "Can I say something first?"

Dion looked at Winter. He lit a cigarette and clinked is lighter shut. "Shoot, Win."

"I'm not totally sold that she's not a Changer anymore. I mean, she failed the acid test, man."

Krystal stiffened her stance.

"We could always acid test her one more time," Jimbo said. "Put everyone's mind at ease."

"She's not a Changer." Fred looked at Thomas. "A Changer can recognize another Changer by looking into their eyes. Thomas and I both checked her. She's one hundred percent human."

Krystal tossed her beer bottle into a nearby recycle bin and turned to face Jimbo and Winter. She stood tall, feet apart, shoulders squared, hands in the pockets of her duster. "I'm not a Changer. And right now I can't say exactly what's going on with those bastards. But I can tell you one thing that's *not* going to happen. No one…*no one* is going to acid test me again. *Ever.*"

CURTIS SAVORED THE PLUSHNESS OF the high-back executive chair in Levi's conference room. The room temperature was perfect. His Mohawk notwithstanding, the absence of hair over his entire body felt good. The sterilization chamber had invigorated him. He felt strong but relaxed.

Angelica looked up from her tablet. "So, Mr. Dyer. I can't stress the importance and permanence of the position in which you're placing yourself. You understand that once you undergo the Change, you are indebted to our organization?"

Curtis's vision blurred as he looked across the table at Angelica. Every thought he'd had since the acid testing at Punk headquarters was interlaced with Krystal Peterson, the Changer. Every move he'd made began and ended with thoughts of Krystal. At this moment he wondered if he was in love or obsessed. *Fuck it. I love you, Krys.* He committed. His eyes focused on Angelica DeMone. "Yes, ma'am. I understand."

"Go, buddy!" Johnny said.

Levi looked at Dr. Rasmus. "Have this man prepped for the Change. Program his knowledge base for level three security and access. We will upgrade based on his performance through the first thirty days. I expect him to be a valuable commodity, so I want to move quickly but cautiously."

Dr. Rasmus nodded. He tapped the electronic tablet in front of him. "Consider it done."

Butterflies fluttered in Curtis's stomach. He didn't hide his elation. "Thank you, sir." He smiled. "You won't regret this."

Angelica twirled her stylus slowly through her fingers. "Oh, we're not worried about regretting our decision, Curtis. We will be in complete control."

The conference room door swished open, and two security guards entered with two medical attendants dressed in white.

One of the attendants spun a wheelchair around and settled it beside Curtis. "Please move into the chair, sir."

Curtis pushed his executive seat back and sat in the wheelchair. He gazed at the backs of the two security guards leading him out of the conference room and through the War Room. As he entered the wide sterile hallway once more, he wondered if his rank in the Changers' organization would be above that of the guards that walked before him. He wondered about Krystal's rank in the organization. He smiled and sat back to enjoy the ride. *Guess I'll find out soon enough.*

CHAPTER 14

Video on Cell

Nico met the Three Amigos at the city limit sign on the highway leading west out of Tremayne. He pulled his Bear-Cat off the road in front of Will's and switched off the ignition. The steel driver's door felt cold and wet on his hand as he pushed it closed. He strapped his left arm to his side and walked back to meet the trio.

Will, Adam and Joey stood in a tight circle at the rear of Joey's idling truck.

Joey motioned to Nico as he walked toward the three friends. "Get back here by the exhaust where it's warm."

Nico bumped fists with the three. "Long day today, guys." He puffed fog with each word. "I can't wait to get back to headquarters and give Dion the scoop on everything that happened in town."

"Yeah," Will said. "We still have three hours on our shift. Looks to be an easy night." He glanced toward Tremayne. Lights reflecting off the moist evening air cast a halo over the city. "Things seem to be getting back to normal since Dion lifted the alert."

"Finally." Nico turned around to warm his backside from the vehicle's exhaust. "But I'm talking about earlier with all those kids."

"That was weird," Adam said. "I've never seen anything like it."

Joey rubbed his hands together. "Whadda you guys figure they were up to, anyway?"

"I don't know, man." Will shrugged. "Why is it every time something goes wonky I automatically assume the Changers are up to no good?"

"With young people, though?" Joey said. "I've never seen 'em mess with kids."

"Yeah," Adam agreed. "But you're not talking about those little twerps being Changers, right? I mean, all the Changers I've ever heard about are adults."

"They wouldn't be setting a good example." Nico grinned. "Not for recruiting purposes, if you know what I mean."

"C'mon, guys." Will frowned. "You're just throwing out random comments. We're smarter than this. Let's say this activity by these weird kids has something, anything, to do with the Changers. What's the deal?"

Adam stared at the PUNK SECURITY decal on the side of Joey's truck. His eyes narrowed. "And did they attack that lady in the alley, or was it someone else?"

Joey tipped his chin at Nico. "You went to the hospital to see her. What did she have to say?"

Nico shook his head. "She was unconscious when I was there. Probably sedated. Dion sent Winter and Lace, though."

"Did they talk to her?" Joey asked.

"Nope," Nico said. "That was a couple hours ago. She was still out of it."

Will looked at Joey and Adam. "We should see if we can get in and talk to her before we leave town."

"Good idea." Nico stepped out of the circle. "I'm gonna head back to headquarters. Catch up with me when you get back."

"You got it," Will said.

The Three Amigos watched Nico as he sauntered back to his BearCat.

"It's good Dion put that guy in charge of security in Tremayne," Will said.

"Yeah," Joey agreed. "He's got a cool head, and he's tough for only being eighteen."

"He's a good leader," Adam said. Joey flinched when Adam feigned a punch to his friend's stomach. "We just need to get *him* to start believing it."

He shoved his hands into the pockets of his parka. *The paper!* He pulled out the wad he'd found in the alley and uncrumpled it. "Hey, guys, check this out."

Will tipped his chin up. "What is it?"

Joey took the paper from Adam. "Looks like a receipt." He shrugged.

"Flip it over," Adam said.

"Hmm…it's hard to read."

Will held out his hand. "Lemme see it." He examined the back side of the crinkled paper. "It *is* kinda hard to see." He held the receipt next to the red glow of the vehicle's taillight. "*HELD NIDEQ OH CELL?*"

"What the heck's *NIDEQ?*" Joey said.

Adam snatched the paper from Will. "Pretty sure it says '*HELP. VIDEO ON CELL.*'"

"Well, that makes sense," Will said. "Who do you s'pose wrote it?"

Adam shook his head. "Hard to say. I found it in the alley right before I discovered those stupid kids throwing rocks at that lady."

Joey shrugged. "So, maybe she wrote it?"

"I don't know."

"We still have to talk to her." Will tightened his bandanna and zipped up his parka. "Let's head to the hospital."

The Three Amigos turned and trotted to their vehicles. Will made a wide U-turn and headed toward Tremayne. Adam and Joey followed like a train, perfectly distanced and tracking in sync with Will's BearCat.

NICO BRAKED HIS ARMORED VEHICLE at the main gate to the Punks' compound a mile from the Perimeter Wall. As he pulled slowly toward the entrance, a Punk dressed in all black exited the guardhouse.

Nico rolled down the driver's window. "Hey, Ace."

Ace slung his AR-15 behind him. "'Sup, Nico? You look like I feel after an all-nighter."

"Long day, man."

"Heard you had a little skirmish with some kids or something." Ace jerked a thumb over his shoulder. "Radio was going crazy for a while there."

"Yeah." Nico scraped his hair behind his right ear. "Weird stuff." He stared ahead toward the Perimeter. "I gotta update Dion. I'm sure you'll hear the details eventually."

"Bad shit?"

Nico squinted. "I don't know what to make of it. I thought things were strange before the Chybrid attack." He shook his head. "But now…"

Ace motioned to the guardhouse. "Well, get home, man. I can tell you need a break."

The boom arm swung skyward as Ace backed away from Nico's truck.

Nico left his foot on the brake, his right hand draped over the steering wheel. "Hey, Ace?"

Ace stepped back to the driver's window. "What is it, man?"

"You ever feel like we bit off more than we could chew?" Nico stared at his left hand lying limp in his lap. "Like no matter what we do, the Changers are gonna have their way?"

A gust of wind pushed Ace's collar against the back of his neck. "Like the Punks should surrender, or just stop trying to defend ourselves against the Changers' insanity?"

Nico looked at Ace. "I don't know what I mean. They practically wiped us out. If it wasn't for Krystal, everyone at the Perimeter would be dead right now. Then where would we be? Could what's left of us survive?"

Ace placed his hand on Nico's shoulder and squeezed. "Krystal had help, man. There's help on the inside—inside the Changers. A lot of them don't like what's happening to this country, same as us."

Nico took a deep breath. "I'm sure you're right. I better go. I'll catch you later."

"Chin up, dude." Ace pounded his fist on Nico's shoulder. "We're Punks. We always find a way." He backed away once again.

Nico left the driver's window open. The rear tires chirped on the wet asphalt as he accelerated through the checkpoint and headed toward Punk headquarters.

The Three Amigos parked parallel on the curb outside Tremayne Medical Center. Nearly every parking stall was occupied. The heavy mist in the air was gradually turning into an irritating drizzle.

Will hopped down from his vehicle and slammed the door. He pulled on the handle to check the lock. "Must be visiting hours," he said, eyeing the parking lot.

"Well, hopefully that lady is up and awake," Adam said.

The trio walked abreast up the wide walkway to the main entrance. Small groups of visitors huddled for warmth in random spots under a wide awning in front of the ten-story building. The friends strode through automatic sliding doors and stepped up to the receptionist's station in the main lobby.

Will made a quick assessment of the activity behind the counter. A doctor and a nurse were trying to reconcile information between a patient's medication history and what the doctor had actually ordered. Another nurse was on the phone. Two other nurses, half-sitting on the back counter, were engaged in casual conversation. The lone receptionist—a short, stocky redhead—mindlessly shuffled paperwork from one side of her computer keyboard to the other.

"Excuse me, ma'am," Will said to the receptionist.

She didn't look up. A new priority struck her, and she jotted something down on a sticky note before getting up from her chair and waddling to the back of the station.

Will eyed her activity, making his own evaluation of its importance. He raised a hand to catch her attention. "Excuse me, ma'am."

The woman glanced up at Will from the back counter. She pursed her lips and sighed.

"We need some information on a patient," Will said, his hand still in the air.

"We're very busy tonight," she said. "Please be patient."

Will looked at his friends. "Adam, get ahold of Nico and find out what room our victim is in."

Adam clicked his shoulder mic and stepped away from the counter toward the visitors' waiting area.

"She's being kinda disrespectful," Joey said. "Doesn't she recognize our security parkas?"

"I thought about that." Will reached inside his vest and pulled out his ID. He held it up toward the receptionist. "Ma'am?"

"She's flat out ignoring you, bro." Joey glanced over his shoulder. "Here comes Adam."

Adam walked swiftly past his two friends. "Let's go, guys. Room 504."

Will and Joey followed Adam around the side of the receptionist's station. They hurried through a wide, highly polished corridor to a set of elevators.

When they stepped into the elevator, Joey pushed the button for the fifth floor. He looked at Will. "What was the deal at the reception desk?"

Will shook his head. "I don't know. Seems like our authority wasn't recognized—at least not by that woman."

Adam glanced up at the lighted numbers above the doors. "Based on that lady's treatment and what we heard from Nico, the Punks' status in Tremayne isn't what it used to be."

"Kind of a sudden change, don't you think?" Joey said.

"Agreed," Will said as the elevator slowed to a stop and the doors opened.

The trio walked off the elevator and surveyed the directional sign in front of them.

"Well, Rooms 500 to 520 are to the left." Will took a deep breath. "Let's see if our status means anything up here."

CHAPTER 15

Minds of the Children

FOUR SETS OF TWENTY-FOUR DESKS, each two rows deep, faced four different directions in the brightly lit circular classroom. A video orb in the center of the room hung suspended by a single rod from the high ceiling. Images cast on the walls from the orb were regulated by the four teachers according to their group of students.

Dr. Rasmus and Angelica waited in the observation room outside the classroom.

"It's nice the way you have this set up, Rasmus," Angelica observed. "Twenty-four students per instructor is manageable. I have a question, though."

Dr. Rasmus stood with his hands folded behind his back. He raised an eyebrow. "What's on your mind?"

"I notice the students are not wearing earbuds or headphones of any type. How do they manage to remain focused on their respective instructor without distraction from the other teachers?"

Xander smiled. "It's a matter of elementary sound wave cancellation."

"Wait." Angelica raised her hand. "Keep it simple. Layman's terms. I don't need a scientific explanation."

"Okay." He shrugged. "Monitors in the floor and ceiling detect the sound waves emanating from specific locations within the classroom. Those sound waves are then precisely matched in pitch and frequency, and an exact opposite sound is inserted into the area behind the second row of students in each group. The sound is effectively canceled."

"Hmph." Angelica glanced into the classroom behind the glass. "So, if I throw out a five, and the system throws out a negative five, the effect is zero."

"That's good," Xander said. "Just think of your numbers in terms of sound waves."

"I suppose you could have used four separate classrooms."

Xander nodded. "Yes, but we conserve space much in the way we conserve energy. Why use more space if technology can enable us to use less?"

Angelica checked the time on her cell. "I suppose." She turned from the observation window and sat down in a nearby chair. "I thought Levi was supposed to be here by now."

Dr. Rasmus remained in place, gazing into the classroom. "Hmm. He'll be here soon, I'm sure."

Levi stepped off the elevator with Johnny Logan on level nine in the Underground City.

"This is the most important project you've undertaken, Logan." He smoothed the lapels on his blue sport coat. "I expect perfection."

"Yes, sir." Johnny smiled.

Levi glanced up. "And wipe that stupid look off your face. Reserve your dumbshit tough-guy demeanor for the outside. There's no place for it inside the City."

"Just trying to stay in character, sir. Keeps the lowlifes off guard."

The two walked in silence down the wide corridor. Since level nine was reserved for top-security Changers, they encountered few personnel, save for the occasional pair of guards on routine patrol. Levi's wingtips clicked conspicuously on the highly polished floor. When they reached the door to the classroom observation area, Levi stopped and turned to Johnny.

"I have to tell you, Logan." Levi looked slightly upward and locked eyes with Johnny. "Dr. Rasmus and Ms. DeMone are top-notch professionals—"

"Yes, s—"

"Shut up." Levi stepped up to Johnny. "Stepping and fetching like you're doing right now makes you look weak. Either that, or you're a phony. Get your act together. I need everyone firing on all cylinders."

Johnny stared at Levi, squelching the "yes, sir" on the tip of his tongue.

Levi held his gaze. "That's more like it."

Two guards stationed by the door appeared oblivious to Levi's verbal beatdown of Johnny. They stepped to either side of the portal a split second before Levi waved his hand over the palm reader.

Angelica stood quickly when she heard the door swish open behind her. She brushed the wrinkles from the front of her black pencil skirt and checked the time on her cell again.

Dr. Rasmus turned to face the door. He smiled. "Leader." He nodded at Johnny. "Logan."

"Good evening, Doctor." Levi turned to Angelica. "I trust our distinguished doctor has adequately briefed you on our SOUL Chybrid children."

Angelica's eyebrows involuntarily rose. She glanced through the window at the students in the circular room. "Those are Chybrids?"

Dr. Rasmus smiled. "I was waiting for your arrival, Leader."

"Great," Levi said as the four Changers moved to the observation window. "Let's get started."

The four instructors in the room each faced their respective groups of students. The instructor on the north engaged his class in a nonstop lecture. There was no image from the video orb for these students. All the children in this class were well-behaved and attentive. From the east class, the instructor called upon students with their hands raised. He answered questions as the students took notes on their electronic tablets. From the west wall, the instructor remained busy discussing multiple images cast from the orb in front of his class. The students were relaxed and laid-back in contrast to the north and east classes. The south instructor stood silent, his arms folded in front of him. Not all the children in his class remained in their seats. Some leaned on the tables, conversing with other students. Others walked up and down the single aisle, disrupting the flow of the instructor and harassing their classmates.

Angelica gazed at the southern group of students. "Are we to take it some groups are less refined than others? There's a marked difference in discipline between classes here."

"My thoughts precisely," Levi said. "It does seem some of these SOUL Chybrids are in need of further development."

Dr. Rasmus smiled. "You mean, they don't all appear to be heartless, all-knowing, perfect automatons?"

Levi glanced sideways. "I expect perfection, Xander."

"And that you have. You are observing perfection, Leader."

Johnny crossed his arms. "It's obvious."

Angelica stepped back and looked up at Johnny. "Seriously?"

"Sure," Johnny said. "Every kid isn't the same. Some are studious, some are rowdy, some are average and others are geniuses. If you want these SOUL Chybrid children to appear realistic, you gotta mix it up. We still program them and we retain control, correct?"

"Yes!" Dr. Rasmus looked at Levi. "This man is a good choice to coordinate the project in Bystander territory, Levi." He nodded to Johnny. "A good choice indeed."

Levi's gaze remained fixed on the activity in the classroom. "Just as I have said." He nodded. "I have the utmost confidence in Logan. Our new team is the cream of the crop, yourself included, Doctor."

"So is this it?" Angelica asked, thumbing her tablet screen. "My impression was there would be a demonstration of the SOUL Chybrid children."

Dr. Rasmus stood with his hands folded in front of him. He swiveled toward Angelica. "This is just the introduction, Ms.

DeMone. Thorough testing demands we expose the subjects to real-life situations in a variety of environments."

Angelica looked around the room. "This is hardly real-life, Doctor."

"The demonstration is not here. We currently have a group of test subjects in Tremayne—"

"Speaking of," Levi interrupted. "I have received reports of disruption of the peace in Tremayne. Disruption caused by gangs of youths. Might we use our new subjects to quell some of this errant activity?"

"We might, and we will." Dr. Rasmus raised a hand. "The disruptive youths in Tremayne are our own SOUL Chybrid children, currently residing with various Bystander foster families." The doctor smiled. "Well, most of them. Some of the local residents have actually begun to warm up to our Chybrid children."

Angelica frowned. "And we are in control of these little hooligans? What's the purpose, Xander?"

"It's an experiment." Rasmus glanced at Johnny. "We programmed the behavioral circuits in this group specifically to defy authority. Additionally, their emotional chip is minimal to the extreme."

Angelica seated herself on a nearby couch. She crossed her legs and tapped the face of her tablet. "Pretty sure I want a drink. I'm calling for refreshments."

"Very well," Levi said, motioning to additional seating around a smoked-glass coffee table.

Dr. Rasmus made himself comfortable at the end of a couch as Levi seated himself at the opposite end. Johnny sat on a love seat facing Angelica.

The door to the observation room swished open. Two male attendants dressed in blue tuxedos entered, each pushing a sturdy brushed-titanium cart on wheels.

Levi smiled. "Splendid idea, Ms. DeMone." He glanced at Dr. Rasmus. "Martini?"

Angelica ignored Levi's politeness. "Give me a vodka shot, now," she said to the first waiter. "Then fix me a vodka Collins."

"Yes," Rasmus agreed. "A martini is perfect."

Levi held up two fingers to the second attendant.

"Whiskey, straight," Johnny said.

Angelica downed her vodka shot and looked at Dr. Rasmus. "So, Doc. We're deliberately turning juvenile delinquents loose on the good citizens of Tremayne. Do tell."

The doctor wouldn't be rushed. He savored a long sip on his martini and slid the cocktail glass onto the coffee table in front of him. Grabbing the plastic lightning-bolt-shaped toothpick that pierced the olive, he swirled the liquid for a moment before settling back onto the sofa. He gazed across the table at Angelica and slowly slipped the olive off the pick. He held the olive between his front teeth momentarily before sucking it into his mouth and waggling his eyebrows.

Levi watched the doctor's every move and smiled.

Johnny sipped his whiskey, eyeing Angelica over the rim of his lowball glass.

Angelica stared at Rasmus, expressionless. *What a putz*, she thought. "Well?"

Unfazed by Angelica's mild rebuff, Dr. Rasmus swallowed his olive and smiled. "With the emotional chip at a minimum, we have observed the SOUL Chybrid children conducting certain activities that the average person might find objectionable."

Levi slung his arm across the back of the couch and turned toward the doctor. "But you said some of the local children have taken a liking to these Chybrids."

"Yes, Leader." Rasmus leaned forward and retrieved his martini from the table. "We placed these extreme personalities in Tremayne to confirm what we already knew—"

"Which is?" Angelica said.

Rasmus slowly turned his gaze from Levi to Angelica. "As I was saying." He turned back to Levi. "We already knew we would attract the fringe child, the kid on the edge."

"Explain," Johnny said.

"Gladly." The doctor leaned forward, elbows on his knees. "These target kids have almost no conventional home life. They're not on the street—yet—but they're close. In many cases, they may as well be. They come and go from their 'homes' as they please. They have no parental support or discipline."

Johnny finished off his whiskey and raised a finger to the number one waiter. "Kind of like the street gangs among the Bystanders that were eradicated decades ago."

"Ah," Rasmus said. "But the Bystanders didn't eradicate the gangs. History tells us they did themselves in."

"He's right," Angelica interrupted. "You can't keep killing each other nonstop year after year and expect to survive as a group."

"Correct." Rasmus sat back. "It's only too bad the Changers had nothing to do with that. You must admit the Punks played a huge role in ending that scourge."

Levi downed the remaining half of his martini. "We had those gangs in the palm of our hands. They were on our side."

"Leader." Rasmus raised his hand. "If I may speak freely."

Levi nodded.

"We mollycoddled them—"

"We gave them everything they wanted. Ingrates!"

"That's precisely my point," Rasmus said. "The Punks, on the other hand, gave them nothing except self-respect."

"Exactly," Johnny said. "The Punks helped them rebuild their neighborhoods, gave them jobs and showed them how to become members of a peaceful society. Why do you think so many former gang members joined the Punks?"

"Enough!" Levi stood and turned to the waiters. "Gimme another martini."

"Can we move on?" Angelica said. "I'm all for seeing a demonstration of the new SOUL Chybrid children." She looked at Dr. Rasmus as she swirled her drink. "Let's see if we can get this right without making new little gang members of these delinquents."

Rasmus smiled and motioned for a second martini. "All part of the plan, team." He stood and stepped over to the waiter's cart to retrieve his drink. "As Mr. Logan so aptly alluded to, we have complete control over the actions and minds of these Chybrid children. And the children of Tremayne will follow the Chybrids." He smiled and held his cocktail in the air. "Once we possess the minds of the children, we will control the world."

Levi regained his composure and raised his glass to the doctor. "Yes! I only wish I had employed you sooner, Xander. Truly, you are light-years ahead of Dr. Felix Yaz in terms of knowledge, imagination and scientific ability." He glanced at Angelica. "Speaking of that, Ms. DeMone. What's the latest report on the whereabouts of that dreadful traitor, Dr. Yaz?"

CHAPTER 16

Yaz

SILVER STOOD UP QUICKLY WHEN Dr. Yaz's transport cube came to a stop. "*Finally*, we've arrived *somewhere!*"

Felix waved his hand over a small pad on the wall, and the door to the tiny portable room opened. He motioned to Silver. "After you, Ms. Long."

Silver stepped into Felix's spacious living quarters. Her jaw dropped and she stopped short as she gazed around the six-sided room. Her knees weakened. The hair on the back of her neck bristled. "Wha…" Vertigo swept over her. "What is this place?" Unconsciously, she reached for something to catch her balance when her hands landed on something hard. "Yaz? Yaz?" She gripped the chrome railing across the back of a chair and aimed her butt—way off target. She missed the seat and plopped onto the carpeted floor.

Felix rushed to Silver and knelt down beside her. "Ms. Long, let me help you. The sensation you are experiencing is from the transport cube. It's only temporary. Come, sit."

Silver waved him off. "No. I'm fine," she said, remaining on the floor.

"Here," Felix said, moving the chair next to Silver. "I insist. Help yourself, but let me get you some water."

Silver's heart pounded in her chest as she leaned back on her elbows and surveyed her surroundings. The hexagonal room contained floor-to-ceiling video monitors on four walls. There was an opening to additional rooms on the fifth wall. The door to Felix's transport cube occupied a small space on the sixth wall next to a wet bar. The glass-covered ceiling was open to the sky. Indirect violet lighting illuminated the baseboards around the entire room.

A control panel sat blinking directly front and center of the monitor walls. Three of the monitors displayed multiple pictures within pictures. The fourth monitor wall was framed by a light bar with a faint yellowish glow. Silver was mesmerized by the curious mix of colors—mostly a dark bluish-green hue—swirling within the frame. Her eyes glazed as she stared at the black, almost three-dimensional center of the framed wall.

"Ms. Long?"

Silver felt a tug on her left arm as Felix struggled to break her involuntary trance.

"Ms. Long, get up, please."

Silver squeezed her eyes shut and opened them again, forcing herself to break away from the daze-inducing sight in front of her. She allowed Felix to help her into the adjacent chair.

"What the hell, Felix?" Silver rested her elbows on her knees and rubbed her palms into her eyes. She looked up at the ceiling again. "Are we still in the Underground? Are we even on the ground at all?"

"You will know more, all in good time." Felix smiled and stepped behind the wet bar. "I'm going to bring you some water. Then we can talk."

Silver scrutinized the constantly changing images on the monitors: Tremayne downtown. Tremayne garment district. Tremayne City Park. The Changers War Room. Every floor, every elevator, every restaurant and business establishment in the Changers' Underground City. Punk headquarters. The Perimeter Wall. Various locations occupied by Punks. Every train platform in southern and Central California.

"What is this?" She spun her head toward Felix. "Felix, what is this? My team never had such a sophisticated security system." Her hands were trembling. "No wonder I was demoted. I should have known about this."

Felix walked around the bar and pulled another chair next to Silver. "First, Ms. Long, please take a deep breath and drink some mineral water. I do need you to remain calm."

Silver looked sideways at Felix and grabbed the tumbler from his hand. She drank fast, swallowing half the water before forcing the glass back into his hand. "There." She gestured toward the monitor walls. "Now explain...*this*!"

Felix gazed at the side of Silver's face. Wisps of stray black hair meandered over her ear, touched her neck and intertwined with the long peach fuzz on her neck. She looked vulnerable, scared. Felix couldn't remember a time Silver Long had ever touched his heart. But tonight, his heart went out to her.

"Relax, Ms. Long...Silver."

Silver inhaled deeply and slowly exhaled, her shoulders slumping forward ever so slightly. "I guess with everything I've seen, it shouldn't be a shock to know you monitor all these places. I should learn to stop being surprised when it comes to you." She looked at Felix. "And sure, dispense with the 'Ms. Long' and call me Silver."

Felix smiled inside and stood. "I do not yet have monitors everywhere—only the locations you see here, plus a few others. That I have the capability to act as a spy and observe activity in so many places is only a fraction of my capabilities." He walked across the plush carpet to the control panel in front of the four monitor walls.

Silver kicked off her pumps and stood slowly. "Word in the Underground is the new number one scientist is way ahead of you, Felix. Not just intellectually, but in terms of imagination and the ability to work with others toward a common goal." She stood still for a moment, then moved tentatively toward Felix and stood beside him. She caught herself gazing again at the swirling, multicolored monitor and diverted her eyes to Felix. "But I'll give you a chance. You say this spying operation of yours is only a fraction of what you can do?" She shrugged. "Okay, surprise me some more."

Felix raised an eyebrow. "Be careful what you ask for." He tapped a number of buttons on a touch pad in front of him. A holographic monitor appeared, suspended midair in front of the control panel. He removed his sport coat and tossed it on a chair behind him.

Silver folded her arms across her chest. "What, you have to *prepare* or something?"

"Just making myself comfortable." He turned to the monitors. "Okay, now choose a location, any location you see on any of the monitors."

Silver smirked. "All right…" She paused. "Let's see. There." She pointed at a live image of the city center in downtown Tremayne.

"Very well," Felix said. He looked past Silver and motioned to a table. "Pick up that ball. That one, there."

Silver picked up a red rubber ball and squeezed it.

"Now, take that marker and write your initials on the ball," Felix said.

Silver did as instructed and marked the ball with two huge letters: SL. She turned it over in her hand and tossed it to Felix.

Felix caught the ball and placed it in front of him on the table housing the control panel. He glanced at Silver. "You may want to sit down again."

Silver snorted. "I'm fine." She swiveled at the waist and surveyed the room again. "Titanium walls, a secret transportation box around the Underground, flashing lights and wall-sized monitors. Hoop-de-doodle. If you can impress me with a rubber ball, there's no hope left for me anyway. Do whatever you're going to do."

Silver watched as Felix flicked his fingers in the air toward the holographic screen in front of him. The yellowish glow around the darkened multicolored wall glowed steadily brighter.

Felix pointed to the monitor with the live image of Tremayne. The main intersection at the city center was busy. Traffic lights flashed and changed with the flow of pedestrians and vehicles. "Watch this. Then keep an eye on that monitor."

Silver turned to Felix in time to see him toss the ball at the swirling, dark-colored wall. As the ball hit the wall, the yellow lights flashed, then dimmed as the ball disappeared. Silver blinked, did a double take, then remembered the monitor. She looked again at the other wall as Felix flicked away at the virtual screen.

The image on the screen enlarged as Felix zoomed in to a crosswalk at the intersection. The rubber ball bounced slowly into the crosswalk. Felix stopped the camera long enough for Silver to read her initials on the ball, then released the view back to live action.

Silver dropped her arms to her side. She stared at the monitor, mouth open.

Felix turned to her. "Tell me, dear. Has the great Dr. Xander Rasmus perfected real-time teleportation?"

CHAPTER 17

The Team of Four

KRYSTAL RECLINED ON THE HUGE black leather sofa in Dion's quarters at Checkpoint One. Ryker and Winter were involved in another death match at the pool table in one corner of the room while Dion and Jimbo watched the activity from behind the bar.

"You didn't call the pocket," Ryker said. "Shot doesn't count."

Winter stabbed her cue stick into the carpet and placed her free hand on her hip. "What, so we're playing cutthroat rules?"

Ryker smiled. "You betcha, girl. Now pull your ball out and hand me the cue ball."

"You suck," Winter said. "I don't think any of your *rules* are official. I think you just make up this shit."

"He's making it up," Krystal said. "But rules are rules."

Winter shot Krystal a look and threw the cue ball at Ryker.

The ball struck the palm of his hand as he flinched and ducked. "Ow! Damn, Win."

A cold breeze swept into the room when Jasper and Lace entered.

"Beer time," Jasper said.

"Me too," Lace agreed.

Jimbo opened two bottles and slid them down the bar top as the two punks stepped up.

"Nico's on his way in, bro," Jasper said.

Dion dumped the contents of an ashtray into a can under the bar. "Awesome." He lit a cigarette and clinked his Zippo shut.

Lace hopped onto a barstool and swiveled around to face the room. "So, Krys. Are you starting to feel more at home? Kinda like the old days?"

"Actually, I feel better. Most of the time before—when I was a Changer—I felt like shit. I mean, I loved you guys." She glanced at Winter. "All of you. I was leading this miserable double life."

"How miserable could it have been," Winter said. "You were living forever, girl." She puffed up. "I mean, check it out. Good-looking, Curtis Dyer was in love with you, you were about to get your own place here at headquarters—"

"And my life was committed to the fucking Changers," Krystal said, sitting forward. "I don't know what you don't get about it, Win."

"Ease up, Win," Lace said. "No one walked in her shoes."

Jasper set his bottle on the bar top and swung around. "How long are we gonna flog this dead horse? So, yeah, Krystal was a Changer. But she's not now. We voted her back in, man."

"Was she feeding info to the enemy?" Winter asked. "We don't know that."

"We do," Lace said. "She said she wasn't, so in my mind she wasn't."

"It's our code, dude," Jimbo said. "Punks are loyal to Punks. We do what we think is right and what's good for the Punks."

Winter looked at Jimbo. "Don't call me dude, Jim." She turned to Krystal. "I'm having a hard time letting it go, Peterson—"

"But you have to," Lace said. "Krys is one of us. I feel like she always was."

Ryker held his hand up. "Toss me a beer, Jim."

Winter tossed her cue stick onto the pool table. "What, so shit's gettin' real? Have your say, Ryk."

Ryker caught the bottle Jim tossed him. He popped the top with a bottle opener attached to one end of the pool table. He held the bottle cap up and snapped his fingers, hurling the cap—Frisbee style—back to Jimbo.

He took a triple swig and looked at Winter. "Krys is in, just like you, me and the rest of these people. Let it go, Win."

Winter's shoulders slumped. She looked at Krystal. "It's hard for me to say I'm sorry, Peterson. I hate the Changers with everything in me. What they've done to this country, to this world…"

"I get it," Krystal said. "Dammit, Win. Just know I'm on your side. I always was. I hated the Changers as much as you. I still do."

Two-way radio communication sounded in the ceiling speakers. *"Nico here. Copy, Jimbo?"*

Jimbo strode to the far end of the bar and tapped a button on the control console. "Go, Nico."

"Where's Dion?"

"Head on over to Dion's quarters. Everyone's here."

"You got it. I'm out."

Krystal stood from the couch and approached Winter. The room went silent when Winter folded her arms across her chest.

Krystal's eyes locked on Winter's. "Me and you are gonna have a beer sometime real soon," Krystal said.

Winter didn't flinch. "Fat chance."

"Real soon." Krystal held up two fingers to Jimbo. She caught the first bottle and turned back to Winter. "The next one's yours."

Winter held steady, her eyes fixed on Krystal. Jimbo winced when the second bottle left his hand and flew toward Winter's head.

Krystal set the first bottle on the coffee table behind her. Without looking she reached up in time to intercept the second bottle midflight. She felt Winter's hair on the back of her hand.

Winter closed her eyes then slowly opened them. The hardness left her face.

Krystal swore to herself she saw a smile—barely perceptible—cross Winter's face. She popped the two bottles open and handed one to Winter.

"I got your back, Win." She took a swig of her beer. "Have mine."

A light knock from outside sounded on the door a split second before Nico entered.

"Come on in, buddy," Dion said.

"Hey," Ryker shouted from across the room. "Shut that door. It's cold out there."

Nico managed a grin. "You're telling me." He kicked the door closed and blew warm breath into his hand.

Dion extended a fist across the bar. "You look like you need a warm-up. What'll it be?"

Nico bumped his fist on Dion's. "Got any hot chocolate?"

"Comin' up," Jimbo said.

Krystal stepped around Winter and strode toward Nico. "So, is this the badass I've heard so much about that's in charge of security in Tremayne?"

Nico extended his hand to Krystal. "Hi, I'm Nico. You must be Krystal Peterson?"

Krystal bumped Nico's fist and smiled. "It's nice to meet you. Yes, I'm Krystal."

Nico nodded. "It's nice to meet you, too."

Ryker racked the balls on the pool table and hung his stick on the wall. "So, bro, we've been anxious to get your report."

Fred Garrison sat across a small dinette table from Thomas Dennis in the pair's temporary quarters at Checkpoint One.

"I feel detached, Thomas."

"Yeah, me too."

"We escaped the Changers to help put an end to their dreams of world domination." Fred glanced at the digital clock above the door. "Now, here we sit. Big dreamers, us."

"Didn't you think Krystal would sort of rely on us to help figure things out?" Thomas shook his head. "Seems like she doesn't even need us."

Fred looked down at his cell, vibrating on the table. "What the?" He held the device up to Thomas. "You recognize this?"

Thomas frowned. "No. Three numbers: 4-6-25. What kind of ID is that?" He looked at Fred. "Are you going to answer it?"

"Think I'll let it hit my voice mail. See if they leave a message." The vibration persisted. Fred sat forward and looked at the cell again. "Should have stopped by now. What the heck?"

"Hell, just answer it," Thomas said. "Hang up if you don't like it."

"I'm putting it on speaker." Fred touched the cell to connect the call. "Hello?"

"*Fred, my friend. And hello to my friend Thomas, as well.*"

"Felix?" The two responded in unison.

"*How have you two been doing?*"

Fred leaned forward on his elbows toward the cell. "Physically, okay. Emotionally, it's been a roller coaster."

"We wondered if we'd ever hear from you again," Thomas said.

"*Of course, of course. What's this about your emotions? I heard you made contact with Krystal—or she with you.*"

Fred sensed Felix had a smile on his face. "Yes, we are with her now." He glanced at Thomas. "Well, not exactly *with* her. We're at the Punk headquarters at the Perimeter."

"Yeah," Thomas said. "She's in a meeting of sorts, I guess. They have us tucked away in this little studio apartment." He looked around the room. "More like a motel room."

"*I trust you are becoming acclimated to the human lifestyle. At least from the Punks' perspective.*"

"Honestly, Felix, they're not really letting us in on anything," Fred said.

"*Most curious. There is much to do. Krystal is going to need all the help you can give. You must stick together.*"

Thomas sat back. "We feel like outsiders."

"*That's enough! Krystal will need you two. The Punks need you, whether they know it or not. And the world needs you. Now pick your chins up off your laps and man up!*"

"We can do that, Felix," Fred said. "But we're going to time out in a few months. That's not something we're looking forward to correcting."

"A small issue. Stop worrying about the little things. I'm going to send you additional help—someone else to add to your team."

"So we'll be a team of four?" Thomas frowned. "I can't imagine anyone who's left in the Underground that would give up the Changer lifestyle."

"Big boy panties, Thomas. Big boy panties. Now I want both of you to go to Krystal. Interrupt her meeting if you must."

"We're under guard here, Felix," Fred said.

"I'll let Krystal know you're coming. Just do as I say."

"So we know some shit went down in Bystander territory," Ryker said. "And it seems minors—children—are at the center of it."

"I guess you could say that," Nico said. He retrieved a tall mug of hot chocolate from the bar top. "There's a lot going down, but we're not sure what to make of it."

Dion walked around the bar and sat in his favorite chair next to the leather sofa. "Make yourself comfortable, buddy. Start from the beginning."

Nico hoisted himself onto a barstool and turned to face the room. "Well, today started out kinda like I expected." He sipped his drink, eyeing the group over the rim of his steaming mug. "I figured it was gonna be pretty quiet since Dion hadn't lifted curfew or given the all clear signal to the city manager. Then Will called me on the radio and said Krystal Peterson..." He glanced in her direction. "...had pretty much taken out all the Chybrids that were attacking us here at the Perimeter."

Krystal smiled. "For the record, everyone did a helluva job holding down the fort before I got here. Punks died to protect this place and our cause. And to protect the Bystanders."

"I understand," Nico said. "I was here for the big battle before Dion sent a bunch of us to Tremayne to set up a defense there."

"You've seen a lot for your age," Krystal said as her cell buzzed. "Hi, Felix...Yes, they are...Yes...Yes, of course...Yes, we'll talk later."

"He stepped up," Dion said. "When a whole ton of Punks ran for safety in the tunnels, Nico stuck it out. He's one of us, that's for sure."

"Agreed," Ryker said.

Silver stood behind the wet bar in Felix's quarters. "I can't believe you contacted those dregs."

Felix took off his glasses and tucked them in the top pocket of his shirt. "You underestimate their abilities, dear."

Silver rolled her eyes. "Seriously, Felix—"

"And their value. They are top scientists. They have guts."

"I'll admit it takes guts to turn tail and run away from the best thing that ever happened to them." Silver cracked open another bottle of mineral water. "They were elite among the elite."

"Precisely why they are so valuable on the outside. They are among a new elite team of three, soon to be four."

Silver sipped her water and replaced the cap. "Team of three?" She looked up, feigning thought. "Let's see, there's stupid Garrison." She held up her thumb. "Then there's idiot Dennis," she said, holding out her index finger. She looked at her hand, then at Felix. "That's a team of two by my count."

"Obviously you have forgotten Ms. Peterson—"

"Ha! That's rich! So you've got those two teaming up with Peterson?" She smiled and shook her head. "You're losing it, Felix."

Felix folded his hands in front of himself and smiled. "Remember I said there is soon to be four."

Silver dropped her hand. "And the illustrious Dr. Yaz completes the team of four?"

Nico sipped his hot chocolate. "So anyway, things seemed to be looking up once I got the call from Will. I was glad the Three Amigos were on their way to help me out. Those guys are cool."

Jimbo leaned on his elbows on the countertop from behind the bar next to Nico. "So what happened?"

"Well, I'm starting to relax once I know Will and them are heading to Tremayne. Then I noticed some kids—I've never seen them before then—messing around in one of the alleys. So I called out to them and told them they should go home until the all clear comes."

"From what I hear, they gave you a hard time," Dion said.

"Yeah, they did. I mean, nothing I couldn't handle, but yeah. So basically, I had to take one of 'em down. I called for backup and had the big guy taken to the police station."

Winter leaned against the pool table. "We should be able to handle a bunch of young pukes. What made all this such a big deal?"

"The bad happened when the Amigos got there. Adam started looking around, and he found some kids in another alley. They were throwing rocks at this lady—"

Lace looked across the room and nodded her head at Winter. "The assault victim?"

"So Adam busted them, right?" Jasper asked.

Nico shook his head. "Nah, they got away. But the lady, oh man, she was messed up. She was probably in her midforties, and she was unconscious. Looked like she got beat up pretty bad. For sure she's gonna need some dental implants. Those kids dropped a rock on her mouth big enough to knock out a couple of teeth. Plus, I'd be surprised if she doesn't lose an eye. Long story short, paramedics took her to Tremayne Medical Center."

Winter tipped her chin at Lace. "Yeah, that's the lady Dion sent us to question. She was unconscious when we got there. Doctors said they were still running tests and they didn't know when she'd be ready to see visitors."

"Yep," Nico said. "That's the lady. She was still out of it when I went to see her, too. So before I left Tremayne, Will said they were going to go try to talk to her."

Dion glanced up at Ryker. "Guess we'll know more when we hear from them."

"Hey, Dion," Krystal said. "I need to have Garrison and Dennis in here."

Dion tipped his chin to Krystal and squinted.

Krystal held up her phone. "I'll explain later."

Dion nodded to Jimbo. "Make it happen, bro."

"Come over to my side of the room, dear," Felix said.

Silver sighed and rolled her eyes. "Fine, Felix. I owe you, but I'm getting tired. Surely you have room in this place to set me up for the night." She swiped her pumps from the floor and met the doctor at the control console.

"I have something for you," he said, producing a small titanium container. "There is a combination on the outside. You must remember the code. I will not write it down, and you mustn't either."

Silver looked down at the container. "Fine." She held out her hand.

"Now follow me around the railing here."

Felix led her toward the multicolored teleportation wall and took her hand as she stepped down onto the platform.

"Not…too…comfortable with this, Felix," she said, gazing at the wall.

Felix smiled and pointed to his right. "See that monitor there? That's where Ms. Peterson is meeting with the Punks at their headquarters."

Silver frowned. "And that's real time, right?"

"Of course," Felix said.

Silver watched the live remote images as Fred and Thomas entered Dion's quarters. She saw Krystal greet the two as the door closed behind them.

"Amazing, your technological ability, Felix," Silver said.

"The combination is *4-6-25*. Don't forget it."

The blood rushed from Silver's face as she turned to the doctor. "Felix—"

He smiled. "Time for the team to meet their fourth member."

Silver turned to look at the teleportation screen. "Wh—"

Felix placed his hand firmly in the center of Silver's back and pushed hard. The dim yellow frame glowed brightly as Silver passed through the opening.

KRYSTAL MOTIONED TO THE BAR. "You two want something to drin—" She thought she must have blinked. Maybe her heart—or her brain—skipped a moment in time as Silver Long tumbled onto the floor in front of her.

Krystal jumped backward and whipped her 9mm pistol from the holster. She pointed the gun at the figure on the floor before the sight registered in her mind.

Winter mimicked Krystal's stance, pistol drawn. "What the hell, Peterson?" she shouted.

Silver paused on all fours, disheveled locks of silky black hair thrown forward across her face. She looked up at Krystal before glancing slowly around the room. "You bastard, Felix," she whispered.

CHAPTER 18

End of a Punk

On Levi's orders, Changers medical technicians had prepared the VIP operating room on level eleven for Curtis Dyer. The VIP OR was equipped with highly advanced neural lace technology that was not available to regular recipients of the Change procedure.

Four attendants pushed Curtis on a gurney through a narrow hallway toward the OR. A custom mix of fentanyl and diazepam fed through an IV in Curtis's arm had relaxed him to a state of immobility, but he remained conscious and semi-aware of his surroundings.

He smiled as his mind drifted to Krystal. Lights in the ceiling changed from sharp and clear to a blurry white glow as the technicians guided the gurney through a doorway into the operating room.

Whirring and clicking sounds blended with muted voices from several other attendants and medical assistants in the room.

"Welcome to the Change, Mr. Dyer."

Rasmus, Curtis thought. *Good. I have the best overseeing my procedure.*

"Hey, buddy. I'm right here with you. Nothing to worry about."

It was Johnny Logan. *Yeah. Real reassuring.*

"I want you to relax," Xander said. "The procedure will take several hours. But you will not remember a thing when it is all over."

Curtis felt pressure on his forearm. Someone's hand, he imagined. He thought of speaking, but no words came. The white glow in the room faded to gray. Shadowy blobs moved in and out of his view as voices came and went in his head.

"...the static recharge system has been implanted..."

"...heartrate is good. We're ready for deployment of the nanobots..."

Curtis unconsciously attempted to swallow. Pressure at the back of his throat produced a gag reflex. Unaware his eyes were closed, they shot open. All was dark gray.

"Doctor, patient cognition is at an unacceptable level."

"Increase the sedative, please," Xander said.

"Dude, that tube is huge."

"Silence, Mr. Logan. Nurse, deploy the nanobots."

The sensation of drowning overwhelmed Curtis. Flashes of bright white cut into the gray as he strained to turn his head to the side.

"That's godawful," Johnny said. "He's choking on that black shit you're forcing down his throat!"

A flash of clarity came and went. *I'm in a pod! Can't move. Can't breathe.*

"Doctor, brainwaves indicate the patient is awake."

"Increase the sedative!" Xander barked.

Curtis gagged again. His chest heaved. *Help! Someone help!* He couldn't hear his own voice as the room spun in circles. *Help,* he thought as the room faded to black.

Unaware of the four hours that had passed, Curtis heard Xander's voice.

"Good work, everyone. The Change is complete. Level two security and information protocols have been embedded."

"Dude," Johnny said. "Levi said to load level three, not two."

"As if it's your business, Logan. I know where we're headed with this man. He is targeted to be in our leader's inner circle. I know Levi will approve."

"Your decision, man."

"Ladies and gentlemen," Dr. Rasmus announced. "Curtis Dyer is now a Changer. Get this man out of the pod and into recovery."

CHAPTER 19

Destination Demo

CURTIS STOOD IN FRONT OF the floor-length mirror in his new quarters in the Underground City. He eyed his naked body and smiled. "Hmm, I kinda like the bald look." Keeping his eyes on the mirror, he turned to one side and flexed. "Yeah."

He turned around to survey the room: Soft-gray walls outlined above and below with indirect blue lighting. A fully equipped wet bar in one corner. A nice, modern, blue leather sofa with chrome trim, a matching love seat and chair, and a large glass coffee table. A huge desk sat in one corner facing the room.

He glanced into the bedroom. "Might as well get dressed." He smiled again. "Although it's a shame to cover up such a killer body."

When he reached the bedroom, he opened the top dresser drawer and retrieved a pair of microfiber undershorts. He started at a tone from the ceiling speaker and looked up. *What th—?* The tone sounded again, followed immediately by a knock on the door. "Oh shit," he whispered.

Curtis hurried through the living area to the door and swiped his hand over a panel on the wall.

"Dude, looking good!" Johnny said from the corridor outside. "You'd best get dressed. We're about to head out."

Curtis moved his hands to his hips. "Head out? Where?"

Johnny stepped past Curtis into the room, and the door swished shut. "Tremayne, my friend. We're gonna view the new SOUL Chybrid children in action."

"SOUL what?"

Johnny looked around the room. "Damn, dude. They got you set up nice."

Curtis relaxed and smiled. "Yeah, I like it. I could really get used to the Changer lifestyle—"

"Well, get used to it dude. You're in it for the long haul." Johnny swiveled to Curtis. "Get dressed, get dressed, man. Time's wasting and the boss is waiting."

"Oh." Curtis hurried into the bedroom and finished dressing. *Jeans and a T-shirt, just like I like it*, he thought. He glanced out into the living area, then back into the closet. *Hmm…sport coat, too, I guess. Since Logan looks a little dressy.*

"All right, I'm ready," he said, stepping into the living area.

Johnny shook his head. "That'll never work, dude."

Curtis smoothed the lapels on his sport coat. "What? Is the coat too much?"

"The coat's fine. It's that face."

Curtis glanced at the mirror behind the bar. "What, should I do my Mohawk? I kinda like being bald. I think I look more sophis—"

"We're going to Tremayne, Dyer." Johnny wasn't smiling. "You can't be seen looking like yourself. You're missing, remember? You want people asking questions? You want to be found?"

Curtis dropped his hands to his sides. "Well…"

Johnny turned toward the door. "Whatever, man. Just look like someone else before we get there."

Curtis followed Johnny to the door and out into the hallway. "I got time, right? It's all the way to Tremayne. Southern Cali to Central is four hours, at least."

Johnny strode quickly through the wide corridor. "We're taking the Hyperloop. We'll be there by daybreak—that's less than an hour. Best get changed."

Curtis walked swiftly to keep up Johnny's pace. His mind raced. This would be his first public change to alter his outward appearance. "Got it," he said.

LEVI TURNED TO GREET XANDER and Angelica as the two stepped off the elevator into the Hyperloop terminal. "Where's Logan and Dyer?" he snapped.

"I thought they'd be here," Angelica said.

"Agreed," Xander said.

Levi checked his cell. "Well, you two are right on time." He glanced at the open door of the hyperspeed train. "Which means they're late."

An adjacent elevator door swished open. Curtis and Johnny stepped out and strode toward the waiting trio. Levi frowned and tapped his wrist, even though he wasn't wearing a wristwatch.

"We're ready, Leader," Johnny said.

Levi glanced past Johnny at Curtis. "He's not."

"He'll change on the way, sir," Johnny said.

Levi turned and moved onto the train. The others followed and seated themselves.

Curtis stepped in after Johnny and selected a seat at the rear of the car. He gazed around the interior of the tube-shaped vehicle and marveled at the technology. He felt like he was on a spaceship. As he watched the door close and lock in place, the forward movement was immediate. Curtis's head involuntarily pushed back against the headrest as the Hyperloop accelerated. He closed his eyes and concentrated on changing his appearance.

KRYSTAL STRODE SWIFTLY ACROSS THE open expanse of the Punks' compound in the early morning hours the day after her reunion with the group. Recent rain and plunging temperatures gave way to the dreaded tule fog overnight. The previous day's wind was nonexistent. Sodium vapor lights on posts lining the concrete walkways fought in vain to penetrate the haze.

Her ears prickled at the sound of gritty footsteps behind her. She stepped off the sidewalk and backed away until the concrete faded into the mist. *Long stride*, she thought. *Tall. Confident.* Her timing was perfect when she moved back to the sidewalk and thrust her hand into the path of the oncoming figure.

"Whoa, shit!" Ryker said. He skidded to a stop and grabbed Krystal's wrist. "Scare the hell outta me, girl!" He loosened his grip as Krystal stepped in front of him.

"Funny," Krystal said. "But that wasn't my intent." She glanced toward the depot, squinting through the fog. "Where you headed, anyway?"

"Breakfast. Same as you, I'm assuming."

"Yeah, I got my appetite back today."

"Fog sucks today," Ryker said. "And it's freezing out here." The pair walked toward the Depot more by instinct than sight. "Fred and Thomas breakfast guys?"

Krystal smiled to herself. "They'll both eat pretty much any time." She looked up at Ryker. "But, yeah. They're breakfast guys."

"What about our new addition?"

"Silver?" Krystal cringed. "I guess, Ryk. I never made it my business to care about her. I still don't…not really."

Ryker swiped a thumb under his bandanna, clearing a stray lock. "Yeah, you guys have some history. I get that. What's Dr. Yaz say about it? If he's as smart as you say he is, he sent her for a reason."

"I only spoke briefly with him about it. I know she'll be an asset—if she's actually on our side."

Ryker nodded toward the door to the Depot. "Well, I guess she's a breakfast person."

Krystal watched as Silver flung the Depot door open and stepped inside. "I guess."

When the pair reached the Depot entrance, Krystal stepped in front of Ryker and grabbed the door handle.

"Wait." Ryker placed his hand over hers.

Krystal glanced up, and her eyes locked on his. When she felt his skin through fingerless gloves on her wrist, she stepped back and shoved both hands into the pockets of her duster. "What?"

Ryker raised both hands in a no-foul gesture. "Whoa, Krys."

She gazed out into the thick mist, then back at the door. "You said 'wait' and then I said 'what.' So, *what?*"

"All right. I was about to say I think we need to start with a good attitude here." He paused and leaned around to view her face. "Okay?"

"I gotta be honest, Ryk. There's gonna be some big-time tension for a while till she proves herself to me. I know you guys are all enamored with this *new girl*—"

"Ha!" Ryker smiled. "I'll admit she's hot. But it takes more than looks to win any of us over."

"That bugs me. The fact you even mention her looks."

Ryker shrugged. "Guys are visual beings. Always have been."

"And you see that first?"

"We're getting off track here. But yeah, I noticed she's a beautiful woman. But that doesn't affect my loyalty to us—the Punks. And it doesn't affect my judgment." He grasped her shoulder and turned her to face him. "First and foremost, it doesn't change your standing with me."

Krystal leaned her back against the exterior wall of the Depot and folded her arms across her chest. It felt frozen against her back, but she stayed, unflinching. "Might as well clear the air here. Where do I stand with you, Ryk?" She tipped her chin up. "Where do I stand with any of you?"

Ryker matched Krystal's stance. "I'm gonna go deep here. Three months ago, you were a good, solid commander with the Punks. You were working your way up. Today, I'd put you at the top."

Krystal raised an eyebrow. "At the top? Like you and Dion?"

"Dion and I have a long history. We're brothers. You're right up there with him in my eyes."

She looked down at her boots. "You've known me a little over three years. Big difference there."

"Right. But time has nothing to do with it. I know what you've been through and I know what I've seen in you. Today, I'd trust you with my life. You gotta believe that, Krys."

Krystal stood upright. "I'm glad you said that. Trust me when it comes to Silver Long. My history with her won't cloud my judgment." She studied Ryker's face. "And I won't let you down."

Ryker stepped forward and opened the door. "I know you won't. And that works both ways." He smiled and swept his arm toward the opening. "After you!"

With the Hyperloop well under way, the five Changers released their lap belts and swiveled their seats to face the aisle.

Johnny glanced at Curtis, then did a double take and smiled. "That's it? That's your look?"

"What?" Curtis said. "I don't look like myself anymore, right?"

"Logan," Levi snapped. "Get this man up to speed. He is seriously lacking in some of the finer points of the Change."

Curtis did his best to not appear bewildered when he looked at Johnny. *What?* he mouthed.

Angelica was mildly amused. "You look a little…nerdy."

Johnny shot a look at Levi, who wasn't smiling. He turned back to Curtis. "Take on a look that you want to live with. You know, one that's *you*. Your personality." He nodded encouragement. "One that you want to keep while you're with us." He leaned toward Curtis and spoke softly into his ear. "Get handsome, like me."

Curtis nodded. "Ah, got it."

"I take it breakfast will be served shortly, Leader?" Xander asked.

"Yes, Doctor," Levi said. "I expect it momentarily."

Angelica eyed the far end of the compartment. "I see refreshments are on their way."

A male attendant in a white jumpsuit, pushing a lightweight carbon fiber cart, strode swiftly down the narrow center of the car. He stopped one row of seats in front of the Changers and pressed a small button in the ceiling. A cover in the floor between the passengers slid sideways, giving way to an oval platform that rose automatically to table-height. The attendant bowed. "Fresh-squeezed orange juice for all."

Curtis swiveled his chair to the table and looked at Johnny. "How's this?"

Johnny looked at Curtis and sat up straight. He nodded. Then he nodded again. "Yes, Dyer. That's more like it. That's the ticket. What do you think, Leader?"

Levi smiled. "Yes, Dyer. I believe you're a quick study. You're going to work out fine."

Johnny turned to Angelica. "I'd say he's one handsome devil, wouldn't you, Ms. DeMone?"

Angelica glanced up at Curtis while placing a napkin in her lap. "Yes. Ooh, baby," she said, expressionless. "Where's my quiche? I'm ready for breakfast."

CHAPTER 20

Dead-End Doris

THE WAITING ROOM ADJACENT TO the Intensive Care Unit on the fifth floor of Tremayne Medical Center was quiet. Hospital staff had dimmed the lights overnight. The Three Amigos had waited out guests and family members well past visiting hours.

Will sat slumped in a thinly padded orange-and-chrome chair and gazed out through the floor-to-ceiling windows on the street-side wall. Fog. Lights from the parking lot fought to reach the third level of the hospital. Anything above the fourth floor looked like a wet wall of smoke reflecting the interior lighting.

The doctor on duty meandered into the darkened waiting area and stopped. He pulled an electronic tablet from his white coat and flipped a finger on the surface, scrolling the screen upward. He looked up at the Three Amigos. "Anyone here have a relation to a..." He glanced at the tablet again. "...a Ms. Doris Givenzy?" He looked up, seemingly impressed with himself at having properly pronounced the name.

Will stood quickly and turned to greet the doctor. "Room 504?"

Adam nudged Joey hard in the ribs. "Heads up, bro."

Joey's eyes fluttered open as Adam stood.

The doctor slipped the tablet back into his lab coat. "That's correct," he said to Will. "Are you a relative?"

Will glanced quickly at Adam, then back at the doctor. "Well, yes. Sort of."

The doctor removed his glasses and tucked them into a top pocket. "We ran her name through our database. We also contacted the Tremayne Police Department. Neither search turned up any relations to this woman."

"Uh—" Will began.

"She's a Changer," Adam blurted out.

The doctor raised an eyebrow. "Really? And how would you know?"

Adam glanced quickly around the room, as if the right words were floating somewhere in the air. "Uh…*we're* Changers. We're here on the highest authority from the Underground. Any information you have about Ms. Givenzy, you can tell us."

"Sounds like a crock to me," the doctor said. "You all look like Punks."

Adam stepped up to the doctor. "If I have to prove anything to you, our leader isn't going to like it."

The doctor smiled and looked down his nose at Adam. He folded his hands in front of himself. "I'll take my chances. Prove it, young man."

Joey sat on the couch, silently listening to the banter. He speed-dialed Dion.

"*Joey? It's four o'clock in the morning. What's up, buddy?*"

"Yeah, Dion. I'm sorry about the time. I gotta talk fast. We got a situation here at the hospital. Adam kinda told the doctor we're Changers—"

"*What? You guys are working way past your shift.*"

"Okay, wait. Let me finish. We can get information on this lady if we can prove we're Changers. Does Krystal—or anyone there at headquarters—know what we can tell this doctor that will convince him to tell us about her?"

"*Holy shit, Joe. Gimme a minute.*"

Joey held the cell to his ear and turned around in his chair. "Hey, guys. I got our authorization coming right up."

The doctor kept his arms folded and swiveled to address Joey. "Well, welcome to the morning, Rumpelstiltskin." He glanced at a digital clock on the wall. "I really don't have time for your nonsense. There are other patients I must see."

"*Hey, Joey?*" Dion said.

Joey turned back around in his chair. "Yeah. Go ahead, Dion."

"*Krystal's in a meeting right now. I pulled one of the other Rogue Changers out for this. Let's hope it's worth it.*"

"Okay. Sorry, Dion. It's pretty important."

"*Here's Thomas.*"

"All right—"

"*This is Thomas. Joey?*"

"Yeah, it's Joey. Here's the deal—"

"*I already know the deal. Listen up. All hospitals and law enforcement have a set of codes they use to verify the Changers' authority. I'm going to send a code to your phone right now. When the message comes in, it'll look like an unknown number—no ID. The message will have a code in the image. Just tell that doctor to scan your code into his system. They'll give you everything you need.*" He chuckled. "*I'll be surprised if he doesn't offer up his firstborn son when he sees the level of authority from this code.*"

Joey smiled. "Got it. I'll wait for the code. And thanks, Thomas."

"Well, kids," the doctor said. "I've had about enough waiting. I'll have hospital security escort you out."

Joey's phone buzzed. "Wait." He looked down at the screen. "What you'll actually be doing is scanning the code on my cell." He looked at Will and Adam. "If you know what's good for you."

The doctor dropped his hands to his sides, and his shoulders slumped. "Oh, fine! Give me that thing!" He stepped up to Joey and held his hand out without looking.

Joey slapped the phone into the man's hand. "Might want to check your attitude."

The trio followed the doctor to the nurses' station. The doctor grabbed the edge of a monitor and swiveled it around to face him.

He placed the phone over a near-field communications device and looked at the monitor.

CHANGERS NORTH AMERICA
SECURITY LEVEL 10

The doctor caught himself with a hand on the countertop as his knees weakened. He looked up at the nurse across the counter.

Her eyes were sympathetic. "Doctor?"

The doctor breathed deeply and turned to face the Three Amigos. He smiled weakly and leaned against the countertop with both elbows.

"Well?" Will said. "We asked nicely before. We'd like any information you have on Ms. Givenzy."

"And we'd like it now," Joey said.

The doctor, still supporting himself with both hands, turned to the nurse. "Please get them whatever they need." He turned back to the three. "The nurse will get you any information we have. And…and please accept my sincerest apologies for any misunderstanding."

"Misunderstanding on your part," Adam said.

The doctor nodded profusely. "Yes, yes. Misunderstanding on my part. If there is anything else you need, please don't hesitate to contact me." His hand trembled as he reached into his top shirt pocket and retrieved a business card.

Will looked at the card but made no attempt to reach for it. "Dr. Smith." He looked up at the doctor. "Seriously? You're Dr. *Smith?*"

The doctor nodded again. "Yes. Yes, I am. Dr. Smith. Dr. Stanley Smith." He took another deep breath. "Now, if you will address Nurse Jones, she will help you."

"Smith and Jones," Joey said. "Doesn't that figure."

Adam turned to the doctor. "Well, thank you, *Dr. Smith.* Thank you for your cooperation."

"Yes, of course. Any time," the doctor said as he hurried down the hallway toward the restroom.

Will moved over to the nurses' station and placed his hands on the counter. "Nurse Jones."

"Yes, sir. I understand you are seeking information on the assault victim, Ms. Givenzy."

"That's right. We'd like to see her now."

Nurse Jones's hands trembled. "Well, sir." She glanced down the empty hallway where the doctor had been, then looked back at Will. "Well, sir. You can't see Ms. Givenzy."

"You saw the authorization—" Joey began.

"Yes, yes. I saw it," Nurse Jones said. "But Ms. Givenzy died three hours ago. We spent the last three hours trying to find a next of kin to notify. We found no one."

"Where's the body?" Will asked.

The nurse fidgeted with a stylus on the counter. "Well, the body was taken to the basement morgue for immediate disposal."

"Disposal?"

"Why, yes. You know the policy, correct? With no family or friends to notify, Ms. Givenzy has already been cremated."

Will looked at his two friends. "Well, Ms. Jones. It would have been wise to check in the waiting room *before* you cremated her instead of *after*. Don't you agree?"

"I am truly sorry, sir." The nurse reached under the counter. "We have her clothes." She placed a clear plastic bag on the counter in front of Will. "And her other belongings."

Will picked up the bag off the counter and reached inside. He pulled out items of clothing and handed them to Adam, one at a time. *Shoe, shoe, sweater, bra, blouse. Where is it? Where is it?*

He turned the bag upside down over the counter while the nurse watched. *Skirt, bracelet, watch. Cell phone!* Will shoved the device into the back pocket of his jeans and looked at his friends. "Adam, grab the rest of that stuff. We're outta here."

CHAPTER 21

Amok Raymond

DION SAVORED THE SCENT OF freshly scrambled eggs and sizzling bacon when he entered the control room inside the Depot. Jimbo sat in his usual spot at the communications control console, staring at a huge monitor on the wall.

"Fucking cold today," Dion said.

"You're telling me." Jimbo swiveled his chair to face Dion. "Fog's so thick, you get wet just steppin' outside."

Dion rubbed his hands together. "Breakfast smells good." He glanced at a side door leading to the dining room and tipped his chin up. "Who all's in there?"

Jimbo lit a cigarette and dropped his lighter on the bar top. "Let's see. Ryker, Krystal, Winter, the two Rogue Changers, and Silver, whatever she is."

"You need to get it straight, bro." Dion shrugged off his duster and hung it over the back of a barstool. "Krys says she's a Rogue Changer. Anyone who's been a Changer but doesn't want to be one anymore. That makes three Rogues in there, plus two Punks—Ryk and Win."

"And Silver?"

Dion shook his head slowly. "I guess that remains to be seen. It appears Silver's on our side at this point."

"I don't trust her, man," Jimbo said.

"No, but I trust Krystal to keep an eye on her."

Jimbo took a long drag on his cigarette. "I don't even fully trust Krystal, bro."

Dion walked toward the dining room door. "I know, man. You and Winter. I think you'll come around."

Jimbo swiveled back to the comm console. "We'll see. Just lookin' out for the Punks, that's all."

Dion pushed the dining room door open and stood in the entryway. He surveyed the diners and inhaled deeply. "Damn that smells good."

RYKER GLANCED UP AND RAISED his hand to the Punk leader when Dion entered.

Fred turned around in time to see the door close behind Dion. "Boss is here, guys."

Winter remained stone-faced. "Didn't know he was in on this meeting."

"He needs to know everything that's going on," Ryker said. He nodded to Krystal. "But Krys is in charge here."

"Morning, everyone," Dion said as he grabbed a chair from an adjacent table.

Ryker slid his chair closer to Krystal to make room for his friend. "You order yet, bro?"

Dion flipped the chair around and sat down between Ryker and Winter. "Yep. I called in a few minutes ago." He glanced up at Thomas. "Thanks for handling that with the Amigos."

"No problem," Thomas said. "Shows what a team of Changers and Punks can do."

Winter looked across the table at Silver. "Punks and Changers. Punks first, guy. Remember that."

Silver smiled. "A little early for you, Winter? You sound testy."

"He's right, Win, whatever order you wanna say it." Dion took a sip of his orange juice. "Thanks to Krys, we dodged a bullet. Her ability to take down the Chybrids was due exclusively to Changers technology. You can't dispute that."

"So what are they up to now?" Ryker asked.

Krystal speared a sausage bite with her fork and swirled it around the maple syrup on her plate. "I got some good info from Felix, guys. You can forget about the fucking mechanical Chybrids ripping us to shreds."

"Seriously?" Winter said. "So you're the savior of the Punks and you singlehandedly eliminated our biggest threat?"

Krystal popped the sausage bite into her mouth without looking up. "Let's get one thing straight here." She took three long swigs from her ice water and set the glass back onto the table, then looked up at Winter. "The Changers' ultimate goal is world domination. First, they're aiming for North America. Right now, they control the entire western half of this continent. Whatever phase this is in their timeline, they want North America next. Those mechanical Chybrids weren't our biggest threat."

"Really?" Ryker said. "If not for Felix and you with those skull-buster bullets, we were goners."

Fred leaned onto the table with both elbows. "You have a point, Ryk. But we know the Changers. It's like this. They go for the jugular each time they move forward. But they always have another phase coming."

"Like a backup plan?" Dion asked.

"Not exactly," Fred said. "They go for the jugular, and they still want to stomp on your skull when you bleed out. They don't care. They're that ruthless."

Winter leaned back in her chair. "So the next phase is them stomping on our skulls—"

"Which was in their plan all along," Krystal said.

"I have to pee," Silver said, standing up. "Where's the restroom around here?"

Dion pointed toward the kitchen. "Head through that little alcove back there."

"So, Krys, what's the word from Felix?" Ryker asked. "Are we ready for the Changers' skull-stomping?"

Krystal looked at Ryker, then she gazed at the elite team of Punks seated around the table. "Absolutely not."

Jimbo got up from the control console and stretched. He walked to the Depot entrance and opened the door. The color of the thick fog had changed to a lighter shade of gray as the sun began to rise. He turned and grabbed his duster off of a coatrack near the door before stepping outside. He lit another cigarette and stuck the lighter into his duster pocket.

All sound outside was muted by the thick mist in the air. Jimbo squinted toward the glow of a light post along the concrete pathway in front of him. A wisp of moisture drifted out of place, no longer part of the stationary cloud. He reached around his back and pressed a hand to his waist. *Yep, 9mm in place.* He squinted into the mist again as a shadow approached. The sound of grit crunching on the sidewalk indicated footsteps.

He shifted his duster around his back and pulled his 9mm from his waistband. "Hey."

No answer.

From behind him, Jimbo heard unintelligible banter from the two-way radio inside the Depot. "Heads up, man. Who's there?" *Where the hell is security?* he thought.

He stood as still as possible, his pistol hung from one hand at his side. His ears prickled at the dead silence.

At the breakfast table, Dion glanced behind him toward the door to the communications room. Banter on the radio had caught his attention. No reply from Jimbo sparked his concern. "Excuse me, people." He pushed his chair back and stood. "I'll be right back."

The communications room and bar area were quiet and empty when Dion entered. The door to the outside was closed. No Jimbo. *Taking a leak, maybe,* he thought.

The two-way crackled. "*It's Will, Jimbo. Do you copy? We're 10-19, heading in from the medical center.*"

Dion glanced up at the electronic map on the wall. Three lighted dots representing the Three Amigos' Lenco BearCats moved along the highway toward the Perimeter. He pressed a button on the control console. "*Will, it's Dion. I copied.*"

"10-4, Dion."

Dion walked slowly toward the Depot door to the compound. He opened the door, just a crack, and looked outside with one eye. The heavy air drifted inside, cooling the skin on one side of his face. The hair on his neck bristled. He glanced down and saw Jimbo's 9mm handgun lying on the concrete walkway. Jimbo had his back to the door. Raymond had one arm around Jimbo's neck. The other hand grasped a pistol, the business end pressed against Jimbo's temple.

CHAPTER 22

The Xander Plan

"I TRUST THE QUICHE IS TO your liking, Ms. DeMone?" Levi said.

Angelica dabbed the corners of her mouth with her napkin. "I've had better." She folded the napkin and laid it vertically onto the empty plate in front of her. "But I'll give you that it's not bad for a Hyperloop transportation-type meal."

"I'll speak to the head chef," Levi said.

Curtis smiled and looked at Levi. "My waffle and bacon were excellent."

Johnny glanced at Levi, leaned into Curtis and cupped a hand over his mouth. "Ix-nay, buddy. He didn't ask you."

Levi smiled. "That's quite all right, Logan. I'm happy to see Mr. Dyer feels comfortable enough to speak freely."

"Yes, Leader. I was just—"

Levi held up a hand. "He is part of my inner circle, Logan. Just as you are. Mr. Dyer is a valuable addition to our staff." He nodded at Johnny. "Kudos to you, of course, for bringing him to me." He looked at Curtis, then back at Johnny. "But that's as far as things go with you. Mr. Dyer is his own man. He may speak to me any time, any place."

"About anything?" Johnny asked.

"About anything and…" Levi gestured around the table. "…about *anyone*."

"So you want us narking on each other?" Johnny asked.

Xander had ordered wine for breakfast. He took a sip and placed the glass back onto the table. "Checks and balances, Logan." He smiled at Johnny. "You have something to hide?"

Johnny dropped his fork onto his plate without taking the last bite of his omelet. He sat back. "I got nothing to hide, Rasmus." He pointed at Curtis. "It's just that…I thought I was going to be his mentor. I thought I was going to supervise him."

"The doctor is correct, Logan," Levi said. "We have checks and balances. We all keep each other honest." He looked at Angelica. "Would you agree, Ms. DeMone?"

Angelica nodded, feigning subservience. "Oh, yes, Levi. We all keep each other honest." She put a hand on Xander's forearm. "How's that wine? I'm getting to the point where I feel the urge to have some myself."

"Splendid," Xander said. He winked at her. "Takes the edge off meetings like this."

Levi raised his water glass to Xander. "I'm glad you reminded us we're all in a meeting here. We'll reserve pleasure for our trip back to the Underground. For now, why don't you brief us all on your progress with the SOUL Chybrid project and what we should expect from our little excursion today."

Johnny swiveled his seat toward Curtis. He looked directly into Curtis's eyes. "Don't think you're *in*, buddy. You keep your nose clean and talk to me first before you speak to our leader again."

"Are we interrupting something, boys?" Angelica asked, staring at Johnny and Curtis.

Johnny sat up in his chair. "My apologies. Go right ahead."

"As I was saying," Xander began. "We have conducted stringent testing of the SOUL Chybrid children within the city limits of Tremayne. We have deliberately programmed the SOUL children to the limits of compassion—having little to none. Of course, this is merely an experiment and the activities of these Chybrids have not been received to any degree of favor by the Bystanders. That is, the citizens of Tremayne."

Curtis sat staring at Xander as his eyes glazed over. The doctor's words faded to background noise as Curtis's mind drifted to Krystal. He imagined the day they would be reunited. His eyelids closed as he felt her hand on his face, his lips touching hers, their bodies pressed together. He felt her arms around him, the skin of their cheeks touching. *She'll be so happy we're both Changers now*, he thought.

"And we expect the SOUL Chybrid children to become citizens themselves, students in public schools and active members of society among the Bystanders," Levi said.

"That's correct," Dr. Rasmus confirmed. "Our plan is to migrate the SOUL Chybrids into Bystander territories as full families. We will push the population of the SOUL Chybrids into North America at a limit just below that which the Bystanders' social services can support, without being a complete burden to their system."

"Excellent." Levi clapped his hands together once.

Curtis's eyes shot open.

"Once the SOUL Chybrids have become integrated into society, they will be used to influence the youth of the Bystanders. We will program the Chybrid children at all levels of intelligence and personalities. The Bystander children will naturally be inclined to side with our SOUL Chybrids, thus—"

"Thus making them oblivious to the fact we intend to absorb them to maintain our own lives," Angelica said.

Xander leaned back in his seat and looked down his nose at Angelica. "Well, that's putting it bluntly. But, yes."

Sounds fucked up, Curtis thought. *The Punks won't stand a chance to get anyone onto their side. Not without the youth. Hmm, I'm a Changer now. So is Krystal. I'm not sure I care.*

"Yes!" Levi said. "As you have so eloquently stated, Doctor, when we capture the minds of the children, we will rule the world!"

"Precisely," Xander agreed. He turned to Angelica. "But let me address your point about absorbing the lives of the Bystanders. We have developed the SOUL Chybrids to a new level. This level will lessen the need for direct absorption of the human Bystander by a regular Changer. As you will soon see, the SOULs will absorb the Bystanders on our behalf and become container vessels of our life-extending enzyme."

Levi smiled.

The white-suited attendant brought Angelica's wine and set it on the table.

She picked up the glass and lightly sniffed the edge of it. "Do tell, Doctor."

Xander didn't hide that he was enjoying his time in the spotlight. He looked at Curtis. "Mr. Dyer. You have not yet had the need to absorb your first life, am I correct?"

Curtis nodded. "Yes, that's correct."

"Since you have been trained in the absorption of human life to extend your own, you know the details. Sadly, when we absorb a life, we leave the remnant of the body behind." His mouth curled into a snarl. "You know, that shriveled pile of skin and bones that's leftover for our 'collection team' to clean up—"

"The collection team is used for mass absorption operations only, Xander," Angelica clarified.

Xander took a deep breath to hide his irritation at the interruption. "Yes. And when you absorb a life in a single event…" He glanced at Angelica. "You must dispose of the remains yourself, or leave it for someone to discover." He frowned. "Can get messy, you know."

"Yes, sir," Curtis said.

Xander held up a finger. "But." He looked around the table. "But our new adult SOUL Chybrids have the ability to absorb a human and store the life-extending enzymes of the human body within specially built capsules. The capsules are protected within the Chybrid housing for delivery back to the Underground."

"So what about the carcass, the dead human body?" Johnny asked.

Xander sat back in his seat. "That's something we're still working on."

Johnny snorted. "So the dead body just stays where it is, to be discovered by anyone?"

"Yeah, okay, Logan. The point is, we Changers don't have to deal with it. The SOUL Chybrid will absorb the human and walk away. There's no emotion there. No sense of responsibility or remorse."

"Ha!" Johnny sat forward. "I never felt remorse after absorption." He glanced back at Curtis. "I mean, it's the human or me, right? Changers are worth more than any Punk or Bystander." His eyes widened. "Hey, Doc. You s'pose we'll get to see a Chybrid absorb a Bystander when we get to Tremayne?"

Dr. Rasmus finished off his wine and set his glass on the table. He sat back and smiled, resting both hands on the arms of his chair. "One can always hope."

CHAPTER 23

Talking Down

S ILVER STARED AT A ROW of seven urinals on one wall of the black-tiled restroom. On the opposite wall were seven regular toilets inside stalls with privacy doors. She glanced back at the urinals. *What the heck are urinals doing in the ladies' restroom? And what's that low one for, midgets? Oh, wait. I get it. Coed restroom.* She rolled her eyes. *Whatever,* she thought as she chose a stall on one end and entered, fastening the door latch behind her.

She pulled her cell from a back pocket of her pants and sat down on the closed toilet lid. *What the hell, Yaz.* She speed-dialed Felix.

The call buzzed twenty times in her ear before going dead. She looked down at the cell. *CALL ENDED. You little shit.* She speed-dialed the doctor again.

Eight rings later, Felix answered. "*Silver. Hello.*"

"Felix," Silver whispered into the cell. "What have you gotten me into? I don't know if I'm up for this. Have you ever tried to hang out with these savages? And Peterson. She really thinks she's the cat's meow. Acts like she's the boss. This is dumb, Felix. What am I even doing here—"

"*Silver, you must calm down.*"

She cupped her hand over the cell and raised her voice to a loud whisper. "How can I be calm when I don't even know why I'm here. I mean, you just pushed me through your little transport wall-thingy and expect me to wing it?"

"*I told you, you would be part of a very special team. You*—"

"I'm not too far from timing out, you know. I need to absorb someone soon. How's that going to look? Bet you didn't think about that."

"*I've checked your stats. You have six months left, give or take a day. Now, tell me what's happening right now. I don't have a monitor in the Punks' dining facility at this time.*"

Silver took a deep breath and surveyed the inside of the stall. "They're having this breakfast meeting. I think they like getting up early, which for me, you know it's a stretch. So far, everyone seems nice enough. And their leader, Dion. He's better-looking in person than I remember from the images I've seen on our monitors in the Underground. There's one person, Winter. She's a little scary. But nothing I can't handle—"

"*Silver. The meeting. What is it about?*"

"Right. So you said there was going to be this team of four. You know, me and Peterson, plus Garrison and Dennis. But this guy, Ryker, and this Winter character are both in on it. They're talking about going to Tremayne to get a firsthand look at what we—I mean the Changers—are up to. They're convinced the Chybrid attack isn't the end of pressure from the Changers."

"*And you know from experience that their assumptions are correct. You know the Changers will not stop until they have eliminated all opposition to their agenda.*"

Silver's shoulders slumped. "I know. And somehow you've stuck me on the losing side. I'm accustomed to winning, Felix."

"*Do you even realize what an elite team of professionals you are a part of? Look at the history here. Look at the experience.*"

"I suppose I haven't analyzed their individual abilities and talents."

"*Yes, do that. Analyze them. Then realize the sum of their parts is exponentially greater than they are as individuals. And remember that team includes me. And yourself. I am in contact with Peterson, as well as Garrison and Dennis. I will send instructions to you as well.*"

Silver sat for a few moments to absorb what Felix had said.

Felix waited patiently on the other end of the connection.

"Okay, Felix. Thanks for talking me down." She looked down at her lap. "By the way, what's this little metal case with the combination lock you sent me here with?"

"*In time, dear. I assure you, you will know before you need it. Just remember to guard it with your life.*"

"Yeah. Got it," she said before ending the call.

RYKER GLANCED AT THE DOOR leading to the communications room. He slid his chair back from the table and dropped his napkin on his plate. "I'll be right back, everyone. I'm gonna see what's keeping Dion."

Winter looked up at Ryker. "Was thinking the same. Need a hand?"

Ryker waved her off. "Nah, I'm sure it's nothing. I'll let you know."

When he entered the communications room, he saw Dion standing at the door leading to the compound.

Dion glanced back and held a finger over his mouth, then motioned for Ryker to join him.

"What's up, bro?" Ryker whispered.

Dion whispered over his shoulder. "Ray's out there holding a nine to Jim's head. I don't know what his problem is."

RAYMOND SPOKE TO JIMBO THROUGH gritted teeth. "Remember the day your little pet, *Krystal Peterson*, came *home*? You shoulda' been on my side, bro."

Jimbo stood firm. "I'm on the Punks' side, Ray. It's where you should be."

"The Punks are whacked out, man," Raymond said. "Three months ago, they shoulda' killed her ass. Now that fuckin' bitch is back in our ranks. And you voted against me."

Jimbo's muscles flexed against the pressure from Raymond's

grip. "I voted her out, Ray. You heard me. But majority ruled here. I accepted the decision of the organization."

"Every one of you that allowed her back in is dead. That's my goal." Raymond pressed the pistol harder against Jimbo's temple.

"Dude, you can't get any closer with that nine than you are. Let's go inside. Get some breakfast and talk this out."

The sound of vehicles in the distance caught the Punks' attention. Jimbo strained to look sideways against the gun at his head. Fog lights on the approaching trucks did little to cut through the blanket of murk that had settled into the compound.

"Company's coming, Ray. Let's tone this situation down."

"Fuck that, Jim. It's probably those three little pukes that never should have had a vote." Raymond wrestled Jimbo around to face the vehicles. "First you, bro. Then, they're dead."

"THE AMIGOS ARE ROLLING IN," Dion whispered to Ryker. "Ray's got his back to us now. Let's move."

Light from inside the Depot reflected off the fog in front of the two Punks outside when Dion flung the door open. Raymond glanced back and squeezed the trigger a split second after Jimbo dropped to the ground.

Dion lunged at Raymond's knees as Ryker dove over Dion, both fists flying. A hard right cross from Ryker's fist connected with Raymond's temple. The disgruntled Punk crumpled to the ground as Ryker's boot slammed into Raymond's ribs.

Jimbo scrambled to his feet. "Hold up, Ryk! He's out!"

Dion released his grip on Raymond's legs and stood up. He glanced at the prone Punk's right hand, still clutching his pistol. "Grab the nine, Jim. Ryk, get the zip ties."

Jimbo peered into the mist toward the glow of headlights. "The Cats are idling, guys. I can't make out anyone."

"Looks like you guys got everything under control." It was Will.

Dion started. "Will! What the hell, sneaking up like that!"

Adam and Joey followed Will into the light cast from inside the Depot.

"Had to sneak up, bro," Adam said. "Till we could find out what was happening."

Ryker returned from inside with a hefty pair of zip ties and straddled Raymond. "Good job, guys." He gathered Raymond's limp arms and secured them behind the unconscious Punk's back.

Joey stared wide-eyed at the back of the leather-clad Punk on the ground. "Is that Ray?" He looked up at Ryker. "What *was* happening?"

"Can't say yet." Ryker looked at Jimbo. "Guess you can fill us in."

Jimbo brushed the dirt from the front of his leather vest. "I honestly think he intended to take me out." He looked at the Three Amigos. "You dudes were next on his list."

"You mean, *are* next on his list," Will said. "He's not dead, right?"

Dion shook his head. "He'll be fine. But he'll have to make his way without us. He's out of the organization."

"Wow," Will said. "Just like that, huh? No meeting or voting?"

Dion looked Will in the eyes. "You heard what Jim said. Ray was going to kill him, then you three. There's no place for that in the Punks. We have disagreements. But we're family. Family doesn't do what he wanted to do. It's my decision. He's out."

"I'll get security to dump him outside," Jimbo said as he stepped back into the Depot.

Dion turned to Jimbo. "He takes nothing with him. Put him out through the Wall—same gate we sent Krystal out."

"You got it. Any message for him?"

Dion's eyes narrowed. "Nothing worth wasting my breath on. He wouldn't listen anyway."

KRYSTAL PUSHED HER CHAIR BACK from the table in the Depot's dining room. "So the teams are set for today. Winter, you're with Silver. Fred's with Thomas and Ryker's with me."

"Mmm-hmm," Winter said, eyeing Silver. "Ryk's not even here. He's got no say about the *teams?*"

"He's deferred authority of these operations to me." Krystal checked the safety on her 9mm handgun and slipped the pistol into the holster strapped to her thigh. "I'll update him on the way into Tremayne." She strode to the doorway and unhooked her duster from the adjacent coatrack. "Everybody stay in contact with each other." She buttoned her duster to mid-breast and looked up. "Any questions?"

Fred and Thomas pushed their chairs back and stood from the table. "I have a question," Fred said. "Any reason for Thomas and I to change our appearances? Or Silver?"

"Well, you've been to Tremayne, so you might consider it." She looked at the other two Rogue Changers. "To my knowledge, you haven't been to Tremayne." She shrugged. "Change or not—your choice."

"Makes sense," Fred agreed. "So today we're in observe-and-report mode only, right? No intervention."

"Mostly correct," Krystal said. "The adult Bystanders are beholden to the Changers by their own choice. The kids, not so much."

The four walked from the table to meet Krystal at the door to the communications room. "If you see a kid that's obviously in trouble, intervene. But only to the extent necessary to defuse the situation. Intervention, yes. But minimal."

Winter checked her nine and slipped on a figure-hugging leather jacket. "I'm intervening for Punks."

Krystal looked at Winter. "Absolutely, Win. Good point. Punks are always high priority." She surveyed the two teams before her. "I feel good. We have the best of the best here. Let's head out. I'm gonna check on Ryker, then I'll touch base with you all when we hit the city limit."

Krystal stopped short when she entered the communications room. The Three Amigos stood side by side on the opposite end of the room, facing her. Jimbo was in his usual spot in front of the main communications console. Ryker and Dion stood, arms crossed, speaking to two Punk security personnel dressed in black military fatigues. The security guards supported a groggy-looking Raymond between them. Raymond's eyes appeared glassy. The left side of his face sported a huge red welt. His normally slicked-back hair was severely out of place.

"What's going on here, Jim?" Krystal said, taking in the scene.

Jimbo leaned back in his chair, hands behind his head. "Our pal Raymond just tried to take me out. Said the Amigos were next on his list."

"Because?" Krystal asked.

"Because he doesn't like that we let you back in. Said he was gonna take out everyone that allowed it."

Krystal snorted. "Is anyone surprised? He tried that with me when I first came back."

"Looking back, we shoulda known."

Krystal tipped her chin toward Raymond. "So what's happening?"

Jimbo smiled. "He's gettin' the Krystal Peterson send-off. Right through the Wall." Jimbo turned to Krystal. "Care to watch?"

"Wouldn't miss it for the world," she said, walking across the room toward Raymond.

She stopped in front of the Three Amigos and looked into their eyes, one at a time. She felt the recognition from the trio. A kindred spirit stirred inside her. Her eyes moistened as the three held their fists out to her. Without a word she bumped their fists. She lingered momentarily—involuntarily—then turned away.

The Three Amigos watched Krystal as she stepped next to Ryker.

"You're just in time for the send-off," Ryker said.

"So I hear."

The two security personnel gripped Raymond's biceps tightly, turned him around and walked him to the door. Dion and Ryker followed the trio out into the compound with Krystal behind them.

The air was still thick with fog. Lights inside the compound mixed with the increasing daybreak, turning the air white. Visibility was about fifty feet. The group headed around the building toward the thirty-foot-high Perimeter Wall. When the six Punks reached the walk-through gate, two additional security guards greeted them. One guard pushed the door open and stepped back.

Outside the Wall, with no lights, the fog was gray against the day. The first guard at the gate addressed Dion. "Sir?"

The two guards supporting Raymond turned their captive around to face the leader of the Punks.

Raymond's eyes narrowed. "Fuck you, Dion."

Dion stepped up to the new outcast and pressed his chest against Raymond's. "That you're not dead is the last good thing you get from me. You're not a Punk, by your own choice. You did this to yourself. Don't let me see or hear from you again. Physically, you live. But you're dead to me and you're dead to the Punks." He turned his back to Raymond.

Ryker nodded to the two security guards. "Cut his cuffs."

The guards turned him around, and the lead guard used a short five-inch blade to slice the zip ties. He pushed Raymond toward the darkness, but Raymond stopped at the threshold.

Ryker raised his boot to the small of Raymond's back and shoved. The ex-Punk stumbled into the murky fog and whipped around. He stared at Ryker and Krystal. "You're dead, Krystal."

A heavy cloud of gray mist drifted between Raymond and the opening, obscuring the former Punk. A security guard slammed the gate closed.

"You're all dead!" Raymond screamed from outside the Wall.

CHAPTER 24

Convergence

Butterflies swirled in Curtis's stomach as the Hyper-loop slowed in the tunnel under Tremayne's City Hall. The feeling was reminiscent of his first ride as a kid on an elevator. He smiled and absentmindedly ran his hand over his head. The old Mohawk was gone, a thing of the past. His wavy blond hair felt soft and nice against his palm. The butterflies persisted after the vehicle stopped. His mind raced. *Krystal. I'm back!*

"*We have arrived in Tremayne,*" a voice sounded from the Hyper-loop's overhead speaker system. "*Please prepare to disembark.*"

Dr. Rasmus found it hard to contain his enthusiasm. He rubbed his hands together. "I am looking forward to the demonstration, Leader."

"As am I," Levi said, rising from his seat next to the door of the underground vehicle. He stepped into the aisle and waved his hand in front of him. "After you, Ms. DeMone."

Angelica nodded to Levi and stepped off the Hyperloop into the terminal. She surveyed the high ceiling and stainless-steel walls. Vertical strips of blue lighting separated large panels lining the wide thoroughfare. A round glass elevator occupied one corner of the room, its door open.

Levi's wingtips clicked on the highly polished floor as he

strolled over to Angelica. "I like the quaintness of this terminal."

Angelica checked the time on her cell and glanced at the Hyperloop. "How long does it take them to get off that train?" She looked at Levi. "I do have other business in the Underground, Leader."

Levi stood, hands folded behind him, and watched the three remaining Changers step out of the train onto the platform. "I am trusting in our Dr. Rasmus, dear. I am confident this demonstration will be worth our time." He smiled and walked toward a large electronic billboard. "Speaking of which, have you seen our new promotional signs for the SOUL Chybrid project?"

Angelica stood still. "Does it matter? The Hyperloop is for Changers only. This terminal…" She looked around. "Everything here is for the benefit of Changers that use this facility. Which, by the way, is present company. Look around. We're the only ones here. Why are we wasting funds placing promotional billboards in a facility only we use?"

"It's his ego, Ms. DeMone," Xander said as he approached from the Hyperloop. He turned to Levi. "No offense, sir."

Levi ignored the doctor's comment and walked toward the elevator. "Right this way, Ms. DeMone. There are some people you must meet before we proceed."

When Curtis stepped off the Hyperloop, he hurried to catch up with Levi and company at the elevator.

Johnny grabbed Curtis's shoulder from behind. "Hold up, little guy. Our leader specifically ordered me to instruct you in some of the finer points of our organization."

Curtis stopped and turned to face Johnny. "And there's a *finer point* to walking toward an elevator? I think I can handle this."

Johnny reached for a lapel on Curtis's sport coat. "Listen up, buddy—"

Curtis swiped his hand upward, smacking Johnny's arm to the side. "Listen up *what*?" He glanced behind him. Levi, Angelica and Xander were boarding the glass elevator. "You heard Levi. I'm part of his inner circle." He looked Johnny up and down. "Just like you."

Johnny held his hands up in a no-foul gesture. "Whoa, settle down, buddy—"

"And stop calling me buddy. I'm not your *buddy*."

Johnny shoved his hands into his pants pockets and tried his best to appear relaxed. "Yeah, okay, Dyer. One of these days, you're gonna need me to show you a few things or help you out." He tipped his chin up. "I'm here when that day comes."

"Yeah, I'll remember that." Curtis turned and hurried toward the trio on the elevator.

SILVER STOOD NEXT TO WINTER at the driver's side of Winter's Lenco BearCat. "We're riding in this?" Silver said.

Winter double-checked the lock on a lower storage compartment. "It's standard issue, my friend." She looked down at Silver. "You're riding shotgun."

Silver frowned. "What's that supposed to mean? I've never used a gun in my life. I wouldn't know the first thing—"

"I said you're *riding* shotgun. Not shooting one."

Silver crossed her arms. "I'm not doing *anything* with a gun, shot or otherwise. This mission is *observe* and *report*, remember?"

Winter took a deep breath. "It's a figure of speech, a reference to the old days. I'm driving, see." She opened the driver's door and pointed across the cab's interior. "See that little chair over there on the other side? You sit there. There's no gun. Riding there is just referred to as 'riding shotgun.'"

"Yeah," Silver said. "I got it." She stomped quickly around the front of the truck to the passenger side, muttering under her breath. "Now I have to try to learn some ancient bohemian language." A quick slip in the mud caused her to smack her hand on the vehicle's grill. It was wet and cold. She wiped the moisture on her slacks before opening the passenger door. "I'll get you for this, Felix."

FRED STEPPED ON THE RAIL under the driver's door of his assigned BearCat and hoisted himself into the driver's seat. "I finally feel like we might be productive since leaving the Underground."

Thomas was waiting in the shotgun seat. "I agree. I've been pretty antsy." He looked out the windshield at the back of Krystal's vehicle. "I'm damn curious what the Changers are doing now."

Fred fastened his five-point harness, surveyed the dash and flipped the intermittent wipers on. "Controls on this vehicle are intuitive." He glanced at Thomas. "I agree about the Changers. But it's not hard to figure out their direction, only the specifics."

"What do you mean? We're hearing about this thing with children. Changers haven't historically involved anyone younger than eighteen."

Fred glanced in the rearview mirror on the driver's door. Winter's vehicle sat idling behind him. Vapor exiting his own exhaust became indistinguishable from the fog. "I know the children play a role for whatever phase this is for the Changers. But I'm setting that aside to view the big picture first."

Okay," Thomas said, looking across the cab at Fred. "The Changers are technology, first and foremost. Now what?"

"Remember in the old days, tech companies would come out with the newest, fastest computer chips and system parts?" Fred hung his left wrist over the steering wheel. "But even though you'd buy something that was the fastest on the market, you knew they were already working on the next fastest one?"

Thomas shrugged. "Yeah. So?"

"So it's simple. It's all just plain and simple when you break it down. We—you and I—were intimately involved in not only the Change technology, but also the Chybrid project. But even while that was going on, the Changers were working on the next big thing."

"I don't see how that could be," Thomas said. "I mean, we were the Changers' top scientists. We reported to Felix, who developed and orchestrated everything we did." He glanced out the side window. "You mean to tell me Felix was working on something even newer and better as we were developing the Chybrids?"

"Well, there's a variable I hadn't thought of up until we left the Changers."

Thomas turned to Fred. "And that is?"

Fred stared through the windshield. "Levi Aldrich."

Thomas sat for a moment gazing at the side of Fred's face. He raised his brow. "Of course. Levi trusts no one."

"Right. Remember before Felix…what's his name?"

"It doesn't matter. Your point is he gets someone else. He can't have any single person knowing everything."

Fred looked at Thomas. "Except himself. He trades out his latest, greatest scientist for a new one to develop the next big thing."

Thomas shook his head. "I guess that would come in handy if he wanted to use the new technology against his former top scientist."

"Exactly," Fred said. "And against any team that reported to the top guy."

Thomas gazed out the windshield as Ryker opened the passenger door of Krystal's vehicle and hopped inside. "As I think about it, that must necessarily include his entire inner circle. Even *we* were expendable."

Fred chuckled and shook his head. "That's funny in a way. Silver doesn't know it, but she never stood a chance either."

"Only one from that team that's still there is John Logan," Thomas said.

KRYSTAL LOOKED ACROSS THE CAB of her armored vehicle at Ryker. "Ready, partner?"

Ryker smiled. "Let's do it."

Krystal pulled the gearshift into drive and drove forward through the Punks' compound toward the exit. She flipped the mouthpiece on her headset down to check the two-way radio. "Jimbo, it's Krys. Radio check. Do you copy?"

"Loud and clear, Krys."

"10-4, Jim. Who's at the entry checkpoint?"

"You got Ace on duty."

"Sounds good. Ace, Krystal. Do you copy?"

"Ace. Go ahead, girl."

"Hey, Ace. I'm leading a caravan of three Cats, heading your direction. The fog is still super thick here. Can you keep it clear till we get out?"

"*Sounds good, Krys. Traffic's nothing right now. I'll keep it that way.*"

Ryker reached onto the dash and grabbed his sunglasses. "Sun coming up is doing a number on this fog. Looks like a wall of white right now."

"It'll only get worse when the sun hits us full blast," Krystal said. "My eyes are better than yours at adjusting to this." She glanced across at him. "Just means we'll have to get closer to the action."

Ryker stared at the mist through the windshield. "If there is any."

"Oh there'll be action, partner." Krystal pressed the accelerator pedal. "I can just about guarantee you that."

CHAPTER 25

Ray's Way

FELIX RECLINED IN HIS FAVORITE chair in front of monitor wall number three in his quarters. *Hot,* he thought, kicking off his slippers. His eyes flitted about the video display as he reached—without looking—into a metal container on his left. He slowly placed a large cheese puff into his mouth. There was no crunch as he held the snack between his tongue and the roof of his mouth. When the cheese puff was nearly dissolved, he grabbed a glass off the adjacent table and washed the tasty morsel down with ice-cold diet soda.

Hmm. Where to go today? Let's check on my new friends, the Punks. With his right hand, Felix manipulated a stationary mouse and zoomed to a location outside the Perimeter Wall at Punk headquarters. *Goodness, the fog.* He tapped a virtual keyboard on the tray in front of him. Advanced laser imaging technology cut through the murk and brought the huge structure into view. He zoomed again. *Yes. Activity!*

RAYMOND TRUDGED THROUGH THE MUD outside the Wall, heading for Tremayne. He chose the shortest route, knowing it was only five miles before the wide curve would land him at the nearest remote outpost.

He stopped for a moment to rub his hands together. He glanced up at the towering structure and exhaled warm breath into cupped hands. "Fuck!" His jeans were damp and cold on his thighs. He sniffed hard. Swiping his forearm across his runny nose only served to transfer the moisture from the sleeve of his leather jacket to his face. He winced when his arm brushed against the welt on the side of his face.

He began to jog, holding his ribcage and slipping on the uneven terrain with every other step.

FELIX POPPED AND SUCKED ANOTHER cheese puff. He followed Raymond's movements on the monitor. *What are you doing out there, young man?*

He paused and looked up when a ceiling speaker sounded. "*Attention, Security Detail Nine. Subject GPS located on Level Six. Stand by for coordinates.*"

Expressionless, Felix turned his attention back to the monitor. He took another swig of his soda and manipulated the tracking pad. He framed Raymond into a grid on the monitor and tapped a button on the virtual keypad. *We'll just auto-follow you, young man.*

The ceiling speaker sounded again. "*Security Team Nine. Coordinates on Level Six are 33°48'01.4"N 114°31'54.9"W.*"

Felix ignored the voice.

FUCKIN' PUNKS. FUCKIN' DION. FUCKIN' Ryker. Fuckin' Jimbo. Fuckin' Krystal. Raymond found a cadence as he continued his jog, keeping the Perimeter Wall in sight to his right. His upper chest burned as each breath he exhaled added to the tule fog. The thick air was deafening. He stuck a finger in each ear, wiggled them around and swallowed, as if popping his ears would help.

He recited his cadence aloud. "Fuckin' Punks. Fuckin' Dion. Fuckin' Ryker. Fuckin' Jimbo. Fuckin' Krystal."

FELIX SAT FORWARD. *WHAT ARE you saying?* He adjusted the view to see Raymond's face. Felix's lips moved in sync with Raymond's.

Over and over. The same thing, over and over. Felix frowned. *Why, you little… Perhaps Krystal should know about this man.* He tapped the keyboard again and popped another cheese puff.

Krystal's voice came over the ceiling speaker. "*Hi, Felix. What's up?*"

"Mmm…" Felix crunched his cheese puff quickly three times, grabbed his soda and took a quick drink. "Mmm…hmm." He swallowed. "Krystal, my dear. Are you in a position where you can talk?"

"*I'm with Ryker. It's just us. We're in a truck headed to Tremayne.*"

"I trust your judgment. I have been monitoring the Perimeter."

"*I'm going to put you on speaker.*"

"That's fine. As I said, I have been monitoring the Perimeter. Outside your headquarters. There is something you must know about."

"*What is it, Felix?*"

"Well, there is a young man running along the Wall. By his appearance, I thought he was a Punk. But after watching him for just a few minutes, I'm now sure he's not on your side."

"*Is he kind of muscular, faded blue jeans, a black leather jacket with a shit ton of zippers, and scraggly black hair?*"

"That could describe any one of you." Felix smiled at his own joke.

"*Funny, Felix. Is the left side of his face really swollen?*"

"That would be him. I take it he's *not* one of you?"

"*He was, but he's not now. His name's Raymond. He tried to kill one of our top commanders and threatened to kill other Punks. So what's he up to?*"

"I believe he's headed to Tremayne. But presently, he's quickly approaching one of your outposts. This outpost is occupied with two guards."

"*Thanks for that, Felix. We believe he's not armed. If you have time, keep an eye on him at least till he passes the outpost. Let me know when that happens.*"

"Of course I will. Goodbye." Felix disconnected the call and popped another cheese puff.

RAYMOND'S BREATHING BECAME LABORED. HIS jog slowed to a fast walk. Then he stopped. He bent over, using one hand to hold his ribcage where Ryker's boot had connected, and supported himself with the other hand on his knee. He exhaled huge puffs of fog and coughed. Standing upright, he hacked a throat-full of phlegm into his mouth and spit. His knees weakened, and he sat down hard onto the cold muddy surface beneath him. He looked at the slime he'd just coughed up as it trailed slowly down the rock in front of him.

Raising his head, Raymond gazed at the white cloud that was now his world. He squinted into the haze and reached inside his leather jacket. *Yes!* he thought, pulling out his sunglasses. He slipped the pilot-style shades onto his face and hooked the flexible temples behind his ears. He squinted again. A light in the fog. *Outpost!*

TWO PUNKS STOOD OUTSIDE THE remote outpost and warmed their hands over a burn barrel. The bigger Punk swiped a wad of tobacco from his mouth and tossed it into the fire. He stared, mesmerized at the sparks as they floated skyward.

He looked up at his partner. "You see that? That was awesome."

His female counterpart rolled her eyes. "You need to get out more, Slade. That wasn't close to awesome."

Slade backed away from the barrel and shoved his hands into the pockets of his leather vest. "Let's see what you got." He tipped his chin up.

"Tobacco's disgusting. Whether you're *chewing* it—which isn't really chewing it, it's just letting it sit in your mouth and sucking on the juice—or whether you're smoking it."

Slade acted as if he hadn't heard a thing she said. "So, what have you got?"

She ignored him and rubbed her hands together. "You're an idiot."

RAYMOND ROSE TO HIS FEET, keeping his eyes zeroed in on the faint light in the distance. The light was fuzzy, yellow, distorted by the cloud in front of him.

He glanced to the right. Heavy mist hung in the air between him and the Wall. Following the Wall would take him into town, into Tremayne. He knew the light meant the outpost was occupied.

He chose the faint yellow light, veered away from the Wall and resumed his trek. Ten slippery yards forward and the Wall disappeared from view as if swallowed by the fog.

SLADE STOMPED THROUGH THE DOORLESS entrance to the checkpoint guard shack. The thick, moist air muted the sound of his boots on the wood-plank floor. He reached above his head and tugged lightly on a dirty string connected to a chain attached to the single-bulb socket on the low ceiling. *Pop!* The flash indicated the fluorescent bulb had reached the end of its life. *Motherfucker.* He pulled his flashlight out of the utility holster at his waist and clicked it on. He shined the beam onto the chest-high shelves along the back wall. *Jerky, saltines, canned peaches in heavy syrup, three boxes of pretzels, sardines, about ten cans of Vienna sausages, ramen noodles…ramen!*

"Hey, Lace," he said over his shoulder. "Want some ramen?"

No answer.

Slade shuffled to the back wall and selected a packet of the dry noodles—spicy beef. "Hey, girl. You want spicy or not?"

Still no answer.

Slade shivered. He thought about his jacket lying on the front seat of the Humvee parked outside the shack. *This vest ain't cuttin' it, man.* He grabbed a chicken-flavored, non-spicy packet of ramen from the shelf for Lace and laid it along with his spicy beef pack on a small side table before turning to the doorway.

A small cloud of fog swirled between Slade and the burn barrel outside. He clicked his flashlight off and tucked it into his waistband.

Lace stood wide-eyed on the other side of the burn barrel. She wasn't moving.

Slade squinted through the mist. Something was off. He tipped his chin up and mouthed, *What?*

Lace's eyes flitted back and forth from Slade's face, then to his right, then back.

He glanced down at Lace's thigh. *Pistol*, he thought. No pistol in the holster. He reached around to the back of his waistband. *Dammit!* He'd meant to go on a diet. His pants were tight—too tight at the waist. *Dammit! Fuck the Ramen!* His fat, calloused fingers slipped off the grip of his 9mm pistol. He pushed his stomach at the waistband with his free hand, attempting to send slack to the back of his jeans. *Damn!*

Lace bent at the waist and nodded hard, urging Slade, rooting for him with each tug at the handgun.

Slade managed to shove two fingers between the barrel of the pistol and his ass crack. He yanked firmly up, flipping the handgun out of his waistband. The gun clacked hard against the concrete porch in front of the shack. He turned away from Lace and glanced at the ground behind him.

"Not today, motherfucker." It was Raymond.

The seven-inch blade entered Slade's neck vertically, severing his jugular and slicing through the trapezius. His head tilted toward the knife as the bolster sunk into the fatty skin atop his shoulder. He recognized Raymond's voice, but he never saw his face. His right arm went limp as his left arm flailed against the wood-framed doorway behind him. The sensation of falling backward crossed his mind as his heel stopped against the threshold and the fog turned to a misty black. Slade looked up at the guard shack ceiling. His left arm swiped the two ramen packets off the table as his body crashed onto the wooden floor. The knife was still in his shoulder, the handle resting against his cheek.

Raymond didn't look at what he had done. He stared at Lace through the embers floating above the burn barrel as he picked up Slade's nine. Then he smiled. "Now," he said. "You and me are gonna have some fun."

Lace had seen more than she'd planned on seeing when she left the Perimeter four hours ago. She glanced at Slade. She expected blood. All she saw was his face, his eyes open to the shack's ceiling. Her mind flashed to his smile. His tobacco-encrusted smile.

So what have you got? Her mind raced. She couldn't shake his voice. *So what have you got?*

Raymond tucked Slade's handgun into his waistband behind his back. It slipped in easily. "Where are the keys to the Humvee?"

Lace looked at Raymond. His eyes were black. Wild. Evil. *So what have you got?* She turned and ran into the white mist behind her.

CHAPTER 26

I Spy

Tʀᴇᴍᴀʏɴᴇ's ᴄɪᴛʏ ᴍᴀɴᴀɢᴇʀ ʟᴏᴏᴋᴇᴅ ᴜᴘ from his desk when the red light above the corner armoire flashed. He rose from his executive office chair behind the mahogany desk and walked swiftly across the room. The city manager swiped his hand over a pad on the wall, and the armoire door opened to the side, revealing the round glass elevator from the Hyperloop terminal below the city.

The curved door to the elevator slipped silently around to the back, and Levi stepped off first.

"Greetings," Levi said. He extended his hand to the manager.

The portly man bowed and grasped Levi's hand with both of his. "Welcome, welcome, Mr. Aldrich."

Angelica followed Levi and stepped forward, standing at his right side.

Dr. Rasmus walked off the elevator and strolled over to a picture on the wall adjacent to the armoire. "Hmm," he said, eyeing the large painting.

Curtis forced his way past Johnny through the elevator door and positioned himself on Levi's left.

The city manager smiled at Angelica. "I don't believe we've met." He glanced at Levi. "I've become so accustomed to seeing

Ms. Long at your side." He paused. "Uh, Silver. That is correct, no, Mr. Aldrich?"

Levi forced a laugh. "Forgive me, sir. Ms. Long is no longer with our organization. She is…" He looked down at Angelica, clasping his hands in front of him. "…ahem…Ms. Long is pursuing other interests." He smiled at the manager.

The manager turned back to Angelica and reached down to grab her hand. "And you are?"

Angelica held her hand out as if she expected the man to kiss her ring. "I am Angelica DeMone."

"Mr. Manager," the man said.

"Mr. *Manager*?" Angelica snorted. "Okay."

"Angelica is our head of security," Levi said. He motioned toward Xander, who was still gazing at the large painting on the wall. "That man is the preeminent Dr. Xander Rasmus." His huge forced smile appeared unnatural. "Dr. Rasmus, please come here."

Xander swiveled at the waist, then turned back to the picture. "Pardon me, is this a historical depiction of Tremayne?"

The city manager waddled across the room and stood beside Xander. "Yes, this is an artist's rendition of our beautiful city approximately 100 years ago."

Xander crossed his arms and leaned back before proceeding to stroke his chin with one hand. "I like it." He smiled and nodded his approval.

Angelica rolled her eyes, then turned to face Levi and looked up at him. "Leader." She motioned across the room to the pair at the painting. "Seriously?"

"Ah yes," Levi said, turning to his side. "Mr. Manager. Dr. Rasmus. Please join us again."

KRYSTAL SPED PAST THE CITY limit sign and lifted her foot from the BearCat's accelerator.

"I'm glad you finally backed off," Ryker said. "Visibility is like fifty, maybe seventy-five yards."

"I've got about 200 yards on you." She glanced across the cab and smiled. "Enhanced eyesight courtesy of Dr. Felix Yaz."

"Yeah, yeah. I get it." He gazed out the windshield at the endless cloud of fog in front of the truck. "Not to be presumptuous, but you and Felix must have quite a relationship for him to do what he's done for you."

Her smile faded. "You know, Ryk." She shook her head slowly. "He saw something in me. He saw good in me."

"I see it, too," he said.

"Yeah, I believe you. But you didn't see it at first. Not when it mattered."

Ryker turned in his seat to face Krystal. "We've been through this. I was late to the party. But, yeah. You're special, Krys."

Krystal braked and turned right on Habiliment Avenue. Her eyes narrowed. "You guys ever get a bead on Curtis?"

"Sorry to say, we haven't. That guy's an asset. We still have a team on it." He looked at Krystal. "We haven't given up."

"Looks like business as usual for the Bystanders. I say we park near the city center where Nico and the Amigos encountered the activity."

"Sounds good to me." Ryker rolled his window down and poked his head out the passenger window. "Woo, it's cold! Take the public parking up here on the right—across from City Hall."

"Got it." Krystal slowed for the driveway approach and stopped the armored vehicle to allow pedestrians to pass. "There's a lot more people here than I thought there would be."

"I noticed. That means there's a good chance for plenty of witnesses if anything happens."

Krystal selected a parking spot at the end of a row facing the street. "Good chance for plenty of victims, too," she said as she shoved the gearshift into park.

LEVI PUT HIS ARM ON Curtis's shoulder as the five Changers exited the front doors at City Hall. "I expect good things from you, my boy."

"I won't disappoint you, sir."

The two stopped walking. Levi turned to face Curtis and placed both hands on the young Changer's shoulders. A smile split his mouth—his eyes were cold and hard. "Oh, I know you won't." He dropped his arms to his sides as his smile faded. "I know you won't."

Mr. Manager held the door open behind the group. "Stay warm, my friends. You have the key to the city. Please let me know if there is anything you need."

The Changers walked abreast down the wide steps in front of the expansive three-story building to the sidewalk below. Traffic on the street stirred the fog downtown, dispersing the moisture enough to improve visibility.

Angelica's patience had worn past thin. "Where's the demo, Xander?" She snugged the large collar on her wool coat up around her neck.

"Are you cold, Ms. DeMone?" Johnny asked.

Angelica frowned. "Did you just wink at me, Logan?"

Curtis did his best to keep the party on task. He stepped between Johnny and Angelica. "I agree, Ms. DeMone. I'm anxious to see the doctor's demonstration."

"Let's get on with it, Xander," she said. "Before this Goofus and Gallant show gets any more intense."

"Right this way, people," Xander said as he hailed a taxi.

KRYSTAL FLIPPED THE MIC DOWN on her two-way headset. "Fred, it's Krystal. Do you copy?"

Silence.

"Copy, Fred? You out there?"

"*Krys, it's Fred. Go ahead.*"

"Yeah, Fred. You should turn right off the highway onto Habiliment. We're parked a couple blocks down on the right in a lot across from City Hall."

"*Got it, Krys. Over and out?*"

Krystal smiled. "Winter, did you copy that?"

"*10-4, Krystal. We're right behind him.*"

Ryker gazed out the windshield and squinted. "What. The. Hell."

The pair watched a well-dressed man and a good-looking professional woman as they stepped into an electric minivan—the standard vehicle for taxis in Tremayne. Johnny and a young blond guy stood on the sidewalk at the bottom of the concrete staircase in front of City Hall.

Krystal looked up. She felt the skin crawl on her arms. *Logan.* Her mind raced.

Ryker swung the BearCat's passenger door open.

"Wait," Krystal said, grabbing his forearm.

Ryker left one foot resting on the truck's step with the door open. He looked back at Krystal. "That's fucking Logan."

"I know." Her hand maintained its grip on his arm.

"He's the last known connection to Curtis. We need to detain him."

"I'd have agreed in the past. But look at him. He's dressed up, suit and tie. Totally out of character."

Ryker looked back across the street. "Yeah, so?"

"First, we're waiting for the others. We need Winter. Second, we don't know who's with him. I can't see through those tinted windows."

Ryker pulled his leg back into the cab and closed the door. "Who's that blond guy?"

Krystal's eyes narrowed. "I don't know," she said slowly. "I mean, he looks vaguely familiar. But not someone I can put my finger on."

"What about that fancy guy and the woman?" Ryker said.

"No idea."

WINTER FOLLOWED FRED'S VEHICLE INTO the public parking lot and backed into a spot directly behind Krystal's BearCat. She switched off the ignition and turned to Silver. "Look. I've resigned myself to the fact that Krystal's in charge of this operation. You gotta buy in and accept the fact I know more than you about the Punks and the Punks' way. Just follow my lead. We're supposed to be teammates."

Silver leaned against the passenger door and folded her arms. "Okay, I'll accept that. But let's have an understanding. You admit I know more about the Changers and their ways than you do."

"Well—"

"And, you defer to me when it comes to facts about the Changers."

"I'll trust your judgment on that," Winter agreed. "But I gotta tell you, Krystal's word is law on this operation, and my gut trumps everything."

Silver stared at Winter. "Deal," she said, extending her hand, fingers pointed at her partner.

Winter held out her fist. The two looked down at each other's hands, then into each other's eyes. They proceeded to remove their five-point harnesses without completing any semblance of a handshake and exited the vehicle.

FRED AND THOMAS WERE WAITING at the front of Winter's truck. The four walked across the lot to Krystal's vehicle. While the three Rogue Changers waited at the back of the truck, Winter walked around and tapped on the driver's window.

Krystal opened the door and stepped out.

"So what's our move?" Winter asked.

Krystal walked around to the back of the BearCat and opened the rear door. "Take a look at the taxi across the street," she said, snatching her duster from a hook inside the truck.

Winter peered around the front of the vehicle. She caught a glimpse of Johnny immediately before he ducked into the mini-van. Her hand instinctively went to her waist. Her eyes glued to the taxi, she unsnapped the strap over the grip of her 9mm. "Well, well."

Krystal slammed the door and walked back to Winter.

SILVER STOOD WITH FRED AND Thomas near the sidewalk in front of Krystal's truck. "Looks like we hit the mother lode," she said, nodding to the activity in front of City Hall.

Ryker stepped up behind the trio. "So you guys saw Logan, too, huh?"

Fred stood between Thomas and Silver with his arms crossed. "Oh, there's more to see than John Logan." He nodded toward the taxi. "Levi Aldrich is in that cab."

Ryker's eyes widened. "No shit? Krys didn't see that."

"He rolled his window down a few seconds ago," Thomas said. "Then zipped it back up in a hurry when he saw the three of us."

"Nice," Ryker said. "So what's it mean that the Changers' leader is in Tremayne?"

Silver appeared amused. "Something big, my friend."

"Guess we should follow that cab?" Ryker asked.

KRYSTAL STOOD NEXT TO WINTER and watched the taxi pull away from the curb as she buttoned her duster. "We're gonna have to commandeer a vehicle. We can't keep an eye on that van in the Cats. They'll spot us eventually."

"Agreed," Winter said. She looked across the high hood on the BearCat. "Hey, Ryk. Gimme a hand."

Ryker nodded and stepped past the three Rogues. He met Winter on the sidewalk. Traffic across the four-lane road flowed smoothly but almost nonstop.

"They're leaving, Ryk."

"Saw that," he said, his eyes darting anxiously at the steady swarm of vehicles. "I see a limo coming up here."

"Too conspicuous," Krystal said. "There's a full-size van, white, a couple cars behind that."

The trio stepped into the street, stopping traffic in the slow lane. Krystal held her hand in the air as Ryker and Winter trotted on the dashed lines between the two lanes toward the approaching van. Vehicles in the fast lane began to slow. Winter stepped in front of the white van, her right hand in the air. Ryker rushed up to the driver's door and yanked on the handle.

The surprised driver pulled his hands from the steering wheel and backed away from Ryker. "Hey, man! What gives?"

"Punk Security," Ryker said. "We're commandeering your vehicle."

"Hell you are." The driver reached past Ryker and attempted to close the door. "We don't want you Punks around here anymore. Why don't you just leave!"

Krystal turned to the three Rogues waiting by her truck and waved. "Let's go," she shouted.

"Sir," Ryker pleaded. "You will be reimbursed. We have authority to take your vehicle for official use—"

"I got deliveries to make," the man insisted.

"Look," Ryker said. "Walk on over there to City Hall and tell them your vehicle was commandeered by Punk Security personnel. There's a short electronic form to fill out. By the end of the day, reimbursement for your trouble will hit your bank account. Trust me—"

"Bullshit," the man said. "Help! Help! Hel—"

Winter reached past Ryker and grabbed the front of the man's heavy sweater. "Undo the seat belt, Ryk."

Ryker clicked the button.

Winter pulled the man out of the van by his sweater. She shoved him toward the back of the van. "Go to City Hall." She turned around as Ryker hoisted himself into the driver's seat. She slid open the side door and directed Silver, Fred and Thomas onto the bench seat in the way back.

Krystal jumped into the passenger seat up front as Winter hopped in the back and slammed the side door shut.

Ryker steered the vehicle into the center turn lane and pressed the accelerator.

CHAPTER 27

Looking for Lace

Lace knew she couldn't stay on the asphalt surface much longer. Raymond would figure out the keys were in the Humvee, and he'd eventually overtake her.

She rubbed both arms briskly and thought of her parka lying in the back of the Humvee. Her feet were heavy and numb from the cold. Her run had slowed to a trot—her boots scuffing the grit on the old paved road. The sun had refused to break through the fog.

She slowed to a fast walk and glanced over her shoulder before hurrying to the mud shoulder. *I gotta take a break*, she thought as she pulled her cell from a back pocket of her jeans.

Raymond placed one boot between Slade's legs and the other next to the dead Punk's hip. He leaned down and pressed his hands against the front of Slade's jeans. *No keys, but he's got something*. He tried to slip his fingers into the two front pockets at the same time but only achieved one knuckle-depth with each hand. *Damn, Slade. You need to go on a diet, buddy*. He smiled to himself, knowing that was impossible now.

He stood upright and looked around the room. No cutting tool around. He looked back down at the knife he'd used against his former comrade. Slade's lifeless eyes were still open.

"Whadda you looking at?" Raymond laughed out loud. "Gimme that knife," he said, reaching down.

The stubble on Slade's cheek rubbed against Raymond's fingers as he slid the knife up and out. He wiped the blade on each side against Slade's hairy upper arm. "Now," he said, grabbing the edge of the dead man's pocket again. He sliced through the denim to open the pocket and expose the contents. "Brass knuckles," he muttered. "Whadda you got over here?" he asked, moving to Slade's left pocket. He repeated the procedure to reveal a sleek six-inch butterfly knife. "What? No keys?"

He stood upright, tucked his bounty into his jacket pockets and stretched his back momentarily before exiting the guard shack.

FELIX FINISHED DRESSING AND WALKED back into the main living area of his quarters in the Underground. He tapped a light switch on the wall to extinguish the ceiling lights. He looked up through the glass to view the cloudless blue sky above. A holographic display indicated the outside temperature was currently fifty-five degrees.

He glanced across the room. The video display on monitor wall number three showed Raymond sitting sideways in the Humvee at the remote outpost.

Felix speed-dialed Krystal on his phone pad.

"*Hey, Felix. What's up?*"

"Krystal. That young man, Raymond. He has killed one of your people at the outpost."

"*Holy shit, Felix. I'm guessing there was no way for you to intervene. We had two stationed there. Who's dead? And where is the other person?*"

"The man is dead. The young woman has escaped. But Raymond is attempting to use the vehicle on site."

"*That whole scene sucks, Felix. I'm up to my ass in a situation of my own. Call Dion, please. Tell him what happened. He'll get someone out there to handle that mess.*"

"Yes, I'll do that. So sorry I could not prevent the tragedy. I'll contact Dion. Goodbye."

THE KEYS TO THE HUMVEE dropped into Raymond's lap when he pulled down the driver's side sun visor.

"Ooh la la!" he said. "It's party time."

LACE WALKED FURTHER AWAY FROM the road, hoping to avoid detection by Raymond. She turned and looked back. The asphalt surface was out of eyesight now, but that didn't matter—she knew where it was. She squatted down, facing the direction she thought the road was, and dialed Jimbo. She glanced at the time on her cell. *An hour ago Slade was still alive*, she thought.

"*Hey, Lace.*"

Jimbo's voice was strong, comforting. Tears welled in her eyes, and she lost her cool. "Jimbo, Slade's…Slade's…dead." The words stuck in her throat and she cried.

"*What?*" Jimbo shouted. "*What happened?*"

"Oh, Jim. It was Ray. Ray killed Slade."

"*That sonofabitch! Where's Ray now? Where are you?*"

She could tell he was pacing, flexing. It was his way. She knew if he were here, Jimbo would tear Raymond up. She shivered. "I'm by the outpost road that goes into Tremayne. I don't know how far. I started running about an hour ago. I guess I've been here about five minutes or so."

"*Lace, where's Raymond?*"

"I ran, Jim. I left him at the outpost. But the Humvee's there." She swallowed. "The keys are in it."

"*Look, girl, you've been here before. You were promoted because you're strong. Pull yourself out of this funk or whatever you're in right now.*"

Lace's ire outweighed her fear. "Don't be an asshole, Jim. I was promoted two levels because you guys demoted Curtis. I've never been hunted down by some maniac. You can't say I've been here before."

"That's it. Get mad at me. But suck it up if you wanna live."

"Fuck you, Jim."

"Atta girl. I'm sending some trucks out there. I got you on GPS right now. Whatever you do, stay away from the road. Try to stay hidden in the fog."

Lace held the cell away from her head and strained her ears toward the direction of the outpost. Her heart sank, and a familiar weakness flooded her legs as she leaned forward onto her knees. She put the cell back to her ear. "Jim, I can hear the Humvee coming."

RAYMOND CRUISED THE HUMVEE ALONG the rough asphalt road faster than he should have in the fog. *Got you in my sights, Lace.* He'd rolled down the driver's window—the cold air felt good on his swollen left cheek. "Maybe I'll join the Changers," he thought aloud. "Hell, Krystal did that and no one ever suspected her." He shook his head. "She was the stupid one. She got herself caught. Dumbshit."

The Humvee dipped sharply when the front tires hit a nasty rut in the road. The vehicle swerved hard to the right, and the rear end quickly caught up to the front. Raymond spun the steering wheel against the slide. He hit the brakes—too hard. The Humvee spun around, completing the 180-degree trick. The truck's engine died with Raymond facing the road in the opposite direction.

"Woo-hoo! I just did a one-eighty!"

LACE POSITIONED HERSELF FAR ENOUGH away from the road to Tremayne that she couldn't see the asphalt. She moved as quickly as she could through the mucky terrain. Her direction was purely by instinct.

She heard Raymond's antics with the Humvee on the road but felt confident she was undetectable through the mist. Nauseating butterflies roiled her gut when the sound of Raymond's vehicle stopped.

He's close, she thought. She knew she was the prey in a sickening game of cat and mouse.

SIX VEHICLES—FOUR HUMVEES AND TWO BearCats—sped southeastward toward Lace's location. The dirt road was damp but not muddy. Twelve battle-hardened occupants had prepared for a fight. The windows were open to the brisk air. The Punks held their bare arms out or rested elbows on the sills, their skin warmed by adrenaline.

The driver of the lead BearCat accelerated around a wide curve. He knew the dirt back roads connecting the Punk outposts like a brother. The fog parted in front of the armored vehicle, thrust forward and away by the rush of steel.

"Cat One. You copy, Cat Two?"

The driver of the BearCat at the back of the caravan smiled. "*Cat Two. Go ahead, you sissy motherfucker.*"

"Yeah, okay," the lead driver said. "I'm a sissy, but you're at the ass end of this steel snake."

"*Got that right. Dion put the sissies up front. You need us back here to pick your asses up after the battle.*"

The driver in the first Humvee behind Cat One flipped his mic down. "*Vee One. Copy, Cat Two?*"

"*Go ahead, sissy.*"

"*Y'all need us in the Vees to keep you on track so y'all don't kill each other.*"

"*Go back to sleep, you country bumpshit. You'll need all eight of you to take down the four of us in these Cats.*"

"Cat One. Copy, Cat Two?"

"*Yep, go.*"

"Speaking of taking somebody down—I love that Dion sent twelve of us to stomp out that pissant, Raymond."

"*It's Dion's style, man. Ain't it just like him to cure a case of lice by decapitation?*"

"I swear if he's laid one finger on Lace…"

LACE STOPPED WALKING. SHE STRAINED to hear the sound of Raymond's Humvee. A slight breeze stirred the mist in front of her. *He can't be up there. That Humvee was behind.* She spun around and glanced toward the direction of the road. The fog had lifted ever so slightly, exposing the asphalt edge. The hair on the back of her neck rose. Jimbo's words haunted her. *Whatever you do, stay away from the road.*

"Ooh, noo," she whispered. She listened again.

The voice was small, distant. "Oh, Lacey! Where are you?"

Lace ran away from the road. She kept her eyes trained in front of her as they filled with tears. The fog was lifting. "No, no, no," she whispered.

"Marco," Raymond called. "I see your feet!" He laughed.

"No, no, no, no." Lace found a cadence. *So what have you got?* Slade's voice gave her confidence, spurred her on.

"Aw, come on, Lacey," Raymond said. His breaths were long, deep and labored. "I'm coming, Lace." He slid to a stop. "I'm coming, Lace!" he shouted.

"Cat One. Copy, Vee One?"

"*I gotcha, Cat One.*"

"Comin' up on the left, about a quarter mile, we got asphalt. Transition's smooth, but watch your wheel. It's damn easy to flip that buggy."

"*Not a problem, Cat One. Worry 'bout yerself. I'm right on yer tail.*"

The Cat One driver hit the asphalt at an approximate 150-degree angle. The front tires on the armored vehicle left the earth, spun freely, then landed hard on the paved surface as the back tires followed the airborne arc. The driver accelerated when the rear end hit the road and quickly gained control of the ensuing fishtail. He glanced at his partner in the passenger seat. "Get the GPS on Lace. She can't be far from here."

CHAPTER 28

225

LEVI GAZED OUT THE TAXICAB window at a ground-level marquis as the van entered a new Bystander subdivision just inside the Tremayne city limit. "Cute little cracker boxes, Doctor. Are we touring the entire town? What inspires you to bring us here?"

"This is where you will witness the most base demonstration of the new SOUL Chybrid child," Xander said.

Angelica turned around and grabbed the seat back to look at Xander. "Did you say 'the most base'?"

Xander smiled. "I believe I said 'the most basic,' Ms. DeMone."

Johnny turned from the front passenger seat to join the discussion. "You said, 'base.'"

"It seems I'm outnumbered." He nodded to Angelica. "I misspoke. I meant *basic*." He held a hand up to the driver. "The address is right up here on the right. 225."

"PRETTY SURE THEY HEADED UP the hill here," Ryker said.

"They did," Krystal agreed. "Turn right into that new subdivision."

Winter leaned forward from the back seat and looked through the windshield. "It's a cute little area. But middle class, at best.

You'd think these guys would be doing whatever they're doing in a more affluent area of the city."

"Depends on what they're doing," Fred said.

Ryker turned right and cruised slowly up the narrow street. "Taxi's up there parked on the right."

"I see," Krystal said. "Just pass by and we'll get a look."

The five Changers exited the taxi van and moved across the park strip to the sidewalk.

The driver closed the passenger door on the van's curb side and turned to Levi. He held a tablet out to Levi. "Pay here, sir. The tip is calculated in."

Levi looked down his nose at the driver. "You do know who I am." He paused and raised an eyebrow.

"Oh, yes sir," the driver said, nodding.

Levi remained still, staring expressionless at the driver.

The driver froze, the tablet extended. He glanced toward the other passengers waiting on the sidewalk behind Levi. "Uh…"

Levi raised the other eyebrow and folded his hands behind his back.

The driver lowered the tablet and bowed deeply. "Thank you, sir. Please, do have a nice day." He turned and walked back to his vehicle.

"Right this way," Xander urged.

"Sit low, guys," Krystal said, reclining the back of her seat.

Ryker propped his arm on the van's door and held his hand over his face as if shading his eyes from the nonexistent sunlight. "They're ringing the doorbell at that house."

"We need to park somewhere and get over there to see what's going on," Fred said.

Ryker pulled over to the curb five houses down from 225.

A woman in a plaid dress answered the door and stepped back. She wiped her hands thoroughly on her bright yellow apron. "Welcome, friends." She smiled.

Xander stepped in and grabbed the lady's hand. "Ms. Givenzy, let's make some introductions." He turned to his companions. "We have replaced Ms. Givenzy, the Bystander, with our own Ms. Givenzy, a SOUL Chybrid. The resemblance is uncanny if I do say so myself." He smiled broadly, looked at Ms. Givenzy and winked. "Then, we're anxious to see the baby!"

"Yes, of course," Ms. Givenzy said. She started with Curtis. "Mr. Dyer, it's nice to meet you. I'm Doris Givenzy." She nodded to Johnny and extended her hand. "Mr. Logan, it's nice to meet you. I'm Doris Givenzy." Levi and Angelica received the same greeting from Ms. Givenzy.

Ms. Givenzy turned toward the short hallway leading to the back of the house. "Right this way." She stopped at the first door and quietly entered the room.

A stainless-steel crib rested under the room's only window. A young girl sat in a rocking chair, reading social media posts from friends and strangers on her cell. She looked up when the Changers entered.

"Tracy, I'd like you to meet some friends of mine," Ms. Givenzy said, smiling.

The girl stood and placed her cell on the chair.

"I'm Mr. Aldrich," Levi said, extending his hand. He turned to the others. "Dr. Rasmus, Mr. Logan, Mr. Dyer and Ms. DeMone."

"Tracy has just turned eighteen," Ms. Givenzy said. "She's been our babysitter since we brought our precious angel home."

"Bystander?" Johnny asked.

Xander flashed a sideways glace at Johnny. "Of course."

"It's nice to meet you all," Tracy said and turned to the baby's mother. "Ms. Givenzy, I really need to be going. I'm late for dinner right now."

Ms. Givenzy placed a hand on her cheek. "Oh, dear. I was hoping you would have time to feed the baby once more before you leave. You see I have guests."

"Well…" Tracy said.

Angelica checked the time on her cell. "Where do you live, Tracy?" she asked, not looking up.

"Oh, it's about five miles from here. The other side of town."

Angelica looked Tracy in the eye. "We'll take you home. Why don't you go ahead and feed the baby again."

Tracy looked into the crib. The baby was lying on his back. He caught Tracy's eye and produced a four-tooth smile.

"See?" Ms. Givenzy said, smiling again. "He's looking forward to it."

"Well, okay," Tracy said. "I'll get a bot—"

"I have one right here." Ms. Givenzy pulled a bottle from her apron pocket and held it out to Tracy.

The babysitter took the bottle and walked over to the crib. She held the bottle under her chin and bent over to pick up the baby. The little guy reached his arms toward the girl and wrapped them around her neck.

"Goodness," Tracy said. "You really are hungry." She grasped the baby under his arms and attempted to pull him away to reposition him for feeding. She glanced at Ms. Givenzy as the boy clung to her neck. "Goodness, he's suddenly so strong."

Levi and Johnny smiled while the others watched, expressionless.

The baby tightened his grip.

Tracy turned to Ms. Givenzy again. "Can you help, please? He's choking me."

Ms. Givenzy remained still, smiling.

Tracy moved quickly to the boy's mother. "Help, please," she said, bumping into Ms. Givenzy.

The boy squeezed Tracy's neck and drew his head back.

"Please!" Tracy screamed.

The baby slammed his face into Tracy's, locking his mouth around her lips. Her screams became muffled. She flailed her arms, beating the baby on the back.

Curtis lunged toward the girl.

Johnny grabbed the back of Curtis's collar on his sport coat. "Hold up there, buddy."

Curtis's feet went out from under him as Johnny pulled him back and stood him up.

Levi glanced at Curtis and frowned. "Back off, Dyer."

Tracy hurried over to Ms. Givenzy again and slammed the baby into his mother.

The baby's grip continued to tighten as his tiny fingernails dug into the skin on Tracy's neck. She turned and ran toward the other side of the room, slamming the baby into the wall. Tears streamed down her face. Blood seeped out between her cheeks and the cheeks of the creature stuck to her face. As her knees weakened, she fell to the floor, face first. Her skin became soft and withered as life-extending enzymes transferred from her body to the humanlike vessel beneath her.

Curtis dove to the floor and vomited—mostly into a nearby trash can—before he lost consciousness.

Johnny glanced at Curtis and chuckled.

The tiny monster released its grip on its victim and wriggled out from under the carcass. He sat up, smiled and reached his arms up to Ms. Givenzy.

The mother picked up her son and turned to Xander. "Doctor?" she said, holding the baby at arm's length.

Xander turned to Levi. "Leader, would you like to absorb the nutrients from the child? I assure you, it won't harm him."

Levi waved him off. "No thank you. I have had a recent absorption. Perhaps Ms. DeMone?"

"I'm good," Angelica said.

Johnny smiled and raised his hand. "I'll do it."

THE SIX PUNKS HAD STATIONED themselves around 225. Winter stood poised with her back to the east exterior wall, her head turned toward the street. Silver stood beside her.

Fred and Thomas squatted on the west side. Fred faced the street, Thomas the fenceless backyard.

"No windows on this side of the house," Thomas said. "What are we supposed to monitor here?"

"You know, partner. We have to adapt to the Punks' way. Let them take the lead. Right now, we're advising them. Our time is coming. I can feel it."

Krystal crouched and pressed her face against the window at the back of the house. "Curtains," she whispered. "I can't see a damn thing."

"You don't have to *see* anything. Do you hear that?" Ryker asked.

"Yes. It sounds horrific."

"What the hell are they doing here?"

Krystal shook her head slowly. "Clueless Bystanders never should have let the Changers back inside the Wall." Her eyes narrowed. "You never know when Levi and Logan are involved."

Ryker stood and brushed off his jeans. "We gotta do something."

"No." Krystal grabbed Ryker's forearm. "Not now."

Ryker yanked his arm away. "It's not the Punks' way to let something like this go!"

Krystal looked into Ryker's eyes. "I know, Ryk. We're on the same side. Intervention now is the wrong time."

Ryker's ire burned his gut. "Right." He paced. "Right."

Winter whispered into her shoulder mic. "Front door's opening, guys."

Fred and Thomas scrambled to their feet and hurried to the back of the house.

"Caught Winter's message," Fred said. "Figured we'd come back here. She's got a gun and we don't."

"Yeah," Krystal said. "We gotta get you guys out on the range. You should be armed like the rest of us."

"Join me here, everyone," Winter whispered. "They're moving to the sidewalk on the west side of the house."

Krystal motioned to the others as she spoke into her two-way. "On our way, Win."

Winter remained pressed against the house with her hand in the air. Krystal and the others hurried to the east side.

Ryker moved to the front of the line next to Winter. "Here," he whispered. He pulled a small shotgun mic from his belt and handed it to her. "I got it synced to our two-ways." He turned to the others and tapped his ear, signaling them to listen.

Winter held the mic next to the corner of the house and pointed it at the Changers strolling down the walkway toward the curb.

The audio was crystal clear.

"*Damn, that was nice,*" Johnny said. He rubbed his hands on his chest. "*I feel great.*"

The well-dressed man smoothed his lapels. "*As well you should, Mr. Logan. The SOUL Chybrid specimen performed the extraction of the donor's telomerase flawlessly. But it is the ability to retain and store the enzyme and the associated nanobots for redistribution to you that is the true wonder of this technology.*"

Levi clapped his hands three times. "*Excellent, Doctor. Most excellent.*" He turned to the young blond man, placed a hand on his shoulder and squeezed. "*And how are you feeling after your little episode?*"

The blond man's smile was weak. "*I feel fine. So does this mean we don't actually have to absorb a person firsthand? The Chybrid babies will provide the means to extend our lives?*"

"*The SOUL Chybrid is the extraction, storage and delivery system, son,*" Levi said. "*As the doctor said, there must always be a donor. In this case, Ms. Givenzy's babysitter was the donor.*"

The blond man frowned. "*But the babysitter wasn't a donor.*" He checked himself. "*Well, I mean, she was a donor. But certainly not willing.*"

The professional-looking woman touched Levi's arm. "*May I, sir?*"

"*By all means. Our newest addition is still learning.*"

She turned to the blond man. "*You need to get something solidified in your mind. We are Changers. We epitomize technology. Dare I say, we are technology. For technology to thrive, there must exist willing participants. The Bystanders have allowed the Changers into their city, into their lives. They are more concerned with their lust for our technology than for their own lives. Honestly, none of them actually believes they will become a victim to absorption. But their complacency, their apathy, makes them all victims. We give them* technology—*free of charge, mind you*—*and they give us their lives.*" She shrugged. "*The exchange is a given, and we don't feel guilty about it.*"

Levi held up his hand. "*I see our taxi approaching.*" He turned to Johnny. "*I trust you have summoned transportation for yourself and our new addition?*"

Johnny straightened his stance. "*Yes I have, Leader.*"

"*Splendid,*" Levi said. "*I am entrusting you with my latest protege.*" He looked at the young blond man and placed a hand on his shoulder. "*Mr. Logan is one of our best. He will introduce you to some of our Bystander contacts within the city.*" He couldn't suppress his smile. "*Now that we once again own Tremayne.*" He turned back to Johnny. "*Do you have a game plan?*"

"*Yes, I do, Leader,*" Johnny said. "*We're going to start at one end of the city and sweep through to the other. I think we'll begin in Old Town and work our way back to City Hall.*"

"*Wonderful plan,*" Levi said. "*Be sure to make introductions to our associates at the Bystanders' homeless shelter.*"

"*It's in the game plan, Leader.*"

CHAPTER 29

Mama's Boy

THE BIG PUNK DRIVER IN Cat One glanced at his cell on the dash: *Incoming Call 4-6-25*. He looked at his partner. "What the fuck kind of number is that?"

His partner looked at the cell and shrugged. "It's your mama, dude. How would I know?"

"I'm gonna kick your ass when we're done here. Answer the damn thing."

The Punk riding shotgun swiped the device from its mount. He jabbed the answer icon with a calloused thumb and held the cell to his ear. "Mama, is that you?"

The driver backhanded his partner on the temple, dislodging his navy bandanna.

"Hey!" The shotgun Punk dropped the cell in his lap and adjusted his bandanna. "What the heck, man. It's *your* mama!"

"See who it is, dipshit," the driver said.

"All right, man." The passenger turned his attention to the call. "Yeah, hello?"

The driver's hair whipped wildly into his face. He scraped it back and glanced at his partner. "Well?"

The passenger held up a hand and poked a finger into his free ear. "You're kidding, right? Like, *the cat?*"

The big Punk's impatience overwhelmed him. "C'mon, man! Who is it?"

"Okay, yeah. Sure, dude. Fuck off, okay?" The shotgun Punk ended the call and shoved the cell back into the dash mount.

"Well, that was quick," the driver said. "So?"

Shotgun Punk grabbed a handle above him and turned in his seat. "Some dude. Said his name is Felix." He smiled. "I asked him, 'like the cat?'"

"Probably a wrong number." The driver gazed intently through the windshield. "We gotta be close, dude. That outpost is about three miles up the road."

The radio crackled. *"Cat Two. You there, Cat One?"*

"Go ahead, sissy pants."

"Yeah, mama's boy. We're gettin' close."

"What's with everyone talkin' about my mama all of a sudden? You're on my list now, pansy."

"Please, you're scaring me, poopsie. We're gettin' close to the outpost."

"No shit. Good thing we got you on our side."

The big Punk's cell lit up again. *Incoming DION.* He whipped the phone from the dash mount. "Dion. What's up, boss?"

"You guys get a call from a guy named Felix?"

"Yeah, boss. I didn't take the call—"

"Sounds like maybe you blew him off."

"You bet, boss. You know we're on a mission. We're comin' up on the outpost." He glanced at the shotgun Punk and grinned. "It's time to rescue Lace and beat some Raymond butt."

"Yeah, well, Felix is a friend of mine. He's got some valuable information. You guys passed Lace about a half mile back."

The big Punk felt his ears burn. He smashed the brake pedal to the floor and whipped the steering wheel to the left with one hand.

The shotgun Punk smacked a hand into the dash and grabbed the door sill with the other. "Woo-hoo!"

The armored vehicle slid sideways on the narrow asphalt through the clearing fog. The driver expertly spun the steering wheel back to the right and floored the accelerator. The rear tires spun furiously on the paved surface as the Punk spoke into the phone. "Headed back, boss. How the hell does this Felix dude know where Lace is?"

The two-way popped again. *"Holy hellfire, Cat One! You got this country Punk all fired up with that move! We right on yer tail again!"*

"Cat Two. What the fuck, One? Was that you just passed us by?"

"Git with the program, Cat Two. We headin' back!"

The remaining vehicles whipped their U-turns in identical fashion to Cat One. The six trucks increased their speed.

The Cat One driver was still on the phone with Dion. "I don't know how you know where Lace is, boss. We're driving blind here."

"All right," Dion said. *"I'm patching Felix through to you. Stand by. Then do what he says."*

"You got it, boss." The driver placed the call on speaker and handed his cell to the shotgun Punk.

"Hello? This is Felix again."

"We hear you, Felix. Guide us, man."

"I am tracking all six of your vehicles via satellite. Each vehicle is represented by a tiny light on my map. I also have pinpointed the female, Lace. You are close to her. But you will pass her up again if you don't slow down now."

The Punk lifted his boot from the accelerator. "Got it, man. Tell me where she is."

"She is walking slowly, approximately 400 meters ahead to the north."

The driver looked across the cab at the shotgun Punk. They both shrugged.

"That would be on your right," Felix said. *"Approximately 100 meters off the road."*

Visibility had increased to about a quarter of a mile. The driver pointed ahead to his right. "There she is." He veered off the road into the mud and accelerated. The other five trucks followed.

"Nice find, Cat One," Vee One said.

"She's running away, dude," shotgun Punk said to the driver.

The big Punk easily caught up to Lace and pulled in front

of her. The other vehicles split formation at Vee Three and surrounded Lace.

"*Splendid,*" Felix said. "*Now, the man who killed your companion at the outpost is headed toward Tremayne. He is off the paved road as well.*"

"Thanks, Felix," the driver said. "Can we get back to you after we handle Lace?"

"*By all means,*" Felix said. "*Goodbye.*"

The call ended.

RAYMOND RECLINED IN THE DRIVER'S seat of Slade's Humvee as the vehicle slogged through the muddy terrain toward Tremayne. He bobbed his head to a tune known only to him. *Fuck trying to find Lace, man,* he thought. *I'm heading to town, joining up with the Changers.* He chuckled to himself. *They're gonna love me.*

He spotted the Perimeter Wall through the thinning fog. *No fuckin' wall is keeping me out.* He took his foot off the accelerator pedal, pressed the brake and coasted to a stop. He sat for several minutes staring at the Wall before twisting the key to the off position. *Tunnels,* he thought, opening the driver's door.

The former Punk stepped out of the Humvee and stretched, hands in the air. He relaxed, placed his hands on his hips and surveyed the Wall. *Quarter mile or so back was the last entrance I know. Gotta be another tunnel hatch around here somewhere.* He checked his pockets. *Knife, knuckles.* He walked through the mud toward the Wall. *Looks fuckin' big from this side.*

The white paint on the thirty-foot-high structure was sunfaded and dirty from decades of neglect. But the foundation was deep and the construction solid. Raymond shuffled up to the Wall and placed his palm against the concrete. He shook off old familiar feelings—feelings of belonging, of being a respected family member. His stomach turned as he placed his other hand on the cold hard surface.

He looked up to the top of the Wall. *I been there.* He squinted at the bright white sky as tears pooled in his eyes. He shook his head, then stared at his dirty hands on the dirty wall. And the tears streamed down his face. *Tears?* he thought. He stood upright and punched his cheeks. BAM. BAM. BAM. He shook his head again and stepped back from the Wall.

Raymond walked parallel to the huge barrier toward Tremayne, keeping his eyes trained on the rocks, the trash, the debris scattered against the Wall. He knew the Punks camouflaged the tunnel entrances well. Thirty yards in front of him, he spotted three discarded lawn chairs next to a flattened, overturned burn barrel. And he smiled. *A Punk knows Punks. Raymond, you dog. You're gonna be a valuable commodity to the Changers.*

When he reached the burn barrel he bent down, grabbed the edge and hoisted it to the side. He flung the old lawn chairs, one at a time, behind him. *Uh-huh. Just as I thought.* He reached down, grasped the exposed T-handle and turned it. The hatch popped upward.

Raymond smiled again.

CHAPTER 30

Assembling the Pieces

THE HEAVY FOG HAD MOSTLY dissipated by the time Krystal turned her BearCat into the outer Punk checkpoint off the highway. Blue from the sky teased its presence in the waning hours of the late afternoon. The conditions were perfect for a new round of fog to settle in overnight.

Krystal and Ryker had spent the ride staring out the windshield, not talking to each other.

Ryker turned in his seat. "It's not like you to be completely silent this long. What are you thinking about?"

Krystal continued her forward gaze. "God, Ryk, there's so much."

"I'll agree with you there. What we heard going on inside that house was disturbing." He looked out the passenger window. "But I know you. There's more on your mind than that."

"The Changers," Krystal said. "I'm not even amazed at their perversions anymore. Right now, I'm trying to figure out their personnel. I think there's something there."

Ryker took off his black bandanna and stuffed it into an inside pocket of his leather vest. "How so?"

She finally looked at him. "Well, Levi's always Levi. Nothing's changed there that I could tell. And that woman. She's probably

Silver's replacement. The fancy guy doing all the smiling—I'm guessing he replaced Felix."

Ryker ran a hand through his long brown locks. "And there's Logan."

Krystal nodded. "Right. Then there's the blond guy." She tilted her head and her eyes narrowed. "Replacement for Fred?"

"Well, you know the Changers better than I do. Maybe Fred and Thomas will have some insight on that." Ryker looked across the cab. "I'm glad your face stayed the same."

"What?" Krystal started. She looked at Ryker. "Where'd that come from?"

"Just an observation," he said. "Seems to me there's so much going on with you. You're smarter than anyone ever gave you credit for. You have in-depth experience with the Bystanders, Punks and even Changers at the highest levels." He shook his head. "You even pushed your body to its limit when you were a skinny little thing. Now, Felix did this thing—this whatever—to you, making you fucking awesome, physically."

"I didn't ask him for anything." She glanced at Ryker. "I never asked anyone for anything."

Ryker held his hands up. "I know you didn't. I guess I'm just saying I look at you differently than I have in the past." He looked out the window again. "And I'm saying I'm glad your face is the same."

Krystal pulled the armored vehicle into her assigned spot in front of the Depot. She switched off the engine and turned in her seat to face Ryker. "Me too. I like my face, scars and all. Felix is a genius. It was a genius move to leave my face as is. Especially when he had the ability to make me look perfect."

"I agree," Ryker said. The palms of his hands grew suddenly moist. "And I think you look perfect right now."

For a moment, she locked her eyes on his. Then she turned and opened the driver's door. "We better report to Dion."

"Right," he said, exiting the vehicle on the passenger side.

Fred parked two spots away. Winter pulled her truck between Fred's and Krystal's. The four occupants dismounted and met Krystal and Ryker at the front of Krystal's BearCat.

"Well, that was a trip," Winter said.

"Agreed," Fred said. "Thomas and I gleaned some interesting information from that little excursion." He glanced at Silver. "Wondering if you saw what we did, Silver."

Silver crossed her arms. "Are you talking about that new guy? Yeah, I noticed. Very interesting."

"What's so interesting about the new guy?" Winter said. "They all look new to me."

"It's that—" Thomas began.

"Can we go inside?" Silver turned and looked toward the Depot door. "It's starting to get cold again."

ACE SAT BEHIND THE COMMUNICATIONS console inside the Depot. He swiveled around in his chair when the six entered. "Hey, Krys, Ryk, Win." He waved his hand in the air. "And all you other guys." He looked at Ryker. "Dion wants you guys to meet him and the Amigos in his quarters."

Ryker turned to the group. "Ten minutes, people. Dion's quarters."

"Pit stop for me first," Krystal said.

"Me too," Winter agreed.

Ryker hung back to talk to Ace as the others filed out the side door. He hopped onto a stool next to Ace and gazed up at four huge flat-screen monitors on the wall behind the bar. The four monitors showed lighted maps of North America, West North America, the Perimeter area and Tremayne. Several smaller monitors mounted above the large ones displayed real-time video of security camera locations throughout Punk headquarters.

"I see there's been a breach at one of the tunnel entrances," Ryker said. "Any word on that?"

"Not yet," Ace said. "We headed a team out that way a few hours ago."

Ryker reached across the bar and manipulated the camera controls. "No activity around there."

"Yeah, a few of the cameras are wonky. Pops and Geezer are troubleshooting them."

Ryker stood and walked around behind the bar. He grabbed a bottle of beer from the cooler and popped the top off. "You know, Ace…" His voice trailed off.

"What's up, man?" Ace asked. "You look beat."

Ryker took a swig of beer. He stared across the room at the door leading out to the compound. "I dunno. Sure seems like we're hanging on by the skin of our teeth sometimes."

"Like now?" Ace said.

"Yeah. The Bystanders are buying in big-time to the Changers. I mean, most of them don't even want protection from the Punks anymore."

"Why would they, boss?" Ace said. "Heck, the Changers keep giving and giving. And they don't charge the Bystanders for anything."

"Exactly. And they look at us like we're somehow interfering—"

"Interfering with their free stuff." Ace finished Ryker's sentence.

"In a way, I guess we are, bro."

Ryker chugged deep on his beer. "Sucks we need technology, too, Ace." He looked at his friend. "You know?"

Ace shrugged. "Technology's good, man."

"Yeah. The Changers abuse it, though. All for money and immortality."

Ace folded his arms across his chest and swiveled back and forth in his chair. "Ever think about changing our tactics? I mean, what we're doing isn't working. Can't keep doing the same thing over and over if it ain't makin' a difference."

Ryker finished off his beer and set the bottle on the bar. "I'd like to think we're finding a way to do just that with these new additions."

"You mean the Rogue Changers?"

"Yep." Ryker walked to the side door. He turned back to Ace. "Right now, their value remains to be seen."

KRYSTAL AND WINTER MET RYKER as he arrived at the door to Dion's quarters. Krystal opened the door and walked in. Winter and Ryker followed. Ryker stood next to Dion while Krystal and Winter seated themselves on barstools, their backs to the bar.

"Let's get right down to business," Dion said, looking at Ryker. "You want to get us started?"

"Sure," Ryker said. "From what Krys says, the new lineup of top echelon Changers is significant." He turned to Krystal. "Krys?"

"It's my feeling." She glanced across the room at Fred, Thomas and Silver. "First, I'd like to hear what you three have to say about who was at that house today."

Thomas raised his hand. "The most interesting aspect of the Changers personnel today is the new person, the wavy-haired blond guy."

"What about him?" Ryker asked. "We thought they were all new except Levi and Logan."

"Well, they are new." Thomas glanced between Fred and Silver. "But they're not new Changers."

"Yep," Silver said. "The others may be new to Levi's inner circle, maybe even new to their organization, but that blond guy is a new Changer."

"I'm confused," Winter said.

"It's as simple as this," Fred said. "Changers are aware when another Changer is new to the Change. The three of us could tell that guy was struggling to retain his look. Krystal couldn't see it because she's no longer a Changer."

"Yes," Thomas agreed. "We saw his look—his outward physical appearance—fluctuate, ever so slightly. It's something you wouldn't be able to see if you're not a Changer."

"Okay, so he's a new Changer," Ryker said. "What's the significance?"

"Good question," Dion said. "Everyone has to start somewhere, right?"

Silver stood. "Right! Everyone has to start somewhere. But not at the top."

"So the three of us are curious how a brand-new Changer is in Levi's elite inner circle," Thomas said.

Dion folded his arms across his chest. "Got it. Let's sit on that a minute." He looked at the Three Amigos sitting on the couch. "The Amigos have a shift to start in Tremayne. But they have some information they got from the hospital that we all need to hear about." He glanced at a digital clock on the wall, then back at the Amigos. "You guys have to leave shortly, right?"

"You got it, Dion," Adam said.

Ryker stepped over to the bar and sat on a stool next to Krystal. "Let's hear it, guys."

Will stood from the couch and held his hand out to Joey. Joey handed Doris Givenzy's cell to Will.

"This cell belonged to Ms. Doris Givenzy," Will said. "Doris Givenzy is the victim Adam discovered in the alley. The one those stupid kids were throwing rocks at." He looked at Winter. "She's the lady you and Lace couldn't get in to see at the hospital because she was unconscious."

"Okay," Silver said. "So we're all caught up. What about the cell?"

"Fine," Will said. "Long story short is that Adam also found this piece of paper that we think Ms. Givenzy wrote a note on. The note said, 'VIDEO ON CELL'." He swiped the screen and selected the video app on the device. "So, there's no video," he said, looking around the room. "We're pretty sure the lady panicked and she couldn't get a good view or focus on what was happening to her. But there's good audio." He tapped the video to begin playback.

"*Doris Givenzy. These kids are crazy.*" The woman was obviously running. Her breathing was fast and labored. "*I've adopted a child. He was delivered to my house early this month. Ow! Ow! They're throwing rocks at me! Huge rocks!*" The sound of children's laughter accompanied rustling and heavy, unintelligible background voices. The woman continued running. The clicking of her pumps contributed to the din. "*Oh, help me, please! Someone, anyone! Where is everyone?*" More heavy breathing. "*I was kidnapped from my home. Oh, God, here they come!*" A loud metallic crash sounded in the background. More footsteps. Short, fast breathing. "*Doris Givenzy. New subdivision. 225 Maple Street. Tremayne.*"

Will clicked the device off and turned back to the room. "That's it."

CHAPTER 31

Old Town

RAYMOND HALF LIMPED, HALF SKIPPED toward the last tunnel exit. He'd have to exit the tunnel at Checkpoint Four on the east side of Tremayne. Having intimate knowledge of the Punks' lineup in Tremayne worked to his advantage.

Easygoing Red—the one Punk Raymond would never have allowed to be in charge of a kindergarten classroom, let alone a major checkpoint—was stationed at Checkpoint Four.

He smiled inwardly when he thought about using Slade's butterfly knife to cut the surveillance camera wires. With three cameras out of commission behind him—one every quarter mile at each tunnel hatch—he needed one more disabled camera to complete his trek undetected.

THE THREE AMIGOS WALKED TOWARD the door in Dion's quarters at Checkpoint One.

"Hang on a sec." Krystal touched Will's shoulder before he exited. "Monitor frequency one. That's where I'll be."

Will was mildly perplexed. "Sure, Krystal." He shrugged. "But why? We'll be on routine patrol."

Adam turned around from the exterior hallway. "Something happening we should know about?"

"You bet," she said.

"Like?"

Krystal removed her duster and hung it on the wall next to the door. "Think big picture, guys. Let me worry about the details. You know what we saw and heard in Tremayne today. And we all heard the audio on that recording."

"Sure," Will said. "But you did say those Changers flagged another taxi. I don't think we should expect to see them in town tonight, right?"

Krystal's cell vibrated. She glanced at Will. "How many times do I have to say this—put nothing past the Changers." She turned to her phone and tapped the face.

Will looked at Dion.

"Krystal's in charge, guys," Dion said. "Do what she says."

The trio turned and headed to their trucks.

"Thanks for the info, Felix," Krystal said. She ended the call and pointed at Ryker. "We need to head to Tremayne. Seems our pal Raymond is sneaking around Checkpoint Four."

Ryker hopped off the barstool. "Just us?" He glanced around the room.

"I got a bullet in my nine with that bastard's name on it. I'm sure Lace will appreciate it, too. Not to mention Slade. We'll make it quick."

RAYMOND POKED HIS HEAD UP out of the tunnel hatch at Checkpoint Four. He swiped a hand over his forehead and ran his fingers through his hair. "Fog's back." He smiled. "All the better to hide in, my dear," he said aloud to no one. He looked around before hoisting himself up out of the opening. The cold air felt good after his one-mile limp-skip through the tunnel. He ran hunched over for about ten steps before standing upright. "What are you doing, Ray? Be cool. Act normal."

The opening in the Perimeter Wall was thirty yards in front of him. He slowed his walk as he approached the gate. *No cars coming in*, he thought. He pressed his back against the Wall and slowly peeked around the edge at the gate. Four BearCats—two sets of two—sat back to back just beyond the boom arms. There was enough room for an average-sized vehicle to drive a short slalom between the trucks before heading into the city.

Red and three other Punks were gathered around a burn barrel, their backs to the entrance. Raymond relaxed and strolled quietly to Red's BearCat. The driver's window was open. He stepped on the small running board below the driver's door and looked inside. *Yep. Like taking candy from a baby.* He stood on his tiptoes, reached inside and grabbed the handheld two-way radio lying on the console between the seats. Before backing down off the running board, he glanced in Red's direction. *I knew you were useless, bro,* he thought, stepping back to the pavement.

Raymond turned the volume down on the two-way as he walked quietly around the front of the trucks facing the gate. He crept around the back side of a concrete enclosure that housed two large dumpsters and stepped onto the sidewalk. He hooked the radio over his belt and disappeared into the throng of pedestrians.

The Three Amigos pulled their BearCats into a public parking lot in an older business section on the outskirts of Tremayne. The town had managed to spread anew to the southwest, leaving the origins of the city to numerous rejuvenation projects in recent years. Like other cities inside the Perimeter, Tremayne had its own 'Old Town.' Boarded up warehouses and empty strip malls remained for future renewal projects whenever city council members could agree and funds allowed.

Will dismounted his truck first and walked across the rough asphalt parking lot to the sidewalk. He zipped his parka to the neck and fastened the top snap. He gazed across the street at the darkened shop windows and slipped on fingerless leather gloves.

Joey joined Will. "Whadda you make of what Krystal said?" Joey asked. "Does it seem a little paranoid to you?"

"Nah, not at all. That girl knows what she's doing and she knows what she's talking about." He looked at Joey. "She's special, you know?"

"She's one badass woman," Adam said as he stepped up behind his friends.

Will tipped his chin up. "Check those homeless people."

Adam and Joey matched Will's gaze.

"Yeah," Joey said. "They look like the others. They just seem somehow—"

"Out of place?" Adam said. He started across the street.

"Wait," Will cautioned.

Adam ignored his friend and approached the pair on the other side of the street. The dark-haired guy was taller than the dirty-blond. Both wore ill-fitting clothes—obviously too large for them.

"Stay here a sec and see what happens," Will said. He and Joey stood on the sidewalk, arms folded, and watched the interaction between Adam and the homeless pair that had caught his attention.

"They're just talking," Joey said. "Right?"

"So far," Will said.

Joey squinted and held a hand to his forehead to block the glow from a nearby streetlight. "The big guy looks familiar."

"They both look familiar," Will said. "What say we head on over?"

The pair strolled across the street, stepped up onto the curb and stood behind Adam.

"So what's happening, bro?" Will asked.

"Just meeting some of the new people," Adam said, not looking back.

Will hooked his thumbs into his utility belt. "Well, introduce us."

The big disheveled guy extended a hand. His smile was broad, showing top and bottom rows of teeth. "I'm Jake." He jerked a thumb over his shoulder. "This here's my friend Curly."

The boys shook hands with the two.

Jake pointed a dirty calloused finger over the boys' heads. "We're stayin' at Charlie's House, the homeless shelter."

"Yeah," Joey said. "That's a good place. They fixed it up pretty nice in the last year or so."

Adam tipped his chin at Curly. "So how long you guys been there? At the shelter."

"Uh…" Jake began.

Adam stepped between the two and looked up at the dirty-blond man. "I'm asking Curly."

Curly glanced nervously at his friend then looked Adam in the eye. "Um, a couple months?"

"Are you asking me, or telling me?" Adam asked.

Will and Joey stepped between Adam and Jake and nudged the big guy backward. Will placed a gloved hand gently on Jake's chest. "We've been around a lot longer than a couple months." He looked into Jake's eyes. "Never seen you two here before tonight."

Jake resisted any further retreat. He leaned into Will and looked down at him. "You guys hassling us?"

"They're Punk Security, Jake," Curly said.

Jake raised his voice. "I know who they are. Bystanders don't want your *security* in Tremayne anymore."

Adam took Curly by the elbow and guided him about five steps away from his friend. "Step over here. I have a few more questions."

The big guy stiffened and raised a hand above Will's head. "Don't tell him anything, Curly. Punks don't have authority here."

Will and Joey pressed together, blocking Jake from moving toward Adam and Curly.

"You need to relax, sir," Will said. "Nothing's changed with Punk Security. Until the city of Tremayne severs our contract, we're the authority, like it or not."

Jake took a step back and crossed his arms. "Hey, either of you guys got a cigarette?"

"We don't smoke," Joey said.

Adam turned Curly around to face the street and prodded him gently. Curly backed against a full sheet of plywood that covered a window opening on the old brick building.

"What are you doing?" Curly asked.

"Seriously, dude," Adam said. "We all know you two haven't been around here *a couple months*."

Curly shoved his hands into his baggy pants and glanced at his friend. "Okay, so what? We weren't doing anything wrong when you guys drove up. We're just two homeless dudes living at the shelter. We were minding our own business."

Adam's eyes narrowed. *That voice. Where have I heard it?* He looked into Curly's eyes. "Do we know each other?"

"Ahem…no," Curly said. "I…I mean, I've seen Punks around. You know, just around."

Adam swiveled to face Will and Joey. "Hey guys," he shouted. "Move that guy along and come over here."

Curly yanked his hands out of his pockets. "Wait—"

Adam held a hand to Curly's chest. "*You* wait." He spoke into the shoulder mic. "Adam here. You copy, Krystal?"

Will touched Jake's arm. "Come on this way, sir. You need to head back to the shelter for the night."

Jake resisted. "What about my buddy?"

The two Punks grabbed Jake's biceps and guided him into the street past Curly and Adam. A large low cloud of fog drifted between the trio and the sidewalk. "You guys are makin' a mistake, man," Jake said. "Me and Curly, we stick together."

Adam held Curly against the plywood window and watched the three pass by. His radio crackled. "*Krystal here, Adam. Go ahead.*"

Curly pressed hard against Adam's hand. Adam repositioned himself, forcing the homeless man back. "Best stand still, Curly." He clicked his shoulder mic. "Yeah, Krystal. We got a detainee here you might want to question."

"*What's the issue, Adam?*"

Adam shook his head, glad Krystal couldn't see him. "Jeez, Krystal. I don't really know. He's a homeless guy we found hanging out in Old Town with some other guy. There's something about him."

"*I copy that, Adam. Ryker and I came in through Checkpoint Two on the east side. We'll head your way as soon as we can.*"

"10-4, Krystal. We separated the other guy and sent him to the shelter. We still got a few questions for this one."

"Hold him till we get there, Adam."

"10-4. We're about fifty yards west of the shelter, south side of the street. We'll hold him as long as we can. Thanks, Krystal."

Will and Joey walked backward down the street toward Adam and Curly, making sure Jake was well on his way.

"Yo, guys," Adam said, motioning to his friends.

Curly swiped his hand across his chest and knocked Adam's hand away. He lunged forward and pushed Adam toward Will and Joey. Will sidestepped his friend and grabbed the grimy waistband of the man's pants.

"Not so fast," Will said.

Joey grabbed Curly around the midsection, pinning the man's arms to his sides in a bear hug. "Got 'em, Will. Go ahead and cuff him."

Curly didn't go down easy. Adam recovered his balance and mimicked Joey's grip around Curly's knees. The homeless man fell hard, chest first on the cold concrete sidewalk. Will landed a knee between the man's shoulder blades and quickly placed two heavy zip ties around Curly's wrists.

The Three Amigos scrambled to their feet and regained their composure.

Curly struggled to roll sideways. "What the heck, that's police brutality." His chin was swollen and scraped from the fall. "I'm reporting this."

"We're not the police, mister," Will said, looking down at Curly. He straightened his gloves. "Stand him up, guys."

Adam and Joey each grabbed an arm and hoisted the man to his feet.

Will stepped up to Curly and stared up into his eyes. "I don't get your attitude. But I can tell you this—there's something about you." He jerked his head sideways. "You and your partner look familiar to us. Can't put a finger on anything now, but we're gonna find out."

THE HOMELESS SHELTER WAS BRIGHTLY lit inside. Men and women carrying duffel bags, bedrolls and bags full of miscella-neous belongings moved in all directions. It was evident some knew the routine while others were doing their best trying to find their place in the commune. The smell of the night's supper wafted into the foyer from the large kitchen down one of four wide hallways.

Raymond checked into Charlie's House and received two tickets—one for the night's supper, and one for a cot—from the nice lady at the front counter. He stuffed them into a jacket pocket and turned to leave. He walked the short five steps to the exit as a well-built homeless man entered the building. Raymond body-checked the big guy, stopped and flexed. "Don't fuck with me, homeless dude," he challenged.

The man's eyes narrowed as he looked down at Raymond. "You're here, little man. Makes you homeless, too, right?"

Raymond moved closer to the man and pressed his chest against him. "Think you're crazier than me? Don't make me show you crazy."

He stood firm. "Make your move, punk."

"Oh yeah? I used to be a Punk. But I'm too good for that group now."

"Yeah," the man said, smiling. "Me, too."

Raymond turned and pushed the door open. He looked back at the big guy. "I'm gonna remember you."

CHAPTER 32

Familiar Strangers

Levi and Angelica strode swiftly through the brightly lit pedestrian expressway on Level Three in the Underground. The Changer leader's royal-blue suit was impeccable, as usual. Angelica's three-inch pumps clicked loudly on the highly polished floor. Her gait was quicker than Levi's—her black pin-striped pencil skirt forcing shorter steps—but she easily matched his speed as they approached an elevator.

When the pair entered, Levi pressed number seven and turned to Ms. DeMone. "I have invited Dr. Rasmus to meet us for dinner." He breathed deeply. "I can almost smell the steak and lobster now."

"Well, I'm about beat," she said. "I'll be up early tomorrow to start setting up security for the SOUL incursion into Tremayne."

"I have an easy day tomorrow, dear." He smiled as the elevator door opened. "I will be directing my secretaries to set up a conference call with the Changers Global leaders. If all goes well with our new engagement, they will have no choice but to install me as the Changers Global Supreme Leader."

Angelica rolled her eyes and stepped off the elevator. "Can your ego get any bigger? You do realize you're dreaming of being king of the world, don't you?"

Two security guards met the pair as they turned down the hallway on Level Seven and headed toward Levi's favorite restaurant. "In a few short months this dream, as *you* call it, will become a reality," he said. "If you play your cards correctly, Ms. DeMone, you will be at my side."

"My cards?"

"You are not doing well at this point, my dear."

"This place is tighter than it's ever been, Leader," Angelica said. "I'm light-years ahead of your little hussy, Silver Long."

"If that were the case, Dr. Felix Yaz would be in your custody as we speak." He inhaled deeply again and patted his lapels with both hands as they entered the restaurant. "I love this place."

KRYSTAL DROVE HER BEARCAT DOWN the middle of Habiliment Avenue, hogging the center turn lane. Reflective *PUNK SECURITY* decals affixed to the truck—and a thin blue illuminated light bar in the vehicle's grill—prompted Bystander vehicles to yield the right of way. Rush hour traffic and pedestrian activity stirred the air and helped delay the inevitable settling of fog in the downtown area.

"Almost don't even need headlights," Ryker commented. He looked across the cab at Krystal. "Ever see those ancient holograms of Las Vegas? You know, from before the country was walled off?"

Krystal nodded. "Yeah, but seriously, it's not quite that bright."

"Times Square?"

She smiled. "Yeah, I'll give you that. This fog rolling in kinda spreads the lights. Gives the lighting personality."

"Tremayne's definitely got a personality of its own," Ryker agreed.

Krystal's cell lit up. "Looks like Felix. Can you pick up?"

Ryker snatched the device from the dash mount. "Dr. Yaz?"

"*Oh, yes. I was expecting Krystal. Is this Ryker?*"

Ryker put the cell on speaker. "Krystal's here. Go ahead, Dr. Yaz."

"*Hello, Krystal. That young man, Raymond. He has entered Tremayne by way of the east gate, your Checkpoint Four.*"

"We have a crew stationed there, Felix—"

"*Yes, but he just walked through the open gate and into the city.*"

Krystal glanced at Ryker. "Who's covering Four?"

"Red's crew."

"We gotta get serious here, Ryk. Red's a great guy, but he's weak."

"*Krystal. I only saw him enter the city. I have not tracked him inside the Perimeter. He is currently beyond my view.*"

"I hear you, Felix. Any other way for you to locate him, like GPS?"

"*Not at this time. I lost track as he began to mingle with the residents of Tremayne. The crowds are currently very heavy.*"

Krystal shook her head. "Okay, fine. Anything else you can tell us?"

"*Only that he stole a device from one of the Punk vehicles at the gate. I do believe it is a portable two-way radio.*"

Krystal frowned and looked at Ryker. "That's messed up, Ryk."

"I'll deal with Red. The only good news I can give you is his radios aren't chipped for freq one."

She turned to the cell. "Thanks for the info, Felix. Let me know if you find him again."

"*Of course I will. Goodbye.*" The call ended.

THE MAÎTRE D' FAST-WALKED BEHIND Levi as the Changers' leader strode toward his table at the back corner of the plush establishment. The little man struggled to keep up with the two security guards as he waved frantically at various staff members.

Xander stood from the table and greeted Levi and Angelica as a waiter arrived with a tray holding three drinks. Levi seated himself. Xander stepped next to Angelica and grasped the back of her chair.

"If you don't mind, Rasmus," she said. "I'll seat myself."

The doctor turned without a word and sat back down. He looked across the table at Levi and smiled. "Well, good evening, Leader. I have a great report for you."

The security guards stationed themselves on either side of the corner table, facing out into the dining room.

"That's what I like to hear." Levi leaned back slightly to make room for a waiter to place a napkin in his lap. He picked up his martini from the table and held it in the air. "Here's to good reports." A smile crept over his face. "And Changers Global domination."

"Here, here," Dr. Rasmus agreed.

Angelica raised her glass, nodded her head and triple-sipped her drink.

"So, Doctor," Levi said. "I trust your report addresses the SOUL Chybrid babies and their lack of benefit to our recent engagement."

Xander looked genuinely hurt by the remark. "The babies are of great benefit, Leader. They are essential to the long-term progress of the SOUL project."

Levi remained composed. "When I appointed you, Rasmus, it was understood this project, when launched, would be designed to strike the Bystander community fast and hard."

Xander took a gulp from his martini. "Leader, the SOUL Chybrid babies are containers designed to ensure the strike has depth. The container babies will provide longevity." He glanced at the team of waiters approaching the table, thankful for the upcoming break to this conversation.

"I was under the impression the SOUL Chybrid project launch is impending—"

Angelica rolled her eyes and took another swig of her drink. She looked at Xander. "He can't wait to be king of the world."

Levi gazed down his nose at Angelica. "It's 'Global Supreme Leader,'" he corrected. "That *will* happen, Ms. DeMone. Have no doubt. Better sooner than later."

Four waiters brought two trays full of appetizers and a second round of drinks for the party. Levi rubbed his hands together. "I'm waiting for an answer, Dr. Rasmus."

"Apologies, Leader. I'm afraid some clarification is in order." Xander speared a stuffed potato skin with his fork and dropped it onto his plate. "Recall the SOUL Chybrid children in the classrooms. They, and many like them, are currently deployed inside Tremayne. We have many adult SOULs operating there as well."

He looked up at Levi while slicing into his appetizer. "I like to think of the babies as the Changers' life-currency." He popped a bite into his mouth. "They will grow at the same rate as a normal human. In the event we have underestimated the expansion of the Changer population—say, we start to run low on Bystander lives to absorb—we will have the container babies to renew our lives."

Angelica picked at an asparagus spear with her fork. "Like an insurance policy?"

"Exactly," Xander said.

Angelica's cell vibrated as the screen lit up. She picked it up. "DeMone."

Levi frowned. "Trouble, Ms. DeMone?"

Angelica held up a hand. "And how did they get split up?" *Pause.* "I want a complete report within ten minutes."

She set the device down hard on the table and turned to Levi. "Those two idiots, Logan and Dyer, managed to become separated inside Tremayne."

"First, Ms. DeMone, remember those two are held in high esteem by both Dr. Rasmus and myself. They are of equal value to this organization as you are. *You* are the head of security. If anything of a negative nature happens to them, I will hold you directly responsible."

Angelica's eyes widened. "A security detail is currently in Tremayne. I'll have an update on their whereabouts shortly."

Two waiters approached the table pushing two-tiered titanium carts with the group's entrees. Levi looked at the cart holding his huge steak and steaming lobster and smiled. He leaned toward the cart and breathed in the savory scent. "I want you to go to Tremayne immediately and handle the situation personally."

Angelica glanced at the cart with her dinner and back at Levi. "Right now?"

"Of course, right now. This is of the utmost importance."

"Leader, the situation is under control. Surely it can wait until I finish dinner."

"Ms. DeMone." Levi picked up a fork and a steak knife, rested his fists on the table and turned to Angelica. "Unlike Dr. Rasmus, you have yet to prove yourself. That despicable traitor, Dr. Yaz, is still at large. Krystal Peterson is reunited with the enemy. You have no idea as to the whereabouts of Garrison and Dennis. Now, go to Tremayne and get a handle on the situation at hand. Bring Logan and Dyer back to the Underground posthaste. If you can manage to accomplish this simple task, maybe we can discuss your future as security chief."

Angelica pushed her chair back from the table and threw her napkin on top of her untouched meal. She grabbed her cell, turned and walked toward the exit. She tapped the screen on her cell and held it to her ear. "Get the Hyperloop ready, now! I want four security escorts on site, with transportation, when I arrive."

RAYMOND MINGLED AMONG THE BYSTANDERS in Tremayne's Old Town. Still bitter over his exile from the Punks, the chip on his shoulder kept his spirit down. His rank with the Punks' organization had afforded him more prestigious assignments than depressed areas like Tremayne's east side. He hated that at this very moment he didn't feel out of place rubbing elbows with the lowlifes.

He scanned the faces in the crowd but avoided eye contact. Everyone seemed to keep to themselves or their own group. Eye contact meant acknowledgment that Raymond existed, that someone else knew he was somehow a part of the armpit of society. Raymond knew a hierarchy existed among the homeless. There were leaders and lackeys, perpetrators of violence and victims. There were fiercely defended turfs and unfortunate interlopers. But Raymond wouldn't be here long, so figuring out the pecking order mattered little to him. His plan was survival. Until he found a way to join the Changers.

The ex-Punk jammed his hands into the pockets of his leather jacket and stood still in the middle of the narrow sidewalk. He was unfazed by the intermittent brushes and bumps from passersby. He turned and gazed across the street. More of the same. His peripheral vision caught the glow of flickering blue lights coming from the west. *Punks*, he thought, backing slowly into a small alcove—the entrance to a used clothing and thrift store. The tiny shop was closed for the evening.

Krystal slowed her BearCat as she and Ryker entered the undeveloped east end of Old Town. "Foot traffic is heavy," she said.

"All the homeless," Ryker said. "They can't be too far from here. Charlie's House is coming up on the left."

"I see it. Adam said they're about fifty yards down, my left."

The passenger window was down, Ryker's elbow rested on the sill. He pointed across the cab through the windshield. "There."

Krystal braked the armored truck and stopped in the center turn lane. She left all the vehicle's lights on, set the parking brake and turned off the ignition. The two Punks dismounted and walked swiftly across the street.

A small crowd of people had formed a loose semicircle around the Three Amigos and the dirty-blond guy in their custody. The detainee was sitting on the sidewalk, hands secured behind him, his back against the brick building. Ryker pushed through the pedestrians and lookie-loos, making a pathway for Krystal.

"Hey," Ryker greeted. He glanced at the man on the sidewalk. "So, this is the guy?"

"Yeah," Will said. "He had a partner, but we sent him to Charlie's. We figured it was best to separate 'em."

"Okay, here's the plan," Krystal said. "Ryk and I are going back to headquarters. We'll send Fred, Thomas and Silver back to pick this guy up. It'll be a good first assignment for them. I know it makes for a long shift for you, but we need you to hold this guy till they get here."

"No problem," Will said. "One of us can grab something for us to eat. We'll manage."

"Good. I'll have Fred make contact with you when he gets close." She glanced at Ryker, then back at the Amigos. "One more thing. Keep your eyes peeled for Raymond. We heard he made it to Tremayne, this side of town."

CHAPTER 33

Manufacturing People

THE WINTER AIR WAS SEASONABLY cold in the Southern California desert. The stars appeared early in the crisp clear sky.

Felix pulled on his white lab coat and absentmindedly patted his top pocket to confirm the presence of his stylus. He repeated the check of his cell in one side pocket and his tablet in the other as he gazed into the mirror on the wall beside the transport cube portal. He smoothed a hand over his thinning hair and smiled. *I have chosen the good side.*

The doctor waved his palm over the sensor next to the door. Stepping into the cube, he turned and gazed up at the stars through the glass ceiling in his quarters. He folded his hands behind his back as the door swished closed. *I have been in this place too long. I miss the fresh clean air. I miss nature. One day, I'll be out of this place, and I will stand on a mountain, and I will view the stars directly. One day soon.*

IVAN DUNCAN STRIPPED OFF A pair of disposable synthetic gloves and tossed them into a small stainless-steel-lined hole in the countertop. He pressed a button adjacent to the hole and watched the gloves disappear down the vacuum tube. "Sucks we're relegated to manual labor like this, partner."

Marvellus Macey pushed the last of eight high chairs under a wide counter on the opposite wall. He turned and looked at his friend. "Yeah." He surveyed the brightly lit all-white room and placed his hands on his hips. "Cleaning the lab technicians' break room. Who'd have thought?"

Ivan leaned against the countertop and crossed his arms. "You ever think about getting out of here? Like Fred and Thomas?"

"All the time. I never imagined we'd be cut off the way we were. I mean, look. We dedicated our lives to the Changers. It'd be tough starting new out there in the Bystanders' world."

"I agree," Ivan said. "It's enough that we step out of the Underground every so often to absorb a Bystander. But living with them? I don't know. The Underground is our home."

Marvellus frowned. "But what is there for us here? I mean, it's not like we can *work our way up* anymore."

"I guess we could find other jobs here in the Underground," Ivan said.

"Like what?" Marvellus pulled out one of the chairs he had just pushed in and sat down. "Baristas, waiters, taxi drivers?"

Ivan shook his head slowly. "I don't know—" A flashing green light above the door caught his attention. "Heads up."

Marvellus hopped down off the chair and quickly placed it back under the counter as the door swished open.

"Greetings, my friends."

"Felix!" the two said in unison.

"Get changed. We have work to do."

"But, we're clocked in here," Ivan said.

Felix waved his hand. "I have adjusted your schedules. Your supervisor is loyal to me. Now get changed. We'll be visiting a high security lab to view the Changers' latest technology, so look appropriate. Just don't look like yourselves. There are some lab coats in the dressing room."

The two former scientists hurried to the small room and selected appropriate-sized coats. Felix pulled two small credit-card-sized devices from his pocket and handed one to each man.

"Put this card in your pocket. I am carrying one as well. They will override our implanted chips to facilitate access."

The trio had changed their outward appearances by the time they exited the break room. Felix led them down a familiar white corridor to an elevator. He pressed the number ten when they entered. The number ten button flashed in sync with a red light over the elevator's doors.

"Ten's top security," Marvellus said.

Felix turned and looked up at Marvellus. "Of course it is." Felix passed his override card over an adjacent panel. The light above the door flashed green three times, and the elevator began its descent. "When we arrive, follow my lead."

FOUR SECURITY GUARDS WERE STATIONED outside the elevator on the tenth level. Felix nodded to them as the three stepped off. Ivan and Marvellus followed the doctor to an unmarked door at the end of a short hallway.

When the trio stepped through the doorway into the wide corridor, Felix was surprised to see armed guards lining the walls. Estimating a total of 100 guards, he did his best to appear unfazed at the display. A distant humming sound, accompanied by a clicking, pricked his ears. The clicking seemed to follow a one-sixteenth note rhythm. The sound increased in intensity as the three approached a set of double sliding doors on their right. Felix stopped and turned to face the doors. He glanced further down the hallway and estimated an additional 100 guards on the other side of the doors.

The two guards on either side of the double doors nodded at Felix. He placed a hand into his lab coat pocket and pushed his override card against the sensor. The double doors slid open, revealing a small anteroom with a single door opposite the entrance.

A technician in a white lab coat greeted the trio from behind a console that supported a computer monitor and keyboard. "Good evening," the man said. "Welcome to SOUL Central." He scanned his monitor, looked back at the three, then scanned his monitor again while he tapped his keyboard. His eyes narrowed as he looked back to Felix. "Uh, you're here for?"

"Progress and quality control inspection," Felix said without missing a beat.

"Ah." The technician smiled. "Go right ahead." He tapped his keyboard once more, and a loud click sounded from the single door.

Felix led Ivan and Marvellus through the door into a spacious room, two stories high. The humming Felix had heard from the hallway intensified in this room. Multiple robotic arms—the source of the clicking—tapped busily onto circuit boards. The hair on the back of his neck stood up when he saw the glass pods—hundreds of them—with bodies inside. The pods were suspended in rows from the ceiling at four levels. The largest were chest-high from the floor. The smaller pods landed approximately four feet below ceiling height. Felix counted silently to himself. *Ten, twenty, forty, eighty…multiplied by…* He inhaled deeply and closed his eyes.

"Oh my God, Felix," Marvellus said.

Felix stood still, eyes closed, and held up a hand. He exhaled and opened his eyes. "There are 2,400 pods in this room." He looked up toward the ceiling at the stainless-steel scaffolding with ladders to each tier of glass containers. Technicians in white jumpsuits viewed numerous holographic monitors next to each enclosure.

"But who, or what, is in them?" Ivan said.

"These aren't Chybrids." Marvellus looked wide-eyed at Felix. "Are they?"

Felix approached a technician monitoring a display next to a pod in the main aisle. "Excuse me," he said to the man. "Progress and quality control."

The technician paused and turned to Felix. He smiled. "Oh, yes. How may I help you?"

Felix pulled his tablet from his lab coat pocket. "Tell me about this project."

Technical personnel on high security projects were acutely aware that an audit or quality control inspection may include inquiries regarding the technician's knowledge of the project.

The technician stood at attention, hands to his sides. "This is Engagement X. That is, its designation, X, represents the ancient Roman numeral ten. Hence, this is the tenth major engagement by the Changers North America organization targeted toward elimination of the Punks to control North America, with an eye toward the Changers' world domination—"

Felix had begun waving his hand halfway through the man's spiel. "Stop, stop, stop, young man. The fact you have memorized a manual verbatim means nothing to me. It does not tell me you understand what you are doing. Tell me about this project in your own words."

The man folded his hands in front of him. His smile was relaxed. "Well, sir, these…" He turned and motioned to the pods. "These are SOUL Chybrid children. They have sprung directly from the mind of the eminent Dr. Xander Rasmus." He looked up. "The upper tier of pods are occupied by the infants and toddlers. These SOUL babies, when placed in strategic locations with families in Tremayne and other major cities throughout the region, will be used as containers. Once they effect absorption, they will store the captured enzymes we require for life extension."

"And who will be absorbed by an infant?" Felix said.

The technician appeared puzzled. "Why…babysitters, daycare professionals…you know."

"Excuse me," Ivan said. "Is there a danger of an infant absorbing a family member?"

"Of course there is," the man said. "But we tightly monitor and track all SOUL babies and SOUL children. In the event they absorb the family they reside with, we will retrieve the baby and return it to the Underground. Here it will live a perfectly normal life with a Changer family." He held up a finger. "For, as you know, a Changer will not absorb a Changer."

"What about the other tiers here?" Felix said.

"Ah, these are key in our takeover of the Bystanders. The other three tiers are, from the bottom up, high school, junior high and elementary school age SOUL children. We will use these to infiltrate and influence the Bystander population to hate the Punks and love us."

"How do you plan to place these older children?" Marvellus asked. "You can't just flood the cities and towns with hordes of adolescents and expect them to be taken in by someone."

The technician smiled again. "Another good question. We have built, and continue to build, new subdivisions and housing projects within Bystander territories that are capable of receiving the large influx of new people. We have devised entire SOUL Chybrid families." He pointed toward the end of the main aisle. "That room houses the pods that contain the SOUL Chybrid adults."

"But—" Ivan began.

"I've heard enough," Felix said. He nodded to the technician. "Good job, young man." He turned to Ivan and Marvellus. "We must go." He turned abruptly and walked swiftly to the exit.

Ivan and Marvellus fast-walked to keep up with the doctor. "Felix, what's wrong?" Ivan asked.

"I must contact Krystal immediately." Moisture pooled in Felix's eyes. "I was not prepared for this."

CHAPTER 34

Oh Baby

RAYMOND STOOD SILENTLY IN THE thrift store entrance as foot traffic on the sidewalk thinned. The shadow cast from the brick outcropping that formed the alcove cut his face down the middle. He kept one eye in the light, weighing his options. He studied the scene on the concrete walkway—the Three Amigos standing around the shackled homeless guy sitting on the concrete.

Three putrid-green electric taxi vans moved quietly down the center turn lane toward the four. The vehicles stopped in the middle of the street in front of the Punks and their prisoner. Raymond watched the passengers exit the vans and move swiftly to the sidewalk. He squinted through the mist. *One, two, three, four...seven, eight...ten...twelve! Those guys have rifles.* His lips curled into a scowl as he watched a dozen men dressed in dark blue jumpsuits. *Looks like someone else is going to do me the favor of eliminating those little jerks.*

Distance and the heavy night air muffled the voices. Raymond bent his knee and propped a foot against the wall behind him. He pulled Slade's butterfly knife from his pocket and flipped it around in his hand. *Your chickens are comin' home to roost, you little fucks.* He watched the men disarm the Amigos and frisk them against the building. The homeless man remained seated while the armed men placed handcuffs on the three friends.

A thirteenth person stepped out of the lead vehicle. Raymond's eyes widened. He dropped his foot from the wall, stuffed the knife back into his pocket and stood up straight. *Oh, baby. What have we here?* The woman wore a black formfitting pantsuit and black boots with four-inch heels. Her long black hair was slicked back and tied in a tight French braid. Raymond watched her bark orders at the twelve blue suits. She stood with her hands on her hips in front of the homeless guy. *What are you saying?* He decided to move closer.

"Where's Logan?" Angelica said. "And stand up. I thought you were stronger than this."

Joey looked at Will. "Changers."

The Three Amigos stood facing the brick wall of an old abandoned warehouse, their backs to the street. "I can't believe we had our guard down," Will whispered.

Adam studied the reflection of the street behind him in the dirty glass doors. "Who is that woman?"

Will shrugged. "I don't know. Let's just hope Fred and Thomas get here soon."

Curly stood and looked at Angelica. "Angelica, these guys forced Johnny to go to Charlie's."

Angelica didn't bother trying to hide her irritation. "What the hell is Charlie's? And where the hell is it?" She nodded to one of the blue suits. "Cut those things off his wrists."

Joey turned his head slowly to the left. He did a double take. *Ray?*

The disgraced Punk had made his way down the sidewalk and sat down on the concrete one door away from the Amigos. He did his best to look homeless, not realizing it wasn't much of a stretch. His jeans and boots were caked in mud, his hair tangled. Traces of Slade's dried blood streaked his once-cool leather jacket and the back of his hands.

Joey motioned to Will. "Raymond," he whispered.

Angelica pointed at a blue suit. "Get that door open. I know the perfect place for these dregs."

The blue suit slung his rifle around his back and approached the dirty double glass doors to the warehouse. He stood for a moment, eyeing the entrance. He raised his right leg, took aim and slammed his boot into the aluminum-framed structure, dead center between the doors. The door frames swung inward as the safety glass shattered. One frame lost an upper hinge.

"Follow me," Angelica said. "And bring those Punks with you."

Four blue suits followed Angelica into the warehouse. Three others grabbed the Amigos by their collars and shoved them roughly through the newly created opening.

Light inside the warehouse was nonexistent. Will strained his eyes to follow Angelica. A shove on his back caused him to stumble forward. His boot kicked something hard. He pitched headlong into the darkness, and his feet left the floor. He raised his chin as high as he could as his chest hit the cold concrete floor, and he slid. *Dammit!* His chin slammed into something else. He tasted blood as his lip went numb. A hand on the collar of his parka hoisted him to his feet and shoved him forward again.

Angelica stopped at the back wall of the warehouse. She lifted a huge bar from its resting place across a heavily rusted steel door. She used both hands to pull the door open. Years of non-use had taken a toll; rust partially fused the door's hinges in place. Angelica's strength was more than enough to break the weld. The door creaked open and she stepped back. "Get in the hole."

The stench of mold and decaying animal permeated the Amigos' nostrils. Adam retched, suppressing a gag and forcing his dinner down. Will and Joey were not as strong. Their stomachs emptied quickly in front of them, adding to the nearly unbearable odor.

Angelica was unfazed. She pointed at Curly. "Get him in here, too. This'll hold him till we can fetch Logan."

"That makes no sense," Curly said. Two blue suits forced Curly into the room with the Three Amigos.

The four captives stood motionless in the dark and listened to the heavy bar on the outside of the door slam back into place. When the sound of Angelica's boots clicking on the wet concrete floor of the warehouse faded into the distance, Will exhaled. "Hey, guys."

"We're here," Joey said.

Adam scuffed his feet on the floor. "What the hell is down here? Feels like mush on concrete."

"I don't know, besides my barf," Will said.

Joey squeezed his eyes shut, then opened them wide. "Mine, too." He strained to look around. "Damn, it's dark in here. I still can't see you guys."

"Hey, Curly," Will said.

"Yeah?"

"What's happening here?"

Curly shrugged in the dark. "I'm waiting for a ride. You guys are prisoners."

"Ha," Joey said. "Seems like you're in the same boat as us, dude."

"Think again," Curly said. "You guys are in handcuffs, not me."

Will's eyes had adjusted to the darkness enough to see the silhouettes of the other Amigos and Curly. "So this is the Changers' version of *rescuing* you?"

Curly wandered over to the door. He pressed his hands against the seam around the frame. "You know what, guy? I'm not in the mood to answer to Punks about anything the Changers do. Suffice it to say I'll be leaving here shortly, and you won't."

Will snorted. "So you're a lower-level type, huh? Why else would they leave you here to go fetch Logan? You can't be trusted?"

Adam sat down. The seat of his jeans soaked up the wetness from the floor. "The way that Angelica person treated him, he's low level." He grunted. "Got it!" He stood up, his cuffed hands now in front of him. "You guys need to do this. Get your hands in the front. It's way more comfortable."

Curly's face reddened, unnoticed by the Amigos. He turned around to face them. "If you guys only knew. You'd be on my side."

"What, be a Changer?" Will said. "Not on your life. Not on *my* life. I'd die first."

"I can arrange that," Curly said.

RAYMOND SAUNTERED UP TO THE broken glass doors of the warehouse. He glanced at the blue suits waiting in the taxis in the middle of the street, then back into the darkened building.

Two blue suits walked out in front of Angelica. The guard nearest Raymond placed his hand gently on Raymond's chest and pushed him back, clearing the entrance for Angelica.

Raymond puffed up. "Hey, dude!"

Two additional blue suits rushed to block Raymond as their boss exited.

Angelica stopped behind the guards, turned to face Raymond and folded her arms. "What's this? Another homeless person?"

Raymond used both hands to smooth his hair over his scalp. He attempted in vain to brush the dried mud and blood from his jacket as he tipped his chin to Angelica. "Hey, baby." He smiled.

Angelica pushed between the guards and walked up to Raymond. "Oh, really. *Baby?*" She eyed him up and down and smirked. "So what's your story, big guy?"

"Well, I quit the Punks, and I want to join the Changers."

Angelica was mildly amused. "Oh, *really?*" She raised an eyebrow. "Why's that?"

"Oh, I'd be a great addition to your team. I know all about the Punks. I'm Raymond, by the way."

Angelica looked down her nose at Raymond's grimy hand. "That's it?"

Raymond dropped his hand and wiped it on his jeans. He smiled again. "Yeah. And it doesn't hurt that you and me are both good-looking."

"Are. You. Serious." She glanced behind her at the warehouse door. "Come with me, *baby*. Let's see just how good you are."

Raymond's heart pounded in his chest. He pushed himself between the guards, eyeing Angelica's perfect shape as he followed her into the warehouse.

Angelica waited for him and stopped the guards as Raymond entered. "Two of you wait here. The rest can get in the taxis. I won't be long."

Raymond stopped in the light cast from the street, just inside the broken doors. Angelica reached down and grabbed his hand and led him into the darkness. "Oh, your hand is so strong."

"Oh, baby, you're gonna be impressed. I'm gonna leave you so satisfied, you'll be wanting more," he said.

Angelica stopped and turned around to face Raymond. "Let's see what you're made of, big boy." She encircled his neck with her arms and placed her face to his.

Raymond's hands were shaking as he ran them over the smooth material of her jumpsuit. He squeezed gently when he felt the soft curves of her hips and buttocks. He pushed his open mouth over hers and closed his eyes, savoring the scent of her breath.

Angelica's grip on his neck tightened. She pressed her body against his and dug her fingernails into his neck.

"Ow—" His attempt to speak was muffled as he tried to pull his head backward and disengage his face from hers.

Angelica's body moved forward in perfect sync with Raymond's attempt to withdraw. The hair on her scalp prickled her pores as goosebumps rose stiffly under the braid. And her nails dug deeper into his neck. A slight gag released a horde of nanobots from her mouth to his.

Warmth rose from deep within Raymond's chest, extending to his arms, then his legs. The heat became unbearable, and he twisted his head in a vain attempt to dislodge the Changer's grip on his body. The sensation of falling into fire overwhelmed the disgraced Punk, and his skin withered as his muscles shrank, becoming useless. Raymond saw a flash of bright white before losing consciousness.

Angelica stood firm, her feet apart at shoulder width, hugging the limp body of skin that two minutes ago was Raymond. She looked up at the pitch-black ceiling and laughed. "Oh *baby!*" she shouted, opening her arms and releasing the corpse. She glanced toward the two blue suits by the door and swiped her arm across her mouth. "Get over here," she said.

The two guards turned and approached Angelica as she bent over and grabbed the collar of Raymond's leather jacket. "Open that door." She dragged the limp hunk of human skin covered in leather and denim to the barred door. One of the guards opened the door and stood back. Angelica walked to the entrance and slung the corpse one-handed into the room. "Hey, Punks. This guy's going to wait with you. Try not to disturb him. He's a little worn out." And she laughed again.

The guard slammed the door shut, threw the steel bar back in place and led Angelica out the two broken doors to the street.

CHAPTER 35

Not My Mission

KRYSTAL'S CELL BUZZED AS SHE stepped out of her BearCat at Punk headquarters. "Hi, Felix."

Ryker exited the passenger side and walked around to the back of the vehicle. He snatched his and Krystal's dusters from a hook just inside the rear door. He threw the coats over one shoulder and met Krystal at the front of the truck.

"*I have located that man, Raymond, in Tremayne. He is in the old section of town, near the homeless shelter.*"

"Dammit, Felix. I just came from there. I'm at headquarters now."

"*Yes, I know. But there is more. The three boys in Tremayne have encountered trouble. Raymond is with them.*"

She looked up at Ryker. "Where are the three Rogues?"

Ryker checked the time on his cell. "They're probably just about at the city limit by now." He frowned and tipped his chin up. "Why? What's up?"

Krystal fought shaking. "I don't know. Somehow Ray's with the Amigos." She turned back to her cell. "Felix, are the three boys still in the same place with the homeless guy?"

"*Yes. But they are no longer in charge. They were accosted by a group*" *of Changer guards, led by Angelica DeMone. They have been placed inside the building along with Raymond and the homeless man."*

"Wait. Who?"

"Ms. DeMone is the Changers' security chief. She replaced Silver. You must hurry, Krystal."

"Okay. Fred, Thomas and Silver are on their way there now."

"I do not like the sound of that. I would not advise sending Silver at this time. She is unproven."

"Well, it's too late for that. I made the call to send her."

"Okay, my friend. I'll do my best to track them and update you as necessary. Goodbye."

Ryker grabbed Krystal's shoulders and turned her to face him. "Krys, what's happening? You look pale."

She looked into his eyes. "The Amigos are in trouble, and I might have made things worse for them."

He dropped his hands from her shoulders. "How?"

"Look. I made the decision to leave them there in Old Town, knowing full well that maniac Raymond was on the loose."

Ryker looked relieved. "That's it? The Amigos can handle Ray."

"Long story short, Ryk. They got ambushed by a bunch of Changer guards. And now they're housed up in that building with Raymond." She glanced across the compound at the Depot. "And Felix doesn't fully trust Silver." She began to pace. "Some fucking leader I turned out to be."

"Heads up," Ryker said. He tossed her duster to her. "You're the leader of this mission. When you fuck up, fix it. Then move forward." He pulled on his duster, leaving it unbuttoned.

Krystal stopped pacing. She put her duster on and walked up to Ryker. "Thanks. I needed that. Last thing I wanna look like is a frail, emotional woman."

Ryker smiled. "We all have emotions, Krys. You're not frail by any stretch." His ears flushed hot as he embraced her. "And you're all *woman*, like it or not."

For a moment, she felt weak and vulnerable. She allowed herself a split second of comfort from Ryker's embrace before pushing him away with both hands. "We have work to do."

Ryker stood alone and watched Krystal walk swiftly toward the Depot.

FRED TURNED HIS BORROWED BEARCAT right at Habiliment Avenue off the highway. "Not many people on the streets tonight. This town must close up early."

"It's past rush hour," Thomas said. "Businesses probably close early on weeknights."

The two-way radio on the dash cracked to life. *"Fred, it's Krystal. Do you copy?"*

Fred snatched the mic from its mount. "This is Fred. Go ahead, Krystal."

"You guys might be walking into a trap. We just got word from Felix that the Amigos were waylaid by a bunch of Changer guards and Raymond is with them."

Fred glanced across the cab at Thomas. "I copied that, Krystal. So, what do you suggest?"

"That building we directed you to, they're all inside. You've both been trained to use those nines you're packing. Have them ready. If there's any question, shoot to kill."

Silver scoffed from the jump seat behind the security screen. "Ha. This should be entertaining."

"There's no word on how many Changers are there. I have no idea why they didn't kill the Amigos and Raymond."

"So our goal is the same—pick up the homeless guy, return to base. 10-4?"

"That goal is the same. But first and foremost, get the Three Amigos out of there alive. We're rolling additional trucks from inside the city to your location now."

"Got it."

"Just be careful. Contact me as soon as you have a bead on the situation."

"10-4, Krystal."

A HEAVY BANK OF FOG drifted slowly between the warehouse and the three electric taxi vans parked in the middle of the street.

Angelica strode through the broken glass doors and turned down the sidewalk toward Charlie's House. She pointed at two of the biggest blue suits. "You and you. Follow me. The rest of you wait in the taxis."

The two Changer guards chased after Angelica, struggling to match her pace. When she reached the brightly lit entrance to the homeless shelter, she pushed hard on the door. It swung inward, hitting the rubber doorstop on the wall before bouncing back at the guards in tow.

The lady behind the counter greeted the new visitors with a smile. "Hi. Welcome to Charlie's House. How may I help you?"

"Looking for a tall guy named Logan. New resident."

The nice lady scanned a clipboard in front of her and ran her finger down a list of names on the top sheet of paper. "Hmm… Hmm." She looked up. "We don't have anyone here named Logan, ma'am."

"Look again, lady." Angelica glanced at the clipboard. "He might be using a different name. He's a tall handsome guy, but not too smart."

"I heard that." The voice came from behind Angelica. She swung around to see Johnny standing, arms folded across his chest.

She eyed him up and down. "You look like shit, Logan. Come with me." She turned to leave.

"Whoa, Ms. DeMone," Johnny said, stopping at the door. "Mr. Dyer and I are here on orders from Levi."

Angelica turned around and walked up to Johnny. She pushed her breasts firmly against his chest. "You're a drag on this team, Logan. My orders supersede yours. You separated from Dyer—big mistake. Our leader is pissed about it, I'm up way past my bedtime, and I'm not in any mood to hear lame excuses or BS from you. Now follow me and get your ass in the taxi I have waiting for you." She turned and walked toward the waiting vans.

Johnny followed. "I'm reporting your unprofessional behavior, DeMone."

"Report what you want," she said, not turning around. "I'll have your rank for this, if only for the fact I have to be your babysitter and come this far just to fetch and return you to the Underground." She shook her head as she approached the taxis. "You'll be out of Levi's inner circle before the Hyperloop hits headquarters."

Fred cruised past Charlie's House and eyed the four figures on the sidewalk. "Check it out, people. There's Logan and two Changer guards."

Thomas turned in his seat. "Any idea who's leading them? She looks fierce."

Silver crouched up out of her seat and pressed her face against the small side window. "It's that woman that was with Levi at 225 Maple. Probably the bitch that took my place as head of security." She scowled. "Had to be a female, didn't it, Leader?"

Thomas turned around as Fred glanced at Silver in the rearview mirror. "*Leader?*"

"I mean Levi," she said.

Thomas glanced out the windshield. "Warehouse is on the left. Those three vans are out of place, partner. Make a U around them and park on the curb facing the other direction."

"Good idea," Fred said. He passed the three vehicles and negotiated the U-turn, taking all five lanes to complete the maneuver. He pulled to the curb directly in front of the empty abandoned warehouse. "I'm going to leave it running."

"Sounds good," Thomas said, opening the passenger door.

The trio met at the warehouse doors. Fred glanced down the sidewalk toward Charlie's House. "They're not too far away. We better hurry."

Thomas pulled a flashlight from his utility belt and pointed it into the murk. "Holy hell, guys. This place is wretched." Grit on the floor mixed with moisture—a slurping sound accompanied every step.

"I'm waiting here," Silver said. "You two can act like real Punks and play in the mud."

Fred stopped and looked at her. "We're all in this together. You take the good with the bad, whatever side you're on."

"I'm on the winning side, wherever that is," Silver said. "I haven't felt like a winner since I hooked up with the Punks."

"You gotta fight for your side. If you're on the losing team, fight to win, or don't even bother."

Silver rolled her eyes. "You're pathetic, Garrison."

"Hey, guys," Thomas said. "There's a door."

The three Rogue Changers made their way into the darkness to the rusty steel barricade. Fred pressed his ear against the cold damp steel. "Voices." He took a step back and banged his fist on the door. "Hey," he shouted. "Will, are you there?"

"*Fred!*" It was Will's voice, muffled by the barrier. "*We're here.*"

"Are you guys okay? Is Raymond with you?"

"*We're fine. Ray's here, but he's dead. Can you open up?*"

Fred looked at Thomas and motioned to the bar over the door. Thomas slipped his flashlight into his belt and hoisted the heavy bar up. He threw it off to the side and let go. The trio flinched as the metal hit the concrete floor. Fred twisted the handle and pulled on the heavy steel panel. The Amigos were face to face with the Rogues when the door opened.

"Man, are we glad to see you guys," Will said. "Are the Changers still here?"

"They're headed this way," Fred said. "We have to go. Now."

Silver squinted through the darkness into the tiny room. "So that's the homeless guy prisoner?"

"That's him," Fred said. He motioned to Curly. "Let's go. You're coming with us."

"Hell I am, loser."

Fred pulled his 9mm pistol from the holster on his thigh and pointed it at Curly. "Move. Now. I'll shoot you here because I don't know you or care about you. You'll either get into that Bear-Cat out there, or you can lie dead in this smelly room with that Punk on the floor."

Curly walked toward Fred and the other Rogues. He stopped and spit on Fred's chest. "Fuck you."

Fred looked down at Curly's saliva on his jacket. "Oh, really?" He backhanded the man square on the cheek with the butt of his pistol then pushed the business end against Curly's head and glanced at Thomas. "Cuff this asshole."

The party of seven exited the warehouse. Fred held the Bear-Cat's back door open for the Three Amigos and Curly while they piled inside. Thomas hopped into the shotgun seat.

Fred turned to Silver. "Well? Get in."

Silver stood, feet apart, hands on her hips, staring at the approaching Changers. "Hang on a sec, Garrison."

Fred turned and glanced down the sidewalk. The fierce-looking unknown woman was walking swiftly toward him. Logan and the two blue-suited Changer guards followed closely behind. "Silver, we have to get out of here."

Silver remained firm. Her eyes narrowed as the woman approached. "Hey, bitch." She tipped her chin up.

The Changers stopped at arm's length in front of Silver.

"Who are you?" Silver said.

Johnny changed his appearance back to his normal. He smiled. "Hi, Silver. We gonna see a girl fight?"

"Hello, Logan. Who's this woman?" she said.

"Well, girls. Let me make the introductions. Ms. DeMone, this is Silver Long. She is the *former* head of security of the Changers North America organization."

Angelica snorted. "Hmph."

Johnny was enjoying himself. He nodded to Silver. "Silver, this is Angelica DeMone, the new *better* head of security—"

"Let me show you who's better," Silver said. She reached across her body and snatched Fred's 9mm from its unsecured holster.

BAM! BAM! BAM!

Johnny stood paralyzed as Angelica and the two blue suits dropped to the concrete. All three shots were placed perfectly—dead center in the foreheads. Johnny glanced to the street as the ten remaining blue suits exited the taxi vans in the street.

Silver pointed the pistol at Johnny's face. "Call 'em off," she said.

Johnny held up both hands to the guards. "Stop. From now on do whatever she says."

The Changer guards obeyed Johnny.

Silver smirked. "Now get back to the vans and wait for me, little blue boys."

Fred stood agape next to the driver's door of the BearCat. "Silver, let's get out of here. We've accomplished our mission and then some."

Silver dropped the pistol to her side and turned to Fred. "Don't you get it, Garrison? This isn't *my* mission. I was never on your side. You chose the losing side, and I'm a winner. Go ahead and go back to your new *headquarters*." She turned to Johnny. "Get in the taxi, you big lug. We have real work to do."

Johnny smiled, all teeth, top and bottom. "You got it, boss!"

Silver tossed the pistol onto the sidewalk. It clacked across the concrete and slid into the gutter. "It's been fun, Fred. Have a nice life. I'm sure I'll see you around." She walked to the lead taxi and hopped into the front passenger side. She looked at the blue suit in the driver's seat. "Get us to the Hyperloop."

Fred put his hands on his hips and watched the three-vehicle caravan move silently up the street. He turned and watched them disappear into the fog and surveyed his surroundings. Tremayne was silent. Blue strobe lights from six Punk Security vehicles flashed in the distance as the relentless fog continued its push into Old Town. *Now what?* he thought.

CHAPTER 36

I Did It for You

Krystal sat at the bar next to Ryker, Dion and Winter in the Depot at Checkpoint One. She studied the monitor on the wall. Lighted indicators on the electronic map showed the Three Amigos' vehicles were stationary in Tremayne. "Try Fred again, Jim."

Jimbo swiveled around in his chair to face the communications console. "You got it." He tapped a button in front of him. "Jimbo here. Do you copy, Fred?"

"*This is Fred. Go ahead, Jimbo.*"

Krystal sprang from the barstool and hurried toward the comm console.

"Fred, my boy," Jimbo said. "What's your ten-twenty?"

"*We're just leaving town. We got the Three Amigos and the homeless guy with us.*"

"Good to hear, Fred. That explains why the trackers are showing the Amigos' trucks are fixed downtown—"

Krystal pushed her way to the console and nudged Jimbo out of the way. "Fred, it's Krystal. What about Ray?"

"*Raymond's dead.*"

The five Punks in the Depot fell silent.

Winter exhaled. "Well." She looked around the room at her friends. "That's a monkey off our backs, right?"

"*Copy, Krystal?*"

Krystal turned back to the console. "Yeah, Fred. How'd Ray die?"

"*Absorption. But that's the least of our problems.*"

"What else, Fred?"

Radio silence.

"Copy, Fred?"

"*Sorry for the delay, Krys. Silver left voluntarily with Logan and the other Changers. The ones that imprisoned the Amigos.*"

Jimbo jumped up from his stool. "I *knew* it!"

Winter pounded her fist on the bar. "*Never* trusted her."

Bitch, Krystal thought. She stared at the transmit button on the console. "10-4, Fred. What's your ETA?"

"*Give us about fifteen.*"

Ryker gazed at Krystal as she began to pace. "You okay, Krys?" He shot a look at Dion and shrugged.

"All right, everyone," Dion said. "Silver was a bad addition. But let's remember, Krystal didn't solicit her help. Neither did any of us." He looked at Krystal. "Dr. Yaz sent her to us through that portal thing of his."

"Okay, so where do we go from here?" Ryker said.

Dion lit a cigarette and joined Winter behind the bar. "I think we need to start by letting the doctor know what happened."

Krystal stopped pacing and looked at Dion. "My money says he already knows. And Felix—all of us—have a bigger problem on our hands than we did a few days ago."

"You're right about us," Dion said. "That woman knows more about our operation than a lot of our frontline personnel."

Ryker finished Dion's thought. "But how does Silver defecting back to the Changers affect Felix and his ability to help us?"

"That's a problem," Krystal said. "Hopefully Felix didn't allow her fully into his world."

FELIX STOOD IN FRONT OF the monitor walls in his quarters with his hands in his pockets. He watched the ten blue suits, John

Logan and Silver Long abandon their taxis and mount the stairs to City Hall in Tremayne.

Logan waved his palm over the door sensor, and the group entered. When the door to City Hall closed behind the last blue suit, Felix switched all four monitors off and stared at his reflection.

With Silver's redefection to the Changers, his days in the Underground were numbered.

THE DOOR TO LEVI'S PRIVATE elevator slipped quietly closed behind him as he stepped into his quarters. *Ah, what a day. What a great day to be a Changer.* He stopped at the wet bar and gazed at his reflection in the mirror behind the curved countertop. *Today, Levi Aldrich, you are the Leader of The Changers North America.* He smiled. *Tomorrow, Supreme Leader of The Changers Global.*

A familiar chirping sound snapped him out of his episode of self-admiration. He frowned and glanced up at a red strobe flickering over the elevator door. He stepped across the room to the glass side table adjacent to his leather sofa and pressed a button on the tabletop. "Yes?"

A voice came over the ceiling speaker. "*Leader, it's Xander. There has been a development of the utmost urgency that requires your immediate attention.*"

"What's this *development* that cannot wait until the morning? I'm about to retire for the evening."

"*Understood, sir. I have received a report that Angelica DeMone has expired in Tremayne.*"

Levi stood for a moment to process what he had just heard. "My, my, Doctor. Indeed, that is a curious development. Are there any details?"

"Not at this time, sir. We have dispatched a team to recover the body. Incidentally, two of the guards that accompanied her to Tremayne have also expired."

Levi strolled across the room to the bar. He poured himself a small glass of brandy. "And what of Logan and Dyer? She was to bring them back to the Underground."

"Sir, Logan is en route to the Underground with the ten guards who are still alive."

Levi took a deep breath and sipped his drink. "Dr. Rasmus. What of Dyer?"

"Mr. Dyer is arriving at the Punks' headquarters at Checkpoint One as we speak."

KRYSTAL STARTED AT THE SOUND of the BearCat rolling into the compound. She rushed to the Depot door, pushed it open and strode into the yard.

Dion looked at Ryker across the bar. "What's up?"

Ryker hopped off his barstool. "I don't know, but we're gonna find out right now." He buttoned his duster as he walked toward the door.

Dion, Jimbo and Winter followed Ryker. The three stood outside the Depot entrance and watched as Ryker hurried to catch up to Krystal.

Ryker grabbed Krystal's upper arm from behind her. "Krys, what is it?"

Krystal's eyes remained fixed, staring into the fog in front of her. "Cat's coming. It's gotta be Fred and the Amigos."

Ryker gazed into the mist. "I don't hear a thing." He squinted. "Wait, I hear it now." He looked down at her and felt the familiar dance of butterflies in his stomach. "You better button that duster before you catch cold."

Krystal ignored the comment and ran into the mist. She met Fred's BearCat as it moved steadily along the asphalt road toward the compound. She grabbed the exterior rearview mirror and hopped onto the small step below the driver's door of the moving vehicle.

Fred rolled the window down and smiled. "Hey! Fancy meeting you here."

Krystal leaned into the cab and glanced through the security screen into the rear of the vehicle. "Everybody okay back there?" She watched the Three Amigos give her thumbs-up signs, then turned back to Fred. "You guys figure out who the homeless guy is?"

Fred turned into a parking spot and switched off the motor. "Haven't had a chance. Things were so hectic at the end. We just had to get out of there."

Krystal hopped off the small running board and walked around to the back of the truck. The Amigos piled out quickly when she opened the door. "Am I glad to see you guys. Let's get into the Depot and get warmed up."

Fred and Thomas hurried to the back and pulled Curly out the same door. They secured the vehicle and escorted their prisoner along the now-familiar sidewalk. Fred looked past Curly at Thomas. "Place is starting to feel like home, partner."

"Yes," Thomas said. "I have to say, these people actually treat us like family, not just assets to be used up and traded away. Our lives seem to have value to these people."

Ryker waited for the Amigos and walked with them and Krystal into the Depot. "Damn glad to see you guys. You all look beat. Bet we can have Geezer whip up something hot to eat."

Will, Adam and Joey made their way straight through the Depot and into the dining room. The trio fist-bumped Dion, Jimbo and Winter on the short trek to the side door.

Jimbo took his usual place at the communications console and swiveled his chair around to face the room. Ryker followed Dion behind the bar, and Winter seated herself on a barstool between Jimbo and Krystal.

"I gotta say, Krystal," Winter said. "Your boys from the Underground did a helluva job their first time out."

Jimbo held up a finger to Ryker. "Agreed. And I hate to flog a dead horse, but what about the Silver angle?"

Ryker slid a cold bottle of beer down the bar top to Jimbo. "Still an unanswered question in my mind."

Dion popped the top off a beer for himself. "Does that make you question Dr. Yaz's reliability, Krys?"

"Not at all," Krystal said. "I still have confidence in Felix. I don't really know where he went wrong with Silver."

Thomas opened the Depot door and Curly walked in, escorted by Fred. "Heads up, everyone," Fred said. He looked directly at

Krystal. "Had a good look into this guy's eyes. Believe it or not, he's a Changer."

The room fell silent.

Curly scanned the roomful of Punks.

Fred motioned to Thomas. "Gimme a hand here, partner."

The two supported the handcuffed Changer on both sides and helped him into a chair.

Thomas shook his head. "This guy's having a hard time holding his Change, Fred. Look at him."

Fred stood in front of Curly, bent over and looked into his eyes. "I don't know you, guy. But I can see your natural look coming through. Let's have it. Let it go. We know you're a rookie. Show us who you are."

Tears welled up in Curly's eyes. He directed his attention to Krystal.

Fred stood up straight. "He's looking at you, Krys."

Krystal's eyes softened as she stood up slowly from the barstool. She walked across the room and stood in front of the Changer. Her mouth opened but no words came forth. She looked at the bald head, the strong smooth body. "Take his shirt off."

Fred shook his head. "We'd have to release the cuffs, Krys—"

"Do it!"

Fred looked at Thomas, then he glanced behind the bar. "Dion?"

Winter stood and unsnapped the strap on the grip of her 9mm.

Dion glanced at Winter. "We go it covered. Do what Krystal says."

Fred released the cuffs and dropped them on the table. Thomas reached down and yanked the Changer's shirt over his head.

The Changer's tears flowed as his face changed back to its original form.

Krystal felt a weight in the pit of her stomach. Her face fell. "Curtis?"

"It's me, babe."

Winter used both hands to steady her pistol. "Holy. Fucking. Shit."

"Sonofabitch," Ryker said from behind the bar. "No tattoos, no Mohawk. Hell, no hair at all." He glanced at Dion. "But that sure looks like Curtis."

"It's him," Dion said. "That's his voice."

"It *is* him," Krystal said as tears of her own formed. "You're a *Changer*?" She reached out and touched a teardrop on his cheek. "Why?"

Curtis smiled through his tears. "So we'd be the same." He looked at his former friends—his former family—then back at Krystal. "I love you, babe. I did it for you. I became a Changer for *you*."

CHAPTER 37

Silver Rising

Silver Long threw the seat belt off her lap. She stood and walked down the narrow aisle of the Hyperloop and waited by the door. "Get up and get out here with me, Logan. I'll need you for access."

Johnny unfastened his seat belt as quickly as he could. "On my way." He hurried toward the door and squeezed in front of Silver as the vehicle glided to a stop.

When the door opened, Silver grabbed Johnny's shoulder and yanked it backward. She stepped off in front of him and into the loading zone. Johnny followed her swiftly up a short set of stairs to the Hyperloop's highly polished main terminal. Four Changer guards approached the two as they neared the exit at the far end of the room.

The lead guard greeted Johnny. "Good evening, sir. I trust you had a safe journey."

"Indeed we did," Johnny said, breezing past him.

Two of the other guards stepped between Silver and Johnny. She bumped into both as they pressed together to impede her progress. She looked up at the pair. "Logan!"

Johnny stopped at the exit and turned around. "Oh. Hey, guys. She's with me. I'll escort her."

"Very well," the lead guard said, nodding to the others.

Silver caught up to Johnny and followed him out the door and into a familiar wide corridor. They walked abreast around a wide curve toward the nearest elevator. "We better start with Xander," Johnny said.

Silver's eyes narrowed. "What's a *Xander*?"

"Oh, that's Dr. Xander Rasmus. He took over for Dr. Yaz."

Silver smiled to herself. *Yes, I remember, you ditz.* "Fine. But where's our leader?"

"I'm sure he's turned in for the night. He's got a big conference call tomorrow with Changers Global."

Silver snorted. "Start wherever. But I want my security access back tonight."

The two stopped at the elevator. Johnny waved his hand over the adjacent panel, and the doors opened. He checked his cell. "Looks like he's in the conference room on Level Ten." He pushed the number and pressed his hand against the security clearance pad.

They descended in silence until the doors opened on the tenth level. Silver sighed and motioned to Johnny to step off. "Well, let's get this over with."

Two security guards greeted the pair as they stepped into the wide hallway. They remained expressionless as Silver looked directly into their eyes before turning left toward the War Room. Additional guards patrolled in pairs at various intervals down the corridor.

A team of four guards approached the pair as they neared their destination. The lead guard held her arm out, stopping the others. She eyed Silver. "Ms. Long?"

Silver and Johnny stopped in front of the guards. Silver forced a smile. "Hello, Steph."

Steph smiled and glanced at Johnny, then back at Silver. "It's good to see you again."

Johnny placed a hand between Steph and the others and nudged them aside. "We have to go. Resume your patrol, please." He led Silver between the four guards.

Steph turned and watched Silver walk away. "Are you back?" she said.

Silver didn't turn around. "With a vengeance."

Johnny passed through the security door and entered the multitiered War Room. He made his way quickly through the center aisle filled with technicians behind computer terminals. He hopped up the short set of stairs to the glass-encased alcove that housed the conference room.

Xander sat at the head of the large black conference table. He looked up and frowned when the two entered. "Logan. I've been expecting you. Your locator is working nicely." He stood and eyed Silver. "I can't say the same for your companion. Ms. Long, isn't it?"

Silver glared at the doctor. "Get my access, Logan."

"Uh, yeah. Dr. Rasmus, I need you to grant Ms. Long top security access." He nodded. "Just like she had before."

Xander shook his head slowly. "Oh, no. Not without our leader's approval."

"Guess you'd best wake him up, Rasmus," Silver said.

Xander stood. "I'll do no such thing. I don't know who you think you are—"

"Not who I *think* I am, Doctor." She leaned on the table, palms down. "It's who I *am*."

"Who you *are*? Who you *are* is a failed security chief incapable of keeping track of your own prisoners." Xander removed his glasses and matched Silver's posture at the opposite end of the conference table.

"Everyone has the right to be an ass once in a while, Rasmus." Silver stood. "But you seem to be working overtime to accomplish that."

"You don't even know me," Xander said.

"Fine. Then you're always an ass." Silver looked at Johnny. "Get Levi in here."

Johnny peered across the table at Xander. "Whadda you say, Doctor? I'll vouch for her."

"I don't advise it," Xander said.

"I'll take the heat, Rasmus." Silver walked around the table and sat next to Xander. "Let's make a little pact, you and I. You let me talk to Levi. If he grants me full security access to the Underground and reinstates me as head of security, you fall in line behind me. You're number three and you answer to me."

Xander sat for a moment and pondered the offer. He reclined in the chair and crossed his arms. "And if he doesn't?"

"Then lock me up. You'll never hear from me again."

Xander nodded once. "Very well, Ms. Long. I am confident enough that you are making a fool of yourself. I will call Levi. But *you* will speak to him. If you are able to convince him to come here to the conference room…" He held up a finger. "…tonight. Then we have a deal."

Silver didn't hesitate. "Call him."

Xander speed-dialed Levi's emergency number on his tablet and placed the device on the table. He tapped the speaker button and slowly slid the tablet to Silver.

The speaker cracked to life. "*Rasmus! This better be good!*"

Silver's eyes narrowed as a smile split her face. "Hello, Levi."

The Changer leader was livid. "*Long! Where is Dr. Rasmus? And how did you come to possess his device?*"

"Dr. Rasmus is here with me, which is where you need to be as well."

"*Rasmus. Have her arrested. Has Logan returned from Tremayne?*"

Johnny hurried around the table and stood next to Silver. "I'm here."

"*Get a security detail to wherever you are and have that woman arrested.*"

Silver held up a hand to Johnny behind her. "Hang on, Levi. Your new security chief is dead. You need me."

"*You're a failure, Long. I replaced you for cause. Why am I even arguing with you about this? Logan!*"

"Leader," Silver said. "I have located Yaz."

The speaker on the tablet was silent.

"Levi?" Silver said. She looked back and forth from Johnny to Xander. "Hello? Are you there?"

Xander touched the edge of the device with a finger and angled it toward himself. He shrugged and looked at Silver.

Johnny walked around the table to the wet bar in the corner. "Way to go, Long. Looks like you've sufficiently pissed him off. Would suck to be you right now." He poured a triple shot of whiskey and turned to face Xander. He tipped his glass to the doctor. "Or you."

Xander stood and joined Johnny at the bar. "Me? I haven't done anything. You'll both confirm that." He looked up at Johnny. "Right?"

Johnny shrugged. "I'm not part of your little agreement with Ms. Long, Doctor." He downed his drink and poured another. "You're the one that made the deal. Don't even think about bringing my name up to Levi."

Xander's eyes widened. "But—"

"Relax, Rasmus," Silver said. "I'll handle Levi." She stood and moved around to the head of the conference table and seated herself in the chair previously occupied by the doctor. She picked up the tablet and eyed the screen. "He hasn't hung up." She tossed the device roughly back onto the table.

The conference room door swished open, and Levi entered followed by two security guards. His eyes locked on Silver's. "Where is he?"

Silver stood and smiled. "We have much to discuss, Levi."

Levi remained at the opposite end of the table and eyed Johnny and Xander before turning back to Silver. "First things first, Long—"

"Good," Silver said. "We have common ground. First thing is I get my top security clearance back."

"Not so fast," Levi said. "I don't know that you have knowledge of Yaz's whereabouts."

Silver folded her arms. "Top security clearance for Silver Long. Then, information."

Levi frowned. "A poor attempt at humor. Where's Yaz?"

"It's called a conundrum, Levi." Silver motioned to the pair at the bar. "You have your top two members of your inner circle standing around the bar in the War Room, drinking whiskey like it's water." She chuckled. "And yet, here I am. And here you are. You want information you can only get from me. Information your new security chief was unable to provide. She was a poor choice, by the way. Not even smart enough to keep her guard up."

"Leader—" Johnny said.

Levi raised his hand. "Shut up."

"Give me top security clearance, Levi." She glanced at Xander and Johnny. "And make me second-in-command. Dr. Rasmus is weak."

"He's top-notch. So is Logan," Levi said. "So was Ms. DeMone."

"And yet, here I am," she said. "I found Yaz. I eliminated Ms. DeMone. Logan brought me to the Underground. Logan brought me to the War Room. Rasmus allowed me to stay. Rasmus dialed your hotline. Who's stronger?"

Levi stood still, staring at Silver.

"Be a true leader, Levi. Security chief. Second-in-command. Top security clearance."

Levi looked at Xander. "Make it happen. Now."

CHAPTER 38

Love

K RYSTAL STOOD ALONE OUTSIDE THE door to the Depot. She stared silently into the fog through red-rimmed eyes. Across the compound, two Punk guards stopped for a smoke break under the yellow-orange mist of a sodium-vapor light. A burst of laughter from the pair reached her ears. *Can't even remember the last time I laughed.* She pulled her hands from her duster pockets and rubbed her face. She ran her fingers over the acid scar on her right cheek—her thoughts drifted to the night she was branded by the Punks.

A sliver of light crept out of the Depot. "Care for some company?" It was Ryker. His voice was somehow comforting.

Krystal folded her arms tightly across her chest. "Sure."

He let the door close slowly behind him and stood next to her. "I'm sorry about Curtis. No wonder we couldn't find him."

"Yeah."

Ryker looked down at the side of her face. "Are you still in love with him?"

"Love?" Krystal leaned back against the Depot wall. "A person can build a wall around their heart, you know? And your heart's there, safe behind that fortress you built. Then someone comes along and chips away at your heart's wall. One by one they remove the bricks and expose your heart. And you hate that someone sees it, because you know it's dark."

"That's not you, Krys," Ryker said.

Krystal nodded slowly. "Yeah, it's me." A tear fell. "Curtis lit a fire in my heart. He made it appear bright and shiny with that fire." She looked up at Ryker. "So you know what I did? I rebuilt the wall and snuffed out the fire."

"He made choices, Krys—"

"I did it. I forced him to become a Changer." She looked up as her eyes filled with tears. "God, I suck."

Ryker stood in front of her and cradled her face with both hands. "Do you still love him?"

"Don't you get it? No! I don't love him now!" She pushed his hands away. "That's why I suck. The wall's up. My heart is dark, safe again. There's no room for love in a world like this."

Ryker's arms hung at his sides. "Whatever happens in this world—any world—there's room for love."

She forced her hands back into the comfort of her pockets. "Not for me, there isn't."

He gazed past her at the Depot door. "You just need the right person to break down that wall again. Permanently, so it can't be rebuilt."

Krystal turned to the Depot door and grabbed the handle. "I need to see him. Now." She flung the door open and walked inside.

Ryker turned around, leaned against the wall and lit a cigarette.

The two Punk guards walked slowly up the sidewalk and stopped in front of him. "Evening, boss," the tall one said. "Everything okay?"

Ryker took a hit on his cigarette and exhaled slowly. "Yeah. Anybody got a hammer and chisel?"

JIMBO SWIVELED QUICKLY IN HIS chair at the communications console. "Hey. Krys." He jerked a thumb over his shoulder. "Dion's in his quarters with Fred and Thomas. He wants to see you and Ryk, ASAP."

"I got something to do first," she said, hurrying toward the side door.

"No can do, girl. He said as soon as you two get done with whatever you were doing, get to his quarters."

Krystal stopped and glared at Jimbo.

He held up both hands. "Don't shoot the messenger with those darts. Just get your butt in there."

Without a word, she pushed the side door open and stormed down the hallway toward Dion's quarters.

DION AND WINTER SAT ON stools, their backs to the bar. "I'm sure they'll be here soon," Dion said.

"Krystal will know what to do," Fred said. He settled onto the thick leather sofa and put his feet on the glass coffee table. "You know, Dion. She's the only one of us that's been a Bystander, a Changer and a Punk."

Thomas held up his water bottle. "Well, here's to Krystal." He took a sip and glanced at the door. "Wonder what she thinks of Curtis now?"

"I was in love once," Winter said.

"Once?" Fred said.

"Yeah…"

"So what happened?" Thomas said.

"Ah, it's a long story." She lifted her cell and checked the clock. "How much time you got?"

Dion glanced up when the door opened. "Hey, Krys."

Krystal stepped inside and let the door close behind her. She tipped her chin up at Dion and Winter. "I'd kind of hoped to talk to Curtis."

"We have some information, Krys," Dion said. "Felix contacted Fred and Thomas right after we put Curtis in lockup."

She unbuttoned her duster and slung it over the back of a barstool. "So what's up?"

"First of all," Fred said. "I'm certain Felix is in trouble."

"How?"

"It's Silver. From what he said, he let her get too close to him."

"Yeah," Thomas said. "She knows almost everything about his activities within the Underground. He had a monitor on the Changers' War Room. Levi reinstated her as security chief." He looked at Fred. "She's officially second-in-command now."

"Great," Krystal said. "What are his plans?"

Fred put his feet down and sat forward. "He didn't give us any other details about that. But he's preparing to leave the Underground."

Krystal began to pace slowly when Ryker walked in. "Did he say anything about the Changers' next move?"

Fred stood and walked over to the pool table. He leaned against the edge and folded his arms. "They're already moving. They're populating Tremayne and other major cities in this sector with a new breed of Chybrid. They call them SOUL Chybrids. The SOUL Chybrid is virtually indistinguishable from the average human."

"Populating?" Ryker said. "How, exactly?"

Thomas got up from the sofa and strode across the room to the bar. "Remember that subdivision in Tremayne where we saw Levi?" He leaned over the bar and tossed his empty water bottle into a recycle bin.

"Yep," Ryker said.

"The first phase of that tract is 500 homes. There's four phases planned in that subdivision alone. Plus, they've already begun construction on two other subdivisions and broken ground on a fourth."

"Holy shit," Dion said. "That's 8,000 new homes."

"Sure," Fred said. "And Tremayne City Hall is fast-tracking all the permits and removing any and all roadblocks."

"They gotta be embedded in the city government," Winter said.

Thomas hopped onto a barstool. "They are. The city is also building schools to accommodate the influx of residents."

"Damn." Dion lit a cigarette. "This is bigger than we ever imagined."

Fred shook his head. "It's bigger than you're imagining now. Those housing tracts are for the working class types. They've got plans for luxury subdivisions as well. But think about it, guys. That's a city of a little over a half million people. Just those 8,000 homes will each have families of four occupants."

"Some will have more," Thomas said. "Each home will have at least two adult SOUL Chybrids. Each pair of adults will be assigned a minimum of two Chybrid children of varying ages."

Krystal stopped pacing. "So what's the purpose, Fred? Chybrids aren't going to attack us from Tremayne. They don't need to absorb to extend their lives—"

"The SOUL Chybrids are vessels, containers. The Chybrids will absorb the residents of the city and deliver the nutrients to the Changers."

"They don't need to attack us," Thomas said. "The Bystanders already don't want Punks in their cities anymore."

"He's right," Ryker said. "It's only a matter of time before the Bystanders kick us out. If the Changers control the government, they'll come and go at will. From what you're saying, absorptions won't be an issue." He shrugged. "The government will find a way to make it all okay."

"If they even have to do that," Thomas said. "The Chybrid children will infiltrate the schools and influence the Bystander kids. Felix said they're going after the minds of the children first."

"We've got weapons," Winter said. "Why not just take them down?"

Dion snubbed his cigarette into an ashtray. "After the last attack, our force isn't half what it used to be. Besides, being *persona non grata* in Bystander territory isn't going to endear us or our fleet of BearCats to the residents when they get everything they need from the Changers."

Ryker agreed. "Sure. We protected them from the Changers. They don't need our protection now."

"It gets worse," Fred said. "This ground we're sitting on right now. It's inside the Perimeter. Inside the Wall. The Changers have a fierce army they didn't have to use last time out. They practically decimated you guys with the mechanical Chybrids. Their army stayed home. But that won't happen this time."

"*This* time?" Krystal said.

Fred shook his head again. "Yeah. The plan is to kick the Punks to the outside. Outside the Wall. Then they seal it up and everything inside the Perimeter fulfills their goal."

Butterflies roiled Krystal's gut. The hair on the back of her neck bristled. "Human breeding farms."

The room fell quiet as all heads turned to Krystal. She stood, feet apart, and folded her arms across her chest. Her eyes narrowed as her gaze flitted between the Punks and Rogue Changers.

Dion broke the silence. "What do you say, Krys?"

"I say we don't have much time. Honestly, at this point, we're gonna play catch up." She uncrossed her arms and addressed the group. "First, we clean up all loose ends, starting in Tremayne." She pointed at Dion. "Pull Red out of Tremayne. He's not quite a liability, but he's not our best. Have Jimbo get hold of the Three Amigos and Nico. I want one Amigo at each main checkpoint in Tremayne—east, west and south. Put Nico at the north. Put our best teams together to support them—ten Cats to back them up at each checkpoint. I'll follow up with instructions.

"Next. Ryker, Winter and Jimbo will team up with me. So get Lace in here. Put her on the comm console to replace Jim." She turned to Fred and Thomas. "You two call Felix and try to determine what he has left to be done in the Underground—and what his ETA is for exit." She glanced at her cell. "Everyone meet in the main conference room in the morning. Seven o'clock sharp."

"You got it, Krys," Dion said. "Anything else?"

"Yeah. We got a loose end in lockup that only I can deal with."

"Curtis," Ryker said.

"Right." She snatched her duster from the barstool and headed to the door. "And there won't be any voting or group decisions on this one. I'll handle it."

Krystal exited Dion's quarters and turned down the stark gray concrete walkway toward the Punks' lockup facility. Fog drifted over the sidewalk that led to the lockup, blurring the lights mounted atop poles that lined the path. She swung her duster off her shoulder. Without breaking stride, she slipped the long coat on and buttoned it, waist to chest.

Two guards stood casually at the door to the building. "Hey, Krystal," the lead guard said.

"Evening, guys," she said, stepping past them and twisting the doorknob. "Stand up straight and stay on alert."

The two Punks complied as the door closed behind Krystal.

It was warm inside the cinder block building. No one was stationed at the counter in the foyer. Krystal glanced up at the six flat-screen monitors behind the counter. One monitor showed the two guards outside at the entrance. Another screen displayed an interior hallway and a row of caged cells with barred doors. She noticed Curtis was in cell number one, with two guards stationed at the cell door. She walked through a door behind the counter and into a short hallway.

The guards parted without a word when she walked in. "You two can beat it," she said.

The pair moved around behind her to the exit. "Call if you need us. We'll be right outside the door."

Curtis stood quickly and walked three steps from the bare bench to the door of the cell. He grabbed the bars with both hands. "Babe!"

Krystal stood out of arm's reach in the center of the hallway. "It's time for you to go, Curtis."

His face dropped. "What are you talking about?"

"I'm not a Changer. And you are."

Curtis squinted and moved his face to the bars. "Wait—" He swallowed. "The Change isn't reversible. Levi told me—"

"He's a liar. It's reversible."

"But I became a Changer for you, babe. Because I love you."

Krystal shoved her hands into her pockets. "And I loved you. And I hated being a Changer. I knew we couldn't be together because Changers and Punks don't mix. But I fought for the Punks because you were a Punk and I could be on your side."

Curtis tried to be cheerful. "I know, babe. I saw you."

"You didn't see the half of it. When the Punks kicked me out, I was devastated. I hated the Changers for what they did to me and for what they do to the Bystanders. Then, I tried to kill Levi. But I even failed at that."

Curtis stood agape.

"Then, along came Felix. He saved me from those bastards. He reversed the Change." She quickly swiped a single tear before it dropped. "And I was so happy because I could be *me*."

"You said you didn't need me…"

"I was wrong. I loved you, Curtis, and I couldn't wait to tell you." She turned her head away. "But you're a Changer."

"Tell me now, babe." Tears welled in Curtis's eyes. "Tell me you love me."

She looked directly into his eyes. "You're in Levi's inner circle?"

"Yes."

"Then I don't love you, Curtis. You're not the man I once loved."

Curtis stood tall. His grip on the cell bars turned his knuckles white. He looked Krystal up and down. "So what? Kill me now?"

"For the love we once had, I'm not giving the kill order. I'm going to have you escorted outside the Wall."

Curtis's eyes hardened. "Just like that?"

Krystal glanced at the door down the hallway. "Guards!"

The two Punk guards entered quickly and stopped between Curtis and Krystal.

"Escort this man to the nearest walk-through. Put him outside the Wall and lock the gate behind him."

Krystal stepped back when the guards opened the door.

Curtis didn't resist as the guards guided him under both arms down the hallway.

She turned and gazed at his back, his disheveled homeless guy clothes and his Mohawk-free head as he walked away.

When the door closed she leaned against the wall and took a deep breath. As she exhaled, she slid down the wall and sat on the floor, knees up. She no longer tried to hold back the flood. Her head dropped into her hands. And she cried. Hard.

Ten minutes later she heard the muted sound of the heavy steel walk-through gate slam shut. She wiped her face with both hands and stood.

All four Punk guards were outside the door to the lockup building when she walked outside. "Heads up, guys," she said. "Gonna be cold again tonight." She buttoned up and strode confidently down the lighted walkway toward Punk headquarters. Her leather duster whipped randomly, furling and unfurling like a black flag.

CHAPTER 39

Exit

L EVI PRESSED A BUTTON ON the table in the conference room adjacent to the War Room on Level Ten in the Underground. "Hold all correspondence until further notice."

A soothing female voice sounded from the ceiling speaker. "*Yes, Leader.*"

He surveyed the Changers seated around the room. Twelve high-ranking military officials were seated at the table. Their midnight-blue uniforms were pressed. Every hair on their heads was in place, slicked back behind their ears. Levi smiled. "I trust everyone enjoyed a restful night's sleep."

Silver sat comfortably to Levi's right. "Dr. Rasmus, do we have an ETA for Mr. Dyer?"

Xander checked his cell. "Approximately an hour." He looked up at Silver. "I'd give him thirty minutes after arrival to freshen up before we see him."

"Sounds good to me," Silver said. "I would say that gives us time to view the unearthing of that dreadful earthworm, Dr. Yaz."

"Splendid idea, Ms. Long," Levi said. He nodded at Johnny. "Mr. Logan, please activate the appropriate surveillance monitors."

Johnny used a remote control to manipulate three curved screens on the wall above the corner wet bar. "You can see the security team in real time on Level Three right now. They are all wearing body cams. We can switch between any one of ten cameras to get the best view."

"So what are we looking at now?" Levi said.

"At this very moment, they are moving toward an innocuous door in Corridor 3-101. As you know, this is the corridor leading to the Executive Parking Receiving Room."

"I see the door," Levi said. "Wire-mesh protection?" He looked at Silver. "I find it hard to believe Dr. Yaz is behind that door, Ms. Long."

Silver smiled. "Wait for it, Leader."

Felix stood in front of the monitor walls in his quarters. He stared calmly at monitor one as he tightened a screw on a cell-phone-sized metal box. He watched the armed Changer guards use a set of bolt cutters to snap the lock across the wire-mesh door. He looked down momentarily at the metal box. A red LED displayed a set of numbers adjacent to a small touch pad. Felix tapped the touch pad, then looked back up at the monitor.

The guards had breached the door and were quickly moving single file down a darkened hallway. Lights on the guards' helmets shone on a solid unmarked door at the end of the tight corridor.

Felix picked up another metal box, identical to the first, from the table in front of him. He placed a panel over one side of the second box and tightened the screws on the panel into the box. The LED on the second box flashed identical numbers, matching the first. Felix repeated this routine—programming seven boxes—as he kept one eye on the monitor.

The guards didn't bother to try unlocking the door. They used a small explosive device to blow the handle off the door. It swung it open, revealing the tiny utility room. The lead guard stepped forward and opened the locker on the wall. He pulled a small electronic code scanner from his utility belt and placed it against the warranty sticker. Green LED numbers on the scanner flashed in seemingly random order.

Felix picked up one of the small metal boxes and walked across the room to his transportation cube. He stepped inside and placed the box on the back wall. He tapped a button on the box, and the LED numbers began to scroll, descending from three minutes in one-second increments. Before exiting the cube, he opened a panel on the opposite wall and manipulated a small keypad inside. He closed the panel and glanced at monitor wall one, closing the transportation cube's door behind him.

The lead guard stepped back from the locker and motioned to two guards behind him. "No code. Blow it."

The two guards moved to the back wall of the utility room and placed explosive devices around the locker, inside and out. "Clear!" All ten guards retreated quickly back down the narrow hallway.

Felix stepped up to the electronic console in front of the monitor walls and tapped the keyboard. He nodded once when he heard the transport cube hum to life behind him.

The explosive devices around the locker detonated, destroying the locker and exposing the tunnel. The Changer security guards moved down the hallway and into the tunnel. The metal passageway echoed the cadence of their boots as they ran two abreast toward the doctor's quarters.

Felix turned to his right and fastened the latches on a briefcase-sized box. He unplugged numerous tubes and wires from the box and let them drop to the floor. Inside the box was a DNA storage and data extraction device containing all the information currently in the Changers' possession. He must guard this device with his life.

The lead Changer guard in the tunnel held up a hand, stopping the others. He listened intently and turned to the guard next to him. "Do you hear that—"

The empty transportation cube rounded the curve in front of the guards. The speed of the cube allowed approximately point one second for the guards to react. The impact on the first four guards was swift and fatal. The speeding metal box pushed the four bodies into the other guards and swept them—arms and legs flailing—back into the utility room. When the cube came to a rest, only the three guards at the rear were able to stand on their own. They quickly felt for pulses and assessed the damage. Four dead. Three with broken limbs, one soaking the leg of his pants with blood from a large gash on his inner thigh.

The new lead guard's headset lay shattered on the floor. He yanked one from an injured guard's helmet. "Break, break, break! Security Base One, Security Base One. This is Unit 1008. Medical emergency at Level Three, Corridor 3-101, 100 yards south of Executive Parking Receiving. Also, send ten backup."

A calm male voice replied. *"10-4, Unit 1008. Medics and backup are en route."*

SILVER AND LEVI STOOD QUICKLY from the conference table in the War Room. Xander sat stunned. Johnny smiled inside and shook his head. The military brass at the table remained seated and did their best to maintain their composure.

"Long!" Levi shouted. "Why was the security team not advised of this?"

Silver placed her hands on her hips. "There's no way I could have known Yaz would do something like this. It does prove he has been located, Leader."

Levi whipped his head around to Silver. "How many of these weapons does he have?"

"That wasn't a weapon. That's a transportation module, like an elevator car. To my knowledge it's the only one." She looked at Xander. "Get word to the backup team that Yaz only had one of those weapons. All systems are go again."

Levi looked back at the monitors over the bar. "You'd best hope so. The reinforcements are on their way now."

THE THREE REMAINING GUARDS WAITED among the carnage. One guard applied pressure to the gaping wound on his partner's thigh.

The LED numbers on the steel box inside the transportation cube reached zero. The cube exploded, sending shards of hot metal, and body parts from the remaining guards, into Corridor 3-101.

The ten backup guards stopped their steady trot toward the entrance to the small side hallway. The lead guard spoke into his mic. "Security Base One, Security Base One. This is Unit 2001."

"Base One. Go ahead, 2001."

"We're going in. Send the coroner and a cleanup detail. Everyone here is dead."

"10-4, 2001."

FELIX EYED MONITOR WALL ONE. *I have given myself enough time.* He placed the briefcase next to the teleportation wall and turned back to the room. He sighed and walked to his bedroom entrance. He placed one of the six remaining metal boxes onto the doorframe, set the timer, then turned to the bar. He placed another box on one of the two barstools. When he was done placing the devices around the room, he walked toward the teleportation wall. He stopped momentarily and tapped the keyboard.

The ten Changer security guards rounded the final corner and trotted down the last metal hallway toward Felix's quarters.

Felix picked up the briefcase and turned around to face the room.

The ten guards were at the entrance. Two guards in the front of the group knelt and drew their weapons, pointed at Felix. The two in the next row remained standing and fixed their guns on the banished doctor.

Felix leaned backward.

The room flashed white simultaneously in six places.

Four shots from the Changer guards sounded as one.

The eminent Dr. Felix Yaz fell through the teleportation wall. The six white flashes merged, engulfing the room and blowing the glass ceiling out into the clear crisp desert sky.

CHAPTER 40

Payback Time

COMPARED TO THE THRONG THAT usually participated in Dion's group meetings in the Punks' main conference room, this crowd was small. But it was Krystal's meeting. With the Punk military fleet severely depleted by the latest battle with the Changers, she had less to work with and fewer tools at her disposal. She chose the best of the organization to step up. And she would demand more from the fewer.

"Okay, listen up," Krystal said. "Everyone in here is considered a first level commander. Each of you will have specific responsibilities, and you will all be expected to fulfill your duties for the sake of your teammates and to ensure our success against the Changers." She gazed at the team of Punks and Rogue Changers seated around the table. "There are no absolutes here. I expect everyone to help anyone where necessary." She glanced at Winter. "Example. If you have to deviate from your plan, no one thinks better on their feet than Winter. She has a good attitude, and she protects the Punks at all cost. Anyone gets lost in the field, if I'm not available, look to her."

Jimbo turned to Winter, and the two bumped fists.

"All right." Krystal glanced at the flat-screen monitor on the wall and manipulated the display by remote control. "Everyone check the screen." She clicked the remote control. "Here is our secondary line of commanders. All of us will need to rely on these teammates for support at some point."

The monitor displayed additional members of the Punks' organization and others, and a short bio below their pictures. The screen showed:

Will / Adam / Joey / Nico / Lace / Pops / Geezer / Drew / Sydney

Fred raised a hand. "I don't recognize two of them. Drew and Sydney."

"They're Bystanders. Two of the only Bystanders we trust. They're on our side and were instrumental in helping us in the last battle. Ryker and I will contact them." Her eyes scanned the players seated at the table. "I'm going to make the team assignments quick. I'll meet with each team and the support players individually, and we'll have additional group meetings only as necessary."

"Thanks, Krys," Jimbo said. "I hate meetings. I'd just rather get down to business and start kicking some Changer butt."

"Agreed," Krystal said. "Now, down to business. Teams are as follows. One, Ryker and me. Two, Jimbo and Winter. Three, Fred and Thomas."

"What about Dion?" Ryker said.

Krystal walked around the table and stood behind the crew. "Dion is the Punks' anchor. Always has been. Now look at the map and I'll show you Dion's role and why it's imperative he remain at headquarters for now." She tapped the remote control and pulled up a display of the North American territory. "The Punks' organization is divided in three sectors—east, central and west. You all know Dion is the west leader. For Fred and Thomas's information, there's never been any official vote, but Dion is the unofficial leader of the three."

"How'd that happen?" Thomas said.

Krystal pulled up pictures and bios of the three sector leaders and positioned them atop their areas of responsibility on the map. She enlarged the center image. "This is Rudie, leader in the central sector. Rudie called on Dion to help defuse an internal uprising among his own members. Several minor factions among the central sector teamed up with the Changers to take over munitions and auto manufacturing plants. Unfortunately, it was a severe Punk-on-Punk war that lasted several months. Courtesy of Dion, the west sector provided a thousand reinforcements to assist Rudie. Dion's cool head and leadership brought Rudie's people together, helped them rebuild and establish a sensible chain of command."

Krystal enlarged the image on the right side of the map. "This is Jasmine, east sector leader. But don't call her Jasmine. She goes by Jas. When the central Punks temporarily lost control of the factories, Jas's crew lost out on several shipments of arms and vehicles. Dion sent hundreds of well-maintained and highly modified replacement trucks while the fighting raged in the central sector. Jas had problems of her own dealing with not only the Changers but belligerent Bystanders who thought they didn't need Punk protection. The vehicles provided by the west came complete with drivers and weapons—just enough to tide over the east until we restored order in Rudie's sector. When the dust settled, Dion gifted all the loaners to Jas."

Krystal returned the image to size. She tossed the remote onto the conference table and crossed her arms.

Fred raised a hand. "So what's this all mean, Krys?"

She walked around the table and stood beneath the monitor, facing the group. "Dion. We lost over 3,000 troops and more than 1,200 vehicles. We're still mourning our dead three months later. The Changers are on the verge of overwhelming us with numbers like we've never seen before."

"That's a fact," Jimbo said.

"What's your proposal?" Dion said.

"Contact Rudie and Jas. Initially we'll need each of them to send 2,500 troops. Five thousand will get us set up. We need their best weapons and vehicles, and battle-hardened Punks."

Dion stood. "The Changers are moving in their territories, too."

"Not like they are here. The west is the Changers' headquarters in North America. This is where Levi lives. If they win here, the central and east won't stand a chance anyway."

"Sounds like a plan. I'll see what they say."

"I don't care *what they say*. Order them. They owe you. It's payback time."

CURTIS LEANED ON HIS HANDS against the wall inside the shower enclosure in his quarters. Warm water from eight shower heads caressed his body from multiple directions. He closed his eyes and relived the scene in Old Town. *DeMone handled that all wrong. What a disgrace. I'm glad that bitch is gone.* He thought about Johnny. *Not a great backup. But definitely knows how to follow orders and stay on task.* He stood up straight and pressed a button on a waterproof panel. Four shower heads closed off. The remaining four sprayed a soapy solution mixed with disinfectant. Sudsing up, his thoughts turned to Silver. *Now there's a woman who knows her stuff. Our leader fucked up trying to get rid of her. What a* leader.

Curtis closed his eyes again and pressed a hand against the waterproof control panel. He activated the full rinse control. He fought with everything he had to hold back the tears. He squeezed his eyes shut tighter and moved a thumb over the temperature control. The water grew hotter as his thumb rested against the button. Krystal's words reverberated in his mind. *I loved you, Curtis, and I couldn't wait to tell you.* Water from the eight shower heads scalded his skin. Curtis cried. *I don't love you, Curtis. You're not the man I once loved.* He felt the outer layer of his skin—paper-thin tufts—fluttering in the blistering spray. *For the love we once had, I'm not giving the kill order.* He pounded the panel, stopping the deluge.

The former Punk moved from the shower into the adjacent drying chamber and supplemented the activity with a small microfiber towel. Stepping into the bedroom, he stopped in front of a full-length mirror. Gray-white blistered remnants of skin speckled the red figure in the mirror. He lowered his head, chin to chest. A vibration began at the soles of his feet and rose quickly, engulfing his body. The mirror flexed. The repercussion shattered the glass shower enclosure—a million tiny beads of safety glass fell to the floor.

Curtis looked up. His body was restored to perfection, tight, muscular and toned. His eyes narrowed. The once bright blue irises faded to gray, then black. *You should have killed me, Krystal.*

A red strobe light over the door caught his attention. He stepped through his bedroom into the living area, stopped at a black glass-topped desk and tapped a touch pad. A monitor on the opposite wall lit up and displayed details of the red alert.

EVENT: MAJOR EXPLOSION
LOCATION: LEVEL 3 CORRIDOR 3-101
STATUS: AUTOMATIC SECURITY DOORS ACTIVATED
INGRESS/EGRESS: AUTHORIZED PERSONNEL ONLY
EXECUTIVE PARKING/RECEIVING TEMPORARILY CLOSED
CASUALTIES: 20 CONFIRMED EXPIRED / 1 MISSING
CAUSE: INTRUDER / FOREIGN ENTITY
DAMAGE ASSESSMENT: IN PROGRESS / FORENSIC DETAIL ON SITE

Curtis shook his head. "Thought you people had your act together." He tapped the panel to extinguish the monitor and went to his bedroom to dress. He selected a formfitting off-white jumpsuit with matching shirt and dress boots. He pulled on a coordinating waist-length tapered sport coat with dark blue buttons. He checked his look in a full-length mirror and smiled. *I kinda like the bald look.*

Two armed guards greeted Curtis as he exited his quarters and headed toward the elevator. The lead guard nodded. "Good day, sir."

"And good day to you, too," Curtis said.

The guards followed him to the elevator and stopped outside.

Curtis stepped into the elevator, pressed number ten and waved his palm over the security pad. When the doors opened on

Level Ten, he walked swiftly past the two guards and proceeded solo down the wide corridor. A newly installed body scanner flashed orange and back to blue as he passed through the door to the War Room. He bounded up the stairs to Levi's conference room.

Silver looked up as the door swished closed behind him. "It's about time, Dyer."

Levi glanced at Curtis. "Mr. Dyer. You are in time for the update on the security breach on Level Three."

"I checked the alert," Curtis said as he approached the conference table. "Something about an explosion?"

Johnny smiled. "It was awesome. Yaz blew the lid off this place."

Levi shot a look at Johnny. "I would hardly call it awesome." He looked at Curtis. "The traitor, Felix Yaz, has caused some minor damage on the third level. The damage is contained to a small area." He glanced at Silver. "Cleanup will be complete soon, correct, Ms. Long?"

Silver backed away from the table and pointed at the monitor above the bar. "Sure, Levi. You can call it minor. But we'll have crews working all day and into the night to restore basic functionality to that section."

Xander stood by the bar under the monitor. "Would you like a drink, Mr. Dyer?"

"Sure," Curtis said. "Pour me some mineral water."

Silver leaned back and crossed her arms. "My, my, Levi. What have we here? This man acts like he has not been taught the pecking order."

"Mr. Dyer is a valuable member of our team, Ms. Long. Please accept him as—"

"I don't need to be defended, sir," Curtis said. He stepped up to Silver and leaned into her ear. "Stay on my good side and I'll make sure you stay on the team."

Silver's eyes widened. "Why you little shit."

Levi held up both hands. "Enough. Rasmus, get this man his drink."

"Seriously, Levi?" Silver said. "You're having the head of development and technology step and fetch for this newbie?"

Johnny laughed.

Curtis took the glass of mineral water from Xander and turned to Silver. He held up the glass toward her and smiled. "Don't forget what I said."

"Dr. Rasmus," Levi said. "How long until all systems are 100 percent on Level Three?"

"The latest report estimates eight hours."

Johnny stepped up to Curtis and whispered into his ear. "What'd you say to her?"

Curtis sipped his water and tilted his head toward Johnny. "None of your fucking business."

"Whoa, dude." Johnny held up his hands. "No need to be hostile. So what's up?"

"This place is disorganized," Curtis said. "Something like this should never have happened."

It was Levi's turn to cross his arms. "Let's hear it, Dyer."

"Okay," Curtis said. "From what I gather, Ms. Long here located Dr. Yaz. Am I correct?"

"Yes. That is correct."

"And if Dr. Yaz is truly the genius I've heard he is, why were guards sent in to apprehend him with nothing more in the way of protection than Kevlar vests and helmets?"

Levi looked down at Silver. "That's a good question, Ms. Long."

"Excuse me, sir," Curtis said. "You would have to have approved of the operation, correct?"

Silver smiled and raised an eyebrow to Levi.

Levi uncrossed his arms and straightened up. "Don't try to put this on me, Ms. Long. You were fully in charge of this operation."

"And why is he here?" Curtis asked, pointing at Johnny. "I thought he was supposed to be in charge of assimilating the new SOUL Chybrid children in Tremayne."

Johnny's face fell. "Well, I was called to be here."

"That's my point," Curtis said. "You shouldn't have been called in. You need to get your butt to Tremayne and do your job. Your services aren't needed here. It's a waste of your talent."

It was Xander's turn to smile. He held his lowball glass of whiskey in the air. "Here's to Mr. Dyer."

"At least I did my job finding Yaz," Silver said.

"And you sacrificed twenty members of an elite security force attempting to apprehend him," Curtis said.

Silver snorted. "A small price."

Curtis took a long sip of his water and placed the glass on the table. He turned to Silver. "So where is Yaz now?"

Silver cleared her throat. Unwilling to admit she may have lost Dr. Yaz yet again, she opted to keep her knowledge of the teleportation device to herself. "Well—"

"We believe we will find his body in the rubble inside the room he destroyed," Levi said. "We are certain this was a suicide mission."

"Don't bet on it," Curtis said. "You've always underestimated the doctor."

CHAPTER 41

Bird to the Monster

JASPER SAT INSIDE THE SMALL guardhouse at Checkpoint One, one mile outside Punk headquarters. He snugged his black bandanna up over his nose and pulled his beanie down to his eyebrows.

His partner paced outside by the boom gate, occasionally warming himself at a smoldering burn barrel. "Hey, Jasper," he shouted. "You need a heat up?"

"Nah, I'm good. Sun's coming up. It'll break through the fog pretty quick."

A dilapidated mid-1970s pickup turned off the paved highway onto the damp dirt road leading to the first checkpoint into the Punks' compound. Rusted steel panels on the truck—precariously bonded to the vehicle's mostly intact frame—flapped in the breeze.

The dirt road was slick. The driver smiled as the pickup fish-tailed on acceleration. He reached down to the dash and turned the music volume up as high as it would go.

Jasper peered into the mist up the dirt road in front of the guardhouse. *What the hell?*

Headlights on the old pickup fluttered in the fog like two out-of-sync strobes. Jasper heard the roar of the engine when the driver pressed the accelerator. He watched the truck veer into the mud shoulder, then back to the road as the driver spun two full 360-degree donuts in the mud.

Jasper heard the music over the driver's laughter. *Promised Land? Guy must like Elvis*, he thought as the pickup skidded to a stop thirty yards from the guardhouse.

The music stopped when the driver turned off the motor and stepped out of the creaky truck.

Jasper motioned to his partner. "Heads up, dude. Foot traffic."

It was definitely a man. His silhouette sharpened from fuzzy gray to black as he moved through the murk toward Jasper. The man's gait was smooth and confident. His black wool fedora tilted left and forward. His matching black suit appeared clean and pressed.

Jasper exited the guardhouse, swung his AR-15 forward off his shoulder and approached the man. "Good day, sir."

The man stopped and bowed slightly. He removed his hat and held it belt-high in front of himself. "Hello. I am here to see Krystal."

Jasper took a step back and aimed his gun at the man's chest. "What's in the briefcase?"

The man looked down at the case in his left hand. "These are my personal possessions," he said, not looking up.

Jasper's partner approached the two slowly, his AR-15 also pointed at the stranger. "I'll get hold of Ace, right?"

"Yeah, do that," Jasper said, keeping his eyes on the man.

The man looked up at Jasper and smiled. "Please. Contact Krystal. Tell her Felix is here."

KRYSTAL STOOD, ARMS CROSSED, IN Fred and Thomas's room at Punk headquarters. "Looks like they issued you two the smallest guest quarters we've got." She surveyed the room. "A hot plate? You guys ever use that?"

"Nah," Thomas said. "But there's good food here. We've been pretty well taken care of." He glanced at Fred. "At least in terms of feeding us."

"I'm getting you guys top-notch accommodations," she said. "You can kiss this place goodbye." She looked at Fred. "You'll move into Curtis Dyer's old quarters."

"Thanks, Krys," Fred said.

"There's an empty suite next to that. You'll set up there, Thomas."

"Awesome," Thomas said. "We do appreciate it."

Krystal put her hands on her hips. "You two are important. We need everything you have inside those heads of yours—experience, intellect, technology."

Fred held a hand to his forehead.

"You okay, Fred?" she said.

He rubbed his head. "We're timing out. I hate to say it, but we're gonna need an absorption soon."

Krystal gazed at her two friends. "You don't need to absorb anymore. You both need what Felix gave me."

Fred looked up. "Do you realize the technology that's required for that?" He glanced at Thomas. "I mean, we brought all that information with us. But we don't have the means to set up any of the computers, the machinery, the whatever."

"We'll come up with a way," Krystal said. "Punks always do."

Thomas shook his head. "You couldn't devise anything that would match up to Felix."

Krystal smiled. "For starters we have you two. I'd say that's a good start."

"I like your enthusiasm," Fred said. "But—"

"Look," Krystal said. "Right now, this place we're living in is one huge black world. Every evil force you can think of is against us. We fight till the end, whatever the end is. I'd rather go down with all my friends standing beside me flipping off the monster, than give in to it."

Thomas couldn't help laughing. "I like that. So, we're literally flipping the bird to the Changers."

Krystal held out her fist. The three Rogue Changers exchanged bumps.

"Now, get your stuff packed up." She turned to leave. "I'll have your new quarters ready by the time you're done."

Fred rubbed his forehead again and frowned. "Hey, Krys."

She held the door open and looked back at Fred. He flipped her off.

Krystal smiled. "Bird to the monster."

LEVI AND HIS ELITE INNER circle wandered around inside the burned-out shell of a room that was once Dr. Felix Yaz's quarters.

Levi gazed up at the opening where the glass skylight had blown out. "How are we so close to the surface, Rasmus? We entered that dreadful little supply room on Level Three. It looks like we're at ground level."

Xander smiled. "The doctor truly is a thinker, Leader. You see, this hallway we entered is on a pressure-sensitive adjustable platform. It rose ever so gently as we walked through. From what I can tell, the floor throughout this tunnel senses when weight is applied—such as when someone is walking on it. As a person progresses through the tunnel, the floor rises. This tunnel is specifically programmed to rise from the third level to here, however high we are. The motion is so subtle, you hardly notice you are actually walking uphill." He turned around to the group. "Ingenious."

"What's so ingenious about it?" Johnny said.

"That should be obvious. When we discovered the entrance to this tunnel system was on Level Three, we all assumed Dr. Yaz's quarters were on Level Three." He gazed at the four other Changers. "Correct?"

"Yes," Silver said. "But you said Dr. Yaz is a thinker. From the looks of this place, surely you mean he *was* a thinker."

"You're delusional," Curtis said. "There are no bodies here."

"He is right," Levi said. "I see nothing but charred debris and twisted metal."

Silver scoffed. "And you think a human could have survived this destruction? His body probably disintegrated in the blast."

Xander folded his arms and looked at Silver. "I'm beginning to side with Curtis on this issue. I'm not convinced we should count the good doctor out just yet."

RYKER RECLINED ON THE LEATHER sofa in his quarters, his long legs stretched across his polished wood coffee table. He started at a knock on the door. "Come in!"

Dion stepped in and quietly closed the door behind him. "Hey."

"Hey, bro. Grab a beer and come check out the news. It's crazy."

The Punk leader stepped behind the small bar and grabbed a cold bottle from the refrigerator underneath.

"You're looking badass," Ryker said. "Special occasion?"

Dion's bleached-blond hair had been freshly cut. Numerous spiked tips had been dyed bright red. "Nah, just routine maintenance."

"So, only a vest?" Ryker said. "Isn't it cold outside?"

Dion shrugged and popped the top on his bottle. "Conditioning. You know."

Ryker sat up, boots to the floor. "All righty, bro. I know you better than that. What's up with you?" He motioned to a matching leather chair adjacent to the sofa.

Dion walked around the bar and sat down. He looked intently at Ryker over his bottle as he triple-chugged.

Ryker picked up the TV's remote control and turned the volume down. He looked at his friend. "Well?"

"We've been doing this a long time, Ryk," Dion said.

"Fighting Changers?"

Dion lit a cigarette. He clinked his lighter shut and placed it on top of the pack on the side table. "Yeah."

"I agree. So...what about it? It's been our lives ever since we were old enough to fix a cocktail."

Dion smiled and stared at the soundless images flickering across the flat-screen. "Yeah, those Molotovs. We were badass little guerrillas."

Ryker sucked a drink from his beer. "Thought we were. That's how it all started with you and me, bro."

"Sometimes I just get tired of the whole thing. Tired of this fucked-up world."

"I hear you. I feel like we haven't progressed in years and the Changers just keep on moving up in the world."

Dion blew a smoke ring. "Yep. It's like all we have is what we have, and it's the same as we've had for the last twenty years, you know?"

"Technology-wise?" Ryker said. "Yeah. But we've done surprisingly well in spite of all that." He leaned forward, elbows to knees. "Look, their tech power increases and we keep shutting them down, right?"

"I guess that brings me to the real reason I'm here." Dion took another swig of his beer. "Krystal."

"What about her?"

"Think about it, Ryk. She brought some high-tech weapons against our high-tech enemy. Without her, Punks were done."

Ryker sat back and rested a boot on his knee. "Right. And your point?"

Dion raised his voice. "My point is, Krystal has all the contacts now. She's connected to some very badass people." He smashed his cigarette butt into an ashtray. "High-tech people."

"Contacts are one thing," Ryker said. "We still have the personnel and ingenuity."

Dion stared into the darkened hallway leading to Ryker's bedroom. "I kind of feel like she's taking over."

Ryker gazed at his best friend. He lit a cigarette. "You gave her authority, bro. She's proving she's a leader. I think she's doing a good job so far."

"She was literally giving *me* orders, right?"

"Yeah, but she's making the right moves, Dion," Ryker said. "What would you have done? Did you have a plan? Did you even know what the Changers were doing? *Could* you have known without Krystal?"

Dion leaned forward and rubbed his palms into his eyes. "You're right. With me in charge we were sitting ducks once again."

Static crackled from the ceiling speaker. "*Hey, Ryk. Ace here. Do you copy?*"

Ryker pressed a button on the side table. "Go ahead, Ace."

"*Yeah, Ryk. You seen Dion? He's not in his quarters.*"

Dion tipped his chin up to Ryker. "Yeah, he's here with me. What's up?"

"*Yeah. Jasper called from the checkpoint. Some guy walked up that's asking for Krystal. Says he's Felix.*"

The two Punk leaders stood quickly.

"Copy that, Ace," Ryker said. "Have you notified Krystal?"

"*That's a 10-4, Ryk. She grabbed Jimbo and Winter and headed out. She wouldn't wait for me to notify Dion.*"

Ryker looked at Dion. "We're on our way to the Depot. Sit tight."

CHAPTER 42

Earth Movers

BY EARLY AFTERNOON, THE FOG had lifted in and around Tremayne. Activity on the west side had increased to an uncomfortable level. Two-room temporary housing units filled the once-empty vacant lots in Old Town. The portability of the buildings facilitated ease of setup and breakdown. Signs on the small structures advertised free housing for the homeless. All one had to do was sign their name and catch the next shuttle to the designated area on the outskirts of Old Town. The lines of homeless families, couples and individuals had become so numerous it was hard to distinguish between those waiting to sign up for their new homes and others awaiting their shuttle to the outskirts.

Will peered through his infrared biocular from a standing position through the center hatch in his BearCat. He attempted to count the number of vehicles headed toward him at Tremayne's west checkpoint. *Gotta be a hundred trucks...at least.* He flipped his headset's mic down. "Nico, Nico. It's Will. Do you copy?"

"Gotcha, Will. It's Nico. Go ahead."

"I'm not really sure why, but there's about a hundred or so trucks rolling this way."

"Copy that, Will. What kind of trucks?"

"Big ones. Looks like they've got those huge earth movers on the back."

"*10-4, Will. The Changers are probably setting up to clear some more land for another housing area.*"

"I'm sure of that, bro. But there's enough machinery coming to scrape land for *ten* new subdivisions."

"*They're definitely stepping up the pace.*"

"I'm heading over there. We gotta stop this. At least slow it down."

"*10-4. Leave six Cats at the checkpoint. It shouldn't take more than four of you. Keep me apprised. I'll contact headquarters.*"

RYKER WALKED OVER TO THE communications console in the Depot and patted Ace on the shoulder. "Move over, buddy."

Dion caught Ace's attention. "Have you heard back yet?"

"Yeah. Jimbo radioed in a minute ago. Said they were just pulling up to the gate."

Ryker's impatience got to him. He tapped the talk button. "Hey, Krys. It's Ryker. Do you copy?"

The response was immediate. "*Stand by, Ryk.*"

Ryker sat back in the command chair and looked at Dion. "Guess we finally get to meet Felix."

"Yeah," Dion said. "Six months ago if you'd told me we'd willingly allow Changers to hole up here, I'd have laughed."

The radio cracked. "*Copy, Ryk? Krystal. It's Dr. Yaz, all right. We're 10-19.*"

"10-4, Krys. Meet us in the Depot."

"*Break, break. Nico here. Ryker, you got the console now?*"

Ryker stepped away to make room for Ace.

"Ace here, Nico. What's up?"

"*Not quite sure yet. Just advising you there's some activity on the west side. A shit-ton of big trucks rolling in with earth movers.*"

Ryker looked at Dion. "More housing tracts already?"

"Copy that, Nico," Ace said. "What's your move?"

"*Will's headed that way. We're gonna try a little blockade. I'll need some direction, though.*"

"Stand by, Nico."

TECHNICIANS MANNED EVERY COMPUTER TERMINAL in the War Room at Changers headquarters. Levi, Silver, Curtis, Johnny and Xander stood dead center viewing a flat-screen on one wall. The convoy of earth movers displayed on the monitor extended more than two miles along the eastbound rural highway.

Levi barked orders to the technician at the control console. "What's that activity?" He pointed at the monitor. "Five miles from the city limit."

The technician glanced at his monitor. He used two touch pads to obtain the proper coordinates and zoom the camera. "Five foreign vehicles, sir."

"Status?" Levi said.

"Hostile, sir."

Silver snorted. "Punks."

"Negotiation time, Leader?" Xander said.

Levi smiled and crossed his arms. "Let me think about this."

Curtis looked at Levi. "There's nothing to think about. Blow through the blockade."

Johnny smiled and gently patted Curtis' shoulder. "I like your style, bud."

The technician pressed a button on the console. "Convoy Unit One, this is Control One. Do you copy?"

"*Control One. Convoy Unit One. Go ahead.*"

"Unit One, you have a hostile blockade in your path. Approximately two miles ahead. Stand by for orders." The technician sat straight and stared at his screen.

Curtis looked at the huge monitor. He recognized the five BearCats. He looked back at Levi.

Levi stroked his chin and gazed at the big screen.

Curtis leaned over the technician and pressed the talk button. "Convoy Unit One. Continue to your destination. Ram the blockade."

WILL HAD PARKED HIS BEARCAT in the center of the highway facing the convoy of earth movers. One BearCat was stationed on either side of him. Two additional trucks filled the gaps behind the three.

He squinted into the sun, pulled his goggles down off his helmet and flipped his mic down. "They're coming in hot, guys."

The driver in Unit Two responded. "*Copy that, Will. I got 'em clocked at about sixty MPH. We activated the highway warning sign at three clicks out. Hope they can read.*"

"*First ten trucks already passed that sign,*" Unit Three said.

"*Unit One, Will. Unit Four here. We're backing out, 10-4?*"

Will cranked the ignition on his vehicle. "All units, pull out! All units pull out!"

His eyes were glued to his right-hand side-view mirror. *Come on. Come on, come on!* He jammed the gearshift into reverse and pressed the accelerator to the floor. The rear of his BearCat bumped into the front of Unit Five. *Move, move, move!* He heard the sound of metal on metal—his rear bumper on Unit Five's front bumper—and smelled the burning rubber from his tires. He never saw the first truck in the convoy when it smashed into his vehicle.

The screech of steel tearing steel pierced through the insulation on Will's helmet and past his headset. The wide bumper on the eighteen-wheeler was constructed like a cowcatcher on a freight train. BearCat Units One and Two were tossed aside. The two Punk trucks spun complete 360s and barrel-rolled before coming to a rest on their sides on the dirt shoulders of the highway.

SILVER TOSSED HER TABLET ON a table adjacent to the main control console. "Well, that settles that, I guess."

Levi's ire rose. "I did not give that command!"

Johnny snickered and jabbed an elbow at Curtis.

"Very ballsy, Dyer," Xander said. "The cute little blockade set up by the Punks did not delay our project at all." He glanced at his watch, then looked at Levi. "Not even one second."

"You have damaged our ability to negotiate with the enemy, Dyer," Levi said.

Curtis crossed his arms. "The Punks are weak. They have no room to negotiate."

Silver gazed at the large monitor on the wall. She watched the convoy of heavy vehicles streaming down the two-lane highway toward Tremayne. "He has a point, Leader."

Curtis turned to leave. "I'm going to get something to eat. Anyone join me?"

Johnny glanced quickly at Levi before following Curtis.

Silver and Xander stood on either side of Levi and watched the two as they walked away.

Levi raised a finger toward the door. "I did not give that command!"

The door to the War Room swished open. "That's a fact. But you should have," Curtis said as he and Johnny stepped out into the corridor.

CHAPTER 43

More Than Friends

Ace leaned forward at the communications console in the Depot. "Nico, buddy. Ace here. You copy?"

"*Gotcha, Ace.*"

"Sorry about the delay. What's the status there?"

"*Blockade didn't work. Those semis blew right through. From what I can tell, we got injuries but everybody's gonna live.*"

"Holy hell, Nico."

"*Yeah. Ambulances headed that way to haul off Will and three others. Unit One and Two trucks are pretty much totaled.*"

"Glad to know everyone's alive. We'll get five replacement Cats headed your way. Send Will's Units Three, Four and Five back to headquarters. We'll roll tows for Units One and Two."

"*10-4, Ace. But don't send just anyone to replace Will. This place has become kinetic.*"

"Got that covered, Nico. I'll roll Lace with the replacements. She can cover that west side."

"*All good, Ace. Just know things are getting crazy here. I've never seen this many people in this city before. We got a plan yet?*"

"We got a plan. Hang in there."

"*10-4.*"

Dion glanced at his cell. "Good job, Ace. I have a conference call in five with Rudie and Jas. When Krystal gets here with Felix, tell her I'll catch up when I'm done."

"You got it, boss."

Dion headed for the Depot's side door. He snatched his leather jacket off a nearby barstool and turned to Ace. "Send Jimbo and Winter back to Tremayne to check on Will and his crew. Any of them healthy enough, bring 'em back here. They'll recuperate a lot faster."

Ryker stood outside the Depot in the Punks' compound. Black shadows faded to gray and blended with the mostly concrete structures when the sun dropped below the horizon.

Just as everything seemed to be drying up, the weather forecast had replaced the fog with rain. He peered into the gray, searching for headlights. As anxious as he was to meet Felix, he found it impossible to quell the battle that was raging between his heart and mind. Butterflies fluttered in his gut when he heard the approaching BearCat. *Krystal's coming.*

He glanced up at the darkening sky, knowing his heart was winning the battle.

Dion sat alone on a barstool in his quarters and swirled a bottle of beer in the condensation on the bar top. He snuffed a cigarette out in an ashtray and immediately lit another before dialing a series of numbers into his cell. He tapped a nearby remote control to transfer the audio to the ceiling speaker.

The call connected to two recipients simultaneously.

"Yo, bro!" It was Rudie. "*Long time, my friend!*"

"*Well, if it isn't my favorite scab rocket and Dion,*" Jas said.

"*I'll scab your rocket,* Jazzie," Rudie said.

Jas chuckled. "*So what brings on a conference call, Dion? What's it been, about six months?*"

Dion managed a weak smile. "First, I've gotta ask you two a question. How's everything going in your territories? In general."

"*Pretty smooth sailing since you guys whooped the Chybrids,*" Jas said. "*Seems the Changers kinda let up on us for a while. We got a little mild activity now, but nothing we can't handle.*"

Rudie agreed. "*Yep. You guys put up such a ruckus, those mothers pulled forces from here and sent 'em west. I gotta agree with Jas, though, as much as it pains me. Changers are steppin' it up lately.*"

Dion took a drag on his cigarette and followed it with a hefty swig of beer.

"*You're awfully quiet, Dion,*" Jas said.

Rudie agreed. "*Yeah. 'Sup, dude?*"

"They're at it again. The Changers. We're swamped. They're overwhelming us."

"*Whoa,*" Jas said. "*What's happening?*"

"Long story short?" Dion said. "Their newest project consists of thousands of humanoids. They're building new subdivisions inside the Perimeter—mostly in Tremayne. Their plan is to populate the big cities with these things and have them assimilate with the Bystanders. We know of one incident where they actually replaced a Bystander with one of these humanoids. They call them SOUL Chybrids."

"*Holy shit, bro,*" Rudie said. "*Changers tried that in one place here. One subdivision. We chased 'em out, though.*"

"That's it?" Dion said. "They're out now?"

Rudie cleared his throat. "*Well, not exactly. We got 'em out of the city, but they set up in a county area. Outside our Perimeter. We let it go since we don't have jurisdiction there.*"

"*You need to go out and hit 'em in the county,*" Jas said. "*We don't let those suckers breathe in the east. Give 'em an inch, you know?*"

Dion walked around the bar and grabbed another beer from the fridge. "Jas is right. But I've gotta tell you two, we have bigger problems here. And I need your help."

"*Anything, Dion.*" Jas sad. "*You know that.*"

"*But they're already movin' here,*" Rudie said. "*I don't know what we could do for you.*"

Dion took a swig. "I need you each to send 2,500 armed vehicles, with troops."

"*No can do, pal,*" Rudie said. "*You just heard we got the same thing going on here.*"

"*That's a lot of force, Dion,*" Jas said. "*We still have to defend our territories.*"

Dion looked up at the ceiling speaker. "If the Changers are successful here, neither of you will have any territory to defend."

The ceiling speaker was silent. Dion checked his cell on the bar top—the call was still connected.

"Guys?"

"*And you'll be commanding our troops?*" Jas said.

"No, I—"

"*Ryker?*"

"Not Ryker either. We have a new addition. It's a long story, but I'm asking you two to trust me."

Jas relented. She sighed. "*Good enough for me. Dion's our brother, Rudie. He's never steered us wrong.*"

"*Okay,*" Rudie said. "*We already owe you, my friend. How soon you need this?*"

"Yesterday."

Ryker greeted Krystal as she stepped out of Jimbo's Bear-Cat. "Hey, Krys."

Jimbo and Winter rounded the truck from the back. "Hey, bro," Jimbo said. "Felix is quite a character." He glanced over his shoulder. "Much better-looking than I had imagined, too."

"I'll grab the gear," Winter said. "Rain tonight."

"Oh, hey," Ryker said. "We got four guys at the medical center. Dion wants you two to head back to Tremayne and do a quick look-see. If they're good, bring all four back here."

Winter's shoulders slumped. "Seriously? Tonight?"

"Yeah. One of them is Will."

Winter sighed and looked at Jimbo. "Let's grab some coffee before we head back out."

"Sounds like a plan, sis," Jimbo said.

Felix meandered around the truck and stood next to Krystal.

He nodded at Ryker. "Hello. I recognize your voice as Ryker." He extended his hand. "I am Dr. Felix Yaz."

"Nice to meet you, Felix. We've all been anxious."

Krystal turned to Felix. "Before you get settled, I'd like you to see Fred and Thomas." She glanced at Ryker, then lowered her voice. "They're both pretty close to timing out. If there's anything you can do—"

"Did you notice that Silver brought a small titanium container with her when she arrived here?" Felix said.

Krystal looked at Ryker. "When she first got here, right?"

"That's right," Ryker said. "When she left for Tremayne that night, I'm pretty sure she left everything here." He thumbed over his shoulder. "It's probably still in her quarters."

"Splendid," Felix said. "I will need that for our friends, Fred and Thomas."

Ryker turned and headed toward the Depot. "Right this way."

Fred dozed peacefully in his bedroom inside his new quarters. He had set the music volume on the ceiling speakers to a whisper.

Thomas sat in Fred's recliner in the living room, channel surfing the news networks. *Dammit. Can't get away from these stupid Changers adoption commercials. What ever happened to that stupid lottery?* He clicked the remote control again and stopped on a twenty-four-hour weather channel. *Rain. Whoop de doodle.* A quiet knock on the door pulled him out of his funk. He tossed the remote onto the coffee table and stretched his arms above his head. "C'mon in."

Krystal and Felix entered and closed the door behind them.

"Hey," she said. "How's Fred?"

Thomas motioned to the bedroom. "He's napping. Not feeling too well." He glanced past Krystal. "Who's this?"

Krystal smiled. "Oh! Let me introduce you." She turned to Felix.

"Wait just a minute," Felix said. He turned his back to Thomas and faced the door. His loose-fitting suit hid the vibration when he changed back to his normal appearance.

When the doctor turned to face Thomas, he smiled. "Thomas, my dear, dear friend." He hurried across the room and the two embraced. "How good it is to see you again!"

Thomas pushed back and held onto his friend's shoulders. "I never thought I'd live to see this day. Dr. Felix Yaz outside the Underground. How have you been?"

"Oh, I am fine. But never mind that. I have heard Fred is not doing so well." He raised his eyebrows. "May I see him?"

"Oh, yes," Thomas said. "He's in here."

The three walked quietly into the bedroom. Felix bent over his prone friend and felt his forehead. "Very clammy." He placed an ear to Fred's chest. "Hmm. Oh, dear." He stood up and looked at Krystal. "I do hope Ryker is successful in finding the titanium case."

Felix turned back to Fred and gently prodded the Rogue Changer's shoulder. "Fred? Can you hear me?"

Fred stirred, moaning ever so slightly.

Thomas started at a loud double rap on the door. He hurried into the living room. It was Ryker.

"Good, you found it," Thomas said. "C'mon."

The two walked into the bedroom, and Ryker handed the titanium box to Felix.

The doctor set the container on the nightstand and tapped the combination into the keypad. "Roll up his sleeve."

Krystal slid Fred's short sleeve up his arm and over his shoulder. She snatched a sterilizing pad from the box and swiped it over his skin.

Felix removed a battery-powered injector and selected a cartridge containing a clear liquid. He pushed the cartridge firmly into the injector and pressed the unit against Fred's deltoid. The injector clicked, releasing the doctor's serum.

"Now what?" Krystal said.

Felix sat on the bed at Fred's feet. He looked up at Thomas.

"You must take an injection as well, my friend. I'm sure you are close."

Thomas rolled up his sleeve. "Hit me."

The doctor repeated the procedure on Thomas, then replaced the utensils into the case. "And now, you both must rest." He glanced at Krystal and Ryker. "I will remain here until they have sufficiently recovered."

Krystal looked at Ryker. "I guess that's our cue to leave."

"Keep us apprised, Doc," Ryker said as the two turned to leave.

KRYSTAL AND RYKER WALKED ABREAST down the narrow concrete corridor between the Punk housing units.

"I'm dog-hungry," Ryker said. "Feel like getting something to eat?"

Krystal looked up at him. "Yeah, I do." Her face softened, and she managed a smile. "It's been a long day already."

When they reached the dining room, Ryker held the door open. "Something smells good."

The pair shrugged off their dusters and found two empty pegs on the wall among a jumbled assortment of leather and denim. They turned to face the noisy room. Punks of every rank, shape, size and color filled most of the tables. The lively atmosphere epitomized the chemistry and sense of belonging cultivated by Dion during his tenure as the Punks' leader.

"Table for two in the corner there," Ryker said.

"Let's do it."

Ryker raised a hand and caught the attention of one of the short order cooks behind the counter. He pointed to the corner table as he and Krystal made their way across the room.

"I don't need a menu today," Krystal said as the two seated themselves.

"Cheeseburger and onion rings?" Ryker said.

Krystal's eyes sparkled as she looked at him. "Is there anything else?"

Ryker glanced up at the cook behind the counter.

The man looked at Ryker and used sign language. *What do you want?*

Ryker signed back across the room. *Two cheeseburgers, two onion rings, two ice waters.*

The cook returned two thumbs-up.

"I didn't know you signed," Krystal said. "How cool is that?"

He smiled. "I'm sure there's a lot we don't know about each other, Krys." He gazed at her over the table. "Tell me something I don't know about you."

Krystal leaned her chair back on two legs and hung her arms to the sides. "Hmm. Did you know I once shot a bullet through Silver's hand with a 9mm pistol?"

Ryker raised an eyebrow. "Interesting. So what brought that on?"

"It was a ricochet off Levi's head."

"Wow," Ryker said, both eyebrows now raised. "So the bullet you fired hit Levi's head first? Holy cow."

"Yeah. It's a long story. But I hate that guy so much I tried to kill him." Krystal smiled. "I guess you could say Silver was collateral damage." She chuckled. "I never really liked her anyway."

Ryker shook his head. "Gutsy move. It's a wonder anyone could even get close enough to that bastard to kill him."

She leaned back to the table. "I got lucky. You'd have to be in his inner circle to get close enough. He's always surrounded by heavy security."

"So what else?" Ryker said.

"What do you mean, 'what else'?"

Ryker placed his elbows on the table and rested his chin in his hands. "What else is in that head of yours? What's in that heart?"

She folded her arms across her chest. "Let's leave my heart out of it."

"I'm not letting you off that easy. You can't hide your heart forever."

Krystal looked toward the kitchen. Her ears burned and she knew she was blushing. "When are those burgers getting here?"

Ryker reached across the table and used a finger on her chin to turn her face toward him.

She didn't resist. She looked into his eyes. *Yeah, okay. You're handsome, rugged, kind and loyal. I could fall for you. Damn you, Ryker.*

"Don't hide your heart from me, Krys."

Krystal snapped out of her trance when the cook arrived. "Two cheeseburgers and onion rings, my friends! Sorry you had to wait so long." He surveyed the room. "You can see how busy it is today."

"Thanks a lot," Ryker said. He glanced at Krystal. "The best things in life are worth waiting for."

"That they are, Ryk," the cook said. "I'll have your waters sent over. Enjoy."

CHAPTER 44

Outside the Box

THE MAÎTRE D' IN THE executive dining room on Level Seven greeted Curtis and Johnny with a bow. "Of course, I have a table reserved and ready for you. Right this way."

The two followed the portly man toward the center of the room.

Johnny grabbed the back of a chair when the man stopped at a large table for two. He sat down and looked up at Curtis.

Curtis remained standing next to the maître d'. He scanned the restaurant. "We'll take a table in the corner. I want my back to the wall."

Their host smiled and bowed again. "Apologies, sir. There are no corner tables available at this time. Rest assured you will get premium service from here and any other table of your choice."

Curtis tipped his chin up toward an empty corner table. "We'll take that one."

Johnny glanced over his shoulder, then looked up at Curtis. He smiled. "That's reserved for Levi, dude." He pulled the chair next to him out from under the table. "Have a seat, man. I'm hungry."

Curtis looked down at the man again. "We'll take that one."

He tapped Johnny's shoulder as he moved around the back of his chair. "Let's go."

The maître d' hurried after Curtis. "This is highly unusual, sir. If our leader comes to dine—"

"Then I'll deal with our leader," Curtis said as he selected the chair in the corner. He seated himself and folded his hands on the table. "Now, bring me two large waffles and a side of bacon."

Johnny walked up to the table and chuckled. "They stopped serving breakfast hours ago. Dinner menu is excellent, though," he said as he sat down opposite Curtis.

Curtis remained silent, his eyes fixed on the maître d'.

The man bowed his head once. "Coming right up, sir." He looked at Johnny. "The usual dinner, sir?"

Johnny couldn't help grinning as he placed his napkin in his lap. "You know, I think I'll have some waffles and bacon as well."

Curtis surveyed the luxurious dining area. The room was crowded. Guests occupied most of the tables. Waiters busily brought trays with drinks and pushed rolling carts with entrees.

He nodded toward the crowd. "There's a lot of nosy people here that seem to be taking an interest in us."

"We're sitting at Levi's table *without* Levi. What do you expect?"

Curtis raised a hand to a passing waiter. "A couple of ice waters and coffee? I take mine black, no sweetener."

The waiter nodded acknowledgment and disappeared into the bustle of patrons and servers.

"You order the same thing more than once and they'll make that your usual," Johnny said.

Curtis was disinterested. "So what's the deal with Levi not being able to make a decision?"

Johnny lifted an eyebrow. "Huh?"

"Back in the War Room. Was there actually any other choice but to ram that convoy through the Punks' vehicles?"

"Oh, that," Johnny said. "Well, it kinda seemed like he maybe wanted to talk to them. You know, negotiate."

"Seriously, Logan?" Curtis placed his napkin in his lap as the drinks arrived.

The waiter dropped two glasses of ice water on the table in front of the pair.

Johnny's ice water had a lemon wedge attached to the rim. His coffee was light brown and frothy. It had obviously been blended with additives. He held up the tall glass toward Curtis. "See? The usual."

Curtis grabbed the waiter's wrist and locked eyes with him. "See this order? Make it my usual."

The waiter nodded and passed his tablet over Curtis's right hand. "You're in the system now, sir."

Curtis sipped his coffee and looked at Johnny. "See? It doesn't take two orders to register my *usual*."

Johnny was impressed. "Never thought about that."

"I'm not surprised," Curtis said. "As I was saying, with regard to that convoy and the blockade, there was no choice. Levi seriously considered negotiating with an enemy that has absolutely no leverage. That's a sign of weakness."

Johnny inhaled deeply when the waiter arrived with a rolling cart containing the waffles and bacon. "Damn, that smells good!" He looked up at Curtis. "I kinda like eating outside the box like this. Waffles and bacon at dinnertime!"

"Get used to it," Curtis said. "Levi hasn't thought outside the box in years. The Punks should have been wiped out a long time ago."

Johnny swiped a chunk of margarine and slapped it onto one of his waffles. "Whadda you mean?"

"What I mean is…" Curtis bit off half a bacon slice. "…the only thing standing in the way of the Changers' victory, is the Changers' leader."

Johnny stopped spreading the margarine and looked up at Curtis. He leaned forward and lowered his voice. "Are you saying what I think you are?"

Curtis shrugged and sliced his waffle into strips. "Levi's a liability. He's not a true leader."

Johnny glanced over his shoulder. Two busboys busied themselves clearing a table. "But he's *our* leader."

"How long has he been the Changers' leader, John?" Curtis hand-dipped a waffle slice into the container of maple syrup. He looked up at Johnny. The syrup dripped off the waffle into the container. "And how long is everyone here going to continue to accept his pomposity and indecisiveness?"

Johnny furrowed his brow, bewildered. His eyes darted around the table at nothing in particular. "Well…"

"Anyone in Levi's inner circle could lead the Changers." Curtis bit the end off the waffle slice and pointed it at Johnny. "You could."

"Hmm." Johnny sat up straight and glanced around the room. "I don't know, man. Someone would have to bump him off, you know?"

"And whoever is capable of pulling that off would become the Changers' leader, right?"

Johnny smiled. "Yeah, I suppose that'd be right."

Curtis sipped his coffee. "When we're done eating, I want to visit SOUL Central where we're making the new Chybrids."

Johnny shrugged. "Sure, okay. But why?"

"I want you to see all the technology Levi has at his disposal. Then you'll see why I think we're wasting it by having him as our leader."

"Think we should mention any of this to Silver or Xander?" Johnny said.

"I'm just thinking out loud," Curtis said. He held up his water glass. "Between friends, right? In my opinion, both of them have what it takes to be a better leader than Levi. They both know how to make a snap decision under pressure." He swigged his water and placed the glass on the table. "Damn, you saw Silver in Tremayne when she took out Ms. DeMone, right?"

"Aw, that was awesome," Johnny said, smiling.

Curtis winked. "Then you get my point."

FRED STOOD BEHIND THE WET bar in his quarters at Punk headquarters. "I don't know what was in that injection, Felix, but I feel like I'm running at 110 percent right now."

"I agree," Thomas said. "I was feeling a little down. I guess I didn't realize how close I was to timing out. I feel like I'm firing on all cylinders, only turbocharged."

Felix smiled. "Splendid." He held up a finger. "Just remember, the serum you received is not a replacement for absorption. The effect is only temporary. You will both feel worse than before in thirty days. Forty-five at best."

Fred opened three bottles of mineral water and walked around to the front of the bar. "So absorbing lives is still in the picture for our immediate futures?"

"Unfortunately, yes," Felix said. "However, as you both have witnessed, a reversal of the Change *is* possible."

Thomas smiled. "Then let's do it."

"That is not an easy proposition." Felix shook his head slowly. "I destroyed all the technology and equipment I used on Krystal when I left the Underground."

"But we have all that information," Fred said. "Thomas and I brought all your plans and calculations and formulas with us when *we* left."

"Yes," Felix said. "And I, too, have the information in my head. The unfortunate situation is that in order to perform the procedure on anyone else, we will need to reconstruct my lab." He sipped his water bottle. "And I am not sure that is possible outside the Underground."

Fred hoisted himself onto a barstool and rested his elbows on the bar behind him. "You know, this is a stretch, but there may be a possibility."

"Are you thinking about Pops and Geezer?" Thomas said.

"Well, yes. Krystal said the Hangar is well equipped and they are geniuses when it comes to fashioning something from nothing."

"From *nothing*?" Thomas said. "A figure of speech, right?"

"Of course," Fred said. "But we have to start somewhere. What do you think, Felix?"

"I would like to meet these two geniuses, Pops and Geezer. I would like to tour their facility." Felix stroked his chin. "We will also require some powerful computers and someone with the ability to both program and operate them."

Thomas and Fred locked eyes. "Drew and Sydney?" Thomas said.

"Exactly what I was thinking," Fred said. "I'll arrange it with Krystal."

LACE IGNORED THE SIGNAL WHEN the semitruck driver in front of her flashed his brights. "I'm in no mood for your bullshit, Changers."

The big Punk riding shotgun chuckled. "Glad Dion gave us this assignment, boss." He pounded a fist into his hand. "I really feel like knocking out some Changers."

"Damn, Cassius," Lace said. "Look how they're totally tearing up this town." She guided her BearCat between two trucks into a forty-acre swath of land that had been cordoned off by the Changers. "How many houses do these assholes need, anyway?"

"Too many," the big Punk said.

Lace steered the truck past a dozen Changer construction workers sitting in a group. Conventional tin lunch boxes rested in various stages of disarray around the men. "Greetings, citizens," one of them said to the pair.

Cassius leaned out the window and held up his middle finger. "Greet this, fuckwad." He held his pose, turning toward the rear as the BearCat passed. He sat back down and turned to Lace. "When are Rudie and Jas's crews getting here? I'm gettin' antsy, you know?"

"I think Dion wants 'em here ASAP," Lace said.

Cassius snugged his well-worn fingerless gloves onto his calloused hands. "Fuck that. What's Krystal say?"

Lace shook her head slowly as she stared through the windshield. "It's the same as what he said. Seems like she's directing Dion now."

The big guy traced a tattoo on his forearm with a finger. "Someone's got to, boss. Sometimes I get the feeling Dion's lost his way, man."

Lace's head jerked sideways. "Don't think that. Dion's our leader. Always has been."

Cassius hung his arm out the window. "Think what you want, man. I'll follow Krystal anywhere." He looked at her across the cab. "Almost the whole crew feels that way."

"Dion gave her the authority she has—"

"But it was her idea to bring in reinforcements when Dion was sittin' on his hands, man," he said. "That was a good move."

Lace smiled. "Yeah, but Dion sent you guys to rescue me from Raymond, right?"

"Okay. I'll admit he's still got it in some ways," the big Punk said. He gazed out the window. "Only wish we could have caught Ray. Fucker."

Lace's two-way radio lit up. "*Copy, Lace. It's Nico. You out there?*"

Lace flipped her mic down. "Gotcha, Nico. Go ahead."

"*Yeah, everything's dead at the north, south, east checkpoints. I know you're just getting into town. Anything happening out that way?*"

Lace steered her truck onto the shoulder of a dirt street inside the newly scraped subdivision. "A shit-ton of Changer activity. We're gonna get out and have a look around." She glanced across the cab and smiled. "I think Cassius is chomping at the bit to stretch his legs. You're welcome to join us."

"*Sounds like a plan, Lace. Break. Adam, Joey, you guys copy?*"

"*Joey here.*"

"*Adam.*"

"*Guys,*" Nico said. "*Leave a couple Cats at your checkpoints and meet at Lace's location.*"

In the Underground, SOUL Central was quiet save for the clicking of numerous robotic arms and the usual drone of humming machinery. Curtis looked up at the series of various-sized pods that contained the SOUL Chybrids. "So Levi put you in charge of the young SOULs?"

Johnny smiled. "You bet."

"Well, that's one of only two good decisions he's made in his lifetime. From the looks of this, Dr. Rasmus was the other."

"Thanks for that, Curtis," Johnny said. "I'd count you as a good decision."

"Kissing my ass, Logan? I was destined to be a Changer. Levi had nothing to do with that."

"Yeah, well, Changers are winners, Curtis. You're not a Bystander or a Punk anymore. You're on the winning team now."

Curtis folded his arms and turned to Johnny. "Don't try to school me. Changers are information and technology. We control it all. That's what makes us powerful. Our technology dictates what the Bystanders see, hear and believe. The poor little Bystanders are tools for us. The Punks are like a boil on the ass of our progress."

Johnny scratched his head. "No offense, but you've become one ruthless bastard."

"That's laughable coming from you," Curtis said. "But how else would I be? When your heart's been fucked over by everyone you ever cared about, you'll be ruthless, too." He glanced up one last time before turning to leave. "We have a lot of work to do. The repopulation of Tremayne is behind schedule."

"How do you figure that, boss?" Johnny said, following Curtis toward the door. "Levi set the timeline for incursion at the end of the month."

"Another stupid decision," Curtis said. "The Bystanders need to be hit hard, fast, and *now*."

The two exited the room and turned down the guard-lined corridor. "Dang, dude," Johnny said. "I agree with you about the Punks. But we still need Bystanders. We can't survive without them. They hold our life source."

"Get off your high horse, Logan. I never thought I'd have to listen to your heart talking."

Johnny stopped. "Dude. Everyone's got a heart. Even being a Changer, you always love *somebody*. Hell, your parents are Bystanders."

Curtis stopped three steps in front of Johnny. He didn't turn around. "Mention my parents again and you're a dead man."

CHAPTER 45

Boy in the Cage

A SEVEN-FOOT-TALL CYLINDRICAL STEEL CAGE RESTED atop a sturdy steel platform inside the Hangar at Punk headquarters. A large padlock secured a heavy hasp on the cage's door. Tim, the thirteen-year-old boy apprehended in Tremayne, sat knees up on the cage floor.

Pops stared up at the damaged front suspension on a BearCat from Inspection Pit Two. "Gonna take some parts we don't have to fix this one."

The boy in the cage looked up. "You guys have shit for vehicles, man."

"Hep." Geezer whipped his glasses off and looked at the boy. "And you got shit fer brains, Little Man."

"That's my name. Don't wear it out," the boy said.

Geezer squatted down and peered under the crippled vehicle. "We could salvage some parts from them totaled Cats."

"Looks like that'll have to be the plan for now," Pops said as he mounted the steps up to ground level.

A heavy surge of cold air drifted into the Hangar when Fred and Thomas entered with Felix.

Pops wiped his hands on a grease rag and tucked it into a back pocket. "Check that, Geeze." He motioned to the trio. "Must be that doctor from the Underground."

Fred smiled and waved as the three approached Pops and Geezer. "Hi, guys. Got somebody to introduce to you."

Felix stopped at the steel cage and crouched in front of the boy. The boy looked up from his cell. "The fuck are you looking at?"

Felix remained fixed on the boy's face. "This is a SOUL Chybrid, gentlemen."

The boy raised a middle finger to Felix, then went back to tapping on his cell.

Fred turned around as the doctor stood up. "Seriously? That explains a few things."

Geezer pointed a rag at the boy in the cage. "Explains why he hasn't eaten a thing since he got here." He looked at Pops. "What's it been, 'bout two weeks?"

"About that," Pops said. He looked at Fred. "Krys brought him from lockup a few days ago and had him put in the cage."

"Probably anticipating Felix's arrival," Fred said. "Speaking of, I'd like you two to meet Dr. Felix Yaz. He's a Rogue, like us."

Pops extended a calloused, greasy hand. "I'm Pops. Nice to meet you, Dr. Yaz." He motioned to Geezer. "This is Geezer. He's smarter than he looks."

"You little shit." Geezer tossed a rag at Pops, hitting him squarely in the face. "I'll introduce myself." He held his hand out to Felix.

Felix shook Geezer's hand. "It's nice to meet you, Mr. Geezer."

Pops couldn't hold back a hearty laugh. "Meet Dr. Yaz, Mr. Geezer." He shook his head and tossed the rag back at Geezer.

Geezer pursed his lips and walked over to the main workbench. He occupied himself wiping hand tools and hanging them on a sturdy backboard. "Mr. Geezer…"

"Hey, Geeze," Thomas said. "We have things to discuss, and you and Pops are going to be instrumental in getting Felix acquainted with your setup here."

"Yeah, okay," Geezer said. "I'll be right there. Just cleaning up after Mr. Messy Pops." He chuckled quietly at his joke.

Felix stood with his hands folded behind his back. He surveyed the Hangar, floor to ceiling. "I am impressed with your operation. It seems you have many valuable tools for fabrication and custom assemblage."

Pops turned to Geezer. "C'mon, old man. Let's give the doctor the grand tour."

ACE ANSWERED THE TWO-WAY RADIO at the communications console in the Depot. "Gotcha, Jasper. Go ahead."

"Yeah, Ace. Got a couple in a souped-up four-by pickup here. Guy says his name is Drew. Says they're here to see Krystal."

"Copy, Ace. That's Drew and Sydney. Krystal's expecting them. Let 'em through."

Dion lit a cigarette from behind the bar. "This is a good move, Krys." He rested his elbows on the bar top and blew a smoke ring. "Bystanders with balls. We need a few more like these."

Jimbo leaned against a 1960s jukebox in the corner of the room, his arms crossed. "You ever see their setup in Tremayne? Me and Win checked it out a few months ago during the acid testing operation."

"Never seen it," Dion said.

"You need to get out more, boss," Winter said. "Holy hell, it's high-tech."

"They're a good addition," Krystal said. "When Ryk and I tapped them for assistance, they were more than willing to pitch in. Seemed eager almost."

"Got that right," Ryker said. "They both took vacation from their jobs to help us out this time."

"How long's their vacation?" Dion said.

Ryker grew antsy. He stepped behind the bar and grabbed a bottle of water. "Three weeks, starting today."

"So what's the plan, Krys?" Dion said. "You're the answer girl these days."

Krystal swiveled around on her barstool to face Dion. "I don't have all the answers, Dion. But my strategy is to surround myself with the best of the best, starting right here in this room."

"She's following your own rule, bro," Ryker said. "Damn, look around you. Who's better than this team *you* formed?" He studied the faces of his friends seated and standing in the Depot. "You, Jimbo, Winter, Ace, Krystal and me. You got the Three Amigos and Lace in Tremayne. Well, except for Will. Pops and Geezer? None better."

Krystal softened. "I'm just adding to an already great team in areas where we don't have expertise, Dion."

"She's right," Winter said. "Punks have muscle. We have brute force. We have determination. But we don't have the technical expertise to go head to head with the Changers. Not at the level they've reached."

"We're being left behind, technologically," Jimbo said. "Comes a time when muscle on might just don't hack it."

Ryker walked back around the bar and headed toward the door. "And that time is now." He lifted his duster from a hook on the wall. "Whatever the circumstances were that brought us Krystal, you made the right choice putting her in charge. She attracted Felix, Fred and Thomas, and now she's managed to get two of the best Bystanders around to help us out. I call that an A Team."

Ace spun around from the comm console to face the group. "Not to be a downer, but it's all hodgepodge, right?"

Jimbo stood up straight and uncrossed his arms. "Whadda you mean, *hodgepodge*?"

Ace was unfazed by Jimbo's posture. "You guys are acting all sentimental, like…" He held up both hands and raised his eyebrows. "…ooh, we're all family, and that's gonna win out over everything. I mean, like, whatever we have in technological know-how and all from Felix and them, the Changers have that tenfold."

"Sounds like you're giving up without a fight, bro—" Dion said.

"No," Krystal said. "He makes a good point. Everybody has to remember we're underdogs here. Let's not any of us underestimate the power of the Changers."

"That's exactly my point, Krys," Ace said. "The second we let our guard down, or get overconfident, we're dead."

"Call it overconfident or anything else you want," Jimbo said. "I'm puttin' my money on the Punks, no matter what."

"Me, too," Winter said.

A loud triple knock on the Depot door broke the tension. Drew cracked the door open and peeked inside. "Room for two more?"

Ryker pulled the door open and wrapped an arm over Drew's shoulder. "Get in here, you two." He embraced Sydney. "Good to see you, Syd."

Krystal stood from the barstool and walked across the room. She faced the pair, hands on her hips. "Welcome back, guys. We got temp quarters set up for you. Get unpacked and meet Ryk and me in the Hangar."

"*Copy, Ace? Copy, Ace? Nico here.*" The voice on the ceiling speaker mixed with heavy background noise and chatter.

All eyes turned toward the comm console.

Ace spun around in his seat. "Ace here, buddy. Go ahead."

"*Things are blowing up here. Holy shit, it's ten o'clock at night and I've never seen so many people and vehicles.*"

"Do you have anything that is automated?" Felix said.

Pops scratched his chin. "Well…not really."

Geezer placed his hands on his hips and stared up at the two-story-high ceiling in the massive manufacturing facility behind the Hangar. "Welp, we converted this place a while back." He pulled his glasses from a top pocket on his coveralls and looked into Felix's eyes. "Used to be an assembly plant for electric cars."

Felix crossed his arms high over his chest. "Curious…" He surveyed the remnant of row upon row of steel framing, I-beam construction and empty supports that once housed computer terminals. He placed a hand on his cheek and looked at Fred. "This has possibilities."

"How long do you think it would take to get it close to what you need?" Fred said.

Felix turned to Pops. "There are inoperable mechanical Chybrid bodies outside the Perimeter, no?"

Pops wiped his sweaty hands on his coveralls and pulled a can of chewing tobacco from a pocket. "I reckon there are. We retrieved all our people from the battlefield out there." He motioned toward the main gate. "Didn't see a reason to pick up any of them mechanical beasts."

"Good idea, Felix," Thomas said. "Fred and I know everything about those suckers."

Fred snapped his fingers. "Of course. They're chock-full of transponders and reprogrammable circuitry."

Thomas's eyes widened. "Not to mention mechanical joints and—"

"Precisely why I chose you two as my top scientists," Felix said.

Geezer looked at Felix above his glasses. "Those robots out there's pretty wrecked up. Not to mention muddy as hell. You plannin' on salvaging parts?"

"Exactly what he's planning," Pops said, glancing at Felix. "We'll get a team together to round 'em up."

"All righty, then. Guess I'll get a place cleared out," Geezer said. He scanned the expansive building. "Corner over there looks good."

Felix looked down at the polished concrete floor and began to pace. "Time is of the essence. We need people."

"Shit," Geezer said. "We got people. Lots of 'em."

Felix stopped, turned around and looked at Geezer. "I am not talking about bodies, Mr. Geezer."

Pops chuckled.

Felix pointed at Fred and Thomas. "I am talking about scientists, technicians. Like these men here."

Geezer yanked the rag from his back pocket and began to polish his already clean glasses. "We got smart guys, too."

Felix nodded once. "I will grant you that. And we need the Punks. But I am talking about people who know mechanical engineering, science and technology—"

"We know a lot of that," Pops said. "We just don't know what to call it."

"I need people who speak my language," Felix said. "I will be calling people from the Underground to join us."

Fred started. "Wait. Who are you calling?"

Felix poked his hands into his pants pockets. "Never underestimate my connections, dear friend. There are thousands of Rogues in the Underground."

"And how long till they time out?"

Felix held up a finger. "That's why I told you time is of the essence."

THE BOY IN THE CAGE stood to stretch his legs. He rolled up his sleeve, tapped the face of a virtual cell embedded in his wrist and held it to his ear. "Hello, Mr. Logan. The Punks are conspiring with Dr. Yaz to retrofit an old assembly plant at their headquarters. Yes, sir. He is alive and he is here. I am not clear as to the purpose of the retrofit at this time. Yes, sir. It may be advisable to dedicate a percentage of resources to this location. Yes. Dr. Yaz has indicated there are a number of defectors within our ranks that currently reside in the Underground. Of course I will. My next update to you will be at midnight, tonight."

CHAPTER 46

The Plot Against Levi

CURTIS AND JOHNNY WALKED SWIFTLY up the wide, brightly lit corridor on Level Nine in the Underground. Their long strides matched perfectly. The cadence of their boots clicked smartly in sync off the polished floor.

Curtis glanced up at one of many surveillance cameras. "You're positive your quarters aren't bugged?"

"Positive," Johnny said. "But I'm just as positive yours are. You haven't been around long enough to have them removed."

"Another insane move by our leader," Curtis said. "It's a wonder he's even in charge of dressing himself."

The pair stopped in front of the door to Johnny's quarters. He turned to Curtis. "Are you kidding? Considering what we're about to discuss, it's no wonder your quarters are still monitored."

Curtis stepped ever so slightly toward Johnny. The two locked eyes. "Considering what we're about to discuss, it's insane *your* quarters are *not* still monitored."

The skin on Johnny's neck burned as he swiped his hand over the security panel adjacent to the door.

Curtis followed him inside and quickly assessed the huge living space. *What's this? Hollywood Regency?* He walked across the room, stepped behind the bar and opened the fridge under the counter.

Johnny smiled as he flopped down on a long red velour sofa. He held a hand in the air. "Hey, toss me one."

Curtis peered into the refrigerator. "Toss you one, what? Where's your cold water bottles?"

"Oh. Well, I don't think there are any cold waters in there. I thought you were grabbing a beer."

Curtis looked up from behind the bar. "No cold water bottles?"

Johnny sat up straight on the sofa. "There's some glasses behind you and some ice in the reservoir there. You'll have to use the faucet for water."

Curtis snatched a lead-crystal tumbler from the shelf behind him and scooped it into the container of ice cubes next to the fridge. He turned to fill the glass from the faucet.

"Can you toss me one, anyway?" Johnny said.

Curtis walked around the bar and stood next to one of the heavily padded barstools. "Nope. Get your own beer."

Johnny hoisted his large frame from the sofa just as the door swished open.

Silver stood at the threshold, preventing the door from closing. She gazed around the room, hands on her hips, mouth agape. "You. Have. Got to be kidding me." A smile she couldn't prevent spread across her face. "Gold shag carpet. Red velour furniture." Her gaze turned to Curtis as she stepped inside. She ran a hand over a barstool. "And leopard skin on your barstools?" She looked across the room at Johnny and laughed. "Where's your velvet Elvis painting?"

Johnny jerked a thumb toward the hallway. "In the bedroom." His eyes widened. "Hey! How'd you open my door? You bypassed my code?"

Silver's smile turned from humorous to smug. "I have my ways. You know. Security chief stuff."

Curtis smiled. "Get Logan a beer, Long."

She tossed her cell on the bar top and stepped behind the

counter. "I will not." She was still smiling. "I'm fixing a drink. But get your own beer, Logan."

A chime above the door sounded. Johnny bent over and tapped a panel on the side table next to the sofa. A monitor above the bar powered on instantly and displayed Dr. Rasmus standing in the hallway outside the door. Johnny pressed another button, and the door slid open.

Xander stepped inside and walked immediately to the bar. "Before we get started, I'm preparing myself a libation. Would you like a beer, Mr. Logan?"

Johnny walked over to the bar. "Nah, I'll get my own."

Curtis stepped away from the bar and seated himself in a large red velour side chair. "When you three are done getting your buzz on, let's get down to business."

Silver moved into the main living area and sat in a chair that matched Curtis's. "Let me remind you, Dyer." She held her highball glass in the air. "You're not the boss of us."

Xander finished preparing himself a martini and popped three olives into his mouth before dropping one into his glass. "Meeting's at midnight, Mr. Dyer. We have a few minutes for casual conversation." He looked up at Johnny. "Wouldn't you agree, Mr. Logan?"

"Get your refreshments, boys," Silver said. "And get in here."

Xander stood behind the bar and continued to munch on olives straight from the jar. "We can start any time, if that suits everyone. We are talking about the impending demise of our hapless leader, no?"

Johnny finally popped the top on his beer bottle. He poured the beer into a tall frosted mug, allowing the head on the beer to grow no more than three-quarters of an inch. He turned and grabbed a triple shot glass and filled it with whiskey. He drank half the shot and dropped the small glass into his mug of beer before quickly gulping half the mug. "You're talking about an assassination."

Curtis crossed his legs and sipped his ice water. "I prefer to refer to it as a necessary change of leadership."

Xander stayed behind the bar with the olives and leaned on the countertop on his elbows. He rolled an olive around in his mouth before slicing it in two between his front teeth. "Levi is surrounded by heavy security. It will be difficult to get next to him—"

"Bullshit," Curtis said. "The four of us have all been in meetings with Levi without a guard in sight."

"The guards are always right outside the door, Curtis," Silver said. "Do you have a method in mind?"

Johnny stepped to the living area and flopped down on the sofa again. "I could choke him out and nobody would hear a sound."

"You've been here longer than any of us, Logan," Xander said. "Why haven't you done it already?"

Johnny shifted in his seat. He glanced back and forth between Curtis and Silver. "I…was…building my team." He sipped his beer.

Silver chuckled. "Team? And what team would that be, Logan? Who would follow you?"

Johnny sat forward. "Lemme tell you something. I got a team of SOUL Chybrid youth in Tremayne that'll wipe my ass if I give the word."

"Might I remind you," Xander said, raising his glass. "The SOUL Chybrids are courtesy of me, Mr. Logan."

Johnny tipped his chin to Xander. "So why haven't you used *your* power against Levi, *Doctor*?"

Silver swirled the ice cubes in her drink. "Because he doesn't have any power." She eyed Johnny. "Just like you."

Xander placed his drink on the bar top and shoved his hands into his pockets. "You say that because you have no idea what's in my arsenal, Long. I have a device in my pocket that could kill you from here, right now. You'd never see it coming." He smiled and sipped his martini. "You would merely cease to be."

"You all sound like the Three Stooges," Curtis said. "You can sit here all night and trade barbs, or we can get serious." He turned around in his chair. "Get over here and join the discussion, Rasmus. Standing over there doesn't make you any less culpable or guilty."

Xander moved hesitantly around the end of the bar. "I'm not guilty of anything. We are having a discussion. Just between friends, no?"

"The terms *assassination* and *change of leadership* were used in this friendly conversation, and your only response was to shove another olive into your mouth." He turned back around as Xander meandered to the main living area. "You're as guilty as anyone here. Now sit down."

"I'm not sure I like your tone, Curtis," Silver said. "You think you're some kind of leader?"

Curtis set his glass on a side table and folded his hands behind his head. "I'm going to overlook your rudeness, Silver." He looked across the coffee table at Xander and Johnny. "We're all here because the Changers are in dire need of a leadership change. Can we all agree on that?"

"I agree," Xander said. "But Levi holds all the cards." He set his drink on the sofa's armrest. "One..." He hooked one forefinger over the other. "He has a massive security team. Two, he has a supremely high approval rating from the citizens of the Underground." Xander glanced at Silver. "What was the latest poll result? Seventy-eight percent? Seventy-nine?" He turned back to Curtis. "Three, he has intimate technical knowledge of the Underground and its operations. Four, he possesses the scientific knowledge of the Change process. Five, he is absolutely the master manipulator." He looked around at the trio of traitors. "Need I go on?"

"Ooh, I'm scared," Silver said. She got up and sauntered to the bar. "Seriously, Rasmus. Are you trying to make him sound undefeatable?" She stepped behind the bar, set her highball glass in the sink and grabbed a clean one from the shelf. "All those assets you just named are held by everyone in this room."

"Yeah," Johnny said, sitting forward. He held a hand up to Silver. "Hey, Long. Grab me another beer, will you?"

Silver held an ice cube over her glass and stared at Johnny momentarily before dropping it into the glass. "Watch my lips, Logan. Get. Your. Own." She mixed her drink and leaned on the bar top, facing the room.

"So, Silver," Curtis said. "There's not one of us in this room that holds all the cards Xander just credited to Levi. Are you talking about a joint effort here? Care to explain yourself?"

"Sure," Silver said. "Not one person has to possess all those things. Once Levi's gone, the new leader would merely need to surround herself with key people…" She held up a hand. "*Loyal* key people who have the knowledge and strength to assist the leader."

"Her?" Johnny snorted. "Sounds a little presumptuous to me."

"Ha!" Silver mock-laughed. "You think you could replace Levi? What do you have?" Her eyes darted around the room as if searching for an answer. "Brute strength?"

"You're a shit, Silver," Johnny said. "If I kill Levi, you'll report to me."

Silver tipped her glass to Johnny. "Okay, if you take him out I'll give you that. You do have strength, but you don't have the balls."

"I'm getting another beer." Johnny got up from the couch and stomped to the bar. Silver moved around the other end and walked back to her chair.

"And you do?" Curtis said.

Silver held her glass loosely and slowly shook her head. "Oh, puh-lease!"

Xander finished his martini with a long gulp. "Then, we are agreeing here and now that whomever of us ultimately kills Levi becomes the new Changers leader. And the rest of us must agree to subordinate ourselves to him?" He nodded to Silver. "Or her?"

"Agreed," Johnny and Curtis said in unison.

"I'll drink to that," Silver said.

Johnny started when his cell vibrated. His eyes widened as he slapped a hand over the right rear pocket of his slacks.

Curtis turned in his seat again. "Thought we agreed to silence communications?"

Johnny ignored the comment and answered his cell. He glanced up at the three Changers in his living room. "Uh, hang on a sec."

Xander raised an eyebrow. "You're taking the call?"

Johnny hurried around the bar. He held the phone to his ear and raised a finger to the group with his other hand as he side-stepped furniture on his way to the bedroom. "Be right back. This won't take long. No security risk here."

Silver looked at Curtis. "Honestly, should we have agreed to follow him? You know. In case he's the one? I mean, he didn't even turn off his cell."

Curtis shrugged. "When you think about it, he's the only one here that can risk a phone call." He glanced around the room. "I mean, it wouldn't be unusual to track him here. It's *his* quarters."

"Ha," Silver said. "My tracking chip is disabled. No one knows where I am unless I use my cell."

Xander set the empty olive jar on the side table. "How is your tracking chip disabled?"

She smiled coyly. "You're not the only scientific genius around here, Xander."

"Oh?" he said. "You're a scientific genius now?"

Silver leaned forward in the red velour chair, elbows on her knees. She lowered her voice. "Maybe not. But I am the master manipulator, not Levi as you so eloquently stated. I've got Levi wrapped around my pinkie. I've been closer to him than any of you." She glanced at Curtis. "And I can do it again. Any time."

Curtis tipped his water glass to Silver, then to Xander.

Silver sat back.

Xander picked up the empty olive jar, glanced inside and put it back on the table.

"Ahem." Johnny's exaggerated phlegm discharge broke the silence. He grinned and rubbed his hands together. "So. When are we gonna do the deed?"

"We?" Curtis said, not looking back at Johnny. "You got a mouse in your pocket?"

Johnny puffed up. "No." He smiled, top and bottom teeth. "But I got a little man in my pocket."

CHAPTER 47

Potshots

D REW AND SYDNEY STRUGGLED TO keep up with Krystal and Ryker as they walked along the concrete sidewalk toward the Hangar.

"Damn, Syd," Drew said. "I didn't realize these guys worked all hours."

"No kidding," she said. "It's after midnight. We should have been in bed an hour ago."

"Get used to it, guys," Krystal said, not breaking stride.

"Welcome to your vacation," Ryker said.

When they reached the Hangar, Krystal shoved the door open and stepped across the threshold in front of Ryker. The others followed.

Drew gazed up at the ceiling as the four hurried across the polished concrete floor toward the door to the manufacturing plant. "Place has possibilities."

"Welders, inspection pits, electronic diagnostics," Sydney said. "Contemporary vehicle repair with high-tech fabrication thrown in. I'm impressed."

"Wait'll you guys see what you're up against in the back," Ryker said. "Tie your hair back."

Two heavy steel doors at the entrance to the manufacturing

plant were propped open. The four entered the wide-open space and stopped momentarily. Krystal quickly surveyed the activity, then headed toward Felix and Thomas.

Drew glanced at Sydney. "No rest for the weary around here, I guess."

"We've got approximately no time left," Ryker said.

Felix turned toward the quartet as they approached. He smiled. "Oh, Krystal! We've been looking forward to some additional support." He peeked over her shoulder. "These must be the Bystanders you have told me about."

"Hey, Felix," Krystal said. She turned to the couple. "This is Drew. This is Sydney. Guys, meet Dr. Felix Yaz. You will learn a lot from him. But right now he needs your knowledge and expertise." She looked at Felix. "These guys have many assets and connections. Use them as you wish."

Felix nodded repeatedly. "Of course, of course. It's nice to meet you two."

Krystal looked up at Ryker, then back to Felix. "We've got to go. There's some activity in Tremayne we have to get a handle on. We'll be in the Depot. Give us a call if you need anything." She fixed her eyes on Felix. "Anything, right?"

Felix nodded again. "Yes, of course, dear." He watched the pair as they walked back through the steel double doorway. "They are good people," he said to no one in particular.

Drew gazed across to the far side of the plant. Geezer was covered in mud, directing a group of Punks who were busy cleaning and sorting what looked like body parts. He tipped his chin up. "What's going on over there, Dr. Yaz?"

Felix turned to look. "Oh. That's Mr. Geezer. He is overseeing the inventory and cataloging of the mechanical Chybrids. His assigned task is integral to our success as we convert this area to a laboratory capable of developing the means to defeat the Changers."

Sydney scrunched her face. "I thought the Changers were defeated."

Felix nodded and placed a hand on Sydney's forearm. "My dear, they are on the move again."

Drew studied the doctor's face. "I hear you are the brains behind the development of the mechanical Chybrids that almost destroyed the Punks."

Felix smiled and looked into Drew's eyes. "And I hear you are a computer genius with a souped-up four-wheel-drive pickup truck."

Drew didn't blink. "I take it you're familiar with computer programming languages. Say, Java, JavaScript, Python, Ruby, PHP, C#, C++, and Objective-C?"

Felix let out a rare belly laugh. "Languages of the past, son. From what I had heard, I believe I may have built you up to a much higher level in my mind."

Sydney looked up at Drew.

"The basics, Doctor," Drew said. "I'll run circles around anyone in Scala, Go, Swift, Clojure, and Haskell, as well."

Felix stopped smiling. "That's impressive, my boy. Do you know Elm, Rust, Kotlin—"

"And Crystal and Elixir," Drew said. "And anything else you can teach me. I have a short learning curve."

"Splendid," Felix said. "Why bother with Elixir?"

Drew smiled. "Pop quiz, Doctor? Much like Phoenix, Elixir provides excellent productivity without sacrificing performance."

"Very good," Felix said. "I believe you will be a quick study when I teach you the computer programming language I have developed."

"And what's that?" Drew said.

"For the operation we are about to undertake, you will need to learn *Felix*."

"Never heard of it," Drew said.

"Of course you haven't," Felix said. "It is my own. The only other person in the world who knows this computer language is Levi Aldrich, the Changers' leader."

ACE SWIVELED AROUND IN HIS chair at the comm console in the Depot.

Krystal waved her hand as she and Ryker stepped into the room. "Hop off, bro. I want to talk to Nico."

"You got it, boss," Ace said, sliding out of the high padded chair.

Ryker sidled up next to Krystal as she slid into the seat vacated by Ace.

"They're gonna need some help," Ace said.

Krystal agreed. "You bet they are." She pressed the talk button. "Nico, buddy. It's Krystal. You copy?"

"*Go ahead, Krystal,*" Nico said.

She could tell he was shouting into his mic. "Nico, give me a quick report."

"*Quick will take too long! We need help now!*"

"Nico. Buddy. Calm and easy. Tell me what's happening."

"*We're surrounded, Krystal. Tons of construction vehicles. Excavators, scrapers, graders, dozers, trenchers and…humongous dump trucks. There must be a hundred, at least!*"

"What's the issue?" Krystal said. "They're construction vehicles."

The sound of sporadic gunfire sounded on the ceiling speaker as Nico keyed his mic again. "*We're under fire, Krystal. Every time we try to move, they shoot. It's like they're playing with us, but with real bullets!*"

Dion nodded at Ryker. "Get Lace on the phone."

"I'm on it," Ryker said.

Jimbo grabbed two leather jackets from the wall hook and tossed Winter's to her. "Let's go."

Winter caught the jacket and slung it over her shoulder. She looked back at Dion. "Get us four each to take with."

Dion pulled his cell from a pocket inside his vest and tapped a series of numbers. Pole-mounted speakers in the compound popped to life. Yellow strobes atop the poles lit up. Dion spoke into his cell. "Team One. Team One. Report to the compound. Report to the compound. Crew members one through eight. Crew members one through eight."

Krystal pressed the radio's talk button. "Sit tight, buddy. We're sending help."

Ryker set his cell on the bar top. "Putting you on speaker. Go ahead, Lace."

"Caught the radio talk, guys. Nico's estimate is pretty accurate. Cassius and I parked in this new plot of land where the Changers are prepping for another subdivision. Once Nico, Adam and Joey arrived, construction stopped and these monster vehicles surrounded us. Sealed up all the exits."

"What about the gunfire?" Ryker said.

"They're taking potshots. It's not an all-out attack. Like they're toying with us. Problem is, we can't drive these Cats outta here."

Dion turned around and manipulated a series of controls on a panel adjacent to the communications console. He glanced up at the wall behind the bar. The main flat-screen monitor displayed an electronic map of North America. He zoomed in to the west sector, then down to Tremayne. "Looks like you guys got the trucks circled up, Lace."

"Yeah, Nico was on top of that. He gave the order to circle the wagons when he saw the Changers sealing up the exits. There's ten of us in Cats, back to back in a circle. They each got three trucks inside. My second and third got squeezed out."

"I see the formation," Dion said. "Got you guys on the map."

Krystal spun in her chair and jerked a thumb over her shoulder. "You're up, Ace."

The intermittent gunfire continued. The piercing sound of ricocheting bullets were heard over the cell's speaker.

"Lace," Krystal said. "Can you tell where the shots are coming from?"

"We're laying low right now. But it's not every vehicle. Near as I can tell, it's the dump trucks."

"They need a distraction." Krystal glanced at Ace. "Get ahold of Jim and Winter. Use tac one. It's secure, and I don't trust we're not being monitored."

"Hey, Ace," Dion said. "Tell everyone else to keep away from the area until we can get those ten Cats outta there. No reinforcements at this time." He turned back to the cell. "That's all, Lace."

Ryker disconnected the call and ran a hand over his head. "Well?"

"Good teamwork, everybody," Dion said.

Krystal strode toward the door. "I'm going to the Hangar and have a chat with Felix. He may know something about these construction vehicles." She caught Ryker's eye.

"Go ahead," Ryker said. "I'll be there in a few."

When Krystal left, Ryker motioned to Dion. The two moved to the far end of the bar opposite the comm console.

Ryker lowered his voice. "Have you heard from Rudie and Jas?"

Dion lit a cigarette and leaned against the rear counter. "Not since that night they said they were sending in troops."

"That's another week down the drain, bro. And another week the Changers have had to beef up."

Dion took a long drag on his cigarette and stared at the bar top in front of Ryker. "They're sending 2,500 trucks each. It takes time to organize a movement that big."

Ryker leaned forward and pointed at the monitor behind Dion. "They outnumber us ten to one in that little corner of Tremayne, bro. If that's any indication, we're more screwed the longer we wait. You need to call those two and find out what they're waiting for."

Dion's ire rose. "No one's waiting! That kind of operation takes time. I'm not calling Rudie, and I'm not calling Jas. Have you forgotten how friendships work? Friends trust friends. If you'd pull your head out of Krystal's ass for five minutes, maybe your mind would be clear."

Ryker sat back. "Low blow, man."

"You want a beer?" Dion said, reaching under the counter.

"Yeah."

WINTER PUSHED HER LENCO BEARCAT to ninety miles per hour as light from the sunrise forced its way over the distant rocky horizon. Pink highlights quickly faded to gray as the daylight exposed the usual blanket of winter clouds over the valley. She followed Jimbo's truck by three car lengths, matching his track like a slot car.

She flipped her headset mic down. "Copy, Jim?"

"*Go, Win.*"

"You catch that action back at the I-5 junction? Another convoy of semis loaded up with yellow earth movers."

"*Saw that. At least another hundred, wouldn't you say?*"

"At least."

"*Break, break. Jimbo, Winter. Ace here. You copy?*"

"Copy," Winter said.

"*Go ahead, Ace,*" Jimbo said.

"*Go to tac one.*"

KRYSTAL STRODE SWIFTLY THROUGH THE Hangar and headed toward the door to the manufacturing plant. Her peripheral vision caught movement in the heavy steel cage adjacent to Inspection Pit Three.

The boy in the cage scrambled to his feet. He gripped the vertical bars with both hands and pressed his face against the steel. "Hey."

Krystal stopped and tipped her chin up. "What's up with you?"

The boy put on his best sad face. "How long you guys gonna leave me in here?"

Krystal wasn't moved. "It's not up to me." Her hands went to her hips. "How long are you gonna sit around and not provide any useful information?"

The boy shifted his feet, trying to appear nervous. "Is that why I'm here? I thought those Punks from the city brought me in here because I was causing trouble with the other kids." He smiled and pushed back from the bars, retaining his grip on them. "So whadda you wanna know?"

"Okay, I'll bite," Krystal said. "What's with all the heavy construction equipment moving into Tremayne, Little Man?"

"Ohh, you know. Building subdivisions." The boy pushed forward and backward on the bars. "And by the way, *Krystal Peterson,* that's my name, don't wear it out."

Krystal started for the door. "I don't have time for your bullshit, *Little Man.*"

He watched her as she walked past the cage and headed toward the back of the room. "We're gettin' a new leader." The boy smiled broadly, exposing his top and bottom teeth.

Krystal stopped. "And what's that supposed to mean?" she said, not turning around.

Little Man swung side to side, still gripping the vertical bars. "Oh, wouldn't you like to know…"

Krystal turned and fast-walked back to the cage. "Listen, you little shit." She placed her left hand around Little Man's fingers on his right hand. "Nobody here cares about you except to use you for information."

The boy's face crinkled. "Ow, you're hurting me," he said.

"Hell I am," she said. "Unless you want to rot in this cage, you'd best start spilling information."

The boy smiled again. "I can't rot, silly. I'm a SOUL kid."

Krystal stepped up to the cage, her face two inches from the cold steel bars. "We already know that, asshole." She pulled her 9mm pistol from the holster on her thigh and pushed the barrel through the cage, pointed at the boy's face. "But it's just as easy to put an end to this miserable little SOUL in the cage as it is to let you rot."

He smiled and pressed his head against the business end of the pistol. "Kill me and you get nothing. Smelly, grungy, burned-up Krystal."

She let go of his hand and backed away from the cage. "I've had enough of your shit, you little monster." She holstered her 9mm and headed toward the manufacturing plant.

Little Man gripped the bars again and eyed Krystal, his face to the bars. "We're gettin' a new leader, we're gettin' a new leader…"

The boy's chanting raised the hairs on her neck. She flipped him off over her shoulder and continued toward the plant.

CHAPTER 48

The Hot Zone

"Copy, Jim?" Winter said. "What say we meet up with Lace's crew. You know, the two Cats that got locked out of the subdivision."

"*Sounds like a good place to start.*"

"*Copy, guys? Ace here. Those two aren't on tac one. We got 'em located on the east side of that subdivision. No activity detected. Go ahead and meet up and find out what you can. Then get back to me.*"

"*10-4, Ace,*" Jimbo said.

Winter followed Jimbo into Tremayne. Traffic in town—both vehicular and pedestrian—felt unnaturally heavy. She closed the distance to his truck, nearly hugging his bumper. The prospect of allowing cross traffic between the BearCats was not something she cared to deal with. She gazed out the driver's window, instinctively maintaining her distance to Jimbo's bumper. Pedestrian traffic overflowed off the sidewalks and into the street. Ordinary, middle-class-looking citizens mingled with the apparent homeless population.

"What a menagerie of humanity, Buster," she said to the big Punk riding shotgun.

"No shit," he said, staring out the passenger window. "What's with the regular Bystanders mixing with the homeless people? Somethin's outta place."

Winter followed Jimbo's BearCat down a long alley. Tall brick buildings lined the alleyway, and Winter's claustrophobia set in. "Definitely gives you a weird feeling."

Buster glanced across the cab at Winter. "You're sweatin', boss. You could back off Jimbo's bumper a bit. Might help."

Winter's eyes glazed. "Just get there, Jim," she said aloud to herself. "Make it quick."

Jimbo turned left out of the alley and accelerated, leaving the depressed Old Town behind. Winter rolled her window up and glanced in the rearview mirror on the driver's door. "Holy shit, I'm glad to be outta that mess."

Buster smiled. "Thought you were losing it for a minute there, boss."

Jimbo's voice cracked in Winter's headset. *"Copy, Win? Two Punk trucks up ahead on the right."*

Four Punks stood in a small circle next to two Lenco Bear-Cats on the right shoulder of the road where the sidewalk ended. All four wore identical black leather jackets, jeans, boots and fingerless gloves. They turned to form a semicircle facing the two second-level commanders as the vehicles pulled to the curb.

Jimbo hopped down the short running board below the driver's door and sauntered swiftly toward the four. "Who's in charge?"

The shortest of the four stepped forward and bumped fists with Jimbo. "Me."

"Right on, Dash." Jimbo looked at the other three. "Everyone good with that?"

The trio held their fists out. Jimbo pounded down on each. "You all report to Dash." He yanked a thumb over his shoulder. "Dash will get his orders from me or Winter. Buster and my shotgun are the same as you guys."

"Who's your shotgun?" Dash said.

"Stormy," Jimbo said. "Call her Storm."

"Got it."

Jimbo tipped his chin to Dash. "So what's the scoop here?"

Dash glanced toward the subdivision, about a quarter of a mile up the street. "We were following Lace into the hot zone, just checking things out, you know. We stopped just outside on the curb. So Nico radios to Lace, and she invites them to join her." He reached behind his head to tighten his gray bandanna. "Along with Adam and Joey, right? I told the guys here to hold up outside the zone." He glanced at Winter and Buster. "No particular reason, just my gut."

"Turns out to be a good move," Stormy said. She motioned to Buster. "Let's have a look-see."

Jimbo crossed his arms, accentuating his chiseled physique. "Just don't get too close. Fuckin' Changers are takin' potshots at random shit."

Dash's eyes widened. "Good advice, Jim. But it's not random. They're shooting at Punks. Actually laughing about it, too."

"Fuckers," Jimbo said. "So what happened?"

"Near as we can tell, the shots are coming from the dumpers. The other machines seem to be used as blockades for the dump trucks. Thing is…" Dash scratched his head through the bandanna. "…we haven't spotted a weak spot on those mothers." He squinted at Jimbo. "You know how those big suckers have a cab where the driver sits? We haven't found it. It appears like the cab that's usually surrounded by glass—you know, for visibility—is just a big iron box."

Jimbo glanced behind the Punk. "Whadda you make of that?"

"Well, I think these trucks, at least the dumpers, were specifically made to be war vehicles. You know, battle-ready fighters. I think the construction earth-mover function is secondary."

"So once again, the Changers designed a machine to specifically wipe out the Punks?" Dash's shotgun partner said.

"Wipe out the Punks? That's what the SOUL Chybrids are for," Winter said. "It sounds to me more like these earth movers are insurance. It's their might-against-might variable."

Jimbo stepped back into the street and positioned himself to face everyone present. "Get it straight in your minds, people. The SOUL Chybrids are being used to overwhelm and fool the

Bystanders. They're not for us. They expect the Bystanders to ostracize and banish us. We've been present in Bystander territories throughout the continent because the Bystanders welcomed us. All these years, that presence had kept the Changers in check. Now that they decided to break our treaty with them, the Changers are slowly but surely turning the minds of the Bystanders to mush through technology, free stuff and propaganda. When the Bystanders see the Changers' side of things—through the influence of the SOULs—they kick us out. We become their enemy." He nodded to Winter. "But she's right about the earth movers. They're here to finish off the Punks physically."

Dash looked at the Punks standing next to him, then back at Jimbo. "So what's our immediate plan, boss?"

Jimbo paced in front of the group. "I got a message from Ace on the way here. All it said was 'set up a distraction.'"

"That's a piece o' cake," Winter said. "We got explosives on the Cats."

"There's the matter of getting those guys out of there," Jimbo said. "Say you blow up one of those yellow monsters in there. Then what?" He turned to see Buster and Stormy walking down the small rise from the new subdivision area.

Buster held up a hand as he approached. He shook his head and looked up at Jimbo. "They're wall to wall. Iron against iron. Or whatever those machines are made of."

"I say blow a hole in the blockade," Winter said.

Jimbo nodded to Dash. "How many dumpers?"

Dash's eyes darted furtively around the group as if looking for the answer. "I don't know. Maybe twenty out of a hundred or so vehicles."

Jimbo raised an eyebrow. "If there's twenty, the math could work as a distraction. We could get them out of there on foot."

"What are you thinking?" Winter said.

"Okay, look," Jimbo said. "There's eight of us here. But that's not the math I'm talking about." He pointed at Winter. "Start prepping the explosives. We got ten trucks inside and twenty enemy vehicles taking potshots at our people."

Winter's headset crackled. "*Copy, Jimbo. Copy, Winter. Ace here.*"

Winter motioned to Jimbo. "Ace on tac one."

"What's the word?" Jimbo said.

Winter nodded as she listened to Ace's voice in the headset. "Yeah, that's too bad, bro. Okay. Yep. 10-4, I'll let him know."

Jimbo held up a hand to the crew. "Hold up, everybody." He looked at Winter. "So?"

"I guess Krystal went and talked to Felix to see if he knows anything about the earth movers." She shook her head. "He knows *about* them. But no details." She glanced around the group. "We're on our own here."

DION AND RYKER SAT ON adjacent barstools at one end of the long countertop, staring at the area map on the flat-screen above the bar.

"Sun's coming up and Changers are moving in," Ryker said. "That I-5 activity is killing me."

"Check out the county highway heading out," Dion said. "Bet those are empty semis."

"They are," Krystal said as she walked back into the Depot.

Ryker swung around. "How do you know?"

"My conversation with Felix," Krystal said.

"I thought there was nothing to offer there," Dion said.

Krystal stepped up to the bar and sat next to Ryker. "Not anything I could give to Jimbo and Winter that would help. He did have *some* information, though."

"Spill it," Ryker said.

Krystal picked up a cork coaster off the bar top and twirled it between her fingers. "He said he heard the plan is to bring in one hundred earth movers per day for the foreseeable future. No end date. No max number."

Ryker opened his mouth. He looked at Dion.

Dion looked Ryker in the eye. "What?"

Krystal continued twirling the coaster. "He said the dump trucks are the weaponized vehicles. But we knew that."

"How to counter what they're doing, Krys?" Dion said. "That's what we need to know."

Krystal stopped twirling the coaster and slapped it down onto the bar top. She turned to Dion. "Numbers, Dion. That's the bottom line. We have to overwhelm the dumpers with more firepower than they're bringing against us. Any of the Changer construction vehicles that aren't dump trucks are being used as barricades and protection against any offensive action."

Dion sat back and placed a hand on Ryker's forearm. "Don't even say it, bro."

"I'm not going to ask you to call anyone." Ryker stared at the map on the wall and shook his head slowly. "By the end of the month, they'll have more vehicles than we will, even after Rudie and Jas show up." He turned to Dion. "They're winning, bro. Slowly, but surely, the Changers are winning."

"Guys," Krystal said. "We still have Felix."

"Seriously, Krys?" Dion said. "He's working on duplicating his Change reversal chamber, right? That's good for something, but…" He rubbed his eyes and ran his hands over his face.

"I talked to him about that," Krystal said. "I talked to him about the earth movers. And I talked to him about defeating the SOUL Chybrids. He's got a plan for each."

Ryker took off his bandanna and shook out the wrinkles behind him. "Damn, Krys. From what you said, he wasn't even involved in the development of the SOUL Chybrids. How can he—"

"He's Dr. Felix Yaz," she said. "My money's on Felix."

JIMBO SURVEYED THE SMALL GROUP of Punks in front of him. "Okay, here's the deal. Each of you has two explosive devices with remote detonators installed. I've got control of when they go off. Get in behind that far side of the circle." He looked continuously back and forth between all the players as he spoke. "You will all get exactly two minutes before I start igniting those suckers. So get in and get out. Don't look back and don't try to get fancy or make any last-second adjustments. Is everyone clear?"

He turned around. "Buster, Storm. You two are pivotal, and timing is critical. One minute after these guys take off on foot, hop in the Cats. Not one second sooner. We don't want to give any indication we're up to anything—no undue attention in this direction from those bastards."

The two nodded their acknowledgment.

He addressed the group one last time. "I'm headed to my truck to get eyes on the guys trapped inside. Everyone, radios on. Wait for my signal. I will say, 'now.' That's all you get. Once your units are set, hightail it back to mine and Winter's Cats. Winter's going in shallow, so she'll be the closest to the escape vehicles. Buster and Storm will haul the others away from the area. All of you will exit the area on either mine or Winter's truck. That's it."

Jimbo turned and walked back to Winter's BearCat. He pulled it away from the curb and backed up with the rear end pointed at the subdivision and the circle of yellow earth movers. He left the keys in the ignition and the motor running. He hopped out, leaving the driver's door open, and trotted around to the rear of the vehicle. He opened the two rear doors, hurried to his BearCat and opened its rear doors before heading to the cab.

From the driver's seat of his vehicle, he pushed the power button on a small monitor on the dash. The screen glowed gray as he strapped his radio headset on and flipped the mic down. "Copy, Nico. Copy, Nico. Jimbo."

"*Nico here. Go, Jimbo.*"

"Everyone's on this frequency, so watch what you say. Give me video on all trucks. I'll switch views as necessary. Time to set it up, buddy."

"*10-4, Jimbo. I'll give the word when we're in place.*"

"Atta boy."

Nico had instructed each member of the stranded crew. When he gave the hand signal, the trucks broke out of their circular formation. Each driver pointed their vehicle in a different direction. Each vehicle was set to move forward to a point between two of the dump trucks. There was one BearCat assigned to draw fire from two dumpers.

"I got your video, Nico."

"*10-4. All my Cats, set the smoke.*"

The top hatches on all ten BearCats in the hot zone popped open. Smoke bombs flew from the hatches—four from each truck—and landed approximately twenty yards in front of the vehicles.

"Now," Jimbo said.

Winter led the Punks from the safe zone up a small rise toward the rear of the circle of earth movers. She stopped behind a large grader and motioned for the others to bypass her and continue around the rear of the machines. She fixed her first explosive device to the grader, stood quickly and hurried to the fourth vehicle in line. She set her second device and remained crouched as she watched the other four Punks make their way around the circle.

"*All Cats are go,*" Nico said.

Lace, Adam, Joey and the other Punk drivers in the hot zone each wedged a crowbar between the dash and the accelerator pedal in their trucks. When the engines revved, they dropped the gearshifts and the BearCats moved forward in ten different directions. The rear doors to the trucks swung open, and the Punks stepped down onto the smoke-filled dirt road.

The sound of rifle shots filled the air. Bullets ricocheted off the moving driverless BearCats.

Shooters in the dumpers continued their barrage, oblivious to the fact their targets were empty.

The Punk farthest from the street set his last explosive and began a sprint back toward Jimbo's position.

Buster and Storm walked calmly but purposefully to the other two BearCats as Jimbo detonated the furthest of the explosive devices. The rifle shots stopped momentarily as shouts from inside the circle began.

The two Punks hopped into the trucks and backed them up to the subdivision entrance. Two graders were perched back-to-back, blocking the entrance.

Smoke from inside the subdivision drifted into the street and quickly covered the two Punk vehicles as Buster and Storm walked to the rear of their trucks and opened the back doors.

The gunfire started back up when Jimbo set off the second, third and fourth explosions.

The driverless BearCats continued their ghostlike treks toward the dumpers. Bullets bounced off the fenders and shattered headlights and windows.

Nico and his group sprinted toward the two back-to-back graders as Jimbo detonated the remaining devices. One by one, twenty Punks hopped and crawled over, under and between the two graders at the entrance.

Buster and Storm stood at the back of the vehicles and counted each Punk as they piled through the open doors into the back of the trucks.

Storm glanced over at Buster. "Ten!"

"Ten!" Buster said as the two rushed around and jumped into the drivers' seats.

Winter sprinted to her waiting vehicle and jammed the gearshift into drive as the last of the four remaining Punks entered the open rear doors. She shouted into her mic. "Got 'em all!"

Simultaneously, the four trucks accelerated away from the subdivision as the bullets continued to bounce off the sacrificial BearCats in the hot zone.

CHAPTER 49

Promotions and Emotions

L EVI SAT COMFORTABLY IN A cushy executive office chair behind his huge chrome-and-glass desk. His royal-blue custom-tailored suit was freshly pressed. He enjoyed the time spent in his private study on Level Ten in the Underground City. The prospect of becoming the Changers Global Supreme Leader was exhilarating. After the last conference call with the Changers Regional Leaders, he was confident he had the necessary votes to seal the position. Today's call would be the confirmation of everything he had worked and fought so hard for. In his mind, the call was but a formality.

He tapped away at a virtual keyboard on the glass surface while gazing at the wall in front of him. The video on the wall displayed five grids, each representing a region of the world controlled by the Changers. One by one the grids illuminated the faces of the Regional Leaders—Europe, Asia, Africa, South America. Levi's real-time image was displayed in the center of the screen with live feeds of the four other Regional Leaders positioned at the corners.

Levi smiled and pressed a button, opening the mic to all participants. "Greetings, Changers Regional Leaders."

Each of the leaders acknowledged with a nod and a smile.

"Insomuch as the votes are finalized, I would like to take this opportunity to have recorded into the permanent record my election as the Changers Global Supreme Leader. If each of you would please enter your vote into the system now, my election, and therefore my title, will become official and immediate."

As the number below Levi's image on the screen grew from zero to four, so grew the breadth of his smile. He glanced down at the keyboard and pressed the all-important vote button. The image displayed a large number five, and the title above his name changed instantly from North America Regional Leader to Global Supreme Leader.

"Splendid!" Levi felt an adrenaline surge. He stood from his chair. "I would like to thank you all for this confirmation of your confidence in my ability to lead our organization. There could have been no other reasonable outcome. I will be in touch with you all individually. For now, carry on." He reached down to the keyboard and terminated the connection.

He stood silent, staring at the display on the wall: a map of the world with all five Changer-controlled regions outlined accordingly. He stood tall and held two fists in the air. "I am Levi, Changers Global Supreme Leader!"

Dr. Felix Yaz stood, arms crossed, atop a raised steel platform in the plant at Punk headquarters. It had been seven days since the work on his expansive new laboratory had begun. He was more than pleased with the progress. The new plant was immaculate and near sterile. Felix insisted that everyone who worked in the plant wear white.

A row of twenty-four robotic arms—assembled using salvaged parts from mechanical Chybrids—clicked busily above circuit boards. Sydney stood at the front end of the row, scanning an electronic tablet. She glanced intermittently at a nearby monitor then back to her tablet, occasionally tapping the device with a stylus.

Drew sat in a barstool-height chair at a high desk in the corner of the plant. An array of monitors—two rows of four—was secured to the wall in front of the desk. He tapped expertly onto a keyboard on the desk while his eyes darted between the monitors.

Pops and Geezer hovered around a group of Punks who were assembling four large glass enclosures near the center of the expansive room. Wires and tubes extended from the glass enclosures upward to a second level adjacent to scaffolding attached to the ceiling and secured to the floor.

Pops walked over to the foreman's platform. He looked up at Felix and removed his white bandanna. "I need a break, Doctor. I been six hours without chew or a cigar." He motioned over his shoulder. "Geezer's gettin' tired, too."

Felix nodded several times. "Oh, yes, my friend. Please take a break. I want no fatigue here. Fatigue leads to errors. We must all remain fresh."

Pops turned and motioned to Geezer. "Let's take a break, you old fart."

Geezer looked across the room through grimy spectacles and waved a white towel at Pops.

"See that, Doc?" Pops said. "He's surrendering."

Felix turned to descend the five steps from the platform. He glanced toward the door and waved.

Krystal waved to Felix as she approached. "We gotta talk, Felix."

"My, what is it, my dear?"

"Fred and Thomas aren't doing so well." She glanced around the room at nothing in particular. "I think your twenty-four-seven schedule has really taken a toll on them."

"I do apologize for that," Felix said. "But much of this operation is for their benefit." He pointed at the four glass enclosures surrounded by the team of Punks. "Those are the conversion chambers. We are making excellent progress."

"We all get that," she said. "But Fred and Thomas look bad. I really think you should pay them a visit."

"Yes, yes. By all means," Felix said, walking toward the door. "I would hate to think my schedule has contributed to an acceleration of their demise."

Krystal walked quickly to keep up with Felix. "I don't even want to hear about their demise. They are extremely valuable. But more than that, they're friends."

Felix and Krystal walked through the door into the Hangar and headed to the exit. "Are they in their quarters?" he said.

"No," Krystal said. "We've moved them to the infirmary."

"Then lead the way, dear."

DION AND RYKER SAT SIDE by side at the main control panel inside the Depot. Ace manned the comm console.

"I gotta hand it to you, bro," Ryker said. "It took a while, but Rudie and Jas are really coming through for us."

Dion smiled. "You bet." He looked his best friend in the eye. "I made that call, you know? The one you said I should make. They took that call like true friends. They upped their minimum, sending at least 5,000 trucks. Each. Now you know why they're taking so long."

"No shit?" Ryker said. "Wow, 10,000 armored vehicles? Holy cow, I didn't know they had that kind of firepower."

Dion shook his head. "Me either. We don't have five thousand left in our fleet. But I guess it stands to reason. They haven't been dealing with the same shit we have."

"Yeah. Changers have made themselves pretty manageable in their sectors. We've definitely taken the brunt."

"Yep," Dion said. "So with seven more days passed, the Changers have brought 700 more earth movers in. At least ten percent of those are war-ready offensive machines."

"Ha!" Ryker said. "And we'll have at least 10,000 in a few days to go up against them." He looked sideways at the Punk leader. "Another case of curing lice by decapitation?" He held out his fist.

Dion pounded a fist down on Ryker's. "Lice by decapitation."

WILL MET KRYSTAL AND FELIX in the main hallway inside the Punks' infirmary. He supported himself on crutches—one leg braced and one arm in a sling. He tipped his chin at the two. "Hey. What's up?"

"Hey, the third Amigo lives!" Krystal said. "We're going to see Fred and Thomas."

"I was just headed that way, myself," Will said. "Let's go."

The trio walked down the hallway and entered a room three doors down from Will's.

Fred and Thomas lay in separate hospital beds, each with an IV on a slow saline drip in their arms.

Felix grabbed a chair and positioned it between the bed. "My friends, how are you feeling?"

"Not good, Felix," Fred said. "Please say your conversion chambers are ready. I'm so weary being a Changer. I so need to be real again."

"We are merely days away, my friend," Felix said. He placed a hand on Fred's forearm. "Please stay strong. Please hang on." He glanced up at Krystal then turned back to Fred. "Remember our friends, Ivan and Marvellus? They have been organizing a mass exit of technicians and scientists from the Underground." His eyes widened in an effort to appear hopeful. "They are coming to help, and our work will progress so much more quickly."

Krystal looked down at Thomas. "How's it going with you, buddy?"

Tears welled in Thomas's eyes. "I'm not sure I care to hang on."

Felix's eyes moistened. "Oh, my dear friend. Please don't say that." He placed his other hand on Thomas's arm. "We have been through so much together."

Thomas's tears flowed from the corners of his eyes and soaked into the pillowcase.

Fred turned his head and looked at his friend in the other bed. "Thomas."

Will tried his best. "Suck it up, you two. A few more days and you'll be as good as Krystal." He looked at her. "No offense."

Fred turned his eyes to Krystal. "I want that scar."

Krystal started. "What?"

"Get Geezer in here. Tell him to burn me the same way he burned you. I want to die with the face of a Rogue, not as a Changer."

"I want the same," Thomas said.

"You're both ridiculous," Krystal said. "This is a hideous scar. And you're not going to die!"

"It's a badge of honor, right, Felix?" Fred said. "Burn me."

"Do it," Thomas said.

Krystal looked at Felix and shrugged ever so slightly. "What do we do?" she mouthed.

Felix nodded.

Krystal turned to Will and jerked her head toward the door.

Will nodded once and turned to leave. "I'll get him." When he reached the door, he hobbled back around to face the two bed-ridden Rogues. "You guys are Rogues of the highest standard." He fought his own tears. "No matter what happens."

CHAPTER 50

The Face of a Rogue

B Y MIDNIGHT THE DAY AFTER his election as Changers Global Supreme Leader, Levi lay in his bed staring at the ceiling. He reached to his nightstand and pressed a button, activating all lights in his quarters. He arose from his bed and removed his silk pajamas. Stopping at the full-length mirror, he admired his naked body and smiled. *I do believe my royal-blue suit is still in order*, he thought. *And who would have anything to say if it weren't? After all, I am Levi Aldrich, Changers Global Supreme Leader.*

He changed into his suit and walked into the main living area. *With the resources I now have available to me, I do believe a remodel is in order. Who would expect the Changers Global Supreme Leader to be crammed into a mere 2,500-square-foot apartment?* He smiled at the thought and answered his own hypothetical question. *Why, no one, of course!* He walked to the bar and poured a lowball glass one-quarter full of bourbon. *I like you, sir*, he said, raising the glass to his reflection in the mirror.

When he finished his drink, he stepped into his private elevator and pressed number ten. Four security guards stood at attention when he stepped off the elevator.

"Good morning, Leader," the lead guard said. "Your private study?"

Levi nodded at the guard, turned and walked down the short corridor. He passed his hand over the security pad on the wall adjacent to the door of his study. The light above the door flashed red, then green, and the door swished open. *Curious*, he thought.

He stepped inside and pressed the "all lights" button on the inside panel next to the door. He heard the lock on the sliding door behind him click. The outer foyer illuminated all lights. But only the desk lamp lit in the large room that housed his main office. He shook his head. "I'm going to have to take this up with our head of facility maintenance," he said. He shook his head as he walked into the darkened office space. "Unacceptable. Just unacceptable."

When he passed over the threshold into his study, the lights in the foyer extinguished. He stood still.

"Changers Global Supreme Leader, huh?" The voice was barely above a whisper.

Levi squinted into the darkness as he repeatedly tapped a button on the wall. "Who's there?"

"It didn't matter that the Regional Leaders voted to promote you, *Leader*. Your days were numbered long ago. You're not the Changers Global Supreme Leader anymore. You're not even North America's Regional Leader."

Levi stood tall and flexed his muscles beneath his royal-blue suit. "I demand you show yoursel—"

The needle sank into the Changer leader's neck before his next breath. "Ow. Wh…" he said, flailing his arms as if swatting flies. "Where are you?"

"So much for the Felix Yaz skullcap you had placed below your skin. You should have asked for neck protection as well."

The Changers' leader felt the wall hit him in the back as he fell. "No," he whispered. "Guards…security…help—"

"It's a changing of the guard," the voice said softly. "Die, Levi. Just die."

Levi remained conscious as his large frame slid sideways down the wall inside his private study. His muscles were useless. He felt the presence of a hand on his head. Fingers dug deep into his neatly coiffed hair. He knew it was messy now. He felt the pressure of his hair pulling against the skin on his scalp. Pressure against his neck.

As the long blade sliced through the skin on his neck, the faint light from the desk lamp blurred, then faded to black as blood from the big man flooded onto the blue carpet. Levi felt the pressure when the blade moved down on both ends, handle and tip. He lost consciousness when his severed head rolled to the side.

The assailant picked up the fallen leader's head and walked to the desk. The head hit the inside of the wastebasket as the surgical-quality blade hit the floor.

The assassin unbuttoned a set of bloodstained white coveralls and let them drop to the floor. Stepping to Levi's wardrobe, the assailant opened the double doors and selected a royal blue suit to match the one worn by the dead Changers leader.

The figure paused momentarily for a change of appearance before walking slowly out of the study and into the foyer. With a hand swish on the panel adjacent to the door, the assassin strode out into the bright white corridor.

At seven o'clock in the morning, Ryker and Krystal stepped into the Punks' dining room at Checkpoint One. "There they are," Ryker said, pointing at a table across the crowded room. The pair removed their dusters and hooked them on the wall by the door.

Dion and Jimbo stood when the pair arrived at the table.

Winter remained seated. "Bout time, guys. I'm hungry."

"You didn't have to wait," Ryker said.

Jimbo chuckled. "Like one pig waits for another, bro. We already ordered."

Dion leaned back in his chair and held up both hands. "Heads up, everybody. I just want to let you guys know, Rudie and Jas have come through for us. There are several waves of reinforcements coming from the central and east sectors. They started last night and will continue to dispatch throughout the next week or so."

"Awesome," Winter said. "And it's long overdue. Yellow machines are stacking up every day outside Tremayne."

Jimbo reached across the table and fist-bumped Ryker. "Yo, dude. Yeah." He eyed Winter. "Time to kick some Changer butt."

"Got that right," she said.

"Not to put any damper on this enthusiasm," Dion said, "but keep in mind, the physical battle against the Changers is only half of what we're up against. We're not slinging bullets at SOUL Chybrids."

"I have to agree," Krystal said. "We're gonna need something special to counter the technology and brainwashing the Bystanders are experiencing."

Ryker motioned to a waiter. "The Changers are changing things fast, that's for sure. But I'm with you from the standpoint of banking on Felix. We've got nothing better from a technology angle."

"Well, there's Drew and Sydney," Krystal said. "It'd be nice to get more Bystanders on our side."

"We gotta get Fred and Thomas healthy," Jimbo said. "We need them, too."

Dion held up a hand. "I agree. But first things first. We need to get ourselves entrenched in Bystander territory again. We need them to rely on us again. Like they used to."

"And we do that by?" Krystal said.

Dion took a sip from his water glass. "I'm glad it was you that asked, Krys. We start by pushing the Changers back out of Tremayne. I'm putting you in charge of the operation. Including our troops and the reinforcements, you'll have at least 15,000 armored vehicles and their related personnel at your command." He held out his fist and looked around the table. "Well?"

Every Punk at the table landed a fist in the center, touching Dion's.

Felix walked quietly into Fred and Thomas's room in the infirmary. He pulled a chair between the beds and sat down. The two patients were barely conscious.

Fred rolled his head to the side and managed a weak smile. "Hey, boss."

Felix smiled. "My friends. I have been experimenting at night with some new formulas to help you. I have something that is only temporary, but it should work to keep you alive until our conversion chambers are complete. I have stopped the simultaneous assembly on all four and have dedicated our resources to accelerate the process for two chambers at this time." He looked back and forth between the two Rogues. "These are for you, as soon as they are ready."

"Felix," Thomas said. "One."

"Excuse me?" Felix said.

"Dedicate the resources to one chamber. For Fred." Thomas stared at the ceiling. "I was serious when I told you I don't want to go on."

Felix scooted his chair closer to Thomas's bed. "My friend. We need you. We must defeat the technological stranglehold the Changers are gaining over the world."

"It's just me, Felix," Thomas said. "I'm tired. My heart isn't in it. I hate the Changers, and I wish I had never been a part. I've absorbed so many innocent people in my life. I have to suffer this. I have to go. It's my payback."

Felix reached into his lab coat pocket and retrieved two injectors. "One of these is for you, my friend. It will pull you through until the conversion chamb—"

"No, Felix," Thomas said. "It's my choice."

Felix reached out and touched Thomas's face. "I see Mr. Geezer has duplicated Krystal's mark on your faces. You look different."

"And I feel different," Thomas said. "I will not die as a Changer. I will die with the face of a Rogue."

CHAPTER 51

The End of the Beginning

RUDIE SAT SHOTGUN IN AN armored Lenco BearCat at the top of a freeway on-ramp in Topeka, Kansas. He tapped the face of his cell.

The answer on the other end was immediate. "*Hey, scab rocket! You ready to move?*"

"Ready than you'll ever be, Jazzie. We got business in Cali."

"*Got that right,*" Jas said. "*Hey, which way you guys going?*"

"I-70 far as we can. Then we dropping onto the 15 down to Barstow and north up their asses to Central Cali. How 'bout you?"

"*I-78 from Gotham, the center of the universe, over to Allentown. We'll hook up with I-70 south of Pittsburgh. We'll be winging it when the 70 ends. See who gets there first, scab boy.*"

"You got tolls that way?"

"*Are you kidding me? We got Punks in every booth in the route and green lights all the way.*"

"Same, same," Rudie said. "I'm in the first wave, baby. We got at least a day's head start on you."

"*All right, Rudie. Drive safe. See you there!*"

"That you will, Jazzie. That you will."

A caravan of 250 vehicles sped westbound on Interstate 10 through the Southern California desert. The vehicles were an eclectic mix of Mercedes, Bugattis, Teslas, and McLarens, intermingled with an array of pickups and vans, econo-boxes and electric motorcycles.

Ivan Duncan speed-dialed Felix from his small quarters in the Underground City.

"*Hello, Ivan, my friend.*"

"Hi, Felix. The first wave is on its way."

"*Excellent. They will be here in a matter of hours.*"

"True. They're all pretty much leaving the Underground at their own pace. Some of the best are in the first wave, though. So that should help."

"*Yes, yes. We need some fast assistance on the reversal chambers.*"

"How are Fred and Thomas?"

"*Not good, my friend. They are barely holding on as the chambers are nearing completion. I am holding onto hope, Ivan.*"

"Okay. Hey, Felix. One more thing. I don't know if it's going to affect how you operate there or not."

"*Yes, what is it?*"

"We're hearing rumblings about a change in our leadership at the City."

"*Are you referring to Levi?*"

"Yes."

"*I don't see how that could happen. And who has taken over as the Changers' leader?*"

"I don't know. We're barely fourth-level security clearance."

"*I see. Well I guess we will find out soon enough. Is that all?*"

"For now. We'll be in touch."

"*Yes, my friend. Goodbye.*"

The top echelon of Changers assembled quietly in Levi's executive conference room. The new leader sat at the head of the table and gazed intently at the other three.

Dr. Xander Rasmus broke the silence. "First, I must express my congratulations. I did not think this day would come so soon."

The Changers' new leader stood to address the group. "Thank you, Xander. The first order of business will be to convey my order of authority. Until further notice, my second-in-command is Mr. John Logan. I expect you all to respect this decision and report to me through Mr. Logan."

Johnny smiled his usual full-toothed, top-to-bottom smile.

Silver slammed her tablet on the conference table. "Bullshit!"

RYKER AND KRYSTAL STEPPED INTO the Hangar from the Punk compound.

"Dion's assignment of you to lead the Punks for this operation was pure genius, Krys," Ryker said. "There was really no other choice."

"It's a big responsibility," she said. "I feel good about it, though."

"Well, you finally got buy-in from Jim and Winter. That's saying a lot."

Krystal glanced at Little Man in the steel cage. He was gripping the bars, his face pressed against the steel. The boy was smiling.

Krystal stopped. "What's the word today, kid?"

"We got a new leader…We got a new leader." He swung his hips in motion with his chant.

Krystal crossed her arms. "Is that so?" She tipped her chin up. "Who's the new leader of the Changers, Little Man?"

"It's your boyfriend…it's your boyfriend…it's your boyfriend…"

Her skin turned cold as the blood rushed from her face. Her legs were weak, and she felt Ryker's hands under her arms. Her mind raced as the room swirled in front of her and she heard Curtis's voice. "*I love you, Krys. I did it for you.*"

www.ingramcontent.com/pod-product-compliance
Lightning Source LLC
Chambersburg PA
CBHW071153100726
47908CB00002B/364